# *Eve's Destiny*

## Mike & Eve Series #1

RENÉE Y. LEWIS

ISBN: 978-1-5356-0705-6

# Contents

# *Chapter 1*



Detectives Mike McGarrett and Samuel Lewis retrieved the drawing of Lucas from the sketch artist and decided to look for him at the Internet café where the young and naïve hackers said they'd first met him. Once Mike and Sam arrived, they approached the cashier behind the counter. Carol smiled at them, noticing that they were both *very* attractive.

The detectives made a very striking duo, which usually caught the ladies' attention. Sam was tall and well built with mocha-colored skin that was smooth as silk. Mike was fair-skinned, tall and rugged with dark, wavy hair. Mike and Sam were aware of their effect on women, which they used to their advantage on occasion, and they, of course, noticed the cashier's admiration. Mike eyed her nametag, flashed his badge and returned her smile. "Hi, Carol, I'm Detective Mike McGarrett and this is my partner Detective Sam Lewis. We were hoping you could be of assistance. Do you recognize this man?" he asked, showing her the drawing of Lucas.

*They can have my assistance anytime and anywhere*, she thought while perusing the sketch. "Yes, actually, I do recognize him. He's not a regular but he's been in the café a couple of times, even recently. You could probably find out more about him from that man over there," she offered, pointing to a young man sitting in a booth hunched over a laptop. "The two of them have met up here a couple of times and seemed to know each other pretty well."

"We appreciate your help, Carol," Sam replied with a smile.

"*Anytime*, detectives," she responded, giving them both a suggestive and lingering stare.

Mike and Sam glanced at each other as they turned to head across to the other side of the café. As they approached the man pointed out by Carol, he looked up and immediately got nervous at the two imposing men headed right for him. Seeing the instant fear in the young man's eyes, Mike figured it might not be too difficult getting the information they needed from him. Mike flashed his badge, and he and Sam squeezed into the booth with him in order to exacerbate his fear. "We were hoping you could help us out. We have a couple of questions to ask you."

"Umm, sure, officers... What do you need to know?"

"Actually, it's *Detective* McGarrett, and this is Detective Lewis. What's *your* name?"

"Umm, Jake... Jake Thom-Thomas," he stammered.

"Well Jake, we were told you might know this man." Jake looked at the sketch of Lucas. Realizing he wasn't their target after all, he relaxed a little.

"That's Lucas," he blurted without thinking, then winced at having given up his friend's name so easily.

"Lucas what?" urged Sam.

"Lucas... Coles," he offered slowly. "What do you want with him?" Jake asked, glancing nervously between Mike and Sam.

"We just want to speak with him. He has information that we need. Do you know where we can find him?"

Jake hesitated for fear of getting his friend in trouble, but it was probably already too late for that. Lucas obviously had done something shady which was about to bite him in the ass. Jake was not going down for him, so he provided both Lucas's work *and* home addresses. Mike and Sam thanked Jake for his cooperation and decided to pay Lucas Coles an unexpected visit at work.

* * *

Once Mike and Sam arrived at Colby Designs, they announced themselves to the security guard in the lobby, signed in at the front desk, and took the elevator up to the Design Department on the fourth floor. They showed the sketch of Lucas to the receptionist, Sherri Wells. Being that it was her first day, she didn't have immediate information as to Lucas's current whereabouts, but attempted to make some inquiries nonetheless.

While Sherri continued her search, a beautiful young woman, Eve Townsend, stepped off the elevator, and Mike and Sam approached her, hoping for better luck. Eve was slender, with just the right amount of curves, wavy brown hair that rested just below her shoulders and light-brown smoldering eyes. When Eve and Mike's eyes locked onto each other's they felt a pull beyond their comprehension, and both seemed transfixed. The transmission between them sizzled with an unspoken connection.

Sam glanced between the two of them and broke the uncomfortable silence by identifying himself and his partner. He flashed his badge. "Hi, I'm Detective Sam Lewis, this is my partner Detective Mike McGarrett, and you are?"

Eve broke eye contact with Mike to acknowledge Sam and scanned the badge he was displaying. She glanced over to the receptionist, once again catching Mike's eyes. "I'll take care of them, Sherri." Grateful for the save, Sherri nodded. Sherri was intrigued by what the detectives could possibly want with this Lucas Coles and with the obvious attraction between Ms. Townsend and Detective McGarrett. Her first day at Colby Designs was shaping up to be *very* interesting.

As Eve and Sam shook hands, she addressed them both, "Nice to meet you, Detective Lewis, Detective McGarrett. I'm Eve Townsend, one of the department managers."

The sound of Eve's soft voice tugged at Mike's heart. Lucas Coles was the furthest thing from his mind at the moment, but he managed to compose himself enough to shake her hand. "It's a pleasure, Ms. Townsend." At each other's touch, an unexpected surge of electricity shot through their entire bodies, and Eve hastily released her hand, slightly embarrassed.

Sam's eyes darted between the two of them, slightly befuddled by his partner's off-balanced behavior. "Ms. Townsend, do you know how we can reach this man?" he interjected while presenting Eve with the sketch of Lucas. "The receptionist didn't seem to recognize him."

Still shaken by her physical contact with Detective McGarrett, Eve was happy to focus on something else. "It's Sherri's first day. She's still getting familiar with the staff." But when Eve looked at the sketch, it was evident that *she* did recognize him. "That's Lucas Coles, he used to manage the IT department but was recently let go from the company. He no longer works here. That's why Sherri didn't know who he was," she explained.

Mike wasn't certain, but he thought he saw Eve shiver. "How recently was Lucas fired?" he asked, recovered from their physical contact.

"Just a couple of days ago, in fact, but I don't know all of the details. It happened so suddenly, and I heard there was a big scene while he was being escorted out of the building by security. I'm sorry I can't be of more help, but I didn't know him very well. I'm fairly new with the company myself. I only met Lucas when I first arrived just two weeks ago to obtain my credentials." Eve shivered again at the memory of their first encounter. "Other than in passing, I haven't had any contact with him, *thank goodness*."

"You didn't like him much?" questioned Mike.

"I didn't really know him *not* to like him, but to be honest he gave me the creeps. There was something very... odd about him, and I'm just happy to not have to deal with him anymore."

"I see." Sam glanced at Mike and thanked Eve for her assistance while handing her his business card. "Please contact us if you can think of anything else, Ms. Townsend."

"Of course, Detective Lewis."

"Is there a number we could reach you at if we have additional questions?" asked Sam.

"Oh, yes, but I don't have..."

Mike handed Eve another business card and a pen. "You can write your number on this."

"Thank you." Eve jotted her office and cell number on the card and handed it and the pen back to Mike.

"Thank you again, Ms. Townsend, you have a good day."

Eve smiled at Mike. "You too, Detective McGarrett, Detective Lewis." Little butterflies fluttered in her stomach. Still drawn to the tall, dark, and handsome detective, Eve watched Mike as he and Sam walked towards the elevators for a couple of seconds before heading down the corridor toward her office.

Sherri smiled to herself. This was definitely an interesting place to work. She would have to dig up the details regarding this Lucas Coles and his abrupt departure.

After he and Sam entered the elevators, Mike couldn't keep his eyes off Eve as she walked down the hall. Before she reached her office, she unexpectedly looked back and stole another glance at him. Just before the elevator doors closed, their eyes met once again and Mike's heart skipped a beat.

Eve realized that she was smiling to herself and wished that she would get the chance to see Detective McGarrett again. Little did she know she would get her wish sooner than she expected.

* * *

During the elevator ride down, Mike caught Sam staring at him with a wry smile. Mike chose to ignore him and looked away. Sam was the best partner that Mike ever had, three years and counting, and you couldn't ask for a more reliable person to have at your side when it counted the most. Mike could tell that Sam was resisting the urge to comment on his unusual reaction toward Eve, and he had to admit that he was slightly embarrassed by his own behavior.

At thirty-one years of age, Mike didn't have a problem attracting *and* getting the ladies. His mixture of rugged and heartbreakingly suave good looks made sure of that. So it was not in his nature to lose his composure over a woman so easily, especially while working a case, and he was grateful to Sam for stepping in and keeping things on track. Mike had to admit that he was very attracted to the lovely Ms. Townsend and very much wanted to—

"So much for surprising Lucas at work," stated Sam, interrupting Mike's thoughts, and sensing the need to bring Mike's attention back to their immediate problem.

"I know," replied Mike, shaking his head, bringing himself back to reality, "I'm getting a bad feeling about this guy. Even Ms.

Townsend had a negative reaction to him. I hope we have better luck catching Lucas at home. Who knows where the hell he is or what he's up to at this point."

Once back in their car, Sam programmed Lucas's address into their GPS system and they headed out. Mike kept thinking of the beautiful Eve Townsend. There was something vulnerable in her eyes. He felt drawn to her and wanted to see her—

Mike's thoughts, *again*, were abruptly interrupted, this time by a call from dispatch. "All units, we received a call about a 10-71 in progress at The Colby Designs building. 462 Broad St, fourth floor, Code 3, repeat Code 3. A woman named Eve Townsend called it in."

Mike's head snapped in Sam's direction. "Eve," he gasped, his heart started to pound and he was instantly afraid for her safety. "Roger, Dispatch, 3-Adam-10 responding."

"What's your 10-20?"

"Five minutes out, but we just came from there. We're headed back," Mike confirmed, "please send backup and paramedics to meet us at the scene."

"Do we know how many shooters we're dealing with?" asked Sam as he made a quick U-turn back to Colby Designs.

"No, Ms. Townsend didn't see the shooters. Only heard the gunshots and screams," answered the dispatch operator.

"So we don't know how many we're dealing with," mused Mike. "Did Ms. Townsend say where she was located?"

"No, the 9-1-1 operator said they got cut off before she could ask."

"OK, we're already on our way back, log it in," Sam replied while turning on the car sirens and lights.

The partners exchanged a look. What did this mean for Eve? Did the shooter discover her calling for help? Was she hurt or... dead? Mike refused to allow those thoughts. She had to be alive.

They last saw her walking down the hallway, but she could have gone anywhere in the building.

Sam had a feeling that Mike would be worried about Eve and hoped that he could remain objective and in control.

* * *

Lucas Coles had returned to Colby Designs enraged, armed with a gun and bent on revenge for being fired and humiliated in front of the entire department. Having worked there, he knew that Phillip Buckman, the security guard at the lobby entrance, was easily distracted by large crowds. Lucas waited outside until a group entered the building and slipped past Phil while he was attending to the patrons. Keeping his head down to avoid the cameras, Lucas took the stairwell to the fourth floor. Coincidentally, two detectives, looking to question him, were simultaneously riding down in the elevator *from* the fourth floor. He exited the stairwell and approached the receptionist. Sherri didn't immediately recognize him from the sketch Detective Lewis had just shown her, and before she could offer him assistance he pointed the gun at her and fired. It happened so quickly she didn't even have time to react or even scream. The force knocked her backwards and she slumped to the floor in a crumpled heap, leaving smeared blood on the wall from the impact.

Lucas didn't miss a beat, and headed directly toward the office corridor filled with unsuspecting victims. He shot at everyone in his path. There was absolutely nowhere for anyone to go, because if they stepped out into the hall they would be in a direct line of fire, making them easy targets. Their only recourse was to take shelter behind their desks or inside of their closets and to remain quiet.

Eve was in her office when the shooting started. She sucked in her breath sharply and her head snapped up in a startled response to that first shot. "What was that?" she gasped, and then her chest tightened, momentarily constricting her breathing. She knew she couldn't panic, and luckily, she was located farther down the hall, which gave her a little more time to react, but not much. She knew those were gunshots and so instinctively reached for her desk phone to call for help, but was unsure of the direction of the gunman or how close he was, so she grabbed her pocketbook, quickly hid in the closet, pulled out her cell phone and dialed 9-1-1.

"9-1-1, what's your emergency?" the operator asked.

"Someone is trying to kill us," Eve managed in a low, shaky voice so as not to be heard by the shooter.

"Miss, could you speak up? I didn't catch that."

Eve started to sob. "Someone is trying to kill us," she repeated a little louder. "Please help us," she begged. The hallway was filled with gunfire, screams, and desperate cries for help.

"OK, what's your name, miss?"

"Eve, Eve Townsend."

"Hi Eve, I'm Sandra. Try to remain calm. I need you to stay on the line. Where are you calling from?"

"Colby Designs," Eve answered, trying not to cry, her body starting to shake uncontrollably.

"What is the address?"

"462 Broad Street, fourth floor. *Please* help us."

"All units, there is a 10-71 in progress at the Colby Designs building. 462 Broad St, fourth floor, Code 3, repeat Code 3." The 9-1-1 Operator returned to Eve, "Eve, the police have been alerted and they're on their way. Do you know how many gunmen there are, can you see them?"

"No, I can only hear the gunshots and the screams..." Eve could no longer hold back her tears. Additional shots startled her and she dropped the phone, losing her connection to the 9-1-1 Operator. "Oh no, no, no... Damn it..."

"Eve, are you there? Eve..." The line went dead as they were disconnected. The 9-1-1 Operator provided the police with all the information she was able to gather and prayed that it was enough.

Eve was frantic, but she remembered that she had Detective Lewis's business card and tried to dial his number too, but it was too dark inside the closet, and her quaking hands kept misdialing his number.

* * *

The high-pitched sounds of the sirens alerted drivers and pedestrians to make way for the police car approaching them at high speed. Being the congested streets of New York City, the car still had to dodge a couple of people who didn't realize which direction the sirens were coming from. Just as the detectives rounded a busy corner, a delivery van started to back out of a driveway. The driver, startled by the sudden appearance of the police car, slammed on his brakes, but not before blocking their path. Sam cursed under his breath and slammed on his brakes to prevent them from crashing into each other. He laid on the car horn and was about to put the car in reverse to allow him some room to go around it, but Mike stuck his head out of the car and yelled, "GET THAT VAN OUT OF THE WAY *NOW!*" The delivery driver, snapped back to his senses, quickly pulled the van back up into the driveway, allowing Sam to get around him.

Mike suddenly remembered he had Eve's office number. He dialed it, but she didn't answer. He tried her cell, but she didn't answer that one either. Not a good sign.

* * *

Lucas, on automatic pilot, traveled down the hallway, continuing his shooting rampage. Eve could hear the shots getting closer and closer, and her coworkers' screams were deafening. She had never been so scared in her entire life. Bullets flew into her office and she cowered further into the corner of the closet. Unfortunately, one of the bullets ricocheted and caught her in the shoulder. She didn't realize it at first until she felt a warm sensation travel down her left arm and then the searing pain that followed. She had to stuff her fist in her mouth to prevent herself from crying out, alerting the gunman to her location. She started to lose blood, and fear and claustrophobia threatened to consume her. Eve felt as if she was going to pass out. As she faded in and out of consciousness, she vaguely heard someone plead, "Lucas! No! Please don't..." then she heard additional gunshots before blackness overcame her.

* * *

Mike and Sam pulled up and parked in front of Colby Designs. They jumped out of the car and raced into the building. The lobby security guard recognized them as the detectives that had just left about fifteen minutes ago. "Hey, where's the fire, didn't you guys just leave here?"

"Look, we have a situation to contain," Sam responded. "We received a call regarding gunshots on the fourth floor, so we need you to keep everyone off the elevators and to not let anyone upstairs except for police backup and the paramedics. If anyone gets off the elevators, make sure they exit the building."

"*Holy shit!* That's the Design Department. Who's shooting? Is anyone hurt—?"

Sam cut him off, "Look, we don't have time for twenty questions. Just do what we asked," he commanded.

"Sure. No problem, detectives."

Mike held up his badge and addressed everyone in the lobby. "Listen up," he announced, "we have an emergency situation and I need everyone to exit the building immediately." But everyone just looked at him with annoyance and stunned silence. "*NOW*, let's move," Mike commanded forcefully, jolting everyone out of their stupor. *What is it with everyone this morning,* he thought, *they're like fuckin' space cadets.* Sam helped the security guard quickly usher everyone out of the lobby, then he and Mike headed to the fourth floor.

They raced up the stairs so the gunmen wouldn't hear them getting off the elevator. Sam stepped out of the stairwell and carefully checked his surroundings to make sure it was safe. He motioned to Mike that it was clear to approach. Guns drawn, they exited the stairwell. When Sam saw the blood smear on the wall behind the receptionist's desk, he checked and found the receptionist, Sherri, lying in a pool of blood. He checked her pulse. She was unconscious and still alive, but barely. *You sure picked the wrong day to start working here, kid,* thought Sam.

Mike noticed a trail of empty bullet casings leading down the corridor past the offices. A chill ran up his spine as he recalled his last image of Eve walking down that very hall just fifteen minutes prior, but he didn't know which office belonged to her. Mike and Sam proceeded forward, trying to assess the damage, and attempted to pinpoint the gunman's present location. They found additional injured victims in their offices and some that weren't so fortunate. It was a bloody mess. Suddenly, they heard more gunshots and quickly headed in that direction with caution, hoping that backup and the paramedics would arrive soon. They had no idea how many gunmen they were dealing with or how many more victims they would find.

Finally, Mike saw Eve's name on the wall. *This must be her office.* But when he glanced inside, she wasn't there. Fear tightened his body, and he was all too aware of the knot forming in his stomach. *Where was she?* He calmed his nerves, relaxed his body and refocused his attention on the immediate threat, locating and subduing the shooters, and then he would find Eve.

Once they reached the end of the hallway, Mike peered around the corner and spotted the gunman, who he recognized as the man they were looking for that very morning, Lucas Coles, and he was alone...

# *Chapter 2*



*May 25<sup>th</sup>, two months earlier...*

Angelo Gennaro waited in his office for his two sons, Nicholas and Anthony. Angelo, a shrewd and very successful crime boss, was not to be trifled with by any means and always eluded any attempts to be taken down by the police department. The Gennaro Family participated in fraud, racketeering, theft, money-laundering, gambling, narcotics, terrorism, human trafficking, and counterfeit goods. You name it.

Angelo's youngest son, Nicholas, had a new business proposition that he wanted to present to him. Nicholas was still green in many ways and, on occasion, a bit too eager to please. This trait usually blinded him to important details that could make or break a business transaction. Angelo loved his son very much but wouldn't allow him to lead the family business astray, and therefore, Nicholas's last name did not afford him automatic access. He needed to earn the right to be involved, just as his older brother, Anthony, had done. Consequently, Angelo did not have high expectations for the outcome of this meeting, but he always allowed Nicholas the opportunity to prove himself worthy of contention. Angelo promised his dear Lily on her deathbed that he would give Nicholas a chance and not shoot him down without provocation. Nicholas was young and slightly immature for Angelo's taste, but with some grooming he could still grow into a mature man, he hoped.

Anthony, the eldest son, was almost as shrewd a businessman as their father Angelo, and served as a consult in terms of new business transactions. Even though the brothers were similar in looks, Nicholas and Anthony had completely opposing personalities. Anthony was mature and self-assured, and Angelo could trust and depend on his judgment. So if Anthony ever displayed the slightest interest in one of Nicholas's ideas, it would give Angelo a reason to consider it.

Nicholas was nervous about presenting his idea to his father. His older brother Anthony usually took on this role, and Nicholas wanted to impress them both. He was waiting outside of their father's office when Anthony arrived.

"So, little brother, are you ready for this?" Anthony announced from behind.

Nicholas cringed. *Little brother*, how he hated when Anthony called him that, as if they were still kids. But that would soon change once he proved himself valuable. *Then* he'd gain their respect. He turned to face his older brother, "I'm as ready as I'm ever going to be, Tony. This is a great idea. Pop is going to approve of it and I know you will too."

"We'll see Nick, we'll see," replied Anthony.

Nicholas was hurt by Anthony's skepticism. "I did my homework and I'm prepared for this," he defended.

"Sorry Nick, I didn't mean to imply otherwise," Anthony apologized, not intending to put Nicholas on the defensive. "So let's do this bro, and good luck," he continued while giving Nicholas an encouraging pat on the back, but it was too late. Anthony could see the annoyance cross Nick's face.

"Thanks Tony." Nicholas could sense the doubt behind Anthony's well wishes and wanted to shove that doubt right up his ass, *but* he had to remain focused on the task at hand. Angelo Gennaro was no pushover, so Nicholas needed to be on his game and appear in control, even if he felt otherwise. He knocked on the door. A resounding "Enter" was bellowed from the other side, and Nicholas nervously glanced back at Anthony.

"Lead the way, little brother," Anthony replied, smiling to show his support.

Nicholas opened the door and they entered.

"Come, sit down, boys." The brothers crossed the room and sat across from their father at his office desk. Anyone sitting opposite of Angelo *always* felt inferior. Angelo was in charge and he made sure that you knew it. "So Nick, tell me about this business idea of yours."

"Well Pop, I know that you are very comfortable with our usual way of laundering money..." Angelo's eyes narrowed, causing Nicholas to pause. Nicholas cleared his throat and continued, "I propose that in addition to using legitimate businesses as fronts to launder our money, we should finally enter the world of technology."

"Technology...so you're suggesting that we use computers and the Internet for money-laundering?"

Nicholas looked his father directly in the eyes, "Yes, that's exactly what I'm proposing." *Stick to your guns,* he thought.

"Our tried-and-true methods are proven and have served us well over the years. Why should we mess with a good thing?" challenged Angelo.

"We don't have to *mess* with a good thing, Pop. I'm suggesting that we launder our money *both* ways. We would continue to use our proven methods while also taking advantage of technology. This will yield greater results much more quickly because the Internet is making it much easier to clean dirty money nowadays. The world had changed, and technology is a big part of it. We don't want to remain stagnant in a progressive world."

"How would this work, Nick?" asked Anthony. Surprisingly, his interest was piqued and he wanted to hear more, which their father took notice of.

"We will obtain customer bank account information, such as their IDs and passwords, which will give us direct access to their money. Then we'd transfer their funds to an anonymous offshore account. That's just a summarization; there are more details involved, of course."

"I need to know what these details are," urged Angelo, "for instance, how would we obtain the customer IDs and passwords? It's obvious that the entire plan hinges on this."

"Yes, it does. We can obtain this information several ways; we'll just have to decide which method will work best for us. Sending out fake emails to customers that look like real emails from their bank, asking them to update their personal account information by using a link provided in the email, is one example and is very commonly used. It's probably the route I'll choose. Once we obtain this info, we'll send a more experienced hacker to the banks in response to a bogus tech service call from the bank manager, who will escort our hacker through security to the main computer rooms. We have several banks on our payroll, so we'll have no problem finding a bank manager who we could *persuade* to work with us. The hacker will tap into the bank's system to gain access to the customers' credit and bank IDs and financial assets. The hacker will take either one thousand dollars from each account or max out the credit cards online with big-ticket item purchases of sixty grand or more on a dummy Internet website where he'll run the charges and then shut the dummy site down the next day. The money will be routed to one of our untraceable, anonymous offshore overseas bank accounts, or I can set up a new account specifically for this mission, if you prefer."

After Nicholas completed his brief explanation, Angelo looked at Anthony. "So, what do you think about your brother's idea? Is this something you feel we should pursue?" Angelo already decided that he would allow Nicholas to put a preliminary plan in motion and perform a test run, but he wanted to see if Anthony was on the same page. This was, after all, his territory of new business transactions that Nicholas was stepping into, and he wanted to give Anthony the courtesy of offering his opinion.

"I think it has promise, Pop. If you give the go-ahead we'll make sure to keep this separate from our current money-laundering method so if it doesn't work out as expected we won't actually lose any money. I say let's give it a try to see if it produces the kind of results we want."

Anthony was on board and Nicholas was ecstatic, but he couldn't get ahead of himself; he still needed his father's final approval to move forward with the plan. After several minutes of excruciating silence, Nicholas finally heard the words he was dying for.

"I agree with Anthony," offered Angelo as he turned to Nicholas, "I want you to implement this new strategy of yours *but* under your brother's supervision. The two of you will work together on this and keep me posted with your progress."

"Thanks Pop, you too, Tony. This means a lot to me, and I won't let you down."

*You'd better not,* thought Angelo, but he kept his thoughts to himself. It was up to Nicholas to either sink or swim. Hopefully with Anthony's supervision, he'd at least manage to stay afloat this time.

* * *

Eve approached Claire Reynolds, her supervisor's Administrative Assistant, and was greeted with a big smile. Claire was a staple employee at Colby Designs San Francisco Branch. Colby was an architectural powerhouse, with locations in several cities across the U.S., and Claire knew the company inside and out. If you ever needed assistance, she was the person to make it happen, and her short, pudgy stature only added to the warmth she exuded. "Hi Eve, he's expecting you dear," she announced, and motioned Eve to go right in.

"Thanks, Claire." Eve worked for Raymond Jones for four years, straight out of college and moved up the ranks under his tutelage. Raymond's stern demeanor belied his sensitive nature, which only a select few witnessed, and Eve was lucky enough to be one of them. She knocked on Raymond's office door and poked her head into the room.

"Come in Eve, come in," Raymond beckoned, "please, have a seat. I'm sure you're wondering why I called you here."

"Yes, I am."

"Then I won't keep you in suspense. Don't worry, it's good news, or at least I hope you see it that way. You might not know this, but our New York City division has opened up a new managerial position in the Design Department and they're currently in the process of screening viable candidates."

Eve was definitely intrigued. "No, I wasn't aware of this."

"Well, that branch has recently acquired several new clients and they need someone to fill this position fairly soon. The problem is they haven't succeeded in finding the right person, and they asked if we had someone here at the San Francisco branch that we could recommend. They'd prefer to hire someone with knowledge of the company processes. I told them I had the perfect person for them... and that person is you, Eve." She was caught off guard and just stared at Ray in disbelief. "Eve, are you okay?"

"Yes, please forgive me, Ray. I guess I'm just surprised by the offer...I wasn't expecting this." After the initial shock of a possible promotion, her excitement started to grow.

"They desperately need help over there with the influx of new accounts, and we believe you're the woman for the job. Even though you've only been with us for four years, you've proven yourself worthy of this consideration. I personally hate to lose you here in San Francisco, but the New York City branch obviously needs you more." Ray leaned forward and rested his crossed fingers on top of his desk. "So...does this offer appeal to you?"

"Yes it does, very much so."

"Do you want some time to think about it before giving your final answer? It's a big decision given the relocation to New York, so I understand if you need a little time to digest everything."

"Yes, the move would definitely be a big change for me," Eve responded. *But the career possibilities are immeasurable*, she thought.

"Why don't you mull it over and give me your decision by the end of the week? We'll need your answer by then to ensure we have time to continue pursuing other candidates if you turn us down."

"I will, and thank you Ray for considering me. You will definitely have my answer by the end of the week, if not before."

Ray sat back and smiled. He knew she would accept the offer. Eve was no fool; opportunities like this didn't come around every day.

After several days of contemplating, Eve decided to take on the challenge and accepted the offer. She needed a major change in her life, and this opportunity couldn't have presented itself at a better time. Now all she had to do was share the news with her closest friends and prepare for her big move. She knew they would be happy about her getting the promotion but would not be thrilled with her moving so far away from them. Eve decided to invite Bonnie, Charles, and Caroline over to her apartment for dinner with the hopes that a full stomach and several glasses of wine would help them digest the news. Eve had to admit that moving away from her friends and her home was not appealing, but this was a great career opportunity she couldn't pass up.

# *Chapter 3*

Nicholas met with Anthony to finalize his plans for the Internet money-laundering scheme. Although grateful that their father had given him approval to move forward with his idea, Nicholas was not pleased that he had to work under Anthony's supervision. He didn't appreciate being babysat by his older brother, but his spotty track record didn't allow him the freedom to protest. So, for now, he'd bide his time until he proved his worth. Actions spoke louder than words as far as their father was concerned, so voicing any grievances at this point would fall on deaf ears.

"So, Nick, have you gotten the computer hackers in place?"

"Yes, I've located several local Internet cafés where potential hackers hang out. They're a dime a dozen, so we have more than enough to choose from to perform the grunt work. All we really need is one exceptional hacker who will be responsible for tapping into the bank's computer system to gain access to the customers' financial assets and then route the money to our offshore accounts."

"Have you lined up potential candidates yet?"

"Yes, and I narrowed it down to a guy by the name of Lucas Coles. He has an educational background and work experience in the field of computer technology and therefore has sophisticated skills beyond hacking. Lucas has a legitimate job and is employed by a corporation, so he wouldn't be an obvious suspect of low-level hacking activities. I'll have him target internet cafés in the city to recruit the low-level hackers we need. This way we keep our hands clean and they won't be aware of the Gennaro Family's involvement. Lucas speaks their language, so he could blend in with the usual crowd and approach potential hackers without drawing suspicion to himself, as opposed to someone from our organization. We would stick out like a sore thumb."

"You've got that right. Listen, I've made some progress as well. I've chosen a couple of banks on our payroll that we'll use to access the customer accounts. Several of the bank managers had debts to repay to our family, so it was easy to *persuade* them to cooperate as you suggested."

"Thanks Tony. I appreciate your help." *Even though I don't need it,* he thought.

"Once you've secured Lucas's cooperation, we can move forward," Anthony added.

"One of our associates is meeting with Lucas as we speak to provide him with our instructions. If Lucas accepts the offer, by the end of the day, all of the main players should be in place, and then we'll put our plan in motion."

"Good work. I'm proud of you, Nick. I'll inform Pop of our progress. I'm sure he'll be pleased that we'll produce some results for him in the near future."

* * *

Eve was putting the finishing touches on dinner when the doorbell rang. "Who is it?" she called out.

"It's us girl, open up," answered Bonnie.

"We're starving," added Charles, which prompted a disapproving glance from Caroline. "What?" he mouthed. But Caroline just rolled her eyes.

Eve opened the door grinning from ear to ear. "Well, we can't have that now, can we, Charles? Get in here. Dinner is ready, so go make yourselves comfortable."

Caroline and Charles entered the apartment, and as Bonnie brought up the rear, she handed Eve a bottle of wine. "This is for you, my dear, for a future occasion."

"Thanks, sweetie, but you didn't have to bring me anything."

"Guests should not arrive empty handed, and it was our pleasure." Eve and Bonnie had known each other since high school. Due to their last names, they were assigned seats right next to each other in homeroom, and they became instant best friends. Bonnie was slender and athletic from many years of playing tennis. Her creamy brown complexion and short haircut caught the eye of many men. Together, she and Eve were never for a lack of potential suitors in high school or college. Then the two of them met Charles and Caroline in gym class while attending college, and they had all been joined at the hip ever since.

Eve placed the wine in her mini-bar while Bonnie, Charles, and Caroline made their way into the dining area, admiring the spread she had prepared for them. "You definitely pulled out all the stops Eve, you've managed to include a favorite item for each of us," Charles garbled with his mouth already full. "Sorry to get a head start, but I *did* mention that we were starving."

Eve shook her head and chuckled, "Yes Charles, you did mention that."

There was never a dull moment with Charles around. He was quite attractive, which wasn't immediately evident. He was tall, lean, and well built, a clear indication that he took care of his appearance.

His wavy blond hair and blue eyes completed the package. It sort of snuck up on you, but if you stopped and really took a good look, a very handsome man shone through all of that goofy and clueless behavior.

Caroline hit Charles in the arm. "Hey, what was that for?" he snapped.

"You could have at least waited for all of us to sit down together, for Christ's sake," retorted Caroline.

"Well, I apologized, didn't I?"

"That's not the point and you know it," Caroline chastised.

"Okay you two, settle down. Are you sure you weren't siblings in another life?" asked Bonnie, although she sensed sibling rivalry was not the *real* source of their bickering.

"Heaven forbid!" responded Caroline, rolling her eyes again.

Charles grabbed Caroline around her waist, pinning her against his torso. "You love me and you know it. You would pass out if I weren't around." Bonnie and Eve snickered at the free entertainment. Charles took every chance he could get to put his hands on Caroline without drawing suspicion, or so he thought. Who could blame him? Although petite, Caroline often reminded Eve of a Barbie doll but with a hint of feistiness. The two of them were perfect for each other.

Caroline looked at them with pleading eyes. "Are the two of you just gonna giggle or are you gonna help me?"

Even in college, Eve and Bonnie always sensed an unspoken sexual tension between Charles and Caroline and wondered what the two of them were waiting for. It was obvious they had a thing for each other, but neither was willing to acknowledge it, at least not openly anyway. Who knew what happened between them behind closed doors, so Eve and Bonnie agreed to let the two of them reveal their true intentions on their own timetable.

Bonnie took pity on Caroline. "Let her go, Charles, so we can eat."

She spoke the magic words. "You don't have to tell me twice," Charles replied, releasing Caroline and grabbing another piece of fried chicken. Caroline just shook her head, mouthing the letters *O, M, G.*

"Charles, you do realize that I have plates and utensils and napkins?" asked Eve.

Charles shot Eve a look. "Okay, smart-aleck, I get the hint. You just had to get your digs in too."

"I couldn't resist, you make it too easy," Eve replied. "I'm really going to miss all of this," she added, feeling melancholic.

Sensing the change in Eve's mood, Bonnie's head snapped in her direction. "What do you mean by that?"

"Umm, well...I have some news that I want to share with you."

"Good or bad?" Bonnie asked hesitantly.

"A little bit of both, depending on how you want to look at it." Eve paused, wanting to find the right words, and decided to give the good news first and then ease into the not-so-good news of her having to move to New York City. She had wanted to break it to them after they had finished their meal, but things don't always happen as planned. "I was offered a new position in the company, a promotion actually."

"Well, that's great news," Caroline offered. "What could be bad about that?

"The position is located at the New York City branch," answered Eve.

"Oh," replied Caroline, not knowing what else to say, which was a first for her.

"That branch has been taking on several new big clients, and the Design Department is having difficulty handling the workload.

Colby Designs want me to take on a managerial role and put me in charge of that department."

The three friends just sat in silence for a minute trying to absorb what this promotion actually meant. Eve would be moving across the country and away from *them*, indefinitely or even permanently. The three of them exchanged glances with each other, but Bonnie was the first to speak.

"I see what you mean by this being good *and* bad news. You'll be leaving us..." she took in and released a breath, "but...you've been given a great opportunity, and I'm sure I speak for all three of us when I say we couldn't be more proud of you. You deserve this promotion, Eve."

Eve was touched by Bonnie's sentiment, but knew her best friend was struggling to hide her pain so as not to spoil her good news. "Thanks Bonnie, I am excited, but...I have to admit that I'm also a little apprehensive."

"Girl, you are fearless," admired Caroline. "I couldn't move across the country on short notice or *at all,* for that matter, especially by myself. You go for what you want and you don't let anything block your path to success. You and Malcolm are alike in that sense."

"Oh *pleeeeeaaaaase* don't pull a Malcolm on us," complained Charles. "That dude moved away and we *never* hear from him anymore."

"I would never do that to you guys, especially since I know how it feels to be left behind..." Eve was immediately overcome by the pain of abandonment. She and Malcolm grew up together almost like siblings. He was mostly a brother figure in their adolescent years until she developed a serious crush on him in her late teens. He was her oldest and dearest friend next to Bonnie. In college, the five friends had been inseparable, until after graduation when Malcolm decided to travel the country in order to pursue his photography career. His travels proved successful, as he became well-known and sought after for his work.

Eve was going to tell him how she felt at graduation until he informed them of his career and travel plans. Eve wasn't sure if Malcolm shared her feelings, and didn't want to influence his career decisions, so she'd never know if Malcolm would have stayed had she told him how she felt. It was as if she had lost her big brother, protector, and first potential love interest all in one fell swoop. As independent as Eve was, she was just as vulnerable, especially when it came to losing the people closest to her. Due to her parents' death and Malcolm's disappearing act, the feeling of abandonment was ever present at the back of her mind, although she tried not to acknowledge it.

Not aware of Eve's discomfort, Charles continued his tirade, "Malcolm didn't even show up to your parents' funeral, and they practically raised him. I still can't believe he did that," he said angrily, "and a sympathy call after the fact does not cut it. You deserved better than that from *him*, Eve."

The girls noticed that the conversation was upsetting Eve, so Bonnie decided to put an end to it. "Charles, we all feel the same way, believe me, but Eve is *not* Malcolm. She's only moving to New York and will be accessible. She's not traveling the country to God only knows where, like Malcolm is. So let's change the topic to a happier note, like eating this lovely dinner that Eve has prepared for us and celebrating her deserved promotion."

Feeling thoroughly reprimanded, Charles apologized sheepishly. "I'm sorry, Eve; I shouldn't have gone on and on like that."

"Don't worry about it. It's already forgotten," Eve replied, but of course, it really wasn't. Charles had hit a nerve. Eve shared Charles's sentiments and missed Malcolm terribly. She never told her friends about her previous feelings for Malcolm but had a feeling that Bonnie always suspected. Eve had long since gotten over her romantic feelings for Malcolm, which was not easy by any means, but she still missed him nonetheless, because he was a major part of her childhood.

Grateful for the rescue, Eve threw Bonnie a wink in gratitude and the four friends enjoyed their meal filled with laughter while reminiscing about the good times they had all shared together.

*  *  *

The Gennaros' business associate met with Lucas Coles regarding his role in the money-laundering scheme. The Gennaro brothers didn't meet with him personally so as to not be identified by Lucas should he ever get caught by the NYPD.

Lucas watched a tall, lean, well-built and *very* well-dressed man approach him. This man was clearly the person he was waiting for.

The man seated himself across the table from Lucas as if he was meeting a long-time friend for lunch. No introductions were necessary. "I see you've taken the liberty of ordering yourself a drink," the business associate stated.

*Of course I did*, thought Lucas. "Well, I needed something to do with my time while I waited for you to arrive."

The Gennaros' associate was not pleased. "We need you to be alert. I have important instructions to give, which you need to follow exactly to the letter."

"Don't worry. I can handle my liquor, and it's only one drink." Lucas was insulted by this man's insinuation. "So, what did you say your name was again?"

"I didn't."

Lucas took a swig of his drink. He definitely needed it. This man was starting to creep him out. "Okay…so exactly who am I working for?"

"You don't need to concern yourself with that. Just do your job properly and you will get paid handsomely. If you are not comfortable with those arrangements, we can find someone else who is."

"Whoa, hold on. I was just asking; that's all. I'm fine with the arrangement."

"Humph, that's what I thought." He provided Lucas with instructions on how to recruit the hackers from the Internet cafés and how to prep them for the upcoming mission. Lucas would also inform the young hackers that a powerful family wanted their services and they were willing to use threats and blackmail to coerce them to comply. In other words, saying no *was not* an option. After recruiting the hackers, Lucas should never meet with them at that café again and the hackers were to never return to the same café again. From that point forward Lucas would personally contact the hackers, using the burner phones he provided, when their services were needed, and if they refused to comply, they were dead, and possibly their families too.

"Are these instructions clear?"

"Perfectly," Lucas answered. The Gennaros' business associate kindly got up and exited the restaurant.

Lucas couldn't believe his fortune. He hit the jackpot with this one and stood to make a shitload of money. Even though Lucas was educated, he wasn't always smart, nor did he make the best decisions. He was quite greedy in fact, which was usually his Achilles heel. A cautious and smart man would have at least attempted to run in the opposite direction when approached with this offer, but Lucas jumped at the chance to make additional money and didn't care who or where the offer came from, a decision he would later come to regret.

# Chapter 4

Eve had a lot to accomplish during her last month in San Francisco. Given the short notice of her promotion and pending move, Colby Designs provided Eve assistance with finding an apartment and agreed to ship her furniture and belongings as well. For her remaining weeks, Eve focused on wrapping up her ongoing projects and creating an action plan for managing her new design team and handling all of the newly acquired accounts at the New York branch.

Eve had a meeting with her supervisor and entered the conference room to find Raymond waiting for her. "There she is!" he exclaimed. "The woman who is going to have our New York City clients eating out of our hands."

"Don't you think that's a bit of an exaggeration, Ray?" she asked modestly.

"Not at all, you're very good at what you do Eve, one of the best we've ever had here at Colby Designs. I have no doubt that you will get that team in shape. So let's get started creating a plan to make that happen."

"Of course, now I've taken the liberty of putting together a couple of ideas of my own," Eve handed Ray her list. "Tell me if you think they work with what you have in mind." Eve closely watched Ray's reaction as he reviewed her ideas. She wanted to firmly solidify that the confidence he had in her was completely justified. Ray's facial expression didn't divulge what he was thinking, so Eve was resigned to wait for his verbal assessment. *I'd hate to be seated across from Ray at a poker game*, she thought.

When he looked back at Eve, he smiled. "I knew I picked the perfect person for the job. You've captured most of the same ideas I have plus a couple I hadn't thought of."

"I'm glad you approve."

"Definitely. You seem to have a firm grip on what the issues are and how to address them." Ray handed Eve his list. "As you can see, our ideas are very similar. You can just combine the two lists, expand upon them and get the ball rolling on your own once you get there. I don't think we need to waste our time continuing with this meeting at all. You have enough on your plate before your big move."

"Are you sure you don't want to have a discussion about this?"

"It's really not necessary, but if you need assistance you know where to find me."

"Thank you, Ray."

"So how *are* the plans for your move coming along? Have you received the apartment listings from Human Resources yet?"

"Yes, and I've been reviewing them. It's a little weird having to choose an apartment without being able to view it in person, but I'm really happy with the choices they've provided, so I'll definitely make my final decision later this week."

"Great...I have to admit that I personally hate to see you leave us, Eve. If they didn't *really* need you in New York I would have kept you here with us. Our loss is *their* gain, plus this promotion will benefit you as you progress further with your career. A career I had hoped would continue to flourish here with us."

Eve was touched by Ray's sentiments. "I expected to do so as well. I'm very happy here, Ray. Your tutelage has been priceless, a privilege that is not lost on me, and I will always be grateful for your confidence in my abilities. I really appreciate this opportunity, and I won't let you or the company down."

* * *

After reviewing all of the apartment listings, Eve finally chose the one that would be her new home. She began to pack, starting with the things she didn't need to use on a daily basis. This would also give her a chance to scale down and get rid of or donate things she no longer used or needed. Eve wrapped up and divided her ongoing projects at the San Francisco office with the other members in her department, and finalized her game plan for tackling her new duties at the New York branch. She had worked at the San Francisco office for the last four years of her life and she had to admit that she was feeling a bit torn. For the remainder of the week Eve finished packing and shipped her things to New York while her friends planned a fourth of July and farewell party for the upcoming weekend.

* * *

"So Nick, Tony tells me that your money-laundering scheme is working according to plan, so far..." Angelo made sure to leave the question of continued success hanging in the air so that Nicholas didn't take his approval for granted.

"Yes Pop, I'm glad to report that it *is* working in our favor. Lucas Coles, the hacker we secured to implement the plan and basically do all of the dirty work for us, is performing his duties as instructed.

Anthony has chosen which banks to use and made sure to obtain the appropriate *cooperation* from the managers."

"How have the two of you decided how to obtain the customer IDs and passwords? You mentioned several possible options to choose from."

"Tony and I decided to use the email scamming method. Lucas is responsible for recruiting several low-level Internet hackers that will send out fake emails to customers which look like real ones from their banks asking them for their personal account information, in an obscure way of course. We usually get up to a hundred responses within an hour. The hackers will then provide this information to Lucas, who will use it to access the customers' accounts from the bank computers."

"I see. How many times a week do you send out these emails?"

"For now we've been sending them once a day, seven days a week, for the past three weeks. If the process continues to run smoothly we'll increase the frequency."

"That was smart and cautious of you, Son," he said, much to Angelo's surprise, since Nicholas hadn't always shown patience in the past. "Please, continue. I'm interested in hearing more."

Nicholas glanced at his older brother to see if he wanted to chime in, but Anthony deferred to Nicholas. This plan was his baby, and he deserved to present its progress to their father. So, Nicholas continued, "Lucas is an IT technologist and programmer at a major corporation, which is why we chose him to meet with the bank managers and access the customer accounts onsite. The low-level hackers aren't as comfortable working in a business environment. He'll also create the dummy Internet corporation websites where he'll run the charges which will direct the money to our overseas accounts, which I've set up especially for this project. Then he'll shut down the sites the following day so they can't be traced. We've made just fewer than sixty-five million dollars in the three weeks since the operation has been at full swing."

"Sixty five million... in three weeks... that's impressive," remarked Angelo. He was quite shocked actually, but didn't convey that particular emotion to his sons.

"Yes, I have to admit that I too was not expecting us to make *that much* in such a short timeframe, but I'm pleasantly surprised," replied Nicholas.

"So are we, little brother," added Anthony to show his support.

*I'm really gonna have to speak with Tony about this "little brother" crap.* "As I stated before, once everything is running smoothly we'll also increase the amount we charge from the accounts along with the frequency of emails, which will increase our profits even more."

"Good, I want you to continue moving forward. Keep a close eye on the players and adjust your strategy accordingly, if needed. We'll schedule another meeting in a couple of weeks to see where we stand at that time."

"Sure thing, Pop." Nicholas was beaming on the inside. He wanted to shout, "*I told you so,*" but he kept his cool. He was finally gaining his father and brother's respect.

* * *

Eve arrived at Bonnie's house to find the place packed with people from all parts of her life. Bonnie must have swiped her address book in order to create the guest list. Eve was touched that her best friend went to all of that trouble to give her a proper send-off, especially since it couldn't be easy for Bonnie to watch her prepare to move across the country. Bonnie saw that Eve had arrived and made a beeline toward her.

"Bonnie, this is outrageous, but wonderful. You didn't have to do all of this," proclaimed Eve while giving her a giant bear hug.

"Nonsense, you deserve it. I'm sure all of your friends that are here to celebrate your success will agree with me."

"Speaking of which, how did you get all of their contact information? I know for a fact that you don't know all of these people personally."

"I have my ways, which is on a need-to-know basis," Bonnie replied as she winked at Eve and quickly walked away before Eve could question her further.

Eve's mouth dropped open as she watched her scurry away. "That woman is too much," she mumbled to herself while shaking her head. Suddenly, Eve was enveloped in someone's arms and a voice whispered in her ear. She broke free and quickly turned around. "*Jackson*! Hey… I didn't know you were coming," Eve stated slowly and nervously.

"I wouldn't miss your send-off party for the world, Eve…You're breaking my heart, you know that, right?"

"What are you talking about?" Eve knew exactly what he was referring to and wasn't in the mood for it. She wanted to enjoy her last night in San Francisco without Jackson's continued advances.

"Eve, I've been chasing you for a while now, but to no avail. Do you think moving across the country will do the trick? I have half a mind to chase you all the way to New York."

*Half of a mind is right*, thought Eve as her eyes grew wide. "Follow me to New York? You *are* kidding?" she asked.

Jackson just smiled, but Charles and Caroline appeared before he could respond, *if* he ever intended to.

"Hey Jack, why don't you give Eve a break this evening?" warned Charles.

"I was only wishing her well with the move and her new promotion."

Charles glared at him. "I'm sure you were."

"Dude, there's no need to get overprotective," Jackson responded, annoyed with Charles's interference.

Charles's body tensed and he put a hand on Jackson's shoulder. "Eve has a lot of other guests that would also like to wish her well. Why don't we give her some time with *them*?" Although posed as a question, it was obvious that it was a strong suggestion, one that Jackson should not argue with.

Jackson glared back at Charles, but only for a moment, and then turned his attention to Eve. "Enjoy your party," he acquiesced, "I'm sure you'll be very successful, your promotion is well deserved." His smile belied what he was really feeling.

"Thank you Jackson," she responded, relieved when he left to mingle with other guests. That smile, of his sent a shiver up her spine.

"Sorry about that," Charles apologized.

"Are you kidding, what are you apologizing for? Thanks for saving me. Good Lord, he's *relentless*."

"Well, you wouldn't have to put up with him if he wasn't my friend to begin with, but Jackson's really not a bad guy, Eve."

"But he's damned aggressive, Charles," added Caroline. "I'm glad you put him in his place. He just can't believe that any woman wouldn't fall under his charms, *arrogant much*?"

"He's always been that way, ever since we were kids; he's harmless, but yes, as you've stated, relentless."

Bonnie made her way over to the trio. "I just saw Jackson, he didn't look too happy. What did I miss?"

"Girl, don't even get me started on that one," responded Caroline. "You know he was up to his usual *sexual harassment* of Eve."

Bonnie was horrified. "I didn't invite him Eve, really. He found out about the party on his own somehow, I swear."

"It's okay Bonnie, Charles got rid of him." Charles didn't always present himself as someone to be taken seriously, *until* you messed with his girls. Then he displayed a side of himself you didn't want to mess with.

"Just *how* he found out about the party is what *I* want to know," Caroline fumed.

"It is creepy for sure. Just as long as you're okay, Eve. This is *your* night, and you're supposed to be having a good time," answered Bonnie.

"I am, thanks to the three of you."

Eve spent the remainder of the party catching up with friends that she hadn't seen or spoken with in a while. Eve was always an ambitious woman, so it was no surprise to anyone at the gathering that she was excelling in her career. Everyone enjoyed themselves while celebrating Independence Day and Eve's success. How fitting, because Eve was one of the most independent women they knew. Bonnie made sure that each guest had a glass of champagne, and they all toasted Eve during the firework display. Many hugs and congratulations were showered upon her.

After all of the attention, Eve wandered off to catch a moment alone, to decompress and take it all in. Keeping a close eye on Eve all night paid off, as Jackson noticed her slip off to be alone. He took this opportunity to make his move and quickly followed suit. He approached Eve from behind, and then glanced around to ensure no one noticed, more importantly, that Charles hadn't noticed. He grabbed her around the waist and turned her around to face him. Eve gasped at the sudden intrusion to her solitude, and then to her dismay she was suddenly in a lip lock with Jackson Harper. Taking full advantage of their isolation from the other guests, he tightened his grip on Eve, and she wasn't able to break free from his arms *or* his lips.

When Jackson finally pulled away, he gazed into her eyes. "You were not getting away from me without at least *one* kiss, Eve Townsend," Jackson murmured. His face was very close to hers and he continued to hold her tightly. He had wanted Eve for a very long time, and he was going to savor this moment.

Eve squirmed, trying to loosen his grip, but was unsuccessful. She didn't want to make a scene and could see him coming in for another kiss. *Where is Charles, he'd put a stop to this.*

Before she could protest, Jackson's mouth claimed hers once again. He pried open her lips with his tongue and went on a delicious but urgent exploration. He finally released her, breathless. He wanted to devour her. "See what you've been missing, Eve." She didn't dare respond for fear of encouraging him. "Speechless, Ms. Townsend?" he chuckled.

"You…just…caught me off guard, that's all," which was true. "I'd appreciate not being *manhandled*, Mr. Harper. You could ask a girl's permission you know."

"You wouldn't have given it, plus it's easier to ask for *forgiveness* than permission. So…am I forgiven, Eve? They were only good luck kisses. I meant no harm," he cooed, feigning innocence. Jackson could be charming at times, but a creepy pain in the ass mostly.

*Good luck kisses? His tongue was halfway down my throat. Where the hell were Charles, Bonnie, and Caroline?!* Eve's eyes scanned the room desperately. "I'm not sure you deserve forgiveness, but since I'm leaving tomorrow I'll grant it this one time, provided you don't overstep again." Her tone was slightly biting, hoping to get her point across. It was all she could do anyway since she was still trapped in his embrace, which worried her a little.

To her relief she was finally set free as his hands went up in a defensive manner, "Duly noted; I won't overstep again. I really like you Eve, but it's obvious you don't share my desires and it was not meant to be for us. I guess I'll have to accept that now, especially since you're leaving, but I'll miss you." With that, he turned and walked away. Jackson had no intention of accepting defeat. He was *not* going to let a little distance keep him from getting what he wanted, what *belonged* to him. So, he could wait a little longer, and make his move when the time was right.

Eve hadn't realized she was holding her breath, and let out a sigh of relief. She would definitely *not* miss Jackson Harper. She finally spotted Bonnie and the others as they approached her. *Great, now they appear.* She decided to shake off her encounter with the "Casanova" wannabe and not mention his inappropriateness. She didn't want to incite another altercation between Charles and his friend. There wasn't any reason for them to be at odds, especially since she was moving away the following morning.

"I hope you enjoyed your party, Eve," Bonnie said.

"I did, sweetie, it was wonderful," *minus the Jackson Harper parts.*

"So this is it, huh?" Charles added. "It looks like the party is starting to wind down."

"Yeah, you'd better go home and get some rest," Caroline stated, "tomorrow is the big day, and you don't want to be exhausted. Did you call a taxi to pick you up?"

"Yes, I arranged for a return trip with my taxi ride here. They should arrive in about five minutes or so."

The three friends walked Eve outside to wait for her taxi. "We'll see you tomorrow morning as planned to escort you to the airport," added Charles.

"Thanks again guys, goodnight." During the taxi ride home Eve was pensive. She had a lot to think about. Tomorrow was the day that her life would change drastically, but was it for the better or worse, she wondered.

# Chapter 5

The next morning, Eve awoke with butterflies in her stomach. She was excited, nervous, happy, and scared all at the same time. She had never lived anywhere other than California, and living in New York City was going to be a big adjustment, but one that she was looking forward to experiencing.

Her flight was at 8:40 in the morning, so she packed her remaining personal items to be shipped with her on the plane and waited for Bonnie, Charles and Caroline to pick her up. They insisted on driving her to the airport to give her a proper send off. When they arrived, Charles started to pack Eve's luggage into the trunk of his SUV.

"Is this all you have?" he asked.

"Uh-huh, the movers took everything else. I really appreciate you guys escorting me to the airport. It would have been difficult if I had to go alone. It's hard enough having to leave you at all."

"We figured as much. It's hard for us to see you leave," replied Bonnie. "I can't believe it's happening already. In just a couple of hours you'll be gone."

"Oh, for goodness' sake," protested Charles, "please don't start this already. I'll have to listen to the three of you boo-hooing all the way to the airport."

"You're such a *man*," stated Caroline.

"Yes I *am*, and you should be used to that by now," retorted Charles.

"And you should be used to what goes along with hanging around the three of us, who happen to be *women!*" Caroline snapped.

"Whoa you two, calm down. Charles is right. If we get emotional and start crying *now*, we might never stop," replied Eve as they all piled into Charles's SUV. Caroline automatically jumped in the front next to Charles while Bonnie and Eve took the back seats. This seating arrangement was just another sign to Bonnie and Eve that there was more to Charles and Caroline's relationship than either one was willing to admit.

"Thank you Eve, the voice of reason," Charles replied, while squinting at Caroline. He started the ignition and they pulled off.

Caroline ignored him. "How did you sleep last night, Eve?" she asked, twisting her body to the left in order to see Eve in the back seat.

"Barely, I was too hyped up after the party and couldn't get my brain to stop churning."

"I'm not surprised," added Bonnie, "you've got a lot going on."

"I know, and thanks again for the party. It really meant the world to me. I can tell it took a lot of time and planning on your part."

"No problem, girl," answered Bonnie.

"It's just too bad that freakin' Jackson had to crash it. I am so tired of his stalking ass," responded Caroline.

"Caroline, is that really necessary? Labeling Jack as a stalker?" asked Charles.

She whipped her head in Charles's direction. "Are you serious? Even *you* had to step in to get Jackson away from Eve last night. He's creepy, Charles."

Eve jumped in, "I have to agree with Caroline."

"Not you too, Eve, please don't encourage her," Charles pleaded.

"But he does give me the creeps. He hounded me again after the champagne toast and fireworks."

"*WHAT*?! Why didn't you say something?" Charles was starting to fume.

"Charles, please calm down. I didn't want the two of you getting into an altercation."

"Did he do something to you, Eve?" She hesitated to answer and glanced at Bonnie. Charles eyed her in the rearview mirror. "Eve, answer me."

"Charles, calm down, you're driving. I'd like us to make it to the airport in one piece."

"Then answer my question or I'm pulling over. *What* did he do to you?"

"Alright already!" Eve sighed heavily. "Jackson came up behind me, and grabbed me and then…"

"Then *what*?" Charles snapped.

"He kissed me and wouldn't let go of me. I couldn't get out of his grip. I looked for the three of you and couldn't find you, but he finally let me go and then he left. That's when the three of you showed up."

"Eve, and you didn't say a word to us," complained Bonnie.

"I would have punched him right in the nose," stated Caroline. "I'm so tired of him. He goes from stalking to manhandling you now? He needs an ass whooping for sure."

Charles silently glared at Eve through the rearview mirror. He was so angry at her for not telling him what Jackson had done to her at the party. But he could understand why she kept it to herself. Eve returned his stare sheepishly. She could tell he was not pleased with her.

"I'm sorry, Charles. Please don't be upset with me. I just didn't want to ruin everyone's mood last night and didn't want to deal with Jackson anymore. Plus I'm about to board a plane and don't know when I'll see any of you again. I don't want to dwell on upsetting issues."

"I understand, Eve, really, I do. I'm not upset anymore. I guess the only good thing about you leaving is that Jackson can't bother you any longer."

"I hardly doubt distance would stop him," added Caroline, "I'd keep one eye open for him in New York if I were you. I'll give you a shout-out if we hear that he's made a spur-of-the-moment trip away." Charles shot her a look. She just didn't know when to let things be.

"Caroline, the last thing Eve needs to be worrying about is whether Jackson will follow her to New York." Little did he know, Jackson alluded to doing that very thing, but Eve was not about to mention that. She wanted this conversation over and done with.

Even though it was morning traffic, it took them over an hour to reach SFO airport, but they didn't mind since it gave them more time with each other. Once they arrived, Eve picked up her boarding pass and checked in her luggage.

Caroline grabbed Eve's hand and whispered, "I'm sorry about earlier, in the car, talking about Jackson. I didn't mean to upset you. Are you okay? Are *we* okay?"

Eve squeezed Caroline's hand. "Of course we're okay. I know you are only looking out for me. Charles has a blind spot when it comes to Jackson. You keep it real and he has no choice but to look deeper at his friend's behavior. But I don't want the two of you at odds over it."

"The two of *us*, there is no us. Don't worry about it. It's all good." Eve thought the lady doth protest too much. She chuckled inside. She was going to miss them all terribly.

Her loyal friends escorted her as far as the security checkpoint and said their goodbyes. There were lots of hugs *and* tears, which Charles contributed to as well.

After Eve made it through security she waved goodbye one last time, suddenly feeling very alone and scared. "Stop it!" she admonished herself. "You're being a baby." She continued to her gate, boarded the plane and settled in her window seat. As the plane taxied to the end of the field she swallowed nervously as a lump formed in her throat. Eve stared out of the window as the plane started to pick up speed. *She was really doing this*, and then the plane was airborne.

Eve had magazines, books, and music, anything to fill the six-and-a-half-hour flight to New York. A lot of good it did her. Due to her lack of sleep she was too tired to focus and found it difficult to concentrate on any of it. Everyone said that she was brave to uproot herself and start a new life somewhere else all alone. Well, she didn't feel very brave at the moment, and the magnitude of what she was doing was starting to sink in. She had inherited a huge responsibility at Colby's New York City branch, and she had every confidence in her ability to achieve the task at hand. Eve would be alone in New York without a support system, and that would be her biggest challenge, but she knew she could handle it. She *would* handle it.

If her parents were still alive, Eve wondered if she would have taken this new position. Having to move so far away from *them* might not have been so easy, but they would have supported her either way because they were very proud of her accomplishments. They might have even urged her to go, and Eve believed that they were looking down at her now in support of her decision. Thinking about her parents calmed Eve's nerves, and she decided to close her eyes and just relax for the remainder of the flight.

* * *

It was half past five in the evening when Eve landed at JFK. She was well rested from her nap and in a better state of mind. She picked up her luggage and hopped in a taxi. During the forty-five minute taxi ride she texted Bonnie, Charles and Caroline to inform them that she had arrived in New York safely and was headed to her new apartment, which would be empty until the movers arrived with her furniture the following day. Then she called her realtor, Jessica Burk, to arrange to meet her at the apartment with the keys.

She was excited, as this was the first time she would see the apartment with her own eyes. It was located on the Upper West Side on Columbus Avenue with easy access to transportation, restaurants, taverns, museums, and of course, Central Park. Eve was most excited about being near Central Park. She had visited New York before with friends, so she wouldn't be so easily overwhelmed by the enormity of it all. Nevertheless, there was a big difference between visiting NYC and living there, so it would still take some time to get used to the new environment. When her taxi pulled up in front of her building, Eve couldn't believe how much she owed the driver. She would have to decide what her regular mode of transportation would be and might opt for the subway, given how easily you could go bankrupt on the taxi rides alone.

She retrieved her luggage and entered her new building. She was amazed at the number of people mulling about at six-thirty in the evening, but it was a holiday weekend after all, and in NYC no less. She buzzed her apartment number, praying that Jessica had already arrived. Her prayers were answered when Jessica's voice crackled over the intercom asking who it was. Eve replied and was immediately buzzed in. She entered the lobby, found the elevators and rode it up to the third floor. She didn't want an apartment too high up. She felt comfortable tackling three flights of stairs in either direction in case of an emergency. The elevator doors opened and she exited, wondering which apartment was hers. Jessica must have timed Eve's ascent, because a door opened and Jessica's head popped into view.

"I see you've made it in one piece," Jessica announced at the sight of Eve approaching her.

"Hi Jessica, it's nice to finally meet you in person," Eve replied.

"Same here, Eve. Come in, come in and check out your new digs."

Eve entered and set her luggage to the side. A smiled spread across her face. "This is really nice."

"I'm glad you like it. You have a nice-sized closet here to your left and you enter the kitchen here," Jessica stated, pointing to her right. She watched as Eve turned on and off the faucets and stove ranges, as well as looked through all of the cabinets and the refrigerator. "As you can see, everything is working in tip-top shape. You do have the superintendent's contact information for future repairs, right?"

"Oh yes, I have all of that information handy."

"Good, now your bathroom and washer and dryer unit is across from the kitchen and next to the bedroom. And this is the living and dining area. Both the living and bedroom areas have large windows as you requested, so you'll receive lots of sunlight."

"Wow, the virtual tour was spot on, but it looks even better in person."

"I'm glad you approve. You've traveled a long way and we really try to make sure that you're happy with the final result. I know the apartment sizes are smaller here than in San Francisco, and since your furniture is arriving tomorrow, hopefully this meets your needs and everything fits."

"It should be fine. I was prepared for this. I knew I couldn't bring everything, so I downsized quite a bit. Donations, eBay, and Craigslist..."

"Smart girl. Well, here are your keys. This one is for the lobby entrance downstairs, this one is for your mailbox, and this is the apartment key."

"Thanks Jessica, for everything. I wouldn't have been able to do this without you. I'll have to make sure to inform Colby that they've chosen a great Agency to partner with for relocating employees. This experience could have been hell on wheels otherwise."

"Thanks, Eve. I really appreciate the praise. Well, I'm sure you're tired from traveling, so I'm going to leave you to your new home. Do you have any questions?"

"No, I'm good for now."

"Great, but if you need anything else you have my number."

"Yes, thanks again."

After Jessica left, Eve gave the apartment another walk-through and decided to take what was left of the day to decide where to place her furniture and give the place a quick cleaning while it was empty. She ventured out into the neighborhood to find the closest supermarket and picked up some essentials to last a couple of days.

By the time she finished cleaning it was 8:30 in the evening New York Time, but due to the three-hour time difference for Eve, it was only 5:30. She ordered takeout and ate her first meal on her living room floor. Wanting to acclimate to New York time, Eve took a hot shower, set up her air mattress and turned in for the night.

* * *

While Eve waited for the movers the next morning, she occupied her time with the material she never had the chance to read on the plane. Once the movers arrived, they placed Eve's boxes and furniture in their appropriate rooms, and Eve spent the remainder of the day unpacking and putting everything in its place. She only took a break to eat a quick lunch, and when she finished unpacking she plopped her weary body on the sofa and looked around. This was home now. Although it didn't quite feel like it yet, but having all of her belongings made her feel more comfortable at least.

She looked at her watch, which displayed 4:30. It should be about 1:30 in San Francisco, so she figured it was a good time to call Bonnie before she took her lunch break.

Bonnie was also thinking about Eve and wondered how she was settling in. Bonnie didn't want to call and interrupt if Eve was still busy with the movers, so she decided to be patient and wait for Eve to call when she was available to speak. Being patient was not an easy task for Bonnie. She missed her best friend and wanted to make sure that Eve was okay. She was about to get her wish when the phone rang, breaking her train of thought. "Hello, Bonnie Stephens speaking," she answered.

"Hello Bonnie Stephens. I hope you're not too busy to chat with a friend?"

"Eve! I was just thinking about you. How are you? I miss you already, girl. I wanted to call but wasn't sure if you were settled. Are you all moved in yet—"

"Whoa, take a deep breath, Bonnie," Eve interrupted with a chuckle, "yes, I'm basically all moved in. I just finished, in fact, and wanted to check in with you before I passed out from exhaustion."

"I'm sorry for babbling. I guess I was getting antsy waiting to hear from you. I've got to get used to this time difference. You're about three hours behind, right?"

"Yeah, it's just after four-thirty in the afternoon here. I figured you were getting anxious to hear from me, so I wanted to catch you before you went to lunch."

"I thank you for that, my friend. You know me so well. So how are you... *really*?"

"I'm exhausted, both physically *and* emotionally. It all sort of hit me like a ton of bricks once the plane took off. I got a little freaked out, but I was okay by the time I landed. Even now, it still feels a bit surreal."

"I can imagine, one minute you have a life in California and the next you have a whole new one in New York. It must feel like you're going to wake up to find that it was all a dream."

"Exactly, it'll probably take a couple of days for me to acclimate to all of the changes. I'm hoping that I'll be too busy at work to dwell on how much I miss all of you and my life back in San Francisco."

"The people at Colby Designs won't know what hit them once you walk through those doors on Monday. So just take the next couple of days to relax and get comfortable with your new surroundings and enjoy your first week in the Big Apple, because I'll guarantee you won't have time for that after this weekend. Listen, you sound pretty tired, so I'm not going to talk your ear off even though I want to. Get some rest and we'll touch base soon."

"Okay, bye Bonnie."

Bonnie was correct. Eve was pretty exhausted and decided to take a nap before dinner, in her own bed this time. When Eve opened her eyes again, the clock read 9:30. She had to blink several times before she convinced herself that she was reading it correctly. The three-hour time difference had definitely caught up to her. It was too late to start preparing a meal and Eve was too tired to be bothered, so she turned over and went back to sleep.

The next morning, Eve awoke early and refreshed, but starved. A good and *long* night sleep was just what the doctor ordered, and she was ready to start her day. After a hearty breakfast, she decided to become familiarized with her new neighborhood as much as she could during that first week while she had the chance. She located several parks to jog in, one of them being Central Park of course, and stocked her refrigerator with enough groceries to tie her over for a couple of weeks. Eve also made sure to locate all of the local fast food and delivery places, because she was sure to need them more often than her own kitchen during the next several months. After a couple of days, she started to feel more comfortable in New York and started to enjoy the time she had just for herself, short-lived as it was.

* * *

It had been about a month and a half since Lucas started working on the Internet money-laundering scheme for his new employers, and everything seemed to be going great. This venture was turning out to be very lucrative for them, but Lucas believed that *he* was doing all of the hard work and should be well compensated for that fact. He was actually being paid very handsomely, but being the greedy bastard that he was, Lucas felt he deserved more.

He decided to siphon extra money for himself by writing a computer program that would transfer a small portion from each of the website transactions into one of his own personal bank accounts. He figured his employers would never notice because they were obviously not savvy with computer programming or they wouldn't have needed *him* to implement their plan in the first place. Arrogant thinking on his part, given he knew nothing about them personally. He had no idea who he was actually dealing with and what they were capable of.

Lucas, however, only had a small, time window to accomplish this task before he was scheduled to shut down the bogus websites. He wished he had come up with this idea sooner, because he could have been reaping the rewards for the entire month. Now he only had the remainder of the day to implement his plan and decided to install the program once he got home from work. Lucas logged off and damn near ran out of the Colby Designs building, but before he could get to the subway, his cell phone rang. He cursed under his breath; he was not in the mood for distractions.

"Lucas here," he snapped.

"Thank God you answered."

"Who is this?" Lucas asked impatiently.

"It's *Jim* from IT," he answered, frantically calling Lucas for assistance, "we need you back here. Two of the servers just crashed."

Lucas cursed under his breath again. "What! Are you kidding me? I just left and everything was working fine. What in the hell happened?"

"We don't know... that's why we called *you*." Lucas hesitated and didn't respond immediately.

"Lucas, are you still there?"

"Yes Jim, I'll be right back," he answered gruffly and then hung up. Lucas was fuming as he stalked up the street back toward the Colby Designs building. He was two beats away from the subway. Had he gotten inside he wouldn't have had cell reception and would be on his way home now. *What good were assistants if they couldn't assist in his absence*? This problem couldn't have happened at a more critical time. He needed to get home so he could install his program.

Visions of dollar signs consumed his thoughts. He arrived back at the IT department to assess the situation, and unfortunately, the problem was dire. His assistants wouldn't be able to fix the server problem without him, and he didn't know how long it was going to take them to complete it. If they couldn't solve the server issues before midnight he would carry out his plan using the computers in the IT department. Lucas preferred to keep his personal business dealings separate from his job, but what other choice did he have? He had plenty of choices, actually, and should have taken this as a sign to abort his asinine plan, but of course, he didn't.

# *Chapter 6*

Eve arrived at the Colby Designs NYC branch bright and early Monday morning. She decided on taking the subway to work and had survived her first morning rush-hour commute. After signing in at the lobby security desk, Eve took the elevator up to the fourth floor, where the Design Department was located. She stepped off the elevator and approached the receptionist, Linda Quinn.

"Good morning Linda. I'm Eve Townsend, the new Manager for the Design Department. I was told to report directly to Nathan Patterson."

Linda's smile was welcoming. "Oh yes, Ms. Townsend. He's expecting you. Good luck on your first day. Just walk down this hallway, make a slight left and continue down the hallway to the end. His office is to the right. I'll let him know that you're on your way."

"Thank you, Linda."

When Eve arrived at Nathan's office, she was surprised to find him standing there to greet her. "Eve Townsend, I presume?" he announced.

"Yes Mr. Patterson, it's nice to finally meet you."

"Call me Nathan, and yes, it's nice to finally meet you after the many phone conversations. Please, come in."

"Thank you, Nathan," Eve replied as she entered his office.

"I have to admit that we are anxious to have you start, not wanting to put additional pressure on you, of course."

Eve smiled. "That's okay. I figured as much. You've been without an active manager for a while now, so it's only natural you'd want me to dive right in. Don't worry; I'm ready to get to work."

"Great, I'm not surprised. Ray implied as much when he recommended that we consider you. He said we would not be disappointed." Eve was touched by the praises Ray bestowed on her behalf. She owed him a lot and would not disappoint either him or Nathan. "I hope that you're all settled in your new apartment and have been able to enjoy a little bit of the city this past week?"

"Yes, I'm all moved in and I took in some of the local sights in my neighborhood. I kept it low key and more relaxing."

"That's good, so… let's go meet the members of your team and then I'll give you the tour of the company, but not before I show you your new office. You passed it on your way to me," he stated while leading her down the hall. "Here we are, right on the corner. I'm surprised you didn't see your name plate."

"I was too focused on finding your office." Eve opened the door and walked in. It was brightly lit and spacious, and the mound of folders waiting on her desk did not go unnoticed.

"So, do you like it?"

"Yes, it's lovely, even with that stack of work on my desk." Eve laughed.

"I know… we're shameless. We didn't even wait for you to arrive before piling it on. That's how desperate we are."

"No worries, I understand. I'll dive right into those after the tour."

"Okay, so let's go meet the team."

The design team was a talented group, but working without an active manager with the influx of new clients proved to be a daunting task. They were excited for Eve's arrival because they needed the guidance that she would provide, as they were floundering on their own, but were also nervous about the possibility of unwelcomed changes because you never knew what direction a new manager might take. Eve informed them that after she finished reviewing the new client accounts she would set up a staff meeting to discuss how they would move forward.

Nathan Patterson proceeded with the company tour starting with IT. "Lucas, I'd like you to meet Eve Townsend, the new manager of our Design Department. She transferred here from our San Francisco branch. Eve, this is Lucas Coles. He manages the IT department."

Eve shook Lucas's hand. "Pleased to meet you, Lucas."

"The pleasure is *all* mine," replied Lucas while ogling her from head to toe, causing a chill to run up Eve's spine. She quickly released her hand, wondering if Nathan noticed that Lucas was practically salivating. Since Nathan didn't visibly react, she decided to let it go for now. This might be typical 'Lucas behavior' that Nathan was oblivious to at this point, and Eve didn't want her first impression to be of someone complaining about a co-worker on her first day.

"Eve, Lucas will be responsible for providing you with all of the appropriate credentials for entering the building and accessing your computer and the software applications. He just needs to take your picture for the ID badge, so we might as well take care of that now while we're here."

"Please step over here, Ms. Townsend." Lucas guided Eve to stand in front of a white screen. "Just look into the camera and smile," he instructed, and then took Eve's picture. "I will personally deliver your badge within the hour, Ms. Townsend." Lucas gave her the creeps, and she was not pleased that he would be coming to her office, but Eve thanked him anyway.

As Eve and Nathan exited the IT department, Lucas took the liberty of perusing Eve's body from behind. *Mm mm, the back view is just as good as the front,* he thought. Although Lucas was appreciative of Eve's physique, he breathed a sigh of relief that she and Nathan were gone. He hadn't noticed them approaching and he could have been caught red-handed. The two of them showing up unannounced was a close call, and Lucas realized that he had to be more careful. After they were safely out of sight, he resumed with what he was working on, even though it wasn't exactly company business.

Once Eve returned to her office she was suddenly overwhelmed by the pile of folders, reports, mock-ups, and designs that surrounded her. She closed her eyes for a couple of seconds and took several deep breaths. She could do this. She had a strategy worked out, and all she had to do was implement it.

Eve decided to review each project individually to determine what stage they were at in relation to its projected completion date. She discovered several projects falling off schedule that needed to become an immediate priority. She also assessed her team's current responsibilities and weighed it against their capabilities and concluded that their skill-sets were not being utilized efficiently. She was going to have to re-allocate some of their duties or hire new employees if necessary in order to maximize production. A complete restructuring of the team was paramount to their success, and she hoped that she wouldn't receive too much push back.

Eve suddenly felt as if she was being watched and glanced up to find Lucas standing in her doorway. She flinched at the sight of him. "Lucas! How long have you been standing there? Why didn't you say something?"

Lucas was too busy giving Eve the once-over, with particular attention to her legs, to announce his presence, that's why. "Sorry Ms. Townsend, I didn't mean to startle you. You were just so engaged in what you were reading... I didn't want to break your train of thought," he responded with a leering smile.

Eve shivered. "Is that my ID badge in your hand?" she asked, trying to move things along.

"Yes, and personally delivered as promised." He entered her office and handed it to her. "You should have access to everything you need, but if you have any problems just give me a call. I'm at your service." He punctuated with a sweeping bow.

Eve resisted rolling her eyes. "Thank you, Lucas. I'll do that," she replied, praying that she would never have to.

"Have a good day, Ms. Townsend."

"You do the same." Eve's relief at not having to deal any longer with Jackson's creepy behavior back in San Francisco was short-lived after being exposed to Lucas's antics, and she wondered what it was about herself that attracted these nutjobs. Lucas was obviously getting away with his inappropriateness in the workplace, but his somewhat harmless behavior could easily escalate if unchecked. As he exited her office she decided to try and keep her distance from that one.

It took Eve the rest of the day to get through the remainder of the projects and employee reviews, and decided she needed to meet with each of her team members individually before their first staff meeting. This would provide her the opportunity to get to know each of them personally before dealing with everyone as a group. She became too bleary-eyed and starved to continue working and realized it was almost seven o'clock, so she decided to call it a day.

*  *  *

The next morning, Eve arrived bright and early in preparation for the string of meetings she had planned. Each employee saw this as their opportunity to shine in front of the new boss and to make the best first impression possible. Each session was an eye-opening experience for Eve. The team members displayed character traits ranging from arrogance and overconfidence to shyness and humility. Coupling this with their actual work performance and knowledge allowed Eve to finalize their assignments. There would be some definite shake-ups in responsibilities from this point on, resulting in some unfortunate surprises for some.

Everyone gathered in the conference room for the group meeting, anxiously awaiting Eve's plans on how they would move forward. It was a long and interesting meeting as she reviewed the status of each project and doled out the corresponding assignments. Some were shocked by their newfound responsibilities and others tried to debate Eve's decisions, but they all eventually accepted their new duties along with her explanations. After all, who were they to argue? If their work was up to par, the San Francisco branch wouldn't have had to send Eve to New York City to help them in the first place.

Over the next two weeks, the team worked closely with Eve to get the projects back on track as well as keep up with new ones. There were long hours and many late nights, and at times Eve felt as if the only people she saw were the members on her team. But it was all worth it as the hard work started to pay off. Each and every one of them could see the benefits of their efforts and dedication. Eve was proud of her team and of herself.

⁎ ⁎ ⁎

So far the Gennaros hadn't realized, more specifically, Nicholas Gennaro hadn't realized, that Lucas was stealing from the profits of the money-laundering scheme, and this made Lucas feel empowered. The Gennaros thought that they were being discreet by not meeting with him personally. He suspected just from the so-called "business associate" they sent to meet with him that the Gennaro family was his employer and in control of this operation, but he didn't let on to that fact for his own self-preservation. Of course, this was all speculation on his part, but it didn't matter to him who they were as long as he got paid.

Unfortunately, Lucas couldn't be satisfied with the handsome payment from the Gennaros and the money he was stealing from them on the side. He figured if he could pull one over on a major crime family he could most definitely do the same at Colby Designs. He hacked into the company's financials and began siphoning money from an account, which he thought would be less noticeable. Unbeknownst to him, Lucas had inadvertently accessed an account the company had flagged to be monitored. A rookie mistake on his part given his hacking expertise, but that's what happens when you let greed override logic and common sense. He abandoned his own mantra of keeping his business and personal dealings separate and would eventually pay the price for it.

Once Colby's security team received the alert that someone had illegally accessed one of the company's financial accounts, they began the mission of tracking down the culprit. This task was not the easiest, even for Colby's top-notch security experts. Lucas's hacking skills kept him off the radar for over a week, but to no avail. They eventually traced the program back to his computer station and were able to follow the money trail to his personal bank account. Nathan Patterson was immediately informed that Lucas was stealing from the company and was given orders to terminate him immediately.

* * *

Lucas was obviously not aware that his transgressions had been discovered. Money continued to be transferred to his personal bank account from Colby's financial account. Nathan had to handle Lucas's dismissal very carefully so as not to alert him of his pending fate. Given the chance, God only knows what he might install in the company's computer system in the name of vengeance and retaliation. For all Nathan knew, Lucas already had something installed to wreak havoc within the company that would automatically be triggered unless he was able to disable it on a regular basis, or something that could be triggered remotely in case he was ever discovered and terminated.

Nathan decided to set up a meeting with Lucas in his office to discuss a bogus server upgrade. They recently had issues with the servers crashing, so Lucas didn't suspect foul play and figured it was about time for an upgrade, as he was tired of repeatedly getting called back to the office to fix them.

Lucas arrived at Nathan's office. He knocked before opening the door then automatically entered. As he closed the door behind him, he noticed two men were present that he hadn't expected, and thought he had interrupted another meeting in progress. "Oh Nathan, I'm sorry to just barge in. I thought we were going to discuss server upgrades. If this is a bad time I can come back later once you've finished your meeting," Lucas stated, feeling uneasy. The two men looked *very* serious.

"That won't be necessary, Lucas, please have a seat." Nathan gestured to one of the chairs next to the two men and Lucas sat down, hesitantly, alarm bells going off. "I won't waste time, so I'll get to the point," Nathan began.

"Get to the point... about what? I thought we were discussing server upgrades," Lucas questioned, wondering why the two men hadn't spoken or taken their eyes off him since he arrived.

"No, we're discussing something more serious than that, and it needs our immediate attention." The two men glared at Lucas, still not saying a single word, and he started to squirm, wondering what the hell Nathan was talking about. "We know about you stealing money from the company," announced Nathan.

*Holy shit!* Lucas could only stare at Nathan. He didn't see this coming and wasn't sure what to say. What *could* he say? He was busted, and he realized the two guys sitting next to him must be some sort of security. He didn't recognize them, so Nathan must have used an outside source. And they were... rather large, to say the least. Now he really started to squirm and babble. "Nathan, I… I'm sorry, I'll stop. I'll remove the program... Please—"

Nathan put his hand up to cut Lucas off in mid sentence. "You are *fired*, Lucas. We can't allow you to continue working here. You *betrayed* this company. Your credentials have been revoked and you no longer have access to the building *or* to our computers. In fact, security is at your work station as we speak making sure you haven't done anything malicious to our systems that will cause irreparable damage."

"I haven't done anything of the sort. I *only* stole money, that's it."

"Isn't that enough? You committed a crime. You're lucky you're not being carted off to jail as we speak. These two gentlemen will personally escort you off the premises, but if you ever show your face here again you *will be* prosecuted."

The two men stood up, pulled Lucas out of his seat and carried him out of Nathan's office. "*Let go of me!*" Lucas cried out. "You don't have to manhandle me; I can walk on my own." The two men ignored Lucas while he continued to shout expletives and obscenities at them. Lucas caused quite a ruckus as they dragged him down the hallway and into the elevator. Once they arrived in the lobby, the security men snatched Lucas's ID badge from around his neck.

"You'll regret this," he began, "I don't deserve to be treated like this—" Before he could finish his sentence Lucas found himself being tossed outside like trash, right onto the New York City streets. As New Yorkers watched Lucas being tossed on his ass he glared at the two security men through the glass door. *Mark my words. Colby Designs will pay for this*, he thought menacingly.

* * *

It was a hot and humid July morning, and Mike and Sam were interrogating two young hackers they caught in the act of scamming bank customers for their IDs and passwords. "Listen, you and your buddy are in serious trouble, so you might as well start talking," advised Mike. "We can go easy on you if tell us what we want to know, but more specifically, *who* you're working for."

"We don't know...exactly."

"You don't *know...exactly*?" Sam asked suspiciously.

"No, really...we don't. Some older guy, a fellow hacker, approached us at an Internet café and offered us the opportunity to work on a much bigger and more lucrative scam than what we normally operate on our own. We weren't interested because we like to do our own thing, but then he threatened to turn us into the cops if we didn't agree to work with him."

"So you were coerced... someone else is pulling the strings?" Mike asked.

"Yeah, and this guy said that if we told *anyone* what we were doing or tried to stop, we were dead. It was a message from some '*powerful family*' that we are all supposedly working for."

Mike and Sam perked up. "Who is this powerful family? We need a name," urged Sam.

"We don't know their name and never met with them directly. This guy only mentioned them but never said who they were."

"Then what's *his* name?" Sam asked impatiently.

They just stared at him, afraid to give up information that would lead back to them.

"Look, if we have to keep dragging information out of you, we'll just throw your asses in a cell and leave you to rot." The two young hackers glanced at each other nervously and one of them spoke up, "Okay, alright, his name...is Lucas."

"Lucas what? He must have a last name," said Mike.

"We don't *know* his last name. It's not like he's gonna tell us his life story."

Sam cast a look of annoyance in Mike's direction before turning his attention back to the boys. "Okay, wiseass, then why don't you just tell us where we can find this Lucas?" he demanded, glaring at the young hackers.

"We don't know that either..." one answered shakily and hesitantly, almost afraid to admit it for fear of further pissing off Detective Lewis.

"Look! You're gonna tell us the truth or we're throwing you to the wolves," warned Sam. "So you've got about five seconds to spill it."

"We're telling you the truth. We have no idea. We never contacted him directly, Lucas always got in touch with *us*. It was as if he had us under surveillance or something, because he would just show up wherever we were whenever he needed us," one of the boys responded rapidly and with increasing anxiety.

Mike and Sam were certain that the powerful family pulling the strings was the Gennaro crime family. This hacking stuff didn't seem like their normal type of crime, but they had a gut feeling the Gennaros were involved somehow. Even though they lived upstate, their criminal dealings always seemed to trickle back down to the city. I guess you go where the action is.

"So what did this *Lucas* have you do?" asked Mike.

"We sent out emails that appeared to come from legitimate banks asking customers for their personal information, in a roundabout way, of course. Then we passed that information to Lucas. What he did with it, we couldn't tell you. We don't have a clue, honest," one replied.

"Really... look, your only hope is if we find this Lucas character, so I suggest the two of you dig into your memory and provide us with a detailed description so that we can identify this man," snapped Sam.

"Sure, we'll do anything you want," they replied, vigorously nodding their heads in agreement, thinking they may have a way out of this after all.

Once they finished interrogating the young hackers, Mike and Sam sent them to work with the sketch artist.

"Good job playing bad cop, Sam. I thought they were going to piss in their pants," Mike joked as they left the interrogation room.

"I wasn't playing. They were working my last nerve. It's too damn hot for this nonsense," Sam replied with a scowl on his face.

Mike chuckled.

Dan, a fellow detective, caught up to them just as the re-entered the squad room. "Dan, please tell us you've got something we can use," Mike pleaded.

"Maybe... I did some research; they're using the common email scamming method called phishing. It's a fraudulent activity where a third party sends an email designed to look like it came from a legitimate company. You've seen the 'fake' emails that will typically ask victims to take urgent action to avoid a consequence, such as loss of service, verify an account change, or receive a reward. They attempt to lure customers to a fraudulent website to input personal information such as credit card numbers or passwords. They could also ask customers to reply to the email or click on a link, which enables malware to be downloaded to their computer. The fake emails can produce about a hundred responses within an hour."

"People actually still fall for this shit?" Sam asked in total disbelief.

"Well yeah, they think they're receiving emails from their own personal banks. That's how authentic they can look. Everyone has gotten one of these emails at one time or another, but most of us ignore or delete them. Once the hackers have the customer's information, they either max out their credit cards online by purchasing big-ticket items or by spending an average of a thousand dollars on bogus purchases."

"Imagine how much money they could get from just a hundred people," said Mike, "if they stole an average of five thousand from each of those hundred customers they could get three and a half million dollars in one week alone doing this just once a day."

"And by the time the customers catch wind of what happened it's too late for them to do anything about it. Plus they can't even trace the goods purchased," Dan added.

"Why is that? Why can't they just investigate the online stores used for the purchases?" Sam asked.

"Because there weren't '*actual*' goods purchased and the online stores don't '*actually*' exist," explained Dan. Mike and Sam shot glances at each other and collectively thought, *what in the hell*? "Let me explain," Dan continued, "the hackers set up dummy Internet corporations, run the charges and then immediately shut the sites down. The companies aren't real, so there's no one to complain to or investigate, and the customers never get the chance to recover any of their money."

"So where is the money going?" asked Mike.

"I figured you'd ask, so I got our techs to research the Internet service providers to determine who's creating these bogus websites.

They weren't able to track who is building the sites, but they were able to track the credit card charges to an untraceable and anonymous offshore bank account in a small island in the South Pacific," Dan answered.

"Were you able to find out who owned these offshore accounts?"

"No such luck. That's what makes this island a favorite financial center for high-end lowlifes. These banks refuse to cooperate with us or confirm or deny our suspicions unless we can prove that specific deposits were made by a felon."

"That figures, but unfortunately we can't prove that a deposit was made by a felon without looking at the offshore accounts to see who owns them," deduced Sam, "this is all designed to prevent us from tracing the money back to the criminals."

"Exactly, it's perfect. And even though the money trail might somehow lead us directly to the hackers, the real people in charge are able to collect the stolen funds unhindered and can simply disappear if things get hot, leaving the poor hackers twisting in the wind, much like our two young boys in lockup."

"Damn it! All of this information leaves us absolutely nowhere if we can't connect the account to the Gennaros!" exclaimed Mike.

"You think the Gennaros are involved? I wonder what Chief Taylor will think about that," replied Dan.

"When Mike and I were interrogating the kids they mentioned a powerful family being in charge. We just put two and two together. It's a hunch on our part, but my gut tells me the Gennaros are up to their armpits in this."

Mike said, "We have to find this Lucas. He's obviously the person they hired to do all of the dirty work, and is most likely the one in charge of the bogus websites. He might be the only link we have to whoever is running this operation." Their Chief would salivate at the possibility of finally catching the Gennaros in one of their crimes.

Since they couldn't trace the stolen money directly to the Gennaros, they needed to connect the dots somehow. Mike and Sam were on a mission to find this Lucas, who seemed like the only plausible lead they had to pursue.

"Dan, Sam and I will head out and try to track down this Lucas," Mike stated. "Can you contact the parents of the young perps in lockup? They can come down and pick them up; we'll let them go with a warning, *this time.*"

"Sure, we might also want to provide some protection for them if we don't track down Lucas, given the threat made to them if they spoke about the scam or tried to quit," requested Sam.

Dan said, "I'm on it."

"The Gennaros have eyes and ears everywhere," replied Mike. "They might already know that the boys are here."

"And since they can't be sure what the boys told us..." Sam left the sentence hanging.

Mike finished it, "Hopefully our protection isn't too little too late."

# Chapter 7



*Present day, July 24th, continued...*
*Colby Designs, New York City branch*

Once they reached the end of the hallway, Mike peered around the corner and spotted the gunman, who he recognized as the man they were looking for that very morning, Lucas Coles, and he was alone.

Lucas had been shooting his way down the corridor and mumbling to himself. Now he was attempting to reload one of his Glock 17 full-size 9mm pistols so he could finish what he started. If Lucas would only stop moving, Mike or Sam could get a clear shot and end this. Finally, Mike got his wish. He motioned to Sam that he was going for it, and Sam was ready to back him up if necessary.

Mike took a deep breath, aimed, and fired. The bullet caught Lucas in the right shoulder knocking him off his feet. He dropped his gun and the remaining bullets splattered across the floor. Lucas hollered as he grabbed his shoulder in pain, shouting expletives as he did so well. Mike and Sam quickly descended upon him, kicked the gun out of his reach, subdued him with handcuffs and secured his second weapon. Lucas's attempt to struggle was in vain, as he was no match for the both of them.

"You've got this, Sam?" Mike asked.

"Yeah, go find her." Sam continued to sustain Lucas while Mike went to look for Eve.

Mike made his way back to Eve's office but didn't know for certain if she was in there, and felt himself starting to panic. Hoping that she was hiding inside, he entered and called out her name. "Ms. Townsend. *Eve*! It's Detective McGarrett. Please respond if you can hear me." Eve was barely conscious and too weak to respond, but she managed to push against the closet door with her leg. Mike saw the door slowly opening and drew his weapon. When he saw that it was Eve inside, he holstered his gun and went to her aid. He knelt in front of her and brushed her hair away from her face.

She looked weak and she could barely keep her eyes open. "Eve, try to open your eyes, it's Detective McGarrett. Eve, can you hear me?" But she was unresponsive. Mike noticed her wounded shoulder and that she was losing a lot of blood. He stripped off his jacket, ripped off part of his shirtsleeve and made a tourniquet to reduce the blood flow. He wanted to lift her out of the closet and lay her on the floor to check for additional gunshot wounds, but he didn't want to move her for fear of causing additional injury. He checked her pulse and it was weak, but at least she was alive.

Sam guided Lucas down the hallway, and as they passed Eve's office Lucas stopped in his tracks at the sight of her unconscious inside of her closet. He liked Eve, and this caught him off guard because he didn't recall seeing her as he sprayed bullets up and down the corridor. Sam looked at Mike with worry in his eyes. "She's alive, Sam, but badly wounded." Sam breathed a sigh of relief for Eve and for his partner's sake because Mike was definitely becoming attached to this woman. Mike glared at Lucas because he didn't care for the way he was staring at Eve. "Get that bastard out of my sight," he snapped.

"Let's move it, buddy." Sam pushed Lucas forward, causing him to cry out in pain. As Sam ushered Lucas away from Eve's office, backup finally arrived, and he instructed them to take Lucas back to the station for processing while he remained at Colby to assist Mike with the injured survivors. When the paramedics arrived, Mike and Sam briefed them on the victims' conditions, and then Sam returned to the station to continue processing Lucas while Mike rode with Eve to the hospital. Mike was hoping to get statements from the survivors and then check on Eve once the others were settled in their rooms.

During the ambulance ride, Eve continued to float in and out of consciousness, never completely waking. "Detective, do you know if Ms. Townsend has any health issues that we should be aware of?" The paramedic assumed Mike knew Eve personally since he was riding along with her in the ambulance. Not to mention the way he was looking at her and holding her hands.

"Sorry, no, I don't. We only met this morning. My partner and I were questioning her about the gunman..." He let out a breath and shook his head, thinking the attack could have been prevented if they had just stuck around for another five or ten minutes.

"If she starts to come to, can you ask her? She might respond to a familiar voice."

"Of course, I'll try." As if on cue, Eve stirred. "Ms. Townsend, can you hear me? Eve, its Detective McGarrett." Mike glanced at the paramedic. "She's not responding."

"It was a long shot. I'll inform the doctors at the hospital and maybe they'll have better luck obtaining the information from a family member. She's still weak, but her vitals are steady at least, and good job with stopping the bleeding. She'd probably be in worse shape if you hadn't."

After arriving at the hospital, Mike made sure that Eve was being treated before taking statements from some of the other victims capable of answering questions. He wanted to question her last so that he could spend more time with her.

Mike approached the ER doctor who was treating Eve. "Doctor Scott, I'm Detective McGarrett. I arrived with Ms. Townsend and the other victims from the shooting. I've already spoken with the others and would like to question her as well. How is she?"

"Ms. Townsend is going to be just fine, but she lost a lot of blood, Detective. Luckily, the bullet struck well off to the side of her shoulder and it didn't hit any major arteries or vital organs, so I expect her to make a full recovery."

"That's good news."

"Yes, she was one of the lucky ones; it could have ended much worse. We currently have her on antibiotics and pain medication and we gave her a tetanus shot just to be on the safe side. She will most likely be discharged tomorrow, and she'll be in a lot of pain for a while but the antibiotics and pain medication will help with that. We've collected all of the bullets that we removed from the victims. You can pick them up as evidence for your investigation whenever you are ready."

"Thank you, Doctor. Did Ms. Townsend awaken at all while treating her? Were you able to discern any previous health issues? The paramedics asked, but I wasn't able to provide that information."

"Yes, she managed to say that she was a heart transplant patient."

"A heart transplant patient? Wow, I never would have guessed, she's so young and vital. Will it cause her complications with this injury?"

"No, we just need to make sure that any medication we prescribed doesn't interfere with her anti-rejection meds."

"She's still taking anti-rejection meds?"

"Oh, she'll have to take those for the rest of her life. The heart will always be a foreign object in her body, so the medication helps prevent her body from rejecting it."

"I see... will I be able to visit with her now?" Eve's condition was currently stable, much to Mike's relief. He was given the okay to question her but was warned that she might be a little groggy from the loss of blood and pain medication and he shouldn't tire her out.

When Mike entered Eve's room, she was resting with her eyes closed, and he thought she was asleep. Despite his desire to speak with her, he didn't want to disturb her after the harrowing experience she'd just endured. He stared at her for few moments before deciding to leave. Eve was so beautiful, and it tugged at his heart to see her lying in that hospital bed knowing how easily she could have been taken away from him. Eve stirred and opened her eyes just as Mike turned toward the door.

Mike heard movement and glanced back. "Oh, I'm sorry, Ms. Townsend... I didn't mean to wake you," he apologized.

Eve smiled at the sight of him. "That's okay," she replied softly, "did you need something from me?"

"Yes, do you remember me? I'm Detective McGarrett. You met me and my partner this morning, we were asking about Lucas Coles." Eve winced at the sound of Lucas's name. Mike hesitated before continuing. "This is probably the last thing you want to be doing right now, but I was hoping to take your statement about the shooting, if you're up to it."

Eve definitely recalled meeting Mike and his partner and was pretty sure that Mike was the person who found her in her office closet. She had gotten her wish to see him again, but unfortunately it was under less desirable circumstances than she had hoped. She was still shaken from the experience but felt strong enough to tell him what she could recall about the shooting, although she didn't think it was much. She was hiding inside of her closet for the entire ordeal and didn't actually *see* anything.

"Yes, I remember you, Detective. I'm a little tired, but I can try to give you my statement. It feels like a dream, and I still can't believe what happened; it just... doesn't seem real."

Mike pulled up a chair to the side of her bed. "It's the pain medication. Dr. Scott said you would be a little groggy. You can start whenever you're ready, but take your time, okay?"

Eve nodded and began to relive her experience. "After you and Detective Lewis left, I went straight to my office and was there the entire time... it all just happened so fast. I heard the first gunshot and then I hid in the closet. Then there were more gunshots, but I was able to dial 9-1-1 before the gunman reached *my* office, and when he did, he starting shooting inside..." Eve paused and shuddered as she remembered the sound of bullets ricocheting around her.

Mike noticed her agitation and put his hand over hers to soothe her. "It's okay. Like I said before, take your time."

The touch of Mike's hand was comforting to Eve. She looked up at him, took a deep breath and continued, "One of the bullets struck me in the shoulder and I tried not to cry out so he wouldn't hear where I was located, but I never saw the gunman's face. I only heard his voice and then someone called out the name 'Lucas,' pleading for him not to shoot. I assumed it was Lucas Coles from the IT department, the man you were asking me about this morning." She couldn't remember much more other than hearing more gunshots as Lucas proceeded down the hallway.

"It *was* Lucas Coles," Mike replied. "I only wish we hadn't left when we did; we might have been able to apprehend him and prevent the shooting from ever happening."

"So, you caught him?"

"Yes. Detective Lewis took him into custody, so you don't have to worry."

Eve breathed a sigh of relief. "Did the shooting have anything to do with why you were looking for him?"

"No, we needed him for something entirely different. We had no idea any of this was going to happen or if the two incidents are related," although Mike had a suspicion that they were. "I'm so sorry you had to go through this," he continued, and squeezed her hand ever so gently.

"Thank you *and* Detective Lewis for saving me... for saving everyone." Mike smiled reassuringly. Eve felt as if she could trust the detective with her life, and she ached to be in his arms. She hardly knew the man but needed him nonetheless.

"You don't have to thank us; it's our job to protect you. I just wish we had done a better job at it." With his hands still covering hers, Mike reassured her that she and the others were safe and that he and Detective Lewis would be available if she needed anything. He didn't want to further upset Eve by telling her that she had actually lost some of her coworkers that morning. She would find out that heartbreaking news soon enough. He yearned to hold Eve in his arms and protect her from additional pain, and it was difficult to hold back what was brewing inside of him. Their eyes were once again locked, neither understanding the longing they felt for each other. "I really shouldn't keep you up, Ms. Townsend," announced Mike reluctantly. "You need to rest."

"Okay, thank you, Detective." Eve watched Mike as he walked toward the door. Before exiting Eve's room he glanced back and smiled, just as she hoped he would, and she smiled back.

Mike didn't want to leave Eve's side, but he had to return to the station to bring Sam up to speed and make sure they put Lucas Coles away for good. He had a promise to keep.

# Chapter 8

"Good, you're back," stated Sam upon Mike's return. "How are Eve and the other survivors?"

"They're holding their own given what they've just experienced, and Eve is doing okay, thankfully."

"That's good news."

"Yeah, given she's a heart transplant recipient."

"Say what now?"

"I know, I never would have guessed it either. She had the transplant during childhood."

"It's a wonder the emotional stress from the shooting didn't put too much strain on her heart," surmised Sam.

"My thoughts exactly. Her outcome could have been a lot worse than it was."

"Luckily it didn't turn out that way. She seems to be a pretty strong woman. Were you able to speak with her and the other victims?"

"Yes, I took their statements. I got as much information as I could under the circumstances. Most of their stories are aligned, but they're all probably too traumatized to recall everything, so I'll set up meetings with them next week after they've recuperated and had some time to decompress."

"We should be receiving the identifications of the victims that didn't survive."

"I'm *not* looking forward to informing their families, Sam."

"I know, but it has to be done, and soon, before the media starts plastering everything all over the news. I'm sure Colby's employees have already started contacting people about the shooting, so the word will spread and friends and family will start wondering if their loved ones are safe or *not*."

"You're right, I know. I picked up the bullet rounds the doctors removed from the victims in the hospital and logged them into evidence along with Lucas's weapon. Where's Lucas now?"

"He's being processed and having his wound checked out, *and* after being Mirandized, he immediately 'lawyered up' and hasn't spoken a single word since. The lawyer is on his way as we speak."

"Oh really..." Mike shook his head in disbelief. "Sadistic psychopath... he knew exactly what he was doing. He'd better not try to plea that insanity bullshit either. We didn't even get the chance to question the bastard." Mike's anger was increasingly evident. "When Lucas's lawyer arrives, let's put them both in the interrogation room. We'll just have to question him with his lawyer present and persuade them to cooperate."

"Listen, I know you're worried about Eve, but you have to remain professional and not do anything stupid to jeopardize this case," warned Sam.

"I won't, don't worry. Let's just try to figure out how Lucas got into the Colby building. He was fired, and I'm sure they revoked his access, but he managed to get past the security guard and all the way up the fourth floor. Colby Designs need to seriously upgrade their security measures."

"I know... we'll have to question Lucas's boss. Maybe he can provide some insight into Lucas's frame of mind and tell us why he was fired in the first place."

"And who knows if the threat is even over?" added Mike. "What if Lucas wasn't acting alone or if there was a specific target and someone else might return to finish the job?"

"We need to see if our techs can retrieve any data from both his work and home computers. We might get some answers as to his motive, and if we're lucky we might even be able to find some evidence linking him to our case *and* the Gennaros."

"And kill two birds with one stone by putting both Lucas and the Gennaro Family away for a long time."


Mike and Sam entered the interrogation room and sat at the table facing Lucas and his lawyer, Gabriel Brown, who was in his mid-thirties, balding, and round in the waist area. His clients usually consisted of professionals that called upon him for business or personal grievances. Lucas had hired him on the contingency that he was planning to sue Colby Designs for wrongful termination of employment and emotional distress. Now here Gabe sat, across from two detectives regarding *homicide* charges. He was so far out of his league and tried desperately not to appear incompetent and unsure of himself. Lucas, on the other hand, just leered at the detectives as they sat across from him, especially Detective McGarrett, who he remembered hovering over Eve in her office after shooting him in the shoulder and tackling him to the ground.

Mike wanted to wipe that expression right off Lucas's face, but they needed Lucas to talk, so Mike resisted the urge to lunge across the table and mop the floor with him.

"Detectives," began Gabriel, "I'm glad to see you awaited my arrival before attempting to interrogate my client." Both Mike and Sam ignored him, keeping their attention on Lucas.

"So, Mr. Coles, care to explain why you went on a shooting massacre at Colby Designs this morning, injuring sixteen people and *murdering* five others?" began Sam.

Lucas didn't respond. He didn't intend to. He did, however, give Detective Lewis the courtesy of acknowledging the question by flicking his gaze at him, but he remained silent.

Sam returned his stare unflinchingly. "I repeat. *You* are responsible for murdering five people. People you knew *and* worked with and you have nothing to say about it?"

"My client doesn't have to say anything," reminded Gabriel. This invoked a quick and seething look from Mike, causing Gabriel to flinch a little. Mike smiled on the inside. Lucas's lawyer appeared to be easily intimidated, which they could use to their advantage if needed. Lucas was well aware of his lawyer's shortcomings in this particular situation, but he didn't have anyone else to call on such short notice. It didn't matter. He only needed Gabriel's presence in order to protect his rights and hopefully get him out on bail.

"You *are* going down for this shooting, Lucas. You were caught in the act. *But...* things could go a little easier for you if you provide us with some information," Mike offered.

Lucas shifted his gaze from Sam back over to Mike and a tiny smile formed. *So, they want information, do they*? Lucas remained silent. He'd let them say whatever they had to say and then make them squirm until *he* was ready to talk, now that he had a little leverage.

"Exactly what type of information do you need from my client?" demanded Gabriel.

"Information regarding an Internet money-laundering scheme," replied Sam, staring directly at Lucas.

Lucas's eyebrows rose slightly. *How did they know about that?* He thought.

*Ah, a reaction other than smirking at us. We've obviously touched a nerve*, thought Sam. "We were at Colby Designs this morning to question Lucas but, as you know, he was no longer employed there. We were on our way to his home when the call came in about the shooting. We quickly returned to Colby Designs only to find *him* at the scene trying to reload his pistol and continue with his murder spree. We believe that Lucas is involved in this money-laundering crime and want his cooperation bringing down the people in charge of the operation. *Will you cooperate or not?*" Sam asked again.

Gabriel glanced as Lucas, who didn't even acknowledge Gabriel and continued to sit in silence. Gabriel took Lucas's lack of a response as a no. "My client doesn't seem to be interested in your request. What led you to believe that Lucas was involved with this money-laundering scheme?"

Mike and Sam had to be careful how they responded. Even though they had a couple officers guarding the boys and their families, they didn't want to implicate the two young hackers given Lucas's threats to harm them if they spoke to police. They didn't know if Lucas was still in contact with whoever hired him for the money-laundering scheme and if he'd inform them that the two young hackers spoke with the police. "We were given his name, and our police sketch artist was able to produce a drawing of Lucas from a description," replied Sam.

"Who gave you his name?" asked Gabriel.

Lucas knew exactly who gave them his name. Either one or both of those two hackers he hired. There wasn't anyone else involved but the three of them outside of the 'powerful family' that hired them.

Those fucking rats... He warned them if they spoke to the police they were dead, and not only *did* they speak to the police but they had the nerve to give *him* up too. Oh, they were gonna pay for this. Those two boys just landed on his shit list along with Nathan Patterson and this Detective McGarrett.

"That's not important," Mike replied, "what's important is if Lucas is involved and if he will provide us with the names of those in charge of the operation." Mike turned his attention back to Lucas. "Do you plan on speaking at any point and cooperating, or *not*?"

Gabriel looked at Lucas for some kind of hint as to what he wanted and got nothing. Not even a flicker of movement. Lucas remained seated like a statue staring at the two detectives with only two or three movements of his head as he glanced between the two of them during their questions. Lucas gave Gabriel the creeps sometimes, and this was definitely one of those moments. "I will discuss this offer with my client and get back to you. I'd like a few moments *alone* with him, if you don't mind?"

Mike and Sam glared at Lucas and Gabriel. Who the hell did this guy think he was? He was just caught in a shooting massacre and should be jumping at any deal presented to him, but no, he was pulling the silent treatment as if he expected to be saved somehow. Mike and Sam were furious.

"You have five minutes and then he's going back to his cell," stated Mike as he and Sam left the interrogation room.

Gabriel Brown turned to Lucas. "You called me to help you, so start talking. Tell me something."

Lucas had to be careful and make the right decision. He always suspected the Gennaro family was behind the money-laundering scheme, but he didn't have any real proof. If he gave these detectives the Gennaros' name and they weren't involved, he would have made new and very dangerous enemies he did not need. Plus the word about him snitching would no doubt get back to whoever *was* in charge, and they would not be too happy with him either. If he didn't give anyone up he was going down for this shooting for sure, but at least he'd be alive and could get out on parole someday and be free again. Lucas looked at Gabriel. "I have to get back to you about this."

"What? Lucas, are you out of your mind? You *are* involved in this laundering scheme, aren't you?"

"I need time to think this through, Gabe. What I need is for you to get me out on bail. I need to get out of here."

"To do what exactly, finish what you started this morning?" Gabriel snapped angrily.

"What I do with my time is *my* business. I pay you to represent me, *not* run my life."

Gabriel stared at Lucas for a second. "So what am I supposed to tell them?"

"What do you think? Tell them I will consider their offer and get back to them. Just get started on getting me out of here."

Gabriel didn't appreciate being spoken to like a child. He had half a mind to drop Lucas as a client right here and now, but decided against it. He was a little afraid of Lucas, who seemed to have a spiteful and vengeful streak about him, and Gabriel did not want to end up looking at the end of a gun barrel if Lucas managed to get released on bail with the help of another attorney. The door opened, and Gabriel informed Mike and Sam that Lucas needed some time to consider their offer, and then a guard escorted Lucas back to his cell.

* * *

The following morning, Eve was preparing to be released from the hospital when Doctor Scott arrived. "Ms. Townsend, I see that you are ready to get out of here."

"I'm *more* than ready, Dr. Scott. I'm not a fan of hospitals," Eve murmured, remembering the excruciatingly long hours spent in a San Francisco hospital after her parents' car accident. Her mother, Marianna, had died on impact, but her father, Joseph, remained in critical condition for several days. Joseph's hospital room became Eve's second home as she spent day and night at her father's bedside, willing him to open his eyes or reach for her hand just one more time. Her wish was never granted, and then her father's organs started to fail and eventually shut down completely. Ultimately, she'd lost both of her parents.

"You're not the only member of that club; *most* people don't like hospitals. Well, your paperwork is complete, so once the nurse returns with the wheelchair she'll escort you to the lobby. Do you have transportation home?"

"I called a cab."

"Good. Before you leave, I have specific instructions for you to follow to make sure your shoulder heals properly." Doctor Scott handed Eve a list. "Your bandage should be changed at least once every twenty-four hours, and watch out for signs of infection. If it does get infected, *please* come back in immediately."

"I will." Eve was numb and found it hard to concentrate on what Dr. Scott was saying. She just wanted to get out of there.

"You'll also need to perform the rehab moves that the nurse demonstrated for you. Do you feel confident that you can do them by yourself?"

Eve nodded her head. "Yes, I think so," she replied.

"Also, no physical exercise until I give the approval, and get lots and lots of rest."

"I will, Doctor."

"Then you're all set to go, Ms. Townsend. Here are your prescriptions, and I scheduled a follow-up appointment first thing next Friday morning."

"Thanks, Dr. Scott. I'll see you then." As the doctor exited Eve's room, the nurse arrived with the wheelchair. She escorted Eve to the lobby and made sure that she was safely ensconced in her cab before returning to the nurses' station.

During her hospital stay, Eve had a difficult time sleeping. Nightmares about the shooting kept her awake during the night, and she wondered if she would ever get those awful screams out of her head. She prayed that a good night's sleep in her own bed would do the trick.

Eve was glad to be home, but her shoulder hurt, and she was grateful for the pain medication Dr. Scott prescribed for her. Thank goodness she had some leftovers and plenty of fast-food menus, because she wasn't confident that she would be able to cook anything right now with her left arm in a sling. She would definitely have to rely on take out for the remainder of the week. After she finished eating and taking her medication, she called Bonnie to tell her about the shooting. Eve didn't want her hearing about it on the news.

"Hello, Bonnie Stephens speaking."

"Hey, Bonnie, it's Eve."

"Hey girl, what's up? How is New York City treating you?"

"Well... that's kind of why I called you."

"You sound weird, Eve. What's going on?"

"Now don't freak out, but I have some troubling news."

"Don't freak out? It's too late for that now."

"I know, and I'm sorry. But you're at work and I wanted you to be able to brace yourself and not make a scene."

"I appreciate that, but now I'm worried, so just spill it."

"There was a shooting at my job yesterday—"

"*What!*" Bonnie exclaimed a little too loudly, causing some quick glances from her coworkers.

"I was hurt, but I'm okay. I was released from the hospital this morning and I'm home now."

"Oh my God, a shooting... Eve, are you sure you're okay?"

"Yeah, as okay as I can be; I'm still a little shell-shocked, but I only suffered a shoulder wound, so I should be back to normal in a couple of weeks."

"Thank goodness, but you've just moved and have barely been in New York three weeks. I'm not prepared to lose my best friend, Eve."

"Well, I wasn't prepared to get shot, especially at work."

"You must have been scared out of your mind."

Images of the shooting replayed in Eve's head and she shivered. "It was terrifying, but I was one of the lucky ones. Five of my other colleagues didn't survive."

"I'm so sorry, sweetie. Even though you haven't known them for that long it still can't be easy to lose them so tragically."

"I don't think it's completely sunk in yet. It still seems so unreal to me. Our entire department is a bloody crime scene; it's awful."

"How did this happen? *Who* did this?"

"A former employee named Lucas Coles, who wasn't too happy about being fired, I guess. The funny thing is that two detectives came by that very morning asking about him and I informed them that Lucas no longer worked for the company. Not more than five or ten minutes after they left Lucas showed up and went on a shooting rampage. It was horrible. I've never been so scared in my life."

"What did you do?"

"I hid in my closet and used my cell to dial 9-1-1."

"Thank goodness you were able to call for help."

"I know. The two detectives apprehended Lucas. Luckily they were still in the area and close enough to Colby when they received the 9-1-1 call and were able to get back to us quickly."

"How did the detectives find you if you were hiding in your closet? You could have been anywhere in the building when the shooting occurred."

"One of the detectives came to my office to look for me. I guess when he didn't see me inside, he called out my name, I think... It's all a bit blurry to me."

Bonnie was intrigued by this. "So... this detective came looking for you personally?"

"I guess so," replied Eve.

"Interesting," mused Bonnie.

"What do you mean by *interesting*?"

"I just find it interesting that in the midst of all of that chaos this detective took the time to look for you personally, *that's all*."

"That's all, huh? Bonnie, Detective McGarrett and I did meet that morning, and he was probably worried, so I'm sure that's why he came looking for me. Plus, both he and his partner checked on *everyone*, not just me, and then Detective McGarrett followed us to the hospital to take our statements."

"Okay, did he ride with you and the paramedics, or did he drive there in his own car?"

Eve had to think for a second. "I was pretty out of it, but I think he rode with me. I vaguely remember hearing his voice during the ride. What difference does it make anyway?"

"Uh-huh... Eve, I think this Detective McGarrett might be interested in you."

*How could Bonnie possibly know what he was feeling?* "Well, I don't know about that, but um... I do find myself thinking about *him*."

Her interest piqued, Bonnie responded, "Really now, do tell."

Eve sighed. "Okay, let me start from the beginning. Yesterday morning I stepped off the elevator to find the detectives questioning the receptionist, and as I approached them they asked me for my assistance. When Detective McGarrett and I looked at each other... it was as if time had stopped for a couple of seconds and I couldn't move. It was so weird and a little embarrassing to be honest, probably for him too. We both just stood there staring at each other like idiots. Luckily his partner broke the silence by introducing themselves."

"It seems like the two of you were struck by cupid, my friend."

"Oh, stop it, Bonnie."

"Well, you said you were thinking about him, *your* words not mine by the way, *and* he personally escorted you to the hospital."

"He *is* very handsome, but he's probably not allowed to get involved with civilians involved in an ongoing case."

"Maybe you could use the case as an excuse to see him somehow. You're all alone in a new town, so you could play the damsel in distress card and get some personal attention from the nice detective, case-related of course."

"Well, he did give me his card and told me to call him if I needed anything."

"There you go, that was your invitation Eve, and he's already protective of you. I say go for it."

"But Bonnie, I couldn't. That would be too obvious, and embarrassing. I have some pride, you know. I'm sure we'll come into contact again without me having to throw myself at him by playing games. I don't think he'd appreciate me wasting his time on bogus help missions."

"Okay, okay, I won't pressure you about it, for now anyway." Bonnie paused for a couple of seconds. "Eve, speaking of love interests... are you going to contact Malcolm and tell him what happened?"

"Why should I? He doesn't seem fit to return any of our phone calls any more. No matter how many messages I leave him. And he's *not* a love interest," Eve responded with anger.

"Sorry about the love interest remark, but this is different Eve, you were shot. You could have been killed. I can't imagine him not returning your call this time if he knew."

"How is it different? When my parents died he couldn't be bothered to grace us with his presence at their funeral or even call to speak with me personally," Eve responded defensively.

"I didn't mean to upset you, sweetie. Sorry I brought him up. Anyway, Malcolm had his chance. Now it's the hot detective's turn. At least *he's* showing you that he's interested, no matter what you tell me."

"Okay, well, I should let you get back to work, Ms. Cupid. Can you contact Charles and Caroline and give them the news? Tell them not to worry and that I'll call them later this week. I don't think I can deal with the both of them today."

"I can understand that, since I've already tested your patience by bringing up Malcolm. The two of them would just wear you out completely. You just hang in there and know that you can call me anytime if you need to talk. You're still in shock, but the gravity of it all will hit you eventually."

"I know... bye Bonnie, and thanks for listening."

"That's what best friends are for." Bonnie believed that there was a deeper connection other than mutual attraction between Eve and the detective that maybe even the two of them hadn't realized yet or just didn't want to acknowledge for some reason. Bonnie was glad her friend was okay, but it was ever-present in her mind how easily she could have lost Eve forever.

After Eve finished her conversation with Bonnie, she decided to spend the rest of the day relaxing and doing some light reading to take her mind off the shooting. Her brain couldn't handle anything more taxing, and she didn't want to do something that would cause her shoulder to hurt more than it already did. After being inundated with work for the past two weeks, Eve was suddenly stuck with all of this free time on her hands. She was limited to the amount of activity she could do until her shoulder had healed, so she was going to have to figure something out, because she was looking at two weeks of disability time to contend with. Still traumatized and grief-stricken over the loss of her fellow coworkers, she didn't dare turn on the TV, knowing that the shooting was probably plastered all over the news. Eve wanted those images out of her head and desperately needed something else to focus on.

Even though her friends were just a phone call away, Eve was feeling a bit isolated and alone and she found herself hoping to hear from Detective McGarrett, but figured that was wishful thinking on her part. When she allowed herself to daydream about his dark wavy hair, blue eyes and strong build, it put a smile on her face and caused her stomach to flip. There was something very comfortable about being in his presence, and thinking about him helped her to momentarily deal with the awful memories of that tragic incident. She had to admit that Bonnie was right. Detective McGarrett took a personal interest in her and saved her life on that frightful day. Eve didn't know his reasons, but it was clear he was protecting her, and it made her feel safe.

When Eve finally decided to turn in for the evening, she hoped she'd be able to sleep through the night, free of nightmares and hopefully replaced with visions of Detective McGarrett instead.

# *Chapter 9*

Nathan Patterson's doorbell rang early Saturday morning. He was exhausted given the lack of sleep after having to deal with the tragic shooting within his department the previous morning. When he didn't respond quickly enough he heard several loud knocks. Nathan finally stumbled to the front door. "Who is it?" he called out.

"Nathan Patterson, we're detectives from the NYPD," answered Mike while holding up his badge in front of the peephole for Nathan to see.

Nathan opened the door. "Detectives, I guess you're here about the shooting."

"Yes, may we come in? We need to ask you some questions regarding Lucas Coles."

"Of course, I'm sorry it took so long for me to answer the door... I didn't get much sleep, as you can imagine. Come in, please have a seat." Mike and Sam entered the living room and made themselves comfortable on the sofa. "I presume you're also the detectives that captured Lucas?"

"Yes, one and the same," replied Sam.

"We are all in your debt. Thank you. If you hadn't responded so promptly... well, God only knows how many more casualties we might have had." Nathan looked close to tears. "This is my fault; I feel so responsible for all those deaths and injuries."

Mike and Sam glanced at each other. "Why do you say that, Mr. Patterson?" Mike asked.

"Well, if I had turned Lucas in to the authorities, none of this would have happened and those poor people wouldn't have lost their lives. They were members of my team, in my department..."

"Why would you need to have Lucas arrested?" questioned Sam. "Did he commit another crime? Is that why you fired him?"

"Yes, he was stealing money from one of our financial accounts. Lucas is... *was* our IT manager and was very good at his job. We paid him well, so I can't imagine why he felt the need to steal from us. It was very disappointing."

"And you *didn't* have him arrested because..." urged Mike.

"It was his only offense, and he'd been with the company for many years. You would think he'd be more loyal to us. I mean... he's a little 'off,' and some of the female employees found him a bit creepy, but he's never crossed the line or done anything to warrant suspicion of *aggressive* behavior." Mike recalled a similar reaction from Eve when they questioned her about Lucas. "I figured he just got greedy," Nathan continued, "and I decided to give him a break by not throwing him in jail, but he couldn't remain working for us at Colby. I was ordered to fire him and I had him escorted off the premises. He made quite a scene on his way out, but I just don't see how that was enough to make him become unhinged."

"Maybe he felt his many years of employment at Colby also warranted some loyalty from *you* and that he deserved a second chance. Instead, he got tossed out on his ass," offered Mike. "You never know what goes on in people's heads or what can set them off. Most of us have issues that no one is even aware of or how they're affecting us."

"But I had no choice. The decision came from upper management. I just got stuck with the dirty work because he worked in my department."

"We also get the feeling that his being fired was not the only thing that triggered his rampage," offered Sam. "Other factors might have come into play and getting tossed out on his ass was just the straw that broke the camel's back."

"Really, but if he was going to come back for revenge I would think he would have just come after me personally instead of shooting all of those innocent people."

"He might very well have come after you too but didn't get the chance because we got to him first," informed Mike.

That realization hadn't dawned on Nathan. He was damn lucky to be alive. He put his face in his hands and leaned forward, shaking his head, exhausted and grief-stricken. He felt responsible for his employees' deaths, but yet he gets to live out his life because of sheer luck. He raised his head to face Mike and Sam.

"I owe you my life, detectives, and I thank you. How were you able to get to Colby so quickly?"

"We were actually on site shortly before the shooting, looking for Lucas, believe it or not," answered Sam. "We questioned your receptionist, Sherri, but she didn't know anything because Lucas had been fired before she starting working there. But we were able to speak with one of your managers, Eve Townsend. She was also the one who called 9-1-1 when the shooting started. When dispatch put the call through, we recognized the address and returned immediately because we were the closest to the scene."

"It seems that Colby owes Ms. Townsend our gratitude as well. Umm... I'm almost afraid to ask, but why were you looking for Lucas in the first place?"

"That's part of another investigation he's involved in. We needed information from him but we can't discuss it with you," Sam replied, "You understand, of course."

"Yes, I understand. It seems Lucas was more troubled than I realized. How can I repay the two of you? Whatever you need for your investigation, you've got it; just name it."

"We'd like our tech team to go through Lucas's work station. We're hoping to find a connection to the case we've been working on," replied Mike. "It could also lead to an explanation for his shooting rampage, if they're related. He might have been more than just a disgruntled employee."

"Absolutely, our guys have finished with it, so it's all yours, detectives."

"Why were your guys looking at Lucas's computer?" wondered Sam. "If you don't mind me asking."

"We wanted to make sure he hadn't installed some type of malicious software that could harm our systems and other programs doing God knows what. He was very adept at covering his tracks, so if Lucas hadn't chosen an account that was already being monitored, we'd still be in the dark about his thievery."

"I see," Mike pondered, "well, I think we've taken up enough of your time, Mr. Patterson. We'll send our tech team over to Colby now, if that is okay."

"Yes, that's fine. The offices are closed over the weekend, of course, but security at the front desk can let your team in. I'll put a call through and make sure that Lucas's computer is available when they arrive."

"Thank you, again, Mr. Patterson. We'll keep you updated with the progress of the investigation. And if you can think of any other pertinent information, please contact us." Mike handed Nathan his business card as they walked toward the front door.

As Mike and Sam left Nathan's home, Mike put in a call to the tech guys telling them to head over to Colby Designs and go over Lucas's computer with a fine-toothed comb and to also dig into his emails, the browser history, and phone records.

Later in the day, Mike and Sam received word from their tech guys that they didn't find anything on Lucas's computer at Colby Designs linking him to the Gennaros or anything to explain the shooting. Another dead end…

*Chapter 10*

Eve thankfully awoke the next morning nightmare-free, but she still had a difficult time navigating normal day-to-day activities. It was a bitch taking a shower, changing her bandages, and getting dressed, but there wasn't anything she could do except to take things as slow as possible and take her medication until her shoulder completely healed. She was eating breakfast when her phone rang. *Who could be calling so early on a Sunday morning?* When she looked at the caller ID it displayed the NYPD. Eve's stomach performed its usual song and dance, subconsciously hoping it was Detective McGarrett. "Hello, this is Eve," she answered.

"Ms. Townsend, it's Detective McGarrett. I hope it's not too early for me to call?"

Eve smiled. "No, Detective, not at all. I was awake."

"Good, I was afraid you might be sleeping in. I called your hospital room yesterday and was told that you had been released, but I didn't want to disturb you on your first day back home."

If only he knew how much she would have welcomed his call and was actually hoping for it. "It's no imposition. Is there any news about the case?"

"Well, I'm in the process of contacting the surviving victims of the shooting. I know it's a sensitive time for everyone, but I was hoping you would be able to come into the station tomorrow afternoon for follow-up questions."

"I guess I could, but is this really necessary?" she asked. "I already gave you my statement at the hospital." As much as she wanted to see the detective, Eve *did not* want to discuss the shooting again.

Mike could sense her hesitation and understood completely. Why would anyone want to relive that nightmare when they just barely survived it? "No, you don't *have* to, but it would be helpful. I'm re-interviewing everyone to see if you can remember additional information. Sometimes people see and hear things that they aren't aware of at first but might be able to recall at a later time after the initial shock has worn off." Mike was hoping to get pertinent information from Lucas's ramblings during the shooting, anything that could possibly tie him to the Gennaro family or at least explain why he went on the rampage.

"I see... What time do you need to me to come in?"

"Will eleven thirty work for you?" he asked, still sensing her reluctance.

"Sure, eleven thirty is fine."

"Do you need me to send an officer to pick you up? The other victims have family members that can escort them to the station. I'd pick you up myself, but I have meetings scheduled fairly close together throughout the day."

"That's not necessary. I can take a cab, but thank you for the offer."

"Are you sure, Eve?" Mike felt very protective of her.

*Eve? He called me by my first name.* "Yes, I'm sure. It's not a problem."

"Okay, but if you change your mind just let me know and I'll send someone to get you. Thanks again for agreeing to do this. I know it's the last thing you want to be doing right now."

"As long as it helps to put Lucas away, I'm all for it. I'll see you tomorrow, Detective."

"Thank you, Ms. Townsend."

*So it's back to Ms. Townsend.* Eve hung up the phone and tried to put the topic of their conversation out of her mind. She didn't want to think about the shooting today. She was glad to hear Detective McGarrett's voice but was not happy with his request. Suddenly losing her appetite, Eve threw away her unfinished cereal, placed the bowl in the sink and made a mental note to pick up some paper plates and utensils so she didn't have to attempt to wash dishes with one hand.

With all of the changes occurring in her life recently, Eve never had enough time to read anymore. Now she had nothing but time, two weeks' worth to be exact, so she decided to curl up on the sofa with a good book, something light and easy to help keep her mind off the shooting and from having to rehash her experience the following morning. She easily lost herself in the book, and before she knew it darkness had descended upon her and it was time to do her rehab exercises and eat dinner.

After dinner, Eve decided to give her friends, Caroline and Charles a call. Eve called Caroline first and got two for the price of one because of course, where there was Caroline, there was Charles. Either Bonnie had the chance to inform them about the shooting or they had seen news footage at this point. Eve hoped that their initial shock and worry had waned; otherwise, this would not be an easy conversation with the both of them. They, of course, were not pleased with this turn of events and wanted to fly out to New York City and bring her back home where she was safe and under their watchful eye. Eve assured Charles and Caroline that she was okay, and she promised to let them know if she needed anything other than being rescued by the dynamic duo.

Eve decided to go to bed. She drifted into a fitful sleep, tossing and turning while awful memories invaded her dreams. Her nerves about having to rehash her experience the following morning allowed the nightmares to resurface. "Lucas, no…" she mumbled. "Please… someone help us…" Visions of her crouching inside the small, dark closet caused beads of sweat to formulate on her forehead. "No, no, no," she pleaded while thrashing from side to side. Gunshots and screams rang in her head simultaneously. "NOOOOOOO!" she cried out as she sprang upright, drenched in sweat. She was breathing hard through her mouth and she couldn't catch her breath.

The dream felt as real as the original experience. She glanced around, disoriented, and it took a couple of seconds for Eve to realize that she was in her bedroom and *not* her office closet. Distraught, she fell backwards on her bed and cried uncontrollably until she finally fell back asleep from exhaustion.

* * *

Monday morning, Eve awoke with her stomach tied up in knots and bags under her eyes from crying half of the night. She stumbled into the bathroom and stared at herself in the mirror. Ugh, what a frightful sight. She washed her face, brushed her teeth and undressed. After removing the bandages, she examined her shoulder wound, which didn't look too appealing, but it wasn't infected and was actually improving with each passing day. Thank goodness for small favors. She stepped into the shower and let the hot water cascade over her body for a long time, attempting to wash the night away.

After stepping out of the shower, Eve gingerly toweled herself dry, redressed her wound and threw on a pair of comfortable jeans, a white blouse, and her newest accessory, the arm sling, and then she put on a blazer to combat the morning chill. She could only put her right arm in the sleeve and had to let the blazer hang over her left arm. Makeup would have to be her friend that morning, helping to hide the dark circles under her eyes.

She wasn't very hungry and decided to forgo breakfast. The dread of reliving the shooting made her lose her appetite. She opened up her curtains to let in the daylight. It was a beautiful and bright morning as Eve soaked in the sun's rays hoping to garner some strength and positive thoughts, then she headed to the police station.

Eve arrived at the station and informed the officer at the front desk that she had a meeting scheduled with Detective McGarrett. Sam noticed her and went over to reintroduce himself. "I've got this, Lloyd," he said, then turned his attention to Eve. "Hi, it's good to see you again Ms. Townsend, we met the morning of the shooting." Eve's pallor did not escape Sam's attention, and he surmised that she had not slept well for the last couple of nights.

"Yes, it's nice to see you again, Detective Lewis."

"You can follow me. Detective McGarrett and I will escort you to the interrogation room where we're conducting the interviews."

Mike glanced up to notice Sam and Eve approaching and stood up to greet them. He was ecstatic to see her, even if it was under these circumstances, and he was determined to ensure that she was at ease. "Good morning, Ms. Townsend, it's good to see you again." He also noticed Eve's weariness and regretted asking her to come down to the station. She was obviously not ready to be out and about.

"Good morning, Detective McGarrett." Seeing Mike again was almost worth the agony she was about to endure.

Once they entered the interrogation room, Sam helped Eve with her blazer, and Mike noticed her wince. "I see that you're still in pain, are you sure you're okay to do this?"

"Oh, yes. Even with the sling it's going to hurt for a while anyway."

Mike nodded but wished he could take her pain away. "We'll get started so that you don't have to be here any longer than you need to be. Please have a seat." Mike pulled out a chair and Eve sat. "I imagine this might be difficult, but can you start from the time you first met Detective Lewis and me, Friday morning?"

Eve nodded. The sooner she began the sooner she could get this over with. "After speaking with you and Detective Lewis, I went directly to my office. It was barely minutes after you left when I heard a gunshot, which startled me. It's not the kind of sound you expect to hear at work. Then I heard screams and more gunshots. I freaked out for a couple of seconds, not sure of what to do and I didn't know which direction the shots came from or how many gunmen there were. I definitely knew that I couldn't take the chance of peeking into the hallway because I would be easily seen. So I reached for my desk phone to call for help but the gunshots were getting closer, so I hid in my closet instead. I wished that I had gotten the chance to call 9-1-1 before hiding in the closet, but then I realized that I had my cell phone on me and could still call for help. I heard another gunshot, which startled me, causing me to drop the phone during the 9-1-1 call, and we got disconnected. I then tried to call you, Detective Lewis, but I was too nervous to dial your number correctly, so I gave up and tried to stay quiet. The gunshots got louder and louder and then he was shooting inside *my...* office..."

Eve got emotional and instinctively reached for her wounded shoulder. She looked as if she was close to tears, and Mike wanted to comfort her. Eve took a deep breath and pushed through it. "I realized that I had been shot. The pain was unbearable and I started to feel lightheaded. Then I heard someone cry out Lucas's name pleading for him to stop and then a flurry of gunshots and screams moving away from my office. I must have passed out a couple of times, because the only other thing I remember was hearing you call out to me while I was still in the closet and then giving you my statement at the hospital. I'm so sorry that I don't remember much else. I haven't been much help at all, have I?" Eve felt useless because she couldn't provide any new information.

"Are you kidding?" Sam chimed in. "You were very helpful during the shooting. Because of *your* 9-1-1 call, Detective McGarrett and I were able to quickly return to the office building and apprehend Lucas in the act, which saved your life and many others," replied Sam.

"Again, we're sorry for making you and the other victims relive that horrific event, but we must ensure that we have all the facts in place," Mike said in an apologetic tone, focused on Eve's face. Eve still felt this particular visit was a waste of time and that she could be under her covers right now blocking everything out. Her only consolation was seeing Mike again.

Sam observed that the connection between Eve and Mike had not dissipated. He just hoped that Mike could continue to keep his feelings in check and remain objective and clear-minded until this case was officially closed. After Eve finished giving her statement, Mike assisted her with her blazer and got a whiff of her perfume. Although a subtle scent, it aroused him unexpectedly, and he had to stifle a groan.

"Thank you again, Ms. Townsend."

"You too, Detective," she replied with a smile. Sam decided to escort Eve out of the police station and shot a glance back at Mike as they left the interrogation room.

"Ms. Townsend, do you have anyone to help you with your recovery?" Sam asked as he and Eve passed the front desk.

"Unfortunately, no. I'm pretty new in town. I just moved here from San Francisco a couple of weeks ago, so I don't have friends or family here to help me, but I'll manage. Others have it much worse than I do, so I'm not complaining."

"Well, good for you for having a positive attitude, but you know that you could contact Detective McGarrett and me if you need anything."

"That's very kind of you, but I should be fine." Sam and Eve said goodbye, and she left the police station and hailed a cab to take her back home.

When Sam returned to Mike's office, he informed him that Eve was not only new on the job but that she recently relocated from San Francisco. Mike realized that she must have been dealing with this whole ordeal by herself and wished he could check in on her on a more personal level. He was hesitant to do so because he didn't want to blur the lines and confuse her while the case was still ongoing. Eve was obviously vulnerable and not sleeping very well. He didn't want to appear to be taking advantage of the situation for his own purposes.

During the cab ride home from the police station, Eve kept thinking about Mike and how she wished she could lean on him for comfort. It was not in her nature to feel needy, especially towards someone she hardly knew. Why was she so drawn to him? As independent as she was, she felt isolated and cheated. This wasn't how she expected to begin her new life in New York.

Once Eve arrived home, she tried to contact Malcolm, as Bonnie suggested, to inform him about the shooting. Unfortunately, he was still out of the country on assignment, which never made him easy to reach. So Eve left him a message, *again*, and figured he would contact her when he got the chance, which would probably be never. She was annoyed by his lack of contact for such long periods of time, especially when she needed him the most, and she needed him *now*. Eve was, however, grateful for Bonnie, Caroline, and Charles, who were always there for her no matter the distance separating them.

It was almost twelve thirty, and Eve was hungry after skipping breakfast. Now that the meeting with the detectives had ended the knot in her stomach subsided and she was finally able to eat something. After lunch, she retreated to her sofa to re-immerse herself in her book until it was time for dinner, but she was feeling a bit melancholic and couldn't concentrate. Her mind kept racing with unsettling images while searching for answers to difficult questions. Why did Lucas want to kill everyone, and why did she survive and others didn't?

She'd never felt so alone, but didn't know how to cope with the mental stress. Eve ended up just lying on the sofa in a daze until the sun went down, leaving her in total darkness. She got up off the couch, closed her curtains, turned on the lights, and attempted to eat dinner while watching the news. She was so exhausted from not sleeping the night before that she fell asleep on the sofa only to awaken the next morning with the television watching her.

## *Chapter 11*

"We didn't find anything on those computers at Colby Designs," stated Chief Taylor angrily. Mike and Sam were summoned to his office to discuss the lack of progress on the money-laundering scheme.

"Unfortunately, no," Mike answered. "His emails and phone records both at work and home came up empty as well, so he probably used burner phones that couldn't be traced. Lucas was damned good at covering his tracks, and it was just dumb luck that the account he chose to steal from at Colby was already being monitored, or his transgression would never have been traced back to him. Even Colby's IT team have no idea if he was up to anything else. When we searched his house we found plenty of high-end computers, and we wondered why Lucas would take the risk at Colby Designs if he had powerful equipment at home."

"Exactly," responded Sam. "It makes absolutely no sense for him to use company property. If he had used his home computers they might not have been able to trace the theft to him so quickly. Lucas must have known it was a risk but still took the chance. It seems reckless to me"

The chief found this unnerving. "Just because we couldn't find anything doesn't mean he wasn't up to anything else. He was an expert hacker. Damn it! What in the hell is Angelo Gennaro after? What did he need Lucas Coles to accomplish for him and how did they get him to cooperate? Was it greed or fear?"

"We've been working on getting those very answers, but it's still not certain if the Gennaros are involved or not. That's still a supposition on our part. Not to mention figuring out why Lucas went on a shooting massacre," surmised Sam. "I understand losing your livelihood can be devastating, but to gun down your fellow coworkers is a bit over the top if you're getting paid handsomely to do a side job for a crime family. It's not as if he was losing his only source of income. The young hackers said that Lucas used the lucrative payout as a selling point in recruiting them."

"His shooting rampage might have absolutely nothing to do with the money-laundering scheme that might or *might not* be headed up by the Gennaros," added Mike. "The shooting might just be payback for getting tossed out on his ass like garbage. Some people don't respond well to public humiliation, and let's not forget that both Ms. Townsend and his boss, Nathan Patterson, said that Lucas was a little weird. It doesn't always take much to set some people off, especially if they're not quite 'all together upstairs,' if you know what I mean."

The chief was anxious to get to the bottom of this. Every police department had wanted to put the Gennaro Family away for a long time, and for personal reasons he wanted his department to be the one to get it done. "Well, this is all conjecture at this point with too many theories and unanswered questions. Thanks to his lawyer we might never know what Lucas Coles was doing for the Gennaros, but keep digging. We have to find another angle. I want this crime family off our streets, whatever it takes!"

Mike and Sam couldn't rely on getting the information they needed directly from Lucas. Unfortunately, all efforts to question him were fruitless, as Lucas refused to cooperate. He didn't speak a single word, even with his lawyer present. It was as if he were taunting them. He knew the authorities needed him, and he was going to find a way to use it to his advantage. This angered Mike. He didn't like being manipulated or played for a fool.

* * *

Angelo slammed the newspaper displaying the headlines about an employee who went on a shooting rampage at Colby Designs, maiming and killing fellow coworkers, on top of his desk. Nicholas and Anthony jumped at the loud thud. "Did either one of you have any idea that this Lucas was a loose cannon and a *crazy son of a bitch*?"

"Sorry Pop, no, we didn't realize," Nicholas replied sheepishly.

"Sorry, that's all you got? It was your *job*, your *responsibility* to realize. I want answers and solutions, *not* apologies," demanded Angelo. "Your ineptitude and desire to make our family business relevant in the world of technology has put us at risk, Nicholas. Lucas is in police custody and could rat us out at any time. Didn't you check this guy out before you put him in charge of carrying out a major part of this money-laundering operation?"

"He was recommended to me by a trusted ally, so I didn't investigate further. Lucas seemed okay when our associate met with him in person to discuss his role in the operation. Plus, he doesn't *know* he's working for the Gennaros, so he can't implicate us directly, and he's not just some hacker off the street, Pop. He's highly educated in the field of computer technology, which is why he was able to make millions of dollars for us," defended Nicholas.

"Yes, which he was paid handsomely for, but yet he turned around and stole from his own employer. Not only is he greedy, but he's unstable and disloyal, and don't think for one second that I'm taking *your word* that Lucas doesn't know we are involved, Nicholas. I'm very disappointed in you too, Anthony. You were supposed to be supervising this operation to prevent this type of debacle. I expect this lapse in judgment from Nicholas, but *you* should know better."

Anthony was embarrassed at getting reamed in front of Nick and for letting their father down. He suddenly understood how Nick must have felt over the years, constantly being on the receiving end of their father's disapproving tirades. He had miscalculated his younger brother's ability to carry out this operation, but outside of being annoying, Lucas *didn't* set off any red flags when their associate met with him. Anthony prided himself on always being on top of his game, and he was pissed off at himself for letting Nick take the lead on most of the arrangements, allowing him to put the family business in a compromising situation.

Nicholas was offended and hurt by his father's demeaning words, but he *had* screwed up in a major way. His lapse in judgment regarding Lucas put their family and the business in jeopardy, and he knew that it would be a cold day in hell before their father would allow him to have a major role in the business again. This had been his opportunity to shine, and he did for a hot minute while the money rolled in, but his progress was shot to hell the moment Lucas shot up Colby Designs.

"You know that we have to do something about Lucas one way or the other," informed Angelo.

"Let me take care of him, Pop, it's the least I can do," pleaded Anthony with the hopes of restoring his reputation.

"*No!*" Angelo replied sharply. "I'll handle this myself. The two of you have done enough damage. I'll clean up your mess and find a way to eliminate Lucas before he has the chance to implicate us in any way."

* * *

Eve felt a little stiff having slept on the sofa all night and didn't want to move or do anything else, for that matter. When she glanced at the clock, it read ten in the morning. *Wow, I really was exhausted*, she thought. She turned off the television and went back to sleep, in her bed this time, but was only able to grab another two hours before the phone rang. Startled, Eve jumped upward, which caused a sharp pain to radiate from her left shoulder and down her arm. "Goddamn it!" she exclaimed, grabbing her shoulder to provide support. She had to reach for the phone with her right hand and made a mental note to move the phone over to the right side of the bed. "Hello?" she answered brusquely.

"Eve, Its Nathan Patterson. Are you alright?" he asked, catching the sternness of her voice.

"Oh... hi Nathan, I'm sorry about that. Yes, I'm fine. What can I do for you?"

"I wanted to check in to make sure you were recovering okay. How is your shoulder?"

"It hurts... a lot." What else could she possibly say at this point?

"Umm... this must be a difficult time for you."

"I think it's pretty difficult for all of us, Nathan, you included."

"Of course it is, but you just joined us at Colby's New York branch and you don't really know anyone here aside from your coworkers. I thought you might be feeling alone and more isolated than the rest of us."

"I'm in New York City. How could I possibly feel alone *here*? All I have to do is walk outside and I'm immediately surrounded by hordes of people," she joked.

"Eve, you know what I mean, but I'm glad to see you're trying to have a sense of humor about it, *unless* you're using jokes to mask how you really feel."

Eve sighed. "You're right. I do feel alone at times, but I try not to think about it *or* the shooting when I'm awake. Unfortunately, my dreams won't cooperate with that plan."

"So you're having nightmares... well, that's understandable, given what you've experienced. If you need anything during your recovery, please don't hesitate to contact me. I also want you to think about seeing one of our in-house counselors or therapists."

"I'm not nuts, Nathan. Well, at least not yet, anyway. But if that changes, I promise not to go on a shooting rampage. It's already been done."

"Eve, I'm being serious here."

"Exactly, and you're *seriously* bringing me down."

"Okay, I get the hint, but you experienced a traumatic event and should make sure that you deal with your emotional injuries as well as the physical ones. The other victims have their families to rely on for support but, as I mentioned before, *you* don't have that."

"I appreciate the offer, Nathan. I promise I'll think about it, but I'm okay for now." Spilling her guts to a complete stranger was not at the top of Eve's to-do list.

"Well, you just let me know and I'll make sure to put you in touch with our counselors. I want to make sure that you and the other victims have all of the support you need, which kind of brings me to the other reason I called..."

"Oh?"

"The families of our coworkers that didn't survive the shooting are having their individual funerals starting this Thursday and throughout the weekend. They wanted us to inform the surviving victims that you were all welcome to attend, but they understood if your injuries prevented you from doing so. I informed them that we were also planning a memorial service for all of the fallen colleagues next week. We wanted to give them their own time to grieve this weekend and for the injured victims, such as yourself, time to heal so that all of you could attend and pay your respects together as group, *if* you were up to it. I'm hoping we could all gather strength and moral support from each other."

"That's really thoughtful of you, Nathan. I'd love to attend the memorial and pay my respects; just let me know when and where."

"We're aiming for next Monday. I'll be in touch with the location and time... Eve, before we hang up, I wanted to thank you."

"For what?" she wondered.

"The detectives who captured Lucas informed me that you were responsible for calling 9-1-1, which is why they were able to apprehend Lucas so quickly. You probably saved many lives, including my own. If they hadn't arrived when they did, we would have lost a lot more of our coworkers that morning."

"Thanks, I appreciate that, Nathan."

"I'll hold down the fort at the office while you're out on disability. Our clients are aware of the situation and understand our need to recoup while keeping up with the projects with a limited staff. So you just take care of *yourself*, Eve."

"I will, and thanks again." Eve hung up the phone and fell backwards on her bed muttering to herself, "So much for sleeping the day away in total oblivion." Hearing about the funerals taking place this weekend did nothing to brighten her day or lighten her mood. Eve forced herself to get out of bed just long enough eat something and take her medication, clean her wound and change the dressing. She decided to go back to bed the rest of the day, but made sure to set up the phone on the nightstand to the right side of her bed. She really hoped that no one else would actually call today, because she was not in the mood to talk to anyone.

Unfortunately, Eve was awakened not more than thirty minutes later. She was in a deep sleep and it took several seconds for the ringing to register. She slowly opened her eyes and finally realized her phone was ringing, *again*.

*Really?* she thought as she reached for the phone and answered groggily. "Hello"

"Eve, it's Ray. Did I wake you?"

"Ray?"

"Don't tell me you've forgotten me already. It's only been weeks since you left us here in San Francisco."

In spite of her mood, Eve had to chuckle. "No, Ray, I could never forget you. I just wasn't expecting to hear your voice."

"We heard about the shooting, of course, and I wanted to check in on you. Plus, Nathan just called me and said you sounded weird when he spoke with you this morning."

"So he sent you in as backup?"

"In a way, yes. You don't know him that well and he figured you'd be more comfortable opening up to me, if you needed to. Quite frankly, I have to agree with him. You don't sound like yourself, which is understandable, of course."

"I'm still in bed. When Nathan called me earlier the phone startled me and I hurt my shoulder. I was in pain and answered the phone a bit snippy."

"You're still sleeping at this hour? It's after noon. I thought you'd be up by now. Are you not sleeping at night?"

"I try, but I keeping having nightmares about the shooting."

"I'm sorry to hear that and I'm so sorry you were hurt."

"You're not responsible; you do know that, right? I can hear it in your voice, Ray."

"You know me so well. In my head I know I'm not responsible, but in my heart I keep thinking that if I didn't recommend you for that job you would be safe here in San Francisco with us. Plus, Nathan is afraid you might think this is more than you bargained for and leave New York and return to San Francisco. He's been singing your praises for all that you have accomplished in the last couple of weeks and he doesn't want to lose you."

"He never said anything like that to me. Please tell him not to worry. I might be pissed off as hell, but it'll take more than one bullet wound to scare me off. I could just as easily have gotten shot in San Francisco. Guns are everywhere."

"Now that's the Eve I know and love. I was worried there for a bit, but I know you'll be okay. You're a fighter and one of the strongest people I know."

"Thanks Ray, so please pass that on to Nathan so he'll stop offering me grief counselors."

"You might be strong, Eve, but you're not invincible. Talking with a grief counselor may help with your nightmares, at least."

"I'll think about it, but I can't make any promises."

"All right, I won't press. I guess I should let you get back to sleep, but it was nice touching base with you. I'm so used to seeing you every day that it's weird not having you around to bounce ideas off and hash out problems with."

"I know, I miss you too, and tell everyone there I miss them and that I'm okay so they don't worry."

"I will. Talk with you soon, Eve."

"Bye, Ray."

Hearing Ray's voice made Eve a little homesick. Maybe Nathan was right. Not having close friends or family around to talk to was difficult, and hearing Ray's voice *did* lighten her mood and make her feel a little better. Eve snuggled into her pillow and closed her eyes and a little smile formed as she drifted off into oblivion.

# *Chapter 12*

"Ms. Townsend, you've obviously been following the instructions we gave you last weekend. Your wound is almost closed and it's healing well. I don't see any signs of infection," Dr. Scott stated, pleased with the condition of Eve's shoulder wound.

"That's good news," Eve replied with relief.

"Let's check your mobility. If you can handle it, I'm hoping you can shed this sling."

Eve followed the doctor's request and winced in pain.

"I see it still hurts a bit."

"Yeah, but it's manageable, especially once the *medication* kicks in." Eve winked.

"That's good to hear," he responded with a raised eyebrow. He didn't want Eve dependent on the pills. "Well, everything checks out okay, so just continue taking the antibiotics and pain medication until you've completed the prescription. I don't expect any complications, so you *shouldn't* need any refills," he added with a sly smile, "but if you do, don't hesitate to contact me and we'll re-evaluate your needs."

"Thank you, Dr. Scott."

"No problem. You can get dressed, and then you're all set to leave."

Eve decided to visit with some of the surviving victims that were still hospitalized to check on their status. They were grateful that she took the time to visit with them, given she was also wounded and technically their boss.

During the cab ride home, Eve wished she had someone she could call that could come over to keep her company and help avoid boredom. She thought about the suggestion of seeing one of the counselors that Nathan recommended, but she wasn't quite ready to be probed and analyzed. To be honest, what she *really* wanted was to call Detective McGarrett. He and Detective Lewis might have rescued and saved her life, but Eve was hesitant because she didn't want to appear clingy and needy.

Since she had the detectives on her mind and the kindness they bestowed upon her she decided to capture the first time she met them on paper by sketching a portrait of them. Maybe a little art therapy would do the trick, or at least keep her mind occupied. Thank goodness her injury was to her left shoulder instead of the right one, or she wouldn't be able to sketch at all. And without the sling it was a much easier task. After Eve finished the drawing she felt more at ease and decided to give Detective McGarrett a call and at least provide him an update about her progress. Providing positive news was definitely more appealing than whining and complaining.

He was probably out working on the case, but Eve needed to hear Mike's voice even if she only got his voicemail. So she took a deep breath and dialed his number at the police station. She didn't get his voicemail and her heart skipped when he answered, "Hello, McGarrett speaking."

"Detective McGarrett… hi, it's Eve Townsend. I hope I'm not disturbing you?"

Mike knew exactly who it was as soon as he heard her voice. A smile crossed his face as he replied, "Not at all Ms. Townsend. Is everything okay? Is there anything I... um, *we*... can do for you?"

"Yes, everything is fine, which is why I called. I just wanted to give you *and* Detective Lewis an update on my condition." Why was she so nervous? It's not as if she'd never spoken to the man before.

He let out a sigh of relief. "Oh good, you had me worried there for a minute. So I take it your shoulder is healing nicely?"

"Yes, I had my follow-up appointment this morning and the doc gave me the green light. He even freed me from my sling. I still have some residual pain, but that will subside over time. I'm scheduled to return to work in another week, and I'm sure I'll be almost back to normal by then."

"That's great news. I'm glad you called because I was concerned... I was planning to check up on you anyway, especially with the upcoming funerals this weekend."

"So you do know about them? I wasn't sure if you and Detective Lewis were informed."

"Yes, some of the victims informed us while conducting their follow-up statements. They were kind enough to invite us. I also received a call from your department head, Nathan Patterson, regarding the memorial service this coming Monday. Detective Lewis and I are planning to attend and pay our respects, so I assume that we will see you there?" Or at least, Mike hoped he would.

"Yes, I definitely plan to be there, so I will see the both of you on Monday... Well, I don't want to keep you from your work... please say hello to Detective Lewis for me."

"I will, and I'll give him the good news about your recovery. He'll be pleased to hear that you are doing well. Have a good day, Ms. Townsend."

"You have a good day too, Detective."

Mike didn't want their conversation to end and was looking forward to seeing Eve that coming Monday, even though it was for a somber occasion. He would plan with Sam to arrive early enough to maneuver seats next to Eve so that they could provide emotional support for her if she needed it.

Eve hung up the phone and took a deep breath. Thank God she didn't make a fool of herself, or at least she hoped she didn't. Detective McGarrett seemed genuinely pleased that she had called him with the update of her condition. He had a way of making her feel calm, and she hoped the phone call was enough to carry her through the weekend and looked forward to seeing him on Monday. Nathan was correct in his assessment of her using humor to deflect the pain and loss she was experiencing, but it was the only way Eve could get through each day without breaking down. Being around all of the other victims and their grieving families at the memorial service might be the very thing that broke her, so she hoped the detective's presence would be the calming influence she needed to survive it.

* * *

Mike and Sam arrived at the memorial service early as planned. Mike scanned the room for Eve but he didn't see her and hoped that she still planned on attending. Even though she was healing physically, he had a feeling she was putting up a brave front, emotionally. Eve was obviously independent and a fighter, but Mike anticipated that she would actually need some emotional support this morning.

Mike and Sam made the rounds and mingled with the other guests, offering their condolences while awaiting Eve's arrival. The detectives were invited to the service because they single handedly apprehended Lucas Coles and kept in touch with the families regarding their status. Although they weren't able to save everyone, the families could at least sleep at night knowing that the person who took their loved ones away was rotting in jail and in the process of getting what he deserved.

Eve took a taxi to the service and couldn't imagine how she was going to deal with seeing the grieving family members all at the same time, and had a feeling she might end up a basket case. She was glad that the detectives would be there, which gave her some peace of mind. When she arrived, she was immediately overwhelmed by the number of people present. Anxiety started to rise from the pit of her stomach and she thought she was going to have a panic attack right then and there, but then she caught Mike's eyes from across the room. He smiled at her, calming her anxiety for that brief moment in time.

When Mike saw Eve across the room, she looked as if she might faint. He motioned to Sam that he was going to greet her and steered a course through the crowd toward her. "Ms. Townsend, are you okay?"

*Now that you're here*, Eve thought to herself. "Yes, it's just a bit overwhelming when you first walk into the room."

"I thought as much. You looked as if you were ready to bolt," Mike joked, hoping to put her at ease.

"Was it that obvious, or did you read my mind?" Eve asked, thinking that he could come to her rescue anytime he wanted to.

"Yes, I could see it on your face." Mike was confident that Eve would be okay, but he was going to personally make sure of it. He didn't care about the rules at the moment, and this was a perfect opportunity for him to remain close to her without appearing inappropriate. "Detective Lewis is across the room, so why don't you hang out with us and we'll get through this together." Eve gratefully accepted his offer, and he subtly guided her through the crowd of mourning families. "Hey Sam, look who I found."

"Hi Detective Lewis, it's nice to see you again," Eve greeted Sam.

"The feeling is mutual, Ms. Townsend. I hear that you're recovering well."

"Yes, thank goodness." Eve observed the room with sadness in her eyes. "But, is it weird that I feel guilty about surviving? I've had it pretty easy considering what some of the others have endured."

"No, it's not weird at all. Survivor's guilt is quite common. You're probably going to experience a wide range of emotions, but you should allow yourself to feel what you need to feel. Things will get better as time passes. I promise."

"I'm going to hold you to that, Detective."

Sam glanced up. "Oh, I think they are motioning everyone to get seated. Shall we?" He let Eve lead the way. He slowed his step to allow Mike to fall in line behind Eve so that he could sit next to her, and Mike appreciated the gesture.

Eve wanted to pay her respects, but she was really dreading this. Ever since her parents died she hated funerals as well as memorial services. She eyed the photos on display of the five coworkers they lost and thought about how she was robbed of the chance of getting to know them. The realization that she could just as easily have her photo on display as a casualty was not lost on her, and she was completely overwhelmed by the grief that pervaded throughout the room.

Detective McGarrett read her perfectly when she first arrived, because about thirty minutes into the ceremony she felt this all-consuming need to bolt, *again*. While holding back tears, she closed her eyes and tried to shut everything out for a couple of seconds. Mike sensed Eve's distress and placed his hand over hers to let her know that he was there for her. It was all Eve could do not to burst into tears, and she slowly opened her eyes to find Mike looking at her with a worried expression. She gave him a slight smile to portray that she was okay, which, of course, belied her true emotional state. Eve barely got through the remainder of the service and knew that she wouldn't be able to handle much more. She paid her respects and spent some time with the grieving families and decided that it was time for her to go home. The look of sorrow and pained expressions were almost too much to bear, and she just couldn't take much more.

"Ms. Townsend, are you ready to get out of here?" asked Mike, sensing she was ready to leave. "We can take you home, if you need a ride."

"Oh, that's not necessary," protested Eve, not wanting to take them away from the other grieving families who also wanted to thank them for their bravery. She wasn't the only person that Mike and Sam rescued the day of the shooting, and it wasn't fair for her to monopolize all of their time.

"Nonsense," Sam chimed in, "Detective McGarrett can drive you home while I remain here with the other families, and he can return for me later." Mike glanced at Sam and gave him a silent thank you for giving him time alone with Eve. She was touched by the offer and also grateful to have Mike all to herself. Eve and Sam said their goodbyes and Mike escorted her to the car.

Eve was quiet during the drive. "I know that I'm not very good company right now, but I do appreciate you driving me home."

Mike glanced at Eve. "You don't have to worry about keeping me company. I can only imagine what you must be going through, so if you don't feel like talking, it's okay."

"You're very kind and a good person, Detective McGarrett."

"This is true."

Eve smiled at Mike's unexpected response. "Well, it's a good thing I didn't add modesty to that compliment."

"I was joking, of course. I just wanted to see you smile."

"Well, mission accomplished, Detective."

Mike pulled up in front of Eve's apartment building. "Let me find a parking spot and I'll walk you up to your apartment."

"Oh no, that's above and beyond the call of duty. I know I've been a little shaky today, but I think I can make it up to my apartment by myself. You should get back to the service and to Detective Lewis."

"Are you sure? It's no trouble at all." He didn't want to leave her just yet, but he ran out of excuses to be alone with her.

"I'm sure, but thank you for taking care of me. I know that's what the two of you were doing today, so thank Detective Lewis for me as well."

"Were we that obvious? I guess we should rethink our day jobs, huh?" Eve giggled. Mike loved that sound and wanted to hear more.

"Don't worry; your secret is safe with me." Eve got out of the car and headed toward her building. Just before she went inside, she glanced over her shoulder to wave at Mike. He waved back and waited for her to safely enter the lobby before driving off.

As Mike drove back to the service, he smiled at the fact that Eve was able to display some light-hearted humor when she was clearly in distress. He hoped that he was somehow responsible for bringing that out of her today. He was compelled to get to know this woman on a deeper level and be a support system for her if she needed.

When Eve entered her apartment, she was slightly shocked at her change of mood. Just twenty minutes ago she was on the verge of an emotional breakdown, and after the car ride with Detective McGarrett she felt at ease. She kept thinking about the photos of the victims displayed at the service and decided to do some sketches of her teammates. Art therapy seemed to work for her. Each drawing would be based on a personal memory that she had shared with each of them at work. She wanted to remember them from a happier time and not from that last traumatic day they were all forced to experience together.

Mike arrived back at the memorial service and spotted Sam viewing the photos of the victims. It was nice to see them looking happy as opposed to the way he and Mike found them last Friday during the shooting. Like Eve, Sam thought just how easily they could be looking at a photo of her, and didn't know what would have happened to his partner if they hadn't gotten to her in time.

Mike approached Sam, "Hey partner, I'm back."

"So you got Eve home in one piece. How is she doing?"

"I think she'll be okay. Eve was pretty quiet during the drive at first but was in much better spirits by the time I dropped her off. She wanted me to thank you for looking after her today."

"So she figured us out, huh?" Sam chuckled.

"Yeah, I also wanted to thank you for the assist. I really appreciate the time alone with her. You're a good partner Sam, and a good friend."

"No problem my man, that's what friends are for." Sam paused for a second and looked at Mike. "So, how *are* things moving along between you two?"

"Well, I did manage to get a smile out of her."

"Really? That's good progress given how distraught she was throughout the entire service. You must have a soothing effect on her, my friend."

"I'd like to think so," Mike replied with a slight grin, remembering their witty banter at the end of the car ride.

"Dude, you've got it bad," Sam said, observing the goofy grin on Mike's face.

"I know. But I can't help it, and I can't stop thinking about her."

"Then let's close this case so you can get the girl, my friend."

"From your lips to God's ears."

"Hopefully we can get the information we need from Lucas in regards to the Gennaro investigation. So far he's been playing hardball, but he's the best chance we have at getting concrete evidence for a conviction."

Mike and Sam said their goodbyes to the families and headed back to the police station. They had work to do and needed to arrange another meeting with Lucas and his lawyer. Mike and Sam didn't know what changed Lucas's mind, but Lucas was finally ready to talk and apparently had a lot to share.

* * *

Angelo was alone in his office when he made a phone call. "I need you to handle something important."

"Of course, Mr. Gennaro, whatever you need."

"Who do we have on the inside? There's someone I need you to take care of."

"Who is the target?"

"His name is Lucas Coles."

"Consider it handled, boss."

# Chapter 13

A day or two after his arrest, Lucas was transferred to federal prison, where he would remain in custody until his trial. Contrary to his lawyer's efforts, Lucas was thankfully denied bail.

NYPD had leverage over Lucas, of course. The fact that he was caught at the scene of the crime and was responsible for injuring almost a dozen people and the deaths of five others made their case against him very strong. Mike and Sam's chief was willing to strike a deal with Lucas in order to obtain the information they needed because he was focused on a much larger prize. Mike was irate at the thought of Lucas walking for *any* reason, and felt he deserved to rot in prison for the rest of his life. The fact that Eve was one of his many victims only fueled Mike's anger at Lucas's possible release.

Mike and Sam witnessed firsthand the grief and pain that this man caused. But he had to remain professional and not allow his feelings for Eve to cause him to do anything to jeopardize the investigation into the Gennaro Family *and* the case against Lucas. He'd promised Eve that they would put Lucas away, and now he might be forced to break his word, which gnawed at his gut. If Lucas's release came to fruition, he didn't know how they would ever be able to explain it to her and the other victims.

* * *

Lucas headed to the mess hall for breakfast. As a new inmate he hadn't yet clicked with anyone, so he usually looked for an empty seat, ate his meal alone and made his way back to his cell. He happened to glance up and caught the eye of one of the other inmates seated across the room. The steady glare unnerved Lucas, so he quickly glanced back down at his meal to avoid any unnecessary confrontations. *Why is that guy staring at me?* he thought, and decided to finish up quickly and get the hell out of there.

Once he completed his meal, Lucas shot a quick glance across the room to see if he was still being watched. The inmate was no longer there, and he breathed a sigh of relief. On his way out of the chow hall, someone bumped into him but kept on walking without missing a beat. Pissed off, Lucas turned around to confront the inmate but stopped in his tracks. He realized it was the guy he caught staring at him earlier and decided to let it go. *What's that guy's problem?* Lucas was still recovering from a bullet wound and was in no position to put forth his usual cocky attitude. Being the new guy, he figured they were just testing him, and opted not to ruffle any feathers.

If all went well, in a couple of hours he would have the opportunity to get out of this hell hole. His lawyer had scheduled a meeting with the detectives who captured him to discuss a deal with the NYPD to be released from prison and he didn't want to do anything to put his life or his possible release in jeopardy. Granted, he wouldn't be completely free; he would have to be committed for psychiatric evaluation because he did, after all, go on a shooting rampage and was responsible for several deaths.

Lucas only had to provide the name of whoever hired him for the online money-laundering scheme, which they hoped was the

Gennaro crime family. They seemed to want the Gennaros much more than they wanted him, so he was willing to give them up. He didn't actually have any proof of the Gennaros' involvement, but the NYPD didn't know that and he was willing to use whatever he could to free himself.

He still envisioned Eve's lifeless body on the floor of her office. The detectives said she was still alive, and he was glad. He liked Eve and didn't wish *her* any harm. He was, however, not pleased with missing the opportunity to get Nathan Patterson, something he planned on correcting when he got out of prison. He'd also take care of those young hackers and last but not least, Detective McGarrett. *How ironic*, thought Lucas, *that Detective McGarrett's assistance with his release would also lead to McGarrett's demise.*

He barely made it out of the mess hall, holding his injured shoulder, when he started to feel weak. As he got closer to his cell, he started to feel lightheaded. It took every effort he had to make it there. When he finally reached his destination, he stumbled inside and collapsed onto his bunk from exhaustion. A couple of minutes later Lucas heard someone enter and figured it was just his cellmate returning from breakfast. Lucas didn't bother to open his eyes to acknowledge him. He was just too tired and figured he would rest until it was time for lunch and his meeting with his lawyer and the detectives.

Several hours later during lunchtime, the guards arrived at Lucas's jail cell only to find him dead, hanging from the ceiling.

* * *

Mike and Sam were just about to leave the station to meet with Lucas and his lawyer at the federal prison to discuss the deal and

Lucas's possible release when Mike received a phone call. "Detective McGarrett... This is Lucas Coles's lawyer."

"Yes, Mr. Brown, my partner and I were just on our way to meet with the two of you."

"I figured as much and was hoping to catch you before you left. I... I have disturbing news... Lucas was found dead in his cell. He apparently hung himself this morning sometime after breakfast."

"*WHAT!*" Mike exclaimed. "You've got to be kidding me? We'll be there in twenty minutes. Don't touch anything, and make sure that no one else does either." A part of Mike was slightly relieved because Eve and the other victims were free of Lucas Coles, but they really needed information from him and Mike knew the chief would be furious with this latest development.

"What just happened?" asked Sam as they rushed out of the station.

"You're never going to believe this. Lucas Coles was found dead in his cell, hanging from the ceiling. His lawyer thinks he hung *himself*."

"You're thinking he may have had a little help? Maybe from someone who was privy to the fact that he might be singing like a bird this afternoon?"

"You read my mind, partner. I'll arrange for the CSU team to process the scene so that it isn't contaminated before we arrive."

* * *

The CSU team took photographs of Lucas and the surrounding area, bagged all items in the cell and created a detailed crime-scene sketch. Mike and Sam arrived at the federal prison and were taken directly to Lucas Cole's cell where his lawyer was waiting for them while the CSU team finished processing the scene.

"Detectives, I'm glad you guys are here."

"So what in the hell do you think happened?" questioned Mike.

"It looks like Lucas hung himself," replied Mr. Brown.

"We won't know for sure until the ME does her examination, but there doesn't seem to be any signs of a struggle," surmised Sam as he surveyed the scene.

"It looks a little too neat to me," Mike added. "Whether he hung himself or had help, I can't imagine it would be easy either way. There should be more of a disturbance, don't you think?"

"So the two of you don't think Lucas committed suicide?"

"No, we don't. We need to look into whether he had enemies that would want to harm him. Maybe you can help us with that, Mr. Brown."

"Anything said between me and Mr. Coles is bound by attorney-client privilege, Detective McGarrett."

"He's *DEAD*! That *privilege* is absolutely useless to him now."

Mr. Brown just stared at Mike. He was so far out of his league and didn't know what to do at this point and was glad to be rid of this case. He felt bad that Lucas had died, but he was a nightmare of a client and most certainly a liability.

"Fine, don't cooperate with us. Even though that's exactly what we were supposed to be meeting about this morning. Now you're going to remain tightlipped? If you had only convinced your client to talk to us sooner he might still be alive." Mike turned his attention back to Sam. "Maybe one of the inmates had a hand in this, or the 'powerful family' that hired him for the money-laundering scheme. Maybe the autopsy will reveal foul play, which I believe it will."

"I wouldn't get your hopes up, Mike. If this was done professionally I doubt they'd leave us a trace of evidence."

"Well, hopefully the CSU team can turn up *something*, fingerprints, anything..."

After Mike and Sam looked over Lucas's body, they had it taken to the medical examiner, Sharday Mills, hoping the autopsy would confirm their suspicions that Lucas did *not* kill himself, but was murdered instead.

"Where was Lucas's cellmate when all of this went down?" asked Mike.

"He was still in the mess hall," answered Gabriel.

"Has that been confirmed, or are you taking him at his word?" asked Sam.

"The guards confirmed it."

"So he might have seen Lucas there and when he left," Mike responded. "I want to speak with him. Let's find the warden so we can question this guy." Mike turned to Gabriel, "So Mr. Brown, do you have anything else to add that could help us? Did Lucas tell you anything regarding this money-laundering scheme or who hired him?"

"Sorry, Detective McGarrett, but no... you're so sure he was involved in this crime, aren't you?"

"Of course we are. You know just as well as we do that Lucas didn't kill himself. He was a cocky son of a bitch and a coward who'd rather go after innocent hard-working people before he'd ever hurt *himself.* Look where we are, Mr. Brown. We're in a federal prison where Lucas was killed on the very day he was scheduled to make a deal with the police. Open your eyes. Lucas answered to someone and they wanted to keep his mouth shut *permanently.*"

Gabriel looked sheepish at Mike's verbal reprimand. "If you don't need me for anything else detectives, I'll be on my way."

"Then be on your way," replied Sam. Mike just glared at Gabriel as the lawyer turned and walked away from them.

* * *

"So, Joe, you were in the mess hall when they found Lucas hanging in your cell?" Sam asked Lucas's cellmate.

"That's right. I was nowhere near him. I was in the mess hall the *whole time.*"

"And did you see Lucas there?"

"Yeah."

"How did he seem to you?"

"Like he always did. No different, and eating alone."

"Why didn't he eat with you? You *are* cellmates. Didn't you get along?" Sam asked, with one eyebrow raised.

"Now hold on there. I barely knew the guy. He only showed up a couple of days ago. I got my own crew to hang with, and Lucas *chose* to be alone and not get in good with the others. Not my problem he's *antisocial.*" Mike and Sam were not surprised by this remark.

"Did you see Lucas leave the mess hall?" continued Sam.

"Sure, damn near got knocked over on his way out too."

"So Lucas bumped into another prisoner?"

"More like the other way around, and right into Lucas's bum shoulder, the one he got shot in. Lucas was pissed off too, turned around like he was gonna do somethin' bout' it but changed his mind and just left." This got Mike and Sam's attention.

"How did the other guy react?"

"He didn't, never even turned around, just kept on walking like nothin' happened."

"Interesting," mused Mike as he and Sam glanced at each other. "Do you know who this guy is? We'd like to have a chat with him as well."

"No, I don't know who he is and never seen him before. What's with all the questions anyway? Isn't this suicide?"

"Do *you* think Lucas hung himself?" Mike asked.

"Well, didn't he? Wait, you think someone else did the deed?"

"There's always that possibility," Mike responded, "but we're asking the questions here. Did Lucas gain any enemies in his short stint here? He's not exactly the warm and fuzzy type, as you well know."

"Ain't that the truth? But honestly, I haven't heard any rumblings against Lucas, so I can't help you there."

Not the answer Mike was looking for. "Well, thank you for speaking with us, Joe. If you hear of anything at a later time, like who the guy was that bumped into Lucas, please have the warden contact us."

"Sure, detectives. Anything I can do to help." *And to keep you two out of my hair*, he thought.

Several inmates noticed Lucas staggering on his way back to his cell, but others said he was fine in the mess hall, which would indicate that something occurred between the time he ate breakfast and made it back to his cell. If he was so ill that he could barely walk, not to mention his wounded shoulder, how could he have the strength to hang himself? He was more than likely drugged so as to be incapacitated enough to be hung and killed. How convenient that no one was around to hear or see a damn thing or identify the inmate that bumped into Lucas.

✳ ✳ ✳

The following morning, Mike paid Eve a surprise visit, which would be the first stop of many. He knocked, but before Eve could reach her front door, Mike called out to her, "Ms. Townsend, it's Detective McGarrett." Her stomach flipped at the sound of his voice, but when she opened the door she could tell something was wrong and her stomach tensed up instead.

"Detective McGarrett, this is unexpected. Did something happen?"

"I have news that I need to discuss with you regarding the case. Can I come in?"

"Yes, of course, please." She stepped aside and Mike entered.

"Maybe we should sit down, Eve."

Uh-oh, he called her Eve again. She braced herself. "That's not necessary Detective. Is the news good or bad?" she asked, knowing it was most likely the latter.

"A little of both, actually," replied Mike. "Lucas Coles was found hung in his jail cell yesterday morning."

Eve was shocked and mortified and didn't know quite how to respond. She just stared at Mike blankly for a couple of seconds then almost immediately Mike noticed a glint of anger in her eyes. Images of the shooting, her nightmares, and the memorial service had flashed through her mind in that instant. "I would be lying if I said I was sorry Lucas is dead," she announced slowly. "I guess I should have *some* remorse for someone so troubled that he felt he had no other choice than to shoot and kill his fellow coworkers and then hang himself afterward. *But I don't.*" She shook her head and briefly closed her eyes. When they reopened, they were clouded. Eve assumed Lucas killed himself. Mike didn't correct her since he didn't have proof otherwise.

"That's perfectly understandable. You've lost people you've worked closely with and your life was also in jeopardy. You're still traumatized as a result. It'll take time to sort through the many emotions you're probably experiencing, *including* hatred."

"You think I hate Lucas?"

"Don't you, just a little bit? At least a part of you must."

Eve didn't immediately respond. She let out a quick breath, glanced down at the floor and started to bite her lower lip. When her eyes returned to Mike's, she just stared at him uncertainly without answering his question. "So, I guess the good news is that I and the other victims don't have to worry or be afraid of him any longer?" she asked, redirecting the conversation.

Mike realized she was not willing to acknowledge her feelings of hate towards Lucas just yet and decided not to press the issue. Hate might not be an emotion Eve was used to experiencing, and Mike didn't want to add to her discomfort. She had been through enough. "That was my sentiment," Mike responded, "even though, I was hoping to make him *pay* for his crimes, or maybe he did in some way. At least that chapter of your lives is over, and I sincerely hope that all of you can find some closure."

"Since he's dead, can I ask why you and Detective Lewis were looking for Lucas that morning? You said that you didn't know he was going to return to Colby on a shooting rampage and you wanted him for another reason."

"I'm sorry, but... I still can't discuss the details of a pending investigation. I hope you understand."

Eve nodded. "I see. So, there *is* another pending investigation involving Lucas? Should we be concerned? Some of us will return to work on Monday, and I get the feeling that his being fired was not the only thing that triggered his melt down."

"To be honest, I can't really answer that, but I doubt you need to be concerned about returning to work."

Eve wondered if this ordeal was really over, but she didn't think so. It was going to take some more time before everyone completely recovered from this tragedy.

Mike could see the doubt in her eyes and sensed that she needed him. He instinctively moved toward her, reached out and gently pulled her into his arms for comfort and whispered, "It's going to be okay." Eve automatically wrapped her arms around him, and the smell of her perfume stirred something inside of Mike. At that moment in time, wrapped in Mike's arms, Eve never felt safer and believed that everything *would* be okay.

Mike reluctantly released Eve from his embrace and she looked up at him. Their eyes locked and time stood still for several seconds. Now that Eve's part of the case involving Lucas was officially closed, Mike wanted to tell her how he felt about her, hoping she felt the same way, but it was too soon. He wouldn't take advantage of her while she was still vulnerable. He would give her a little more time to process everything and attempt to put this behind her. Mike believed that they were destined to meet the morning of the shooting, and their time to be with each other would come soon, he felt it in his gut.

"I need to make a couple more stops to inform some of the other victims of the news. Are you okay?"

Eve smiled. "Yes, as well as can be expected, I guess. Thanks for telling me about Lucas. I appreciate you taking the time."

"Of course, you take care of yourself. Lucas is dead and he can't hurt you ever again. Try to focus on your recovery and moving forward."

"I will." Eve walked Mike to the door.

"Have a good day, Ms. Townsend."

"You too, Detective."

It had been two weeks since the shooting occurred, and as Mike left, he prayed that she would start to heal now that the worst was behind her.

Eve only had the weekend to get herself together because she and some of the other victims would be returning to work that coming Monday. It would be the first time that she would be returning to Colby Designs since they were all carried out on stretchers.

* * *

Mike and Sam received Lucas's autopsy results, and the ME's findings were a mystery to them. Sharday didn't find any suspicious substances in Lucas's system or any incriminating evidence on his body or clothes. To make matters worse, the CSU team didn't find a trace of anything out of the ordinary that couldn't be explained by daily life in a jail cell. This made it impossible for them to prove that Lucas was murdered, so the investigation of his death would be closed and filed as a suicide. Mike and Sam were at square one with linking the Internet money-laundering scam to the Gennaros.

# *Chapter 14*

Mike swiveled his chair around to face Sam. "I was thinking that we might need to contact those young hackers again. Remember, they told us that when they received responses to the email scam, they passed the customers' IDs and passwords to Lucas?"

"Yeah, and Dan discovered that Lucas used the customer information to run up bogus charges." Sam paused. "Ah, I see where you're going with this. You're thinking we should trace the customer account information to the financial institutions they used?"

"Exactly, those banks would be the ones Lucas targeted, which means that someone on the inside of those institutions is most likely involved as well," said Mike.

"The bank managers are the most logical source. They would have access to the main computing systems and could provide access to Lucas without suspicion. Maybe they were blackmailed into helping or threatened like our young hackers."

"Those boys are the only links we have left to whoever's running this scamming operation, Sam. Maybe we'll get lucky and finally get some evidence to provide the DA to go after the Gennaros, but that's only if the bank managers are willing to cooperate."

* * *

Eve paused before entering the Colby Designs building. This was going to be more difficult than she anticipated. Was she ready for this? She thought she was, but wasn't so confident now that she was standing in front of the building. Well, there was no turning back now. She had to move forward with her life and put the horrific shooting behind her. Although Eve herself was a victim, she was also one of the company's managers and had to resume her role as a leader and be there for her team emotionally. They would look to her for guidance just as they did when she first arrived a month ago. She didn't let them down then, and she wouldn't do so now.

Eve took a deep breath and entered. The security guard gave her a smile. "Ms. Townsend, welcome back. You look well... When I saw them wheel you out of here... I just—"

"Thanks, Phil," Eve interrupted. "I understand your discomfort. It couldn't have been easy for you watching us get carted off to the hospital. You must have felt helpless. It was traumatizing for everyone, but I'm glad you didn't get caught in the crossfire as well." He smiled. "I'll see you later Phil, okay?"

"Yes, have a good first day back, Ms. Townsend." Phil watched as Eve headed toward the elevators. He'd felt more than helpless, he'd felt a little responsible. Lucas got past *him* and into the building somehow, and he felt guilty. It was going to be a long day as the surviving victims returned to work, and as their first point of contact Phil decided to make each of them feel welcomed and at ease.

During the elevator ride, Eve could feel the anxiety threatening to overtake her, much like at the memorial service, but she didn't have Mike's strong presence to carry her through this time. She was on her own and had to deal with it as such. She didn't think she could muster the strength to walk down that hallway so soon, or ever, but she had to.

Eve arrived at the fourth floor and stepped off the elevator and glanced down the hallway. She quickly turned her attention to the receptionist. "Good morning, Sherri," she announced. "You look wonderful. I'm glad you are well enough to return to work."

"Good morning, Ms. Townsend. You look well too." Sherri's voice was a little shaky and she seemed a bit apprehensive, but who could blame her? Eve was surprised that Sherri returned to Colby Designs at all. She was only a temp, and her first day here wasn't exactly a stellar experience. Eve was certain that being shot was not part of the job description she received, and she probably jumped out of her skin every time the elevator chimed. Eve flashed her brightest smile to help put Sherri at ease and gave her a little wink. No other words were needed.

Eve turned toward the hallway and quickly made her way to her office. Her last memory of being in this hallway was of her glancing back to look at Mike as he entered the elevator, and that made her smile. She opened her office door and the smile faded as the memory of hiding in her closet to escape certain death resurfaced. She froze in that spot for several seconds before taking another deep breath and then proceeding inside.

She hadn't noticed at first, but a get-well basket and a beautiful flower arrangement awaited her return. She wondered who sent them and welcomed something positive to focus on. She read the cards; the basket was from her team and the flowers were from Nathan. *How thoughtful*, she mused, but Eve's thoughts were interrupted by a knock at her door. She turned around just as Nathan entered. "Nathan!" she exclaimed.

"Hi, Eve, welcome back. I see you're admiring your gifts. I hope they were a nice surprise, something to help kick off your first day back."

"Yes, they're lovely, thank you." Nathan peered at her for several moments, looking for signs of distress. "Nathan, stop looking at me like that. I'm fine, really."

"Are you sure? If you need another day or so, I understand."

"No, I'm going stir crazy at home and we have too much work here that will continue to pile up. We'd made so much progress together before the shooting, and I hate for us to lose complete momentum. I just want to dive in and try to sort through everything."

"Yeah, but that doesn't diminish what *you've* been through. Everyone handles pain and trauma differently. So my offer stands. If you find your first day more difficult than you predicted, *go home.*"

"Okay... so how is the rest of the team dealing with this? It couldn't have been easy trying to keep the projects moving forward with so many of us out of commission for the past several weeks. Do we need to have a team meeting to rally the troops?"

"Yes, but not today, I don't want to put undue pressure and stress on you and the others on your first day back. Take the day to acclimate and tomorrow we can all meet and make our assessments."

Eve nodded in agreement. "Okay."

"If there is anything we can do to help with the transition, just let me know. You and the other victims carry a heavy mental burden. You survived when five of your colleagues didn't, and you'll have to deal with that somehow. I wasn't even injured and I carry that burden too, maybe because Lucas worked in my department and I feel responsible for not recognizing how disturbed he really was. Maybe I did notice but didn't want to acknowledge it… I just don't know anymore..."

"Nathan, you can't possibly be blaming yourself for Lucas's actions. You didn't put a gun in his hand or pulled the trigger for him. Lucas worked with us every day and yet he was still able to gun us down like animals without a second thought. I heard people begging him to not shoot and he did so anyway..." Eve started to shake and tears formed in her eyes.

"Hey, hey, Eve, I didn't mean to upset you. I'm sorry. I shouldn't be laying my guilt on you. Why don't you sit down? Try to relax and put this out of your mind, okay?"

"Sure, Nathan, I didn't mean to get so riled up. I just get so angry at times... I never know what I'm feeling from one minute to the next."

"That's perfectly understandable. Take a deep breath and try to calm down, *please*. I should leave you alone to get settled. I'll check in on you later."

"Thanks." As Nathan left Eve's office, Eve took stock of her emotions. She was going to have to do better than this if she was going to survive the day. *I'll just focus on work*, she decided.

* * *

Several people entered the break room for their afternoon coffee pick-me-up. "Ms. Townsend, welcome back," one of them called out after spotting Eve across the room.

Eve turned around. "Caitlyn, Anna, Lori, how are you?" she asked, hugging all three ladies.

"That's what we should be asking you. But, you look as beautiful as ever," stated Anna.

Eve blushed at the compliment. "That's very kind of you. I'm doing okay, all things considered. The shoulder is a little sore, but it's manageable."

Lori peered at Eve much like Nathan did earlier. "Are you sure you're okay? We were lucky enough to be at lunch when the shooting happened, and it's still weird for *us* to be here. *You* actually lived through it."

"I know, *live* being the operative word here. Some of our teammates *didn't* survive, so I'm not complaining. I'm lucky *and* grateful to be alive."

"You didn't hang around too long at the memorial," said Caitlyn. "We figured it was too much for you, but… we also saw you leave with that handsome hero detective and figured you were in good hands." The three ladies exchanged some glances before settling back on Eve.

"Girls, what's with the looks?"

"Well, we don't want to overstep or seem nosy, but we were wondering if you and the detective were dating," Lori stated.

Eve chuckled. "No, we are not *dating*. Both Detective McGarrett *and* Detective Lewis were just looking out for me because I didn't have any family members or close friends in town for support. I am the new chick in town, in case the three of you have forgotten," she added while pointing at each of them. Eve was hardly going to share her intimate feelings about the detective with her teammates, especially when nothing had come from it.

Anna felt that their beautiful manager was a tad defensive and figured there was more to it after all. "No, we didn't forget, and that was very thoughtful of the detectives. You and Detective McGarrett just look so good together. It would be nice to have something uplifting come out of this tragedy."

Eve could tell Anna was still fishing, but she was not going to take the bait. She decided to steer the topic in another direction. "Well, Nathan and I are going to have a team meeting tomorrow, just to rally the troops and get a sense of how everyone is feeling. We'll send out a memo to let everyone know."

The girls realized that their fishing expedition had come to an end and didn't want to press their luck. "Okay, well, we had better let you get back to work. You probably have a pile a mile high to rifle through," Caitlyn stated while raising her hand just above her head.

"Unfortunately, yes. And I'm sure the three of you have a lot of work to do as well, so I'll see you later," Eve responded and quickly exited the break room before the girls could sense just how uncomfortable she was.

* * *

Mike was shopping at Whole Foods when all of a sudden he smelled *her* perfume. *You've really got it bad for her if you smell her perfume when she's not even around*, he thought.

"Detective McGarrett?" a soft voice called out.

He turned around and there before him was Eve's beautiful smiling face. *So I wasn't imagining it.* "Please, call me Mike," he corrected, "I think we can dispense with the formalities at this stage. It's nice to see you again, Eve."

*Wouldn't the girls at work love to be a fly on this wall?* Eve thought. Mike always managed to take her breath away, and he was just the distraction she needed.

"You look wonderful. How have you been since we last spoke?" Mike asked. "I wasn't exactly the bearer of good news last Friday."

"I know. Hearing about Lucas's death was a bit of a shock, but I'm doing much better now that the case is closed, of course, and our office floor is no longer a crime scene." Eve hoped she sounded more optimistic than she actually felt. Those fearful pleas for mercy and cries for help were as vivid in her mind as they were the day of the shooting. Her first day back at Colby had been emotionally exhausting.

"We tried to clear your department as quickly as we could. We knew everyone needed some sort of normalcy."

"We appreciated that. Some of us returned to work today, including myself. The rest will return tomorrow."

Mike was pleased with her optimism and sensed that a weight had been lifted off her shoulders. He saw a glimmer of the woman he first met before the shooting occurred. He didn't realize, however, that Eve was just putting up a brave front and his presence accounted for her optimistic mood. She had been on the brink of tears throughout the entire day.

"Do you know Kelly's Bar and Restaurant?" Mike asked.

"I think so. It's near Colby, right?"

"Yes. I wondered if you would like to get together for drinks after work one evening." Since the shooting case against Lucas was closed, it removed the conflict of interest. Mike was originally going to wait a bit before asking Eve out, but she seemed to be handling her recovery well, and he didn't see why he couldn't finally spend some personal time with her.

"Sure, I'd like that."

"Good, I'll call you to set up a time."

"I look forward to it. Have a good evening, Mike."

"You too, Eve," he murmured, not taking his eyes off her. She smiled before leaving to continue her shopping. Mike stared at her as she walked down the aisle. *God, she's beautiful.*

* * *

After he got home, Mike couldn't get Eve out of his head. Later that evening he decided to call her, but he got her voicemail instead and had to leave a message. "Hi Eve, it's Mike McGarrett. It was a pleasure running into you earlier this evening. I was thinking that maybe we could get together for those drinks at Kelly's tomorrow evening. I know that you just returned to work, but I hope you can fit me into your schedule. I'll wait to hear back from you."

Eve was in the shower when Mike called, so she didn't hear the phone ring, but was pleased when she heard his message. She returned his call and agreed to meet with him the following day after work. Mike would pick her up at Colby Designs and they would walk over to Kelly's together. This is what they had both been waiting for since first locking eyes with each other.

# Chapter 15

Mike and Sam headed over to the young hackers' homes, to retrieve the customer information they'd obtained from the email scam. "I ran into Eve yesterday evening after work," said Mike.

Sam glanced at him. "Oh really? Where?"

"In Whole Foods, and I asked her out. I'm picking her up after work."

"Tonight? You most certainly didn't waste any time. Are you sure it's not too soon? I know the shooting case is closed, but Eve is probably still a *little* vulnerable."

"I know, Sam, and I'll be conscious of that. At least now I can provide comfort to her if needed. I think she's doing okay, all things considering. It was her first day back at work and she looked great, *really* great."

Sam smiled at his friend's enthusiasm as he pulled up in front of the apartment building where the hackers lived. "When has she not looked great? But that's beside the point, Mike." He nodded to the officers they'd assigned to guard the young hackers and their families as he and Mike exited the car. "But, I'm happy for you. I know you've been waiting for this."

"Long enough, if you ask me," Mike responded as they approached the building.

Sam pushed the buzzer. "Who is it?" a voice called out.

"It's Detectives Lewis and McGarrett," replied Sam.

"Okay," the voice responded and buzzed them into the building.

The boys' parents were reluctant to have them assist the detectives any further for fear of getting deeper involved in the situation, but they agreed to the meeting. Mike and Sam retrieved the customer information from the young hackers and started working on tracing the accounts to the financial institutions.

* * *

Eve was on cloud nine, anticipating her first date with Mike that evening, something positive to look forward to as she navigated through her second day back at work. She had a lot of difficulty concentrating on her conversation with Nathan, but her mind drifted back to reality at the mention of Lucas's name.

"Have you found Lucas's replacement yet?" she asked, not wanting Nathan to realize she had checked out of the conversation.

"I posted the position immediately after firing him but given the chaos that ensued from the shooting, I didn't get around to looking at any of the applications until last week."

"Are any of them promising? Lucas may have been a creepy nutcase, but he was good at what he did," acknowledged Eve. "Hopefully it won't be too difficult to replace him. His assistants have been doing the best they can, but they are certainly no Lucas."

"I know, and luckily some of the applicants are very promising, so I set up interviews for later this week. I want the managers to meet with them as well. I understand if you're not up to it, given all of the catching up you already have to accomplish this week, but I'd really like you to weigh in on the final decision, Eve."

"I'm fine. I can meet with the interviewees."

Nathan smiled tentatively. "Good, so that's settled… Umm, have you given any thought to, umm, speaking with our grief counselor?"

Eve frowned at the mere mention of the grief counselor. "Yes, I thought about it."

"And…"

She sighed. "I don't think I need to see one. I'm doing okay, honestly, I am."

Nathan didn't seem reassured. "Really? Are you sure?"

"Absolutely, yes. If I were still having nightmares, then I might have considered speaking to them, but I'm *not*, so I'm good." *Good Lord, this conversation is getting old real fast*, she thought.

Sensing Eve's irritation on the subject, Nathan decided not to press her on the issue. "Okay, but I think we should offer the option to everyone else at the team meeting today." Nathan glanced at his watch. "Speaking of, we'd better get over to the conference room. I'm hoping this meeting will help to foster camaraderie and assist with the transition of dealing with the loss of some of our teammates." From the perspective of one of the victims, Eve hoped Nathan got his wish.

* * *

There was lot of bustling as everyone gathered in conference room. Recovered victims, like Eve, were all welcomed with warm embraces and well wishes.

"Okay, everyone, I'd like to start this meeting by welcoming back our colleagues that have returned to us this past week. We are all so grateful that you are well and we wish you a continued and speedy recovery." Nathan paused while everyone clapped, voicing their agreement. "If any of you need *anything* at all, please don't hesitate to ask. We know this can't be easy for you, and we are all at your disposal…"

Nathan let out a quick breath to regain his composure. "Unfortunately, not all of us have returned, and the loss of our five colleagues and friends has left a big hole in our hearts. They will be sorely missed." He paused again to give everyone a couple of seconds to compose themselves. "Now, we might not have all been physically injured, but we were all *most definitely* emotionally injured. We experienced an extremely traumatizing event, and I want to remind you all that we have grief counselors available to help you cope. I'm sure some of you feel that you *don't* need this service, but if you change your mind, just know the counselors are at your disposal. Last but not least, I'd like to give a big thanks to all you who performed double duty to help pick up the slack while our injured were out on disability. It was a very stressful time that could have easily turned into chaos, *but* it didn't. Every one of you stepped up to the plate, kicked it into third and fourth gear, and rallied around each other, as only New Yorkers can do, to make sure our clients were taken care of. I am honored and blessed to have each and every one of you in my department. You should be proud of yourselves, and I thank you."

Everyone applauded while shaking their heads in agreement, appreciative of the kind words and accolades bestowed upon them.

* * *

Nathan escorted Eve back to her office. "So, was I okay? I didn't seem too mushy, did I?"

"No, you were perfect, Nathan. You were truthful and sincere, and that is what's important." Eve gave Nathan a smile to reassure him.

"Thank you. As one of the victims and one of my valuable managers, I know you don't say those words lightly. Eve, you really turned this department around. Most of the credit from what your team accomplished while you were out should be given to you. The processes you put in place made all of the difference. They just had to continue following your lead and perform their tasks as you instructed. I filled in for you when needed and to provide necessary signatures, but that was about all they needed from me. Your team knew exactly what stages the victims were at with their assignments and worked together to keep their projects moving forward."

"That's because I made sure that we kept everyone in the loop with the status of each project, for instance when someone is out sick or on vacation. Thank goodness it came in handy."

"Oh, it did more than come in handy. It kept us running like a well-oiled machine. Our clients were very impressed, knowing the circumstances we were dealing with."

"See, we'll get through this, Nathan, I promise you."

Nathan nodded. "I'll let you get back to work, then. Call me if you need anything."

The only thing Eve needed was to see Mike's face. He was the perfect therapy for her.

* * *

The day could not go by fast enough for Mike and the anticipation was driving him crazy. Sam was getting a kick out of watching his partner get ready for his date with Eve. He had never seen his friend so nervous and happy all at the same time. Mike had a lot of people that cared about him in his life, but could be a bit of a loner at times. He could go for long stretches without a single date and at other times he could be seen with a different woman on his arm every other day, but no one had ever caught Mike's attention the way Eve had, and Sam had a front-row seat to their blossoming romance. As Mike left the police station, Sam wished his friend good luck even though he didn't think he needed it.

Mike arrived at Colby Designs, and when he stepped off the elevator he approached the receptionist, Sherri Woods. "Hi Sherri, do you remember me? I'm Detective McGarrett."

"Of course, Detective, how could any of us forget you *and* Detective Lewis? You saved our lives." She beamed.

Mike smiled. "We were just doing our jobs, Sherri, but I'm glad we were able to help. Sorry we missed you at the memorial service."

"I wasn't recovered enough to attend, but everyone was in my thoughts."

"I'm glad you're okay."

"Thank you. What can I do for you this evening, Detective?"

"I'm here to pick up Ms. Townsend."

"*Oh*, I'll let her know you're here, just give me one minute." Sherri dialed Eve's extension, wondering if this was for business or pleasure.

"Yes, Sherri," Eve answered, hoping that Mike had arrived. She was more than ready to go.

"Hello Ms. Townsend, Detective McGarrett is here to see you." Eve's stomach flipped right on cue.

"Thanks Sherri, I'll be right there," she responded as a warm smile crossed her face.

The sound of Eve's voice provided Sherri with her answer: it was pleasure, for sure. "Ms. Townsend is on her way, but you could have a seat while you wait, if you like." She could sense that the detective was a little nervous.

"Thanks Sherri, but I'll stand." It was a bit surreal for Mike, returning to Colby Designs after the shooting. He wondered if Eve was coping with her return to work as well as she professed. The memories came flooding back to him like a tidal wave and it was unnerving, even to him, even though he was trained to deal with such violence. Mike couldn't imagine how the surviving victims managed to work here again under the circumstances.

The sight of Eve approaching distracted Mike from his morbid thoughts; he was suddenly nervous and felt like a teenager about to go on his first date. They both smiled at the sight of each other.

Sherri smiled inside at the two of them. Detective McGarrett and Ms. Townsend looked perfect together.

"Eve, you look wonderful," Mike announced once she was standing right in front of him.

"Thanks, so do you." Mike and Eve said goodnight to Sherri then entered the elevator. On the ride down, Eve asked Mike how he felt coming back to the Colby Designs building, given the outcome of his original visit.

"I have to admit that it was a little weird. It was difficult to keep the memories from flooding back. I imagine it must have been the same or worse for you and the other victims."

"Sure, it's been… difficult, but it's only my second day back, so I imagine it'll get easier as time goes on."

"It will," replied Mike, trying to be positive. They exited the building and only had a couple of blocks to walk to Kelly's, which was why Mike chose it. He wanted to keep the evening nice and simple for Eve and in a familiar neighborhood. He automatically clasped her hand in his. It felt natural for him to do so, as if they had been dating for months. Eve didn't seem to mind, either. Although it was technically their first date, the connection between them and their feelings for each other were obviously long past the hand-holding point. They fit together like a glove.

After arriving at Kelly's, they grabbed a couple of stools at the bar. "Eve, what would you like, beer, wine…"

"Beer is fine, whatever they have on tap."

Mike ordered a couple of drafts as Eve scanned the room, soaking up the atmosphere. "I like the ambiance. It has a cozy and comfortable feel. I can see why my coworkers love it here."

"That's been my experience as well; I figured you would like it… So, Sam tells me that you're new in town, have you gotten a chance to explore at all? New York can be overwhelming. There's so much to do and it's hard to choose sometimes."

"Unfortunately not, I've only been in town for about a month. I'm comfortable with my immediate neighborhood, but I haven't had the chance to hang out much, given the demands of the new job. I'd been employed at Colby for only two weeks before the shooting happened and then I was homebound for the past couple of weeks recovering from the gunshot wound. What a wonderful introduction to New York. It's enough to make a girl want to return to San Francisco," Eve responded, feeling a little homesick.

The bartender handed them their beers and Mike paid the tab.

"So you're from California? Well, I'm glad you haven't given up on The Big Apple just yet. Maybe I can show you around the city so you start to feel more at home here." Mike was willing to do anything to keep Eve in New York. "So, why *did* you move across the country?"

"I received a promotion and the position was stationed here at the Colby New York Branch."

"They couldn't fill the position locally? Don't get me wrong, I'm *glad* they chose *you* instead."

Eve smiled inside. "I'm glad too, but for some reason they had difficulties filling the position locally and requested a recommendation from the San Francisco office, and here I am."

"Yes, here you are… You must be very good at what you do, Eve, to receive the offer," surmised Mike. Not only was Eve drop-dead gorgeous, but she was pretty damned smart and successful to boot.

"I have my bachelor's in Architecture and I worked as one of the designers at the Colby San Francisco branch for the past four years. You would normally need at least ten years of experience in the field of Architecture and Design to hold a managerial position, so receiving this opportunity is beyond incredible and, I have to admit, a little intimidating at first."

"I'm so proud of you. This is a huge accomplishment."

"I know, and then to come so close to having it all taken away so shortly after I arrived is so… surreal."

"That must have been nerve-racking."

"Well, I felt a bit isolated and I was pretty pissed off. It didn't make any sense to mope around, so I watched TV until it bored me. Then I caught up on some reading and I sketched a little bit."

"So you're an artist too?" he asked. "I'm impressed."

"Well, I don't know if I'd go that far, but I'm pretty good. It was good therapy for me too; it helped me deal with the awful memories and recurring nightmares."

"It's a gift, you know. Being able to draw does not come easily to everyone. I would love to see some of your work if you ever feel comfortable sharing them with me."

Eve played with her beer mug and admitted, "Well, I actually made a sketch of you and Detective Lewis." Mike looked surprised but intrigued at the same time. "I could give it to the two of you as a gift if you like, as a thank you for all of your help. It was nice knowing that the two of you were on the case, and it made me and the other victims feel safe."

Mike was touched at the gesture. "Sam and I would love to have the drawing."

"This is nice, Mike, us hanging out like this. It's given me something else to focus on, something good to look forward to while trying to make it through the workday."

"It's my pleasure, Eve." Mike placed a hand over hers, and she smiled at his touch. "If there's anything I can do to help you cope, just let me know." Mike and Eve both shared a long silent glance between them, their connection deepening. "Eve, I have to ask. Is it just me, or is there something... happening... between us, other than friendship? I'm not imagining this, am I?"

"No, you're not," Eve answered shyly, relieved to finally have it all out in the open.

"Oh, thank God... I mean, I wasn't sure... So much has happened since we first met. I knew what *I* felt, but you were going through so much and I didn't want to burden you—"

Eve placed her other hand on top of Mike's. "You didn't burden me," she interrupted. "You were a source of comfort for me. Thoughts of you helped me through some difficult days."

Mike's heart swelled as he continued to gaze into her eyes. "That's what I hoped, that you knew I'd be there for you if you ever needed me, without feeling pressured."

"Deep down I probably knew that, but I didn't think that anything could happen between us while the case was still pending. And I wasn't sure if you were actually feeling the same way that I was... I didn't want to presume."

"You're right; it would have been a conflict of interest while the case was ongoing. I couldn't pursue you as I wanted to at the time. It was unbearable for me that I couldn't be there for you. And once the case was closed I wanted to give you some time to heal, although Sam kindly reminded me that you might still be too vulnerable, even now."

"Well, that might be true, but here we are." Eve paused for a minute then continued, "So, Detective McGarrett, what else do you do, that is when you're not saving damsels in distress?"

Mike couldn't help but notice the twinkle in Eve's eyes. "Well, I'm a bit of a thrill-seeker," he responded.

"No! You're kidding?" Eve replied, feigning a shocked expression while throwing her hand at the base of her throat.

Mike shot her a quick, side glance while grinning and said, "Okay, wise girl, so you've got jokes now?"

Eve giggled. "I couldn't resist, I mean, come on. You're a Detective. I think thrill-seeking kind of comes with the territory, to some extent anyway."

"Okay, let me clarify, *other* than detective work, I like to race cars." Now it was Eve's turn to be impressed.

"Really? Do you race for fun or do you compete?"

"Mainly for fun. I love the rush you get driving at speeds beyond most people's comprehension. What I especially love is the feeling of complete control in the midst of chaos. Everything is whizzing past you in a blur but, inside the car, it is complete stillness, calmness, there's nothing like it." At least until he met Eve—she gave him that same sense of serenity. At that very moment they were surrounded by hordes of people talking, laughing, and drinking, but when he looked at Eve everything else around them faded in the background; all he saw was her. "I haven't raced in a while, life can sort of get in the way of self-indulgences. I'll have to try and make time for it; I don't want to lose my edge." Mike had a gleam in his eyes.

"I wouldn't worry about that if I were you. So, dare I ask what else you do? I get the feeling there's more."

Mike smiled. "I also go hiking, mostly by myself, and I was also thinking of taking up rock-climbing, *if* I could ever find the time to learn."

"Why am I not surprised?" mused Eve. "You are an interesting character, Detective McGarrett, very interesting."

"I'm glad you think so. What about you, Eve? Are you a thrill-seeker as well?"

"Oh no, I wouldn't say that, but I do love a challenge every now and then. I run marathons as well as shorter distance races."

"No wonder you healed so quickly. You're an athlete and obviously keep yourself in good shape. I'm impressed," *especially since you were a heart transplant recipient*, he thought. Mike wondered if he should bring up the fact that he knew this piece of information, but decided to wait for Eve to mention it. "Maybe we can go running together sometime, unless you'd rather run alone."

"No, that's fine. It's nice to have company on a run every now and then. I've had to put that on hold for obvious reasons, but now that I'm almost healed I can start running again soon." Eve noticed several pool tables across the room and wondered if Mike wanted to play a few rounds.

Mike followed her gaze. "You play?" Mike asked.

"A little," replied Eve. "I'm not an expert by any means, but maybe you can show me a few pointers." There was that twinkle again.

"I would *love* to, Ms. Townsend."

They played a few rounds, as best as Eve could anyway, given her newly healed shoulder. Mike especially enjoyed assisting Eve with her game, since it gave him the opportunity to get close to her without the risk of overstepping his bounds and potentially getting slapped. Eve liked being close to Mike as well, but it was *really* hard to concentrate when his chest made contact with her back and his arms enveloped hers. The air started to thicken around them and electric sparks rippled through Eve's body.

Mike leaned in even closer. "You're not so bad at this, Eve," he murmured in her ear, "but I don't mind giving you a few tips anytime you want."

Eve turned her head slightly and smiled. "I'd like that very much, Detective," she breathed, wanting to feel Mike's lips on hers.

Mike caught his breath and he wanted to kiss her right then and there, but he didn't want their first kiss to be in public. "Since we both have to work tomorrow, I guess we should call it a night. Did you drive to work?"

"No, I took a cab. That's been my main mode of transportation since the shooting."

"There's no need for you to take a cab back. I have my car, so I can take you home."

"That would be nice, thank you."

They enjoyed a nice conversation during the drive and shared a comfortable ease between them. Once they arrived, Mike escorted Eve up to her apartment.

"Why don't you come inside for a minute and I'll get the drawing of you and Sam?"

Eve didn't usually allow men into her apartment on the first date, but Mike wasn't a stranger. He'd already been inside of her apartment, on official business, of course, plus he saved her life so she never felt safer.

When Eve returned and showed him the drawing, Mike was moved. "Wow, it's beautiful, and so life-like. I can't believe you did this. Thank you. Sam is going to love it." He placed the drawing into the manila envelope that Eve provided and looked up at her. "You definitely have a gift, Eve."

Eve was touched; it was the first time she had shared her work with anyone on a personal level and was grateful for the appreciation. "I also did sketches of the victims that didn't survive the shooting and was thinking of giving them to their surviving relatives as mementos."

"I think the families would appreciate you thinking of them and would love the drawings." Mike felt very connected and drawn to her at that moment and didn't want to leave, but since he didn't want to overstay his welcome he started to head out. If Eve was just another fling to him, half of their clothes would have come off by now. Eve walked him to the door. Before he left he turned to her. "I had a wonderful time with you tonight."

"So did I," Eve replied tenderly. Mike leaned in close to her and caressed her cheek with the back of his hand. This caused her stomach to flutter. He'd wanted to kiss her from the moment he first saw her. He tentatively brushed her lips lightly with his. The spark between them was evident, and his mouth covered hers. With one hand holding the drawing, Mike held Eve's head in his other hand as if they were both priceless objects. Eve wrapped her arms around his back for support. When their bodies pressed against each other, a slight groan escaped Mike's throat. The very passionate but tender kiss left them both weak in the knees and a little breathless. They had both wanted *and* needed each other from the first time they met, and it was difficult for them to part with each other that evening.

"Good night, my sweet Eve." Mike's blue eyes bore deep into hers.

"Good night, Mike." Eve was spellbound.

After Mike left, Eve was too weak to move and leaned against the door for support. *Is this really happening or am I dreaming?* No other guy had ever affected her in this way and so quickly. After several minutes had passed she finally made her way into the bedroom to prepare for bed and the following workday.

For the next thirty minutes all she could think about was being in Mike's arms and the touch of his lips against hers. She touched her lips in remembrance then her thoughts were interrupted by a ringing sound and she realized it was her phone.

"Hello…"

"Hi pretty lady."

"Mike, I wasn't expecting to hear from you so soon. Are you home already?"

"Yes, I made good timing for a change and just walked in. I wanted to hear your voice. I miss you already."

"I miss you too."

"I'd really like to see you again, soon."

"I'd like that, Mike, the sooner the better." Eve surprised herself at her forwardness, but getting shot made her all too aware of how short life was.

Mike smiled at Eve's response. "Well, your wish is my command. Goodnight, pretty lady."

"Goodnight, Detective."

Was it possible that they could be falling in love with each other so quickly? Deep down, the both of them knew the answer to that question.

# Chapter 16

The next morning, Mike found Sam getting coffee in the break room and wanted to show him the drawing Eve made of the two of them. Sam could tell the evening went well just by the expression on Mike's face. "I assume you had a good time last night?" Sam asked.

"It was amazing. Eve's is an incredible woman," Mike replied.

"I'm happy for you both. You've wanted this for weeks."

Mike nodded. "The wait has been *unbearable*, but I think it's going to work out for us."

"Well, it's obvious that Eve is into you," Sam replied.

"I think so too."

"You think? *Please*, it was written all over *both* of your faces every time the two of you locked eyes on each other, even from the moment we all first met. *It's disgusting.* I kept thinking 'just get a room already for Christ's sake.'"

"Oh, shut up." Mike chuckled at Sam's bluntness but was encouraged by his assessment and hoped that he was right regarding Eve's feelings for him.

Sam noticed the folder in Mike's hand. "What's that?"

"Oh, wait until you see this, you're going to love it. It's a present from Eve to the *both* of us. She wanted to show her appreciation for the way we handled the case and protected her and the other victims." He handed Sam the folder, and Sam was very intrigued to see what was inside. When he opened it up, he was pleasantly surprised.

"Did Eve draw this?" Mike nodded. "Wow, she is very talented. Tell her I love it. You should have it framed and hung on your wall for everyone to see, but don't tell her. Let it be a surprise for the first time she comes over to your house." Sam continued to look at the drawing and then glanced back up at Mike. "She's a keeper, Mike. *Don't blow it.*"

"Oh, I don't plan to. She's very special to me, and I'm going to make sure that she knows it."

"Now that we've finally got your love life on track, maybe we can be just as lucky with this case. Whenever you're ready, we can head out to some of the local banks we were able to trace the customer accounts to."

"And if we have time we can attempt to reach some of the others across town before they close for the day," said Mike. "Let me put this drawing away in a safe place and grab the bank listing, and then we can head out after you've finished your coffee."

"I'll meet you at your desk," replied Sam.

* * *

Sam and Mike pulled up in front of the first bank on their list. The young hackers breached four banks in total, none of which resided in the same town, which could turn these interrogations into an all-day affair. They entered the first bank, scanning the room for someone in charge, but no one jumped out at them. They approached the information desk and flashed their badges.

"Good morning, Ms…"

"Jones," the young woman working the desk provided, slightly taken aback at the presence of police.

"Ms. Jones," Sam continued. "I'm Detective Lewis and this is my partner, Detective McGarrett. We'd like to speak with the bank manager, please."

Ms. Jones looked concerned and was tempted to ask what this issue was about, but knew they wouldn't divulge that information to her. "Just give me one moment, please." She buzzed the bank manager. "Hello, Mr. Polerno, there are two detectives here to see you… Okay." She hung up and addressed Mike and Sam, "He'll be right out, Detectives."

"Thank you, Ms. Jones," replied Mike.

She took the time to look them both over, discreetly, of course, or so she thought. Mike and Sam always noticed when they were being admired and exchanged smiles as they turned away from the desk in anticipation of Mr. Polerno's arrival.

A tall man of medium-sized build approached the information desk, and Mike and Sam surmised that this was the bank manager. He tried to mask his concern with a smile, but he was clearly nervous at their arrival.

"Mr. Polerno?" Mike asked when the man reached them.

"Yes, he responded, with an outstretched hand.

As they shook hands, Mike made the introductions. "I'm Detective McGarrett, and this is Detective Lewis."

"What can I do for you this morning?" the manager said, his voice sounding a little too chipper.

"We'd like to ask you a couple of questions, somewhere a little more private perhaps?" stated Mike, not wanting to conduct an interrogation in front of bank customers.

"Sure." Mr. Polerno escorted Mike and Sam to his office. "So, you have some questions for me?" Polerno began after they had settled in their seats.

"We are investigating a case which involves the hacking of bank customer IDs and passwords. Some of your customers were unfortunate victims."

The bank manager's heart leaped in his chest and he swallowed hard. "This is the first I've heard of this." He lied as little beads of sweat started to form on his forehead.

"Really? Hundreds of your customers had their information hacked and money stolen from their accounts and you're telling us that this is news to you?" Sam asked, dumbfounded.

"Well, umm, hacking is usually… an Internet breach, correct? They, umm, might have taken their complaints directly to the online customer service department if they noticed anything unusual with their accounts instead of coming directly to us."

"I think having thousands of dollars stolen from you is a bit more than unusual, Mr. Polerno," said Mike.

The bank manager's hands started to shake and he pulled a handkerchief from his jacket pocket to dab the sweat from his forehead. "Well, I didn't mean to diminish the severity of the situation."

"I think that is exactly what you meant to do. We believe that someone accessed those accounts right here on these premises and we believe that you know exactly what is going on, and might possibly be involved."

"*What*! Of… of… course not! I… I have absolutely no knowledge of what you're talking about, detectives, and I resent you stating otherwise."

Mike and Sam cast a look of annoyance between the two of them and then directed their stares back at the bank manager. They didn't have proof that the accounts were accessed on the premises. It was just a hunch on their part, but they were pretty certain that was part of Lucas's job after he received the customer information from the young hackers and obviously struck a nerve.

"Mr. Polerno, you seem a little jumpy and nervous. Are you being threatened or coerced in some way? We can help you if you just tell us who is making you do this," coaxed Sam, hoping to lower Polerno's defenses.

"*No one* is making me do *anything*. I told the two of you that I have no idea what or who you're talking about. Now, if you have nothing else to discuss, detectives, I'd like to get back to work."

Mr. Polerno tried to hide his fear, but his shaky hands and quivering voice, not to mention his beaded forehead, told a different story. Mike and Sam were pretty certain that all of the bank managers were involved, most likely against their will, but nonetheless complicit in the thievery.

Sam handed him a business card. "We have nothing further at this moment, Mr. Polerno, but if you have anything to add or remember something later, please call us. We can help you."

Mr. Polerno took the card grudgingly and placed it inside of the desk drawer. He stood up and shook their hands. "Sorry I couldn't be more helpful, detectives."

"So are we," Mike responded.

They left the office and exited the bank. Ms. Jones smiled at them on the way out. "Have a good day, detectives."

"You do the same, Ms. Jones," replied Mike.

Mike and Sam were certain that they would get the same reaction and responses from the other three bank managers as they headed out to the other banks on the list. Just as expected, those bank managers were also clearly scared and in fear for their lives, and wouldn't admit to their personal involvement. Each and every one claimed to not be aware of this crime against their customers and that it couldn't possibly have originated from their bank.

Another dead end.

* * *

That evening, Mike and Eve talked on the phone for hours, getting comfortable with each other and feeling more connected. That first kiss left both of them reeling and feeling very giddy, which made them anxious to see each other again. Mike asked Eve if she was free for dinner that weekend, possibly Saturday evening. Eve was definitely available, for Mike anyway, and she couldn't wait to see him. Mike would make the plans, something more intimate and special this time, and would contact her with the details.

* * *

At work, Eve grinned like a schoolgirl in anticipation of her second date with Mike, and her coworkers definitely noticed the change in her mood from when she first returned back to work. She was tentative and uneasy for those first couple of days, but now she appeared to be almost joyful again, like the Eve they all met about a month ago, and they wondered what could be the cause of her newfound happiness. Sherri had a feeling she knew the secret to Eve's happy mood but kept Eve's personal business to herself.

Mike called Eve to finalize their plans. "How do you feel about dinner, and some dancing afterwards?" he asked.

"I love dancing, what do you have in mind?"

"That's a surprise, pretty lady, so just make sure to be ready with an appetite and wear your dancing shoes."

"Well, I'll make sure to do just that, Detective." Eve hung up the phone with a big grin on her face.

# Chapter 17

Sam and Mike got word that some of the bank managers they interrogated had suddenly disappeared. They couldn't confirm one way or the other whether the managers left of their own accord or were forced to take a permanent vacation. This confirmed their suspicion of the bank managers' involvement with the money-laundering scheme, but unfortunately they were no longer available to provide the needed information to implicate the Gennaros. Mike and Sam were very frustrated with this turn of events. All of their leads ended up either dead or missing. Mike was in desperate need of something positive to focus on and decided to put all of his attention on his upcoming date with Eve to keep him sane.

*  *  *

It was Saturday night and Mike was anxious, happy, nervous, and any other emotion that he could possibly feel all at the same time. His and Eve's first date was casual and easy-going, which helped break the ice and allowed them to connect on a personal level outside of the Lucas Coles case. But as far as Mike was concerned, this night was special, and he put a lot of thought and planning into making it that way. Mike needed to know for certain if there was merely a strong physical attraction between him and Eve or if there were real feelings developing. He'd never cared about such matters before, making this unchartered territory for him.

Mike nervously fumbled with his tie so he decided not to wear one; it wasn't necessary. Plus, it made him look uncomfortable and stuffy. They were going salsa dancing, so he should loosen up a bit. Mike looked himself over in the mirror to make sure he was presentable then headed out to pick up Eve.

Eve was putting the finishing touches on her makeup. Although this was their second date, tonight felt different, more serious with actual intentions, and she was nervous. Eve wished she had Bonnie or even her mom around to help her get ready and keep her calm. She was still lost in thought when Mike rang the doorbell. She instinctively threw her hand to the base of her throat. *Stop this foolishness!* Eve scolded herself. It was Mike, the man who saved her life and captured her heart, so she had no reason to be nervous. She grabbed her purse and went to greet him.

When she opened the door, Mike was in awe at the sight of her and was almost speechless. She was wearing a burgundy spaghetti-strap dress that framed her body perfectly, silver strapped three-inch sandals that matched her purse, and her hair was pinned up with a burgundy broach with several curly strands cascading down and framing her face.

Eve was left breathless and lightheaded at Mike's appearance. His white shirt fitted his torso like a glove, and the dark slacks and blazer tailored his frame perfectly. He looked rugged and suave all at the same time, and her stomach performed its usual dance routine at the sight of him.

"You look beautiful, Ms. Townsend," Mike said.

Eve smiled. "Thank you, you look very handsome, Detective."

During the drive to the restaurant, Eve glanced over at Mike. "So, do I get a clue as to where we are going?"

Mike smirked and replied, "Nope, but nice try. I told you it's a surprise, so just try to bear with me a little longer. We're almost there." Eve was anxious. She normally liked surprises, but her nerves were getting the best of her.

Mike parked the car in a parking garage and helped her out. *Such a gentleman*, Eve thought. They entered the restaurant and were taken to their seats, where Mike held Eve's chair for her and the waiter presented them with menus. Eve liked the ambiance and felt the evening was starting out on the right foot. She couldn't wait to see how it would progress.

"I'll be back in a few minutes to take your orders. To get started, what would you like to drink?" the waiter asked.

Mike deferred to Eve to order first.

"I'd like an amaretto sour with a splash of ginger ale, please."

"I'll have a Scotch and water, thank you," added Mike.

While they waited for their drinks and perused the menu, another patron popped a champagne bottle, which startled Eve, causing her to jump.

"Are you okay?" Mike asked as he reached for her hand.

"Yes. I'm fine. The sudden loud noise just..."

"Reminded you of the shooting…" he finished.

"Pretty silly reaction, huh?" Eve asked, slightly embarrassed.

"No, not at all. In fact, I think you've been dealing with it all quite well. It's only been a couple of weeks since the shooting, so it's natural that you have some residual uneasiness. A lot of people would still be curled up in a ball, so you have nothing to be embarrassed about."

Eve was comforted by Mike's kind words. "I appreciate that, and it means a lot. *But* enough talk about the shooting," she said while shaking her head. "Let's decide what we're going to eat before the waiter returns with our drinks."

"Your wish is my command," Mike teased with a salute.

When the waiter returned, Mike looked up from his menu. "What are you in the mood for this evening, pretty lady?"

"I'm going to have the grilled salmon with Spanish rice and grilled vegetables," replied Eve decisively.

"I like a woman who knows what she wants," said Mike.

"I always do," replied Eve, with a twinkle in her eye.

The waiter tried to act oblivious as if he wasn't listening; he liked this couple and found it difficult to conceal a little smile.

Mike ordered the broiled trout with mash potatoes and handed the waiter the menus.

"Tell me more about yourself, Detective," Eve asked after the waiter left.

"What do you want to know?"

"Have you always lived in New York?"

"Yes, born and raised. I'm an only child, and my parents live in Yonkers. So they're close enough for me to keep an eye on but not too close to drive me crazy." They both laughed. "So what about you Eve, who did you leave behind when you left San Francisco?"

"I am an only child as well, but my parents were both killed in a car accident a couple of years ago, so I just left behind some really great friends and coworkers."

Mike noticed a slight cloud come over Eve's eyes at the mention of her parents' death and offered his condolences. "I'm sorry. I didn't mean to bring up sad memories."

"It's okay. I can talk about my parents. It's just hitting me a little harder than usual because thinking about them makes me a little homesick, reminding me that I'm far away from my friends back home. One of my closest childhood friends, Malcolm, wasn't able to attend my parents' funeral because he was out of the country on assignment. That really upset me, but my good friends Bonnie, Caroline, and Charles were close by and helped me through the crisis. I really miss them now that I'm so far away from them. They were extremely worried when I told them about the shooting, and actually threatened to jump on the next plane to bring me back home."

Mike noticed Eve kept referring to San Francisco as home. He hoped she would soon start to think of New York as home. "I can understand their reaction," he replied, wondering a little about this long-lost childhood friend Malcolm. The mention of Malcolm seemed to affect Mike more so than the others, and he couldn't help but feel a little twinge of jealousy. He would have to find out more about this elusive friend. "Your friends must have felt helpless, not being able to help you through this crisis as well. They were probably worried about you being out here alone."

"Well, I told them they didn't have to worry. I had two strong, handsome police detectives watching my back," Eve replied with a smile.

Their conversation was interrupted when the waiter returned with their meals. They were both very hungry at this point and had no trouble cleaning their plates as they continued to learn more about each other.

"So, umm, Eve, I wanted to ask you about something I learned during the time you were being treated in the ER. I've hesitated to bring it up because I wasn't sure if reminding you about the shooting would upset you."

"Ask away, Mike. I'll let you know if it becomes too much. I'm curious to know what you learned."

"Well, we were trying to determine if you had any medical issues that would impact your treatment. You were unconscious and nonresponsive during the ride in the ambulance, but the ER doctor said you were conscious just long enough to tell them you were a heart transplant recipient."

"Oh, and you were surprised by that?"

"Well, quite frankly, yes. Are you upset that I know about it?"

"Of course not, Mike. Its pertinent health information, and we were in a life-and-death situation. You and Detective Lewis were trying to save our lives."

"I know. I was just waiting for you to bring it up first, but you didn't… I just wanted you to know that I knew about it."

"I guess it's just a part of my everyday life now so I don't necessarily think of it as something to bring up in conversation. It's not a big deal that you found out. Now you know what to tell the paramedics on my next trip to the ER," she joked.

"Heaven forbid, Eve. I could barely stand it the first time, seeing you unconscious and almost bleeding to death."

Eve reached across the table and put her hands over Mike's. "But everything turned out okay, for the both of us," she replied with a smile.

"It most certainly has," said Mike as his eyes bore into Eve's.

"Uh hum," the waiter cleared his throat, and Mike and Eve glanced up at him. "Would the two of you like to order dessert?" he asked while retrieving their plates.

Mike deferred to Eve. "Whatever the pretty lady's heart desires."

"Why don't we share one? Let's get the molten chocolate lava cake."

That cake was like heaven on a plate. Eve confessed her passion for all things chocolate, and Mike made a mental note for future occasions.

After dessert, Mike paid the bill and they headed out to the dance club. They walked a short distance to a Latin club called Copacabana.

Eve was pleasantly surprised and smiled inwardly. Once they entered, she could hear the music playing in the background and was ecstatic. Mike didn't know that Eve actually *loved* to dance salsa and merengue and was happy to see the pleased look on her face, alluding that she approved of his choice of venue. Mike escorted Eve to the area where the dance floor was located. He noticed the sparkle in her eyes and asked, "Do you want something to drink before we head out on the dance floor?"

"No, I'm okay for now. I'd rather dance."

Mike smiled, looked at Eve and asked, "Hey, why do I get the feeling that you've done this before?"

"Because I have, many times in fact. I grew up dancing salsa. What gave me away?"

"Well, you didn't even flinch when I suggested we head to the dance floor. Some people are reluctant to try dancing salsa for fear of embarrassing themselves by not being able to stay on the beat, but not you. You can't get out on the floor fast enough."

While looking up at Mike, Eve flipped her hair away from her face. "Did you expect me to be reluctant?"

Mike took both of Eve's hands in his and replied, "No. I thought you might be hesitant but figured you would see it as a new challenge and would just go for it. You don't strike me as the type of person who's afraid to try new things."

"When men first meet me, they tend to see a woman that they need to put a protective bubble around. Thank you for being able to see beyond the surface."

"Well, I can't imagine someone who moves across the country away from everyone she knows, survives getting shot and has already returned to work as someone needing to be in a protective bubble. I see a strong woman who knows how to survive and push forward with her life while enjoying it along the way."

She gazed into Mike's eyes and replied, "I appreciate that more than you know."

They both felt very connected to each other. Their bond was deepening as they spent more time together.

"So let's get out there and show everyone how it's done," Mike said, leading her onto the dance floor.

Eve was very sensuous but playful all at the same time. The touch of her body brushing slightly against him caused a tightening in his loins that he hoped was not obvious. Eve was clearly enjoying herself, and he was glad that they were able to have fun together.

Eve was impressed with Mike as well. With salsa dancing the man is responsible for leading his partner, which Mike accomplished very well, and Eve decided that he could lead her anywhere he wanted to. She trusted and felt comfortable being in his arms, and realized she was falling hard for this man.

During the slow ballads, Mike held Eve around her waist and her arms naturally went around his neck. It was like making love to music. He nuzzled her hair with his nose. She felt so good against him and he wanted to kiss her badly. He leaned in and softly brushed his lips across hers. This sent an electric jolt between them and they continued to give each other little kisses for the remainder of the song.

They eventually decided to call it a night. Mike took Eve home and escorted her inside her building. When they arrived at Eve's apartment, she asked if he wanted to come in for a little while. She wasn't ready to say goodnight to him yet. Mike agreed. He wanted to spend more time with Eve and tell her that he truly cared for her and hoped she felt the same way.

"Do you want something to drink? I have red wine and beer."

"Sure, why not? A glass of wine would be nice."

Mike was pretty nervous about what he wanted to discuss and needed to relax. Maybe the wine would take the edge off. They chatted for a bit, and every time Eve looked into his eyes something stirred deep inside of him. Mike decided it was now or never. He sat forward and leaned in closer, and when he took her hand in his she wondered what was happening. Mike had a purposeful look about him, and it was obvious he'd wanted to get something off his chest all evening.

"Eve, I know we've only known each other a little less than a month, and I don't want to scare you away… but from the moment we first met I've felt connected to you and that we were meant to meet each other that morning. I've enjoyed the time we've spent together this past week, and I hope that we could continue to do so." Mike took a deep breath. "Eve, I've developed very deep feelings for you over this short period of time, and I hope that you care for me too, beyond a physical attraction or just someone to date casually."

Eve was elated. She was falling so deeply for this man. Her eyes glistened slightly from the tears she was holding back and she looked at him with loving eyes. "I do, Mike. I just wasn't sure if it was too soon to say so…"

Mike cupped Eve's face in his hands, meeting her lips with his in a gentle and tender kiss. It was so sensuous that it set off fireworks deep inside the both of them. The kiss deepened and everything that they had been feeling and holding inside overwhelmed them. Finally expressing their feelings for each other unleashed a flood of desire they couldn't control, and it completely took over their judgment.

Mike kissed Eve's cheek softly, then his kisses traveled down her neck and lingered above her cleavage. She sighed with pleasure. He slid the straps of her dress down her shoulders and continued to lavish her with kisses as he eased her back against the sofa. His tongue sought hers with increasing hunger and she responded with equal fervor. Their bodies molded into each other. Eve's fingers were tangled in Mike's hair, and then her hands traveled to his muscular shoulders. She stripped his jacket off and let it fall to the floor. Their kiss grew with intensity and she let her nails travel down his back, causing Mike to grind against her. He ached with a deep wanting he had never felt before. Things were moving so quickly that they were pretty damn close to ripping each other's clothes off. Mike wanted to feel her skin and slid his hand beneath her dress to stroke her thigh. Delicious languor spread through her veins and she arched against him causing Mike to groan.

God, she was intoxicating! Eve started to unbutton his shirt and Mike realized that he was losing control of himself and the situation. What was he thinking? Breathless, he abruptly pulled free.

Eve was confused. "Mike, what's wrong?"

He was embarrassed and ashamed of his behavior. He'd waited weeks to tell her how he felt but it took him all of two seconds to jump her.

"Eve, please forgive me. It's only our second date, and I didn't share my feelings with you just to get you to sleep with me. My feelings for you are genuine, and I don't want you to get the wrong impression. I don't want anything to get in the way of this relationship, so maybe we shouldn't rush into something that we might not be ready for."

Well that's a first, a man not wanting to rush into sex. Who knew? Eve was struck by his concern and respect for her virtue.

"I don't think for one minute that you're trying to take advantage of me. You weren't acting alone here, Mike."

"Sex has never meant anything more to me than just sex, but with you, Eve, it's different. We've both developed feelings for each other in such a short time."

"I know, but we don't really know each other very well, do we? So becoming sexually involved is probably not wise at this point."

"Exactly," Mike agreed, relieved that she wasn't offended and understood his position. "I *want* to be with you, *believe* me I do, and it's taken every ounce of strength I have to restrain myself, which is something I'm not used to doing..."

"Don't worry, I understand." Eve replied.

They decided to call it a night to avoid further temptation. They adjusted their clothes as Eve walked Mike to the door. They shared another kiss that damn near brought them to the brink of frenzy again, and they realized it might not be so easy to control themselves as they had thought. They decided to make plans to meet in places where they would be surrounded by other people to help reduce temptation, or at least prevent them from being able to act on it. One could only hope.

# Chapter 18

Mike worked at his desk while thinking of Eve. For a little over a week now he had this permanent grin on his face and his disposition had a marked improvement. His fellow officers noticed this sudden change and wondered what the cause was, all except Sam of course. He knew Eve was the reason for his partner's improved mood. Mike seemed lighter, as if a very large weight had been shrugged off his shoulders. No woman had ever gotten close enough to affect him this way before, until now.

Mike and Eve couldn't get enough of each other and they spent every spare minute they had either together or talking on the phone. It was a whirlwind romance. Everything was moving so fast, and they allowed themselves to be swept away.

Mike wanted and needed to hear Eve's voice, but just as he picked up the phone to call her, Sam appeared at his desk. "Sorry to interrupt, man, but the chief wants to see us in his office pronto. He wants to brainstorm our next plan of attack to take down the Gennaro Family." Mike let out a low groan and replaced the phone on the receiver.

Sam noticed the slightly annoyed expression on Mike's face as they proceeded to the chief's office. "You were about to call Eve, weren't you?"

"Yeah, don't worry about it, I'll call her after the meeting. She's probably busy at work anyway."

"Things seem to be going well. I'm happy for the two of you. Eve is a great catch."

"You don't have to tell me. I'm a lucky man for sure."

Mike's smile returned at the mere mention of Eve's name. It quickly disappeared as soon as they entered the chief's office and saw the look on his face. Mike and Sam glanced at each other, knowing it was probably going to be a rough meeting.

"Good, you're here. We need to make some headway on this case. It's been weeks now. I know that we've had some setbacks: Lucas found dead, whom I know had vital information that we desperately needed; and the missing bank managers... I don't need to continue, do I?" Mike and Sam shook their heads. "So we need to find another lead that ties the Gennaros to the money-laundering case, and by the grace of God to Lucas's murder."

"Chief, the autopsy indicates otherwise," reminded Sam.

"I know that, but the three of us know damn well the Gennaros murdered Lucas to keep him from talking to us and implicating *them*. There's evidence out there somewhere. We just have to find it."

Mike was so over Lucas Coles. He knew deep down the Gennaros were responsible for his death, but he didn't care. He was glad Lucas was dead after what he did to Eve and her coworkers. "We'll do our best, Chief," Mike added reluctantly.

After the meeting they just had with their chief, Mike was in dire need of hearing Eve's voice, so he made a beeline for his desk. "Hey Sam, I need to make that phone call, so I'll catch up with you in a few, okay?"

"Sure, take your time, Mike."

As soon as Mike arrived at his desk he dialed Eve's number. He wanted to get together with her after work and needed to catch her before it got too late in the day to make plans.

Eve was almost out the door to attend a meeting when her phone rang. She ran back to answer it. "Hello, Eve Townsend speaking."

"Is this the Eve Townsend that has completely captured the heart of a handsome detective we both know?"

A smile came across Eve's face at the sound of Mike's voice. "I had no idea that Sam felt that way about me!" she joked.

Mike's mouth dropped open before he let a chuckle escape. "So you're a funny one today."

"I aim to please."

"You always do, pretty lady. Listen, I know this is short notice, but I was hoping I could see you this evening. Are you free?"

"Sure, I was just on my way to a meeting which shouldn't last too long, and then I'm finished for the day. What did you have in mind?"

"How does a stroll in the park sound?"

"It sounds perfect." Anything was perfect to Eve as long as she was with Mike.

"Great. How about Central Park at six? I'll meet you at the 67th Street entrance."

"I'll see you then." Eve went to her meeting but her mind kept drifting back to Mike in anticipation of seeing him later.

Mike met up with Sam to continue working on the Gennaro investigation and Lucas Coles's possible connection to them, and at 5:30, he clocked out to go meet Eve at Central Park.

When Mike met up with Eve, he wrapped his arms around her and gave her a tender kiss. "Mmmm, just what the doctor ordered," he murmured.

"It's been one of those days, huh?"

"Yes, but it's already forgotten, thanks to you."

Eve smiled up at Mike. He took her hand and they walked along one of the park trails. It was a lovely August evening, and they weren't the only ones taking advantage of the nice weather. They passed plenty of runners, parents with baby strollers, cyclists, and people on roller blades.

"You know what, Eve? I find it difficult to believe that you're an only child."

"Really, why is that?"

"Well, you don't act like the typical '*only*' child that gets doted on and ends up turning into a spoiled brat."

Eve had to laugh at his description. "I thank you for the compliment, but am I mistaken or did you not tell me that you are also an only child?"

"You're not mistaken."

"So were you speaking from experience or were you just joking?"

"I have to admit that my parents were guilty, *just a little bit*, of spoiling me on occasion."

"Uh-huh, just a little bit, on occasion you say?"

Mike shot Eve a look and realized she was teasing him. "Just my luck, I have to fall with a comedian. You're really on a roll today, aren't you?"

"You could do worse."

"Believe me, I have. You, my dear Eve, far surpass all those who have come before you."

She stopped in her tracks. "Dare I ask just how many women have come before me?" she asked, staring directly into his eyes.

Mike had to admit he stepped right into that one. "Don't think too badly of me, okay. I've dated quite a lot of women, but no one important and nothing serious until you, Eve."

"Nice recovery. I was wondering how you were going to get out of that one, mister."

"You like that, huh? Am I good or what?"

Eve hesitated.

"Come on, you've gotta give me props for that one. I could easily be in serious hot water with you right now."

"You've got that right, and you might still be..."

Mike pulled Eve closer and whispered, "Well I hope not because I like you, Eve Townsend."

"I know," she replied as she spotted an empty bench. "Hey, let's grab a seat over there."

They sat down and Mike pulled Eve close to him so that he could wrap his arms around her. He loved the smell of her hair; it always smelled like strawberries. Mike noticed an older couple sitting on the bench across from them and pointed them out. "That could be us one day. They look just as happy as we do. They kind of remind me of my parents."

"Do they? Why is that?"

"My parents have always been the affectionate type, not just with me but with each other, and I've been just a little envious of what they have. I've always wanted to experience that close bond with another person, someone that you feel connected to."

"I think deep down everyone wants that. It's comforting to know that there is someone special in the world, just for you, and to know that you are not alone, no matter what."

It was as if Eve was reading his mind. He squeezed her ever so slightly and whispered in her ear, "I don't think I need to be envious of my parents any longer."

Eve turned her head to face Mike and cradled his face with her hand. They shared a long sweet kiss that caused a warm sensation to course through their veins.

"Mike, do you regret being an only child? Not having another sibling around to grow up with?"

"I did at times, but like I said, I was a little spoiled, so being the only kid had its advantages and I liked that. Is that terrible to admit?"

"No, at least you're honest. Let's face it, what kid wouldn't like being spoiled? And you didn't turn out so bad," she added with a wink. "I personally didn't have that privilege because I grew up with my best friend Malcolm, so I didn't feel like an only child. Malcolm's parents were always away on business. He didn't have any other family, so they left him with us most of the time and we were pretty much raised together as if we were brother and sister. I feel more like an only child now than I ever did growing up because I never see Malcolm anymore. We haven't really been a part of each other's lives for quite some time. He might as well have fallen off the face of the earth."

Mike detected a note of hurt and maybe a hint of abandonment in Eve's voice when she spoke of Malcolm's absence. And it probably didn't help that her parents were gone as well. It was as if she had lost her entire family. It clearly bothered her, and he wondered if she realized just how much. He felt guilty for being jealous of Malcolm when Eve first mentioned him. He was obviously a big part of her life, but didn't appear to be a threat to their relationship because he was more of a brother to Eve than an ex-boyfriend, or so he hoped.

"I'm sure he'll resurface and the two of you could reconnect someday. You did tell him about the shooting, didn't you?"

"I tried, but I wasn't able to reach him, *as usual,* so I left him yet another message. I guess someday he'll actually get around to returning one of them. Maybe I'll need to be kidnapped or thought dead before he'd show interest and reappear."

Mike felt for her and got the feeling she didn't want to discuss Malcolm any longer, so he steered the subject in a slightly different direction. "You know what? I always told myself that if I ever had children I would want at least two. That way they wouldn't have to grow up alone like I did, and they would always have each other."

"I want at least two children as well, and for the very same reason."

"I guess we are two peas in a pod, Ms. Townsend." Mike noticed Eve shivering. "Hey babe, are you cold?"

"Just a little bit. It can get surprisingly chilly in the park when the sun in going down."

"Maybe we should get going since we both have work tomorrow?" Mike didn't want to leave yet, but he reluctantly escorted Eve out of the park with his arms around her shoulders to shield her from the chilly air. He wished he had a jacket to lend her, but his arms would have to do the trick. Mike walked Eve to her building, where he parked his car, and they kissed.

"I had a nice time, Mike."

"So did I. I'll call you when I get home."

"Please do."

Eve watched as Mike drove away until she couldn't see his car any longer. They both felt a pang in their heart every time they parted and wished they could spend every minute with each other.

Once Mike got settled at home, he called Eve to let her know that he was home safe and sound. He had only left Eve about thirty-five minutes ago but he missed her already.

* * *

"Umm, did you really have to get rid of the bank managers, Pop?" Nicholas asked his father. Anthony glanced at Nicholas with concern. Second-guessing their father's decisions was never a good idea.

Angelo glared at Nicholas. "Are you questioning my methods?" he demanded.

"No, no, no, I was just asking–" Nicholas started, but was quickly cut off by Angelo.

"You have a lot of nerve asking me *anything* given the position you put this family in. Have you forgotten the type of business we're in, son? Sometimes people have to *disappear*, and if you're not comfortable with that maybe you shouldn't be in this business."

"But it's the Gennaro family business and I'm a *Gennaro*," he whined.

"Then start acting like one. I'm tired of cleaning up your messes. You're not a teenager anymore, so be a man or you will have no place in our business," Angelo barked.

"It's not entirely Nick's fault, Pop. I also missed the fact that Lucas was a nutcase, and until he went ballistic, the money-laundering scheme was working perfectly and made us a lot of money," Anthony added in an attempt to deflect their father's rage away from Nicholas.

"Oh, don't think you're not in deep shit along with your brother. You're lucky it's your *only* screw-up, but a major one nonetheless. I'm not happy at all, and I'm ordering you to finish cleaning this up. Don't look for new hackers, close all Internet and financial accounts associated with this project and make sure nothing can be traced back to us. The cops are just waiting to put our family away, and I don't need the two of you handing us over to them on a silver platter. Have I made myself clear?"

"Yes Pop," both Nicholas and Anthony responded.

"Now go." Nicholas and Anthony quickly exited Angelo's office.

"I'm sorry that Pop was so hard on you, Nick."

"I should be used to it by now and shouldn't have expected anything different. Pop treats me like a child without a brain and doesn't respect me, not one bit. I can't win with him."

"That's not true, Nick. He gave you the chance to implement your plan, didn't he? It just takes time to win his trust."

"Tony, please. I will *never* win Pop's trust." Nicholas turned and stalked away, dejected.

Anthony watched Nicholas as he hurriedly ran up the stairs until he was out of sight and then flinched at the sound of a room door slamming. Anthony was disheartened at letting his beloved mother, Lily, down. He'd promised her on her death bed that he would look after his siblings and shield them from their father's wrath as best as he could. He didn't believe he was doing a very good job of that in regards to Nicholas, and wasn't sure if there was hope for his little brother.

# Chapter 19

It was Friday evening and Eve decided to give Bonnie a call. She hoped that Bonnie was not out on the town, enjoying herself as they used to do with each other. When the phone rang, Bonnie was so focused on her work that she didn't notice that it was Eve's number on the caller ID when she answered the phone.

"Hello, Bonnie Stephens speaking."

"Hey Bonnie, it's Eve."

"Eve, sweetie, how are you?"

"I'm good. I just hope it's not too late to call. You're usually getting ready to go out at this time."

"No no no, don't be silly, you can call me anytime. In fact, I'm not going anywhere this weekend. We have a big project due next week and I want to get as much completed as I can by Monday morning."

"I can call back at a more convenient time if you want."

"Nope, I can take a break for my best friend."

"That's good, because I have news to share."

"Good news I hope, unlike the last time you called to tell me you had gotten shot?"

"Yes, it's good news. In fact, I don't think you'll be too surprised by it."

"You and the detective are dating?"

"How did you ever guess?" Eve joked. "So go ahead and say it."

"Say what? That I *told* you so? I would *never* say that."

"I beg to differ, since those very words just came out of your mouth." Both Bonnie and Eve laughed so hard their stomachs started to hurt.

"Well, I'm glad for you, Eve," Bonnie stated after catching her breath. "As long as you are happy that's all that matters."

"I am *very* happy. We've only been dating for a couple of weeks and it's all still brand new... but it feels as if we've been together for a lot longer."

"I'm not surprised by that. I could tell the two of you were connected right from the very beginning and your feelings for each other were developing before you even started dating, but you wouldn't listen to me... *when I told you so*," Bonnie couldn't resist repeating in a slow and deliberate manner.

"*Stop*, but I'll have to admit you were right." Eve paused for a couple of seconds. "And things kind of got a little out of hand at the end of our second date."

"Did the two of you..."

"No, no, Mike stopped us. He said it was too soon and wanted us to get to know each other better first."

"Well, I'm sold. That man has got it bad for you. If sex were all he wanted he wouldn't have stopped himself. You know how men are." Bonnie hesitated before continuing, "Are you in love with him, Eve?"

"*What*? How can you ask that? It's too soon for me to be in love with Mike... isn't it?" Eve squeaked, clearly taken aback by Bonnie's question.

"If that high-pitched voice is any indication, then I think I've got my answer." Eve remained silent. "Well...*are* you?" Bonnie persisted, already knowing the answer.

Eve hesitated, afraid to say it aloud. "I think, maybe, that I am...at least *starting* to fall in love with him," Eve managed to admit for the first time, even to herself.

"Starting my ass, you are *absolutely* in love with that man, girl. So how do you feel about it?"

"I'm scared."

"Scared of what, exactly?"

"That it's all happening too fast..."

"And?" coaxed Bonnie.

"And that Mike might not feel the same way."

"Do you really believe that, Eve? Because I don't."

"Well, I know that he genuinely cares for me, but that doesn't mean he's falling in love with me or that he is going to."

"Listen, I'm not going to try and convince you of what Mike's feelings are. It's his job to convey that message, so I'll leave that up to him. But..."

"I knew that was too easy," quipped Eve.

"*But,*" Bonnie continued, "I believe that he is already in love with you and won't tell you now because it is too soon and he doesn't want to scare you. That's just my opinion, but what do *I* know?"

"Very cute, so you're a psychologist now?"

"I'm whatever my best friend needs me to be."

"Now that's something we can agree upon. You're the best, Bonnie, and I don't know what I would do without you."

"Well, luckily you won't ever have to find out. Are you going to see Mike this weekend?"

"Yes, he's planned a picnic at the park."

"Now that sounds like fun *and* potentially intimate, so make sure you have protection."

"*Bonnie!*"

"Enjoy yourself, sweetie," Bonnie replied while giggling.

"Don't worry, I will." Eve smiled, shaking her head.

* * *

Mike wanted to get Eve out of the city for a bit and decided to take her to Pelham Bay Park for their weekend picnic. During the drive he took on the role of a tour guide.

"So we're in the Bronx now?"

"Yes, and in case you didn't know, Pelham Bay Park is actually *much* larger than Central Park."

"Really? I didn't know that. I love seeing New York through your eyes, Mike."

"I love introducing you to New York and all of its five boroughs. It can't be easy adjusting to a new city, let alone to an entirely new state. Plus, you were cheated out of time due to the shooting. Those first couple of weeks should have been exciting for you, so we are going to make up for that now *together.*"

"We're certainly off to a good start." Eve paused to look out of the window. "Is this our park?"

"Yep."

"It's beautiful, and so serene."

Mike chuckled to himself at Eve's wide-eyed enthusiasm of a child, which was adorable. "I guess you weren't expecting this, huh?"

"No, I wasn't." She continued to marvel at her surroundings as Mike pulled into the parking lot.

Eve grabbed the picnic basket, Mike grabbed the blankets and they walked hand in hand while looking for the perfect spot. Since Mike made the picnic basket the contents were a surprise to Eve. He liked spoiling her and hoped she would enjoy what he prepared.

"You know, I'm very proud of you for not peeking into the basket," said Mike.

"I wouldn't do that. You said it was a surprise, and I trust that I will love whatever you've prepared," she replied with a sly grin.

"Thanks." Mike spied a nice area where they could set up their picnic. "What about that spot over there?"

"Looks good to me."

Mike started to lay out the blankets. "Eve, do you go on picnics often?"

"Not so much now, but I used to go all the time when I was a kid."

"So it was a regular family affair then?"

"You can say that. Mom loved being outdoors. That's probably where I got it from." Eve smiled at the thought of her mom. She started to open up the picnic basket but Mike deftly interceded.

"I'll take that, you just sit back and relax while I set everything up... So, what are your parents' names?"

"Joseph and Marianna."

"Marianna? That's a lovely name... Was your mom Hispanic?"

"Yes, she was Puerto Rican."

"But not your father I presume? Townsend doesn't sound too Hispanic to me."

"*Es correcto,*" she replied, focusing on the delicious food that Mike was displaying in front of her. She was suddenly very hungry.

Mike looked up. "Do you speak Spanish?"

"*Muy poco,*" she replied, grinning.

Mike laughed. "But your accent is perfect. Why do you only speak it a little bit?"

"My father didn't, plus we also had Malcolm around most of the time. Most of our household conversations were in English so the two of them could understand everything."

"So how did you pick up the language?"

"By hearing my mom talk on the phone with her friends and family, and sometimes she and I would speak Spanish when we were alone with each other. It always made me feel special that she would share a part of her culture with me. It is half of my heritage."

"This picnic must make you miss her and your father. I hope that I can live up to your family memories."

Eve looked at Mike adoringly. "You don't have to live up to anything. We'll create our own memories, and I have to say that everything looks *wonderful*."

"Thanks babe. So, tell me what you want to eat first and I'll fix you a plate."

"Hmm, let's see... I'll start with some of the chopped fruit, a piece of fried chicken and some potato salad please."

"Coming right up, pretty lady."

"Did you make all of this food by yourself?"

"I sure did." Mike handed Eve her plate. "I learned from my mom. We always made Sunday breakfast together and sometimes she let me help with dinner."

"Wow, I'm impressed. Your mom was a good teacher. This all looks delicious. Did you know that I absolutely *love* fried chicken?"

"I didn't, so I'm glad I thought of it. I do have something that I know for a fact you will absolutely love, but it's a surprise."

"Really? I can't wait. Can I get a hint?"

Mike started to fix a plate for himself. "Okay, it's the dessert. And I know you're going to love it." He glanced up, pointing his fork at Eve. "Now that's all you're going to get out of me about that. Just make sure to leave some room in that little tummy of yours."

"You don't have to tell me twice." Eve continued to munch on the fried chicken and smiled as she remembered Charles using those very same words when she made her friends dinner to break the news of her moving away from them, and it made her a little homesick. She snapped her mind back to the present and focused her attention on Mike. "So, what are *your* parents' names?"

"Mark and Carla... Speaking of parents, does it bother you when I bring them up in conversation? I always notice a slight sadness in your eyes when we talk about them."

"No, it doesn't bother me. It's just that some memories hit me a little harder than others, plus I think I'm a little more sensitive these days because of everything that's happened in the last month. I do like hearing about *your* parents, though. They sound like fun people to hang out with."

"They are fun, and you're going to love them."

"I'm sure I will."

Eve was touched by the fact that Mike had already envisioned introducing her to his parents so early in their relationship, and she felt honored. Maybe Bonnie was right that Mike's feelings were deeper for her than she thought. If their relationship progressed into something more serious, Mark and Carla might very well become surrogate parents to her, and she wondered how she would feel about that. She'd been very close with her mother, and her loss left a pretty big hole in Eve's heart. It would be nice to have someone fill that void and provide some motherly advice again, and then maybe she would no longer feel like an abandoned orphan.

"Hey you, where did you go?" inquired Mike. "You looked deep in thought."

Eve snapped out of her reverie again. "Nowhere, I was just thinking about my mom."

Mike suspected there was more to it but didn't pry. "You must be thirsty." Mike held up a bottle of red wine, "Would you like me to pour you some?"

Eve smiled. "Sure."

He handed Eve her wine. "You know what I just realized? I took you to a Latin restaurant/dance club not knowing your heritage. No wonder you could dance salsa so well."

Eve peered at Mike over her wine glass while taking a sip. "Uh-huh, I know."

"You little devil, and you never said a word." Eve just giggled. "Why didn't you say anything?"

"I figured it would be more fun to wait until it came up in conversation and then watch your reaction as you figured it out on your own." Eve cleaned her hands with a napkin and finished her wine.

"Really now," Mike replied, feigning annoyance.

"Yes, you are a great source of entertainment, Mr. McGarrett, plus you can cook and you're not too bad on the eyes either, what more could a girl ask for?"

They both burst into laughter. So much so Mike had to put his plate down. "You're going to pay for that little deception, missy." In one quick motion Mike was headed in Eve's direction. "You think you're so funny, I'll give you something to laugh about."

Eve's eyes popped out of her head at his speed and gasped as he pinned her down on the blanket and started tickling her relentlessly. "Oh... my... God! Pleeeeeaaaaase...*stop*," Eve stammered in between giggles.

Mike finally had mercy and let Eve up as she tried to catch her breath.

"That's not fair, you bully," she whined while hitting him in the arm, "you're bigger than me."

"Who said life was fair?" Mike mumbled.

Mike held Eve close and stared into her eyes while her arms slipped around his neck. He brushed Eve's mussed hair away from her face and caressed her cheek. *You are so beautiful,* he thought.

Being this close to her stirred something deep within him, and Eve suddenly felt weak in his arms. Mike cradled Eve's head in his hand and kissed her deeply. Still kissing her, his hands moved playfully across her body, almost like a gentle massage that tickled her ever so slightly, making her quiver. He caressed her back, her hips and her thighs. He wanted to touch her in other places but restrained himself. He needed Eve and couldn't get enough of her. The feel of her body against his was almost too much to bear, but he *had* to control himself— they were out in public, after all.

Eve felt her body tremble and she returned Mike's kiss ardently. She wanted to rip his clothes off and let him have her right there in the park. It had only been a week since they decided to hold off on making love right away. But he was making her crazy, and she didn't have the strength to push him away. He felt so good she didn't want him to stop.

Try as he might to control himself, Mike felt like he was losing that battle. He leaned Eve backward against the blanket and they continued to kiss each other passionately. He positioned himself on top of her and their bodies fit like a glove. They started to move ever so slightly against each other and a swell of emotion swept through them. Eve whimpered with desire and a groan escaped from Mike's throat. A small voice in his head begged him to get control of himself, but he felt powerless to do so.

All of a sudden they heard a noise. It sounded like a twig snapping, followed by giggles. Mike and Eve sprang upright just in time to see two children emerge into sight, followed by their parents. The family was looking for a spot to enjoy their own picnic. Mike and Eve were so embarrassed at almost being seen by the children, *and* their parents. It was a good thing that things hadn't progressed much further.

"I guess we need to work a little harder at controlling ourselves," Mike joked, slightly breathless.

"I'm glad you find this amusing. Those poor kids could have been traumatized for life," replied Eve.

"Well, we won't have any trouble controlling ourselves now, that's for certain." Although Mike was joking, he was upset with himself because he'd been very close to losing control. If that family hadn't arrived when they did...

Mike and Eve finished off a couple of sandwiches while watching the kids run around playing in the grass. Then Mike presented Eve with her surprise dessert, chocolate cupcakes with chocolate frosting. Eve's eyes widened at the sight of them. "*Chocolate cupcakes!*" she squealed, reaching for one immediately. "Thank you."

"I knew you'd like them. I remembered you mention that you loved all things chocolate at dinner the other night."

"How thoughtful of you," Eve replied in between munches and then gave Mike a quick kiss.

"Mmmm, you taste chocolaty," Mike murmured.

"Don't get too happy, Mister, not in front of the children."

"Ugh, I used to like kids," he groaned.

"*Michael McGarrett*! It's not their fault we can't control ourselves in public." Mike mumbled something under his breath that Eve couldn't quite make out, but she decided to ignore it while resisting the urge to laugh.

"I'll start packing up while you finish eating your dessert," Mike offered.

Mike was quiet during the drive home. He was still thinking about what almost happened in the park but decided not to let it get to him. He was going to focus on the future because was Eve was going to be a part of it. And that put a smile on his face.

# Chapter 20

"This fucking case is cold as ice," stated Sam.

Mike swiveled his chair around to face Sam. "I know, but try telling that to Chief Taylor. He's got a serious hard-on about taking down the Gennaros."

"Well, can you blame him? He lost his son to drugs, drugs *that* family is responsible for selling on the streets."

"Sam, I understand that, believe me, I do, but the chief has to accept some responsibility for his son's behavior. He's the parent."

"Spoken like someone without any children of their own." Sam chuckled.

"Neither do you."

"But I've got nieces and nephews to worry about, so I can relate."

"Okay, you're right, but the chief still has to come to terms with the fact that this money-laundering investigation has come to a screeching halt and we've got other cases to work on. We can't keep pushing new cases onto everyone else just to free ourselves up to only work on the money-laundering case."

"Well, since you've got all the answers, Mike, I'll leave it up to you to break that news to the chief."

"Thanks a lot, Sam."

"Hey, what are partners for?"

* * *

Eve looked up at the sound of a knock on her door to see Nathan entering.

"Hi Eve, have you been able to review the specs for the new hotel project?"

"Yes, I have. This is a real coup for us, winning this bid."

"I know, especially after having to deal with the aftermath of the shooting. I was afraid clients would be a little wary of providing us with a new project of this magnitude."

"Well, Nathan, as you stated, the team didn't let their duties falter, and our current clients' projects didn't suffer as a result. I gather we received some good referrals as being dependable in times of a crisis. Our clients can trust that we can meet their needs in any situation."

"You're right, and we should be proud of that. And to think, that only months ago we were falling behind on *all* of our projects, until you whipped this department into shape."

"You give me too much credit, Nathan."

"Don't be modest, Eve. It was a real coup for *us* that we got *you*."

* * *

Saturday morning Mike and Eve decided to spend the day at the beach and Mike had to admit that he had been looking forward to seeing Eve in a bikini. An image of her flashed in his mind and he had a feeling it was going to be an exciting yet *frustrating* day for him. *Whose bright idea was it to NOT have sex right away? Oh yeah, MINE, you idiot!*

Eve couldn't wait for Mike to pick her up. She loved being with him no matter what they did together, but seeing that body of his was going to be a special treat in itself. Every time he held her in his arms she could feel how toned and muscular he was. Mike definitely kept himself in great shape, and Eve couldn't wait to see it up close and personal.

They enjoyed a nice drive to the beach, and once they arrived they found a nice area to set out their blankets and beach chairs.

"Eve, did you put on enough sunblock?"

"Of course I did."

"Well, let me put some more on you, just in case."

Eve eyed Mike suspiciously. "Just in case?" she asked.

"Yes... I'm just looking out for your safety. I wouldn't want my girl to get sunburned."

"So, I'm *your* girl?" teased Eve. Mike pulled Eve close to him. He could stare into those brown eyes all day. "Yes, you're *my* girl. Do you have a problem with that, missy?"

"Not at the moment, but I'll let you know if that changes."

Mike chuckled. "You do that... but I'm still applying more sun block on you. Believe me, you'll thank me later."

While Mike looked for the sunblock in his bag, Eve started to remove her outer clothing to reveal a lovely golden bikini that complemented the color of her skin perfectly. Eve didn't noticed that Mike was transfixed at the vision she created as she slipped out of her shorts and pulled the t-shirt over her head in an almost seductive fashion. Eve shook her hair free and when she glanced in Mike's direction he quickly looked away and pretended to be digging in his bag for the sunblock. "Let's do this so we can get into that gorgeous blue water, Detective," Eve commanded as she flounced down in the beach chair. She was so unaware of just how beautiful she was and the effect she had on men, especially since Mike was not the only man on that beach appreciating her physique.

Mike sat behind Eve, and in a massage-like motion, he started to apply the sun block to her shoulders and neck then worked his way down her arms and her back. Mike loved the feel of Eve's skin and he had to admit that he was enjoying himself immensely. When Mike finished, he gave Eve some sunblock to apply to her legs as well. The men in their immediate vicinity wished that they were in Mike's position as they watched with envy.

"Do you need more as well?" she asked.

"No, I'm good. I always apply more than needed as a precaution." Although this was true, Mike didn't think he could handle the feel of Eve's hands massaging him at that moment. He was on edge as it was and needed to calm himself down. "Let's go, those waves are calling us."

Mike removed his shirt and shorts and Eve's stomach fluttered at the sight of him. *God Almighty! Is it legal to look that good?* She smiled in appreciation. Mike took Eve's hand and led the way.

From the way Mike and Eve acted you would think that they hadn't been to a beach in years or *ever*. They were splashing water and dunking each other and laughing like two little kids without a care in the world. They were falling in love, and everything they shared together seemed that much more exciting and fun because they were experiencing it with each other. They spent quite a bit of time in the water. Although he occasionally glanced at their belongings he decided to take a break to check on them.

"Aren't you tired yet, energizer bunny?" he asked.

"No."

Mike laughed. "Well, I'm going to check on our things."

Eve was enjoying herself. "Okay. I want to stay a little longer, but I'll come out in a few minutes."

"Don't make me come back out to get you... and be careful."

Mike kissed Eve and swam back to shore. She watched him as he glided across the water. He watched her waving at him as she floated and relaxed in the water. She seemed happy, and he hoped that he had a little something to do with that. She definitely made him happier than he had ever been in his entire life.

When Eve decided to come back to shore, Mike was struck by how alluring she looked as she emerged from the water. The sun caused the water to glisten against her skin, and when she flung her head back and brushed her hair away from her face it appeared to occur in slow motion for him. Mike was completely captivated. How is it that some lucky guy hadn't snapped her up yet? He didn't care because he was that lucky guy now, and he intended to keep it that way. As she got closer, his pulse started to quicken and he felt a tightening in his loins. He wanted her so badly he couldn't think straight. She smiled at him, causing his stomach to clench.

When she reached him, she kneeled over him and kissed him softly. "As much as I wanted to stay out there, I missed you," she whispered.

The tone of her voice and the touch of her lips damn near sent him over the edge. Mike cradled Eve's head in his hands and kissed her hard.

"Wow, I guess you missed me too?" she said breathlessly.

"You have no idea," he replied.

They seemed to forget that they were in public and continued to enjoy a long, sensuous kiss that seemed to last for several minutes. The touch of Mike's hands on her skin made Eve feel as if she would melt, and she never wanted him to let go.

These past couple of weeks had been incredible, and Eve realized that they had spent every weekend together as well. Mike usually visited with his parents on weekends, and she suddenly felt bad for taking their time away from their son. Eve pulled her head back to look at Mike.

"What it is, Eve? Is something wrong?"

"I just realized that we've spent the last couple of weekends together."

"And that's a bad thing?"

"No, of course not, but... when was the last time you visited with your parents?"

Mike was caught off guard by her question. "I have to admit it's been several weeks, probably since we starting dating... Ah, I see where you're going with this."

"You should visit with them this weekend, Mike. They probably miss you and wonder why they haven't seen you. Have you spoken with them recently?"

"Maybe once or twice, but not as often as I normally do. I've been a bad son, haven't I?"

"No. We've just been caught up in our own little world. I would give anything to be able to visit with my parents one more time, so don't take them for granted, Mike."

"Are you suggesting I go *tonight*?"

"Yes I am. But not right this second. I'm not ready to let you go just yet," she said playfully, and Mike chuckled and shook his head.

"What is so funny?"

"So you want to continue to get my blood boiling and *then* send me off to my parents?"

Eve feigned innocence. "It's not intentional, I *swear*."

"I'm sure it's not." Mike smirked. "You know... I must admit that I have been caught up in the two of us and that I've neglected my parents. It's very thoughtful of you to think of them, Eve. Thank you for bringing it to my attention."

"You don't have to thank me. I can share you, but I'll miss you."

Mike caressed Eve's face. "I'll miss you too." Then he gave her a long and gentle kiss. He was *really* going to miss her tonight, for sure. "I'll call them now and tell them that I'm coming over later this evening."

"Good."

Mike dialed his parents, and his mother Carla answered the phone. "Hello?"

"Hey Mom, it's Mike."

"Mike who?" teased Carla.

"Mike *who*?" Mike repeated as he glanced at Eve, who covered her mouth and giggled. "Okay, I guess I deserved that."

"Mike, oh yes, I remember you now. It's just been so *long...*"

"Okay already, have mercy Mom."

Carla laughed. "Well, you did deserve that, Mikey. So to what do we owe the pleasure of your call *today*?"

"I wanted to come over this evening and spend the rest of the weekend with you and Dad. Is that okay?"

"Of course it is. Try to arrive by dinner time so we can all eat together."

"I will, Mom. See you later." Mike looked at Eve. "Can you believe her?"

"Yep," answered Eve, "and I like her already, even though I've never met her."

Mike had a vision of Eve and his mom ganging up on him and he realized that he wouldn't stand a chance against the two of them. The thought of Eve and his mother together put a smile on his face, so Mike decided he would tell his parents about her tonight. He couldn't wait.

# Chapter 21

Mike arrived at his parents' house and let himself in with his key. He found his mother in the kitchen putting the finishing touches on dinner. "What does a guy have to do to get a hug around here?"

Carla's head snapped up at the sound of Mike's voice. She wiped her hands clean and threw her arms around her son. "Mikey, you're here. Let me look at you," she said while taking a step backward.

"Oh *stop*, it's only been a couple of weeks. I haven't changed much, at least not on the outside."

"What does that mean?"

"I'll tell you later. I want to talk to you and dad about something, but we have plenty of time for that. Where is he, by the way?"

Carla noticed how quickly Mike changed the topic. "Your father is upstairs. Why don't you get settled in your room and then tell your father dinner is ready while I set the table?"

"Do you need any help?"

"No, I've got it under control, now get."

"Yes ma'am." Mike kissed Carla on the cheek and went upstairs.

"Don't forget to wash your hands," Carla called out just before Mike reached the top of the staircase. Mike rolled his eyes and shook his head.

Carla noticed a bounce in her son's step and wondered if it had anything to do with what he wanted to talk to them about. Her curiosity was piqued.

Mike dropped his overnight bag in his room and went in search of his father. Mike found him watching the evening news as he usually did while his mother prepared dinner. He knocked on the door, which was slightly ajar. "Hey Dad, I'm here."

Mark turned to Mike. "Long time, no see, Son," he said, grinning from ear to ear.

"Oh my God, not you too..."

"Well, you kind of had it coming."

"I know, and I'm sorry I haven't been around lately, but I promise I won't make a habit of it."

"Just tell me there's a good reason for your absence."

"There is, and I'll talk to you and Mom about it a little later. Speaking of... Mom said dinner is ready, so we had better get downstairs."

After they finished dinner, the three of them remained seated at the dinner table chatting away and making up for the last couple of weekends they lost with each other. Mike didn't realize how much he missed having dinner with his parents. They were very close and could talk about pretty much anything, and at times it felt as if he were hanging out with a couple of friends. He hoped to introduce Eve to his parents one day soon. He had the feeling they would get along perfectly and that Eve would fit right in with their cozy family. And as if on cue, Carla questioned Mike. "So, wasn't there something you wanted to discuss with your father and me? I have to say I'm pretty curious as to what kept you from visiting with us these past couple of weekends."

"Yeah, fill us in," urged Mark.

Mike wasn't prepared for the sudden inquiry. He wanted to give them the news in his own way and he hesitated. Mike's hesitation made Carla concerned. "Is there something wrong, Mikey?"

"Oh no, um... it's good news."

"Well, that's a relief. You had me worried there for a minute, so please tell us what's going on with you."

"Yeah, spill it already," commanded Mark.

"Okay... I met someone." Mark and Carla just looked at him as if they were waiting for the punch line of a joke. When he didn't continue, they glanced at each other in confusion. "Hey, what's with the looks?" Mike asked.

"Well, Son, you've dated plenty of women, but you've never bothered to make a point of mentioning any of them to us before," answered Mark.

"That's true, Dad, but this is different. *Eve* is different."

For Mike to speak of someone specific, his parents knew that this woman must be very special. Sure, a name or two might have come up in passing if Mike happened to talk about an event that he attended, but none of the other women Mike dated or had a passing fling with were ever brought up deliberately in conversation, until now.

"Eve, that's a lovely name," replied Carla.

"She's a lovely woman, Mom."

"How did the two of you meet?"

"Well, that's a complicated story."

"We have all night, Mikey."

*Of course, you do*, he thought, but Mike had to smile. His mom never let him off the hook easily. "Sam and I were investigating a person of interest at Eve's place of employment. We happened to question her about this person and she informed us that he had been fired. After we left, this person returned and went on a shooting rampage within Eve's department."

Carla threw her hands to her mouth in shock. "Oh no! Was Eve hurt?"

"She was shot in the shoulder. But she recovered; she's okay now."

"Well, thank goodness for that," replied Mark.

"You have no idea. Several of her coworkers weren't so lucky, and I'm not sure what I would have done if she hadn't survived."

Carla was intrigued by the depth of her son's feelings at that point in time. "But you had just met her, dear. She affected you that quickly?" Mike nodded yes. "Well, it's only been a couple of weeks since we last saw you. Are you telling us it's *that* serious already?"

"Yes, it is for me. I think it's serious for Eve as well. This is all very new to me, and I don't quite know what to make of it. All I do know is that I need her in my life."

Carla turned to her husband. "Well, what do you know, Mark? I think our son has finally fallen in love."

"It took you long enough, but we're very happy for you, Mike."

"Thanks. I have to admit it's a little scary to be so emotionally invested in someone else this way."

"It comes with the territory, so get used to it. I agree with your father, it's about time, and we're very anxious to meet the woman who has finally captured your heart."

"And she has a definite grip on it, that's for sure. I would love for the both of you to meet her."

"Have you told Eve how you feel?" Carla asked.

"Not in the exact words, but I plan to soon. I'm thinking about cooking her dinner so that we can be alone and have some privacy, and then I'll lay it all out there and pray she's on the same wavelength. I don't want to scare her away."

"That sounds like a plan to me." Carla paused for a second. "Speaking of being alone, have the two of you... taken it to the next level yet, physically I mean?"

"*What*! No Mom, we haven't!" Mike replied, rolling his eyes in embarrassment.

"Well, excuse me for asking, it's just that given how fast things seem to be progressing between the two of you, I just wondered..."

"I guess it's an understandable assumption, especially since we came dangerously close on one of our early dates, but we put on the brakes and decided to spend time to get to know each better before we went that far. That's the reason I haven't visited with you for so long. We've been spending all of our free time together depending on what our schedules allow."

Mark was very proud of his son's ability to be respectful of Eve and careful to protect their relationship. "Don't worry, Son, we understand completely."

"In fact, Eve is the reason that I'm here with you now."

"How so?" Mark asked.

"She realized that I hadn't visited with you since we started dating. So she sent me on my way."

Carla was impressed. "I like this young woman already, and I'm sure we're going to *love* her once we meet her. Is she visiting with her parents now as well?"

"No, she lost her parents several years ago in a car accident, which is why she was sensitive to me losing time with the two of you. She'll never see her parents again, and she didn't want me to take the time I spend with you for granted."

"She lost both of them, oh, the poor thing. That can't be easy for her."

"I don't think it is. I can see it in her eyes when we speak of them, but she's strong."

"I can see how much you care for her. Your eyes sparkle when you talk about her."

Mike was slightly embarrassed. His mother was too observant for her own good. "Yeah, I miss her already. But I missed you guys too, so I'm all yours for the rest of the weekend."

"We're glad to hear it, Son."

* * *

Mike sent his parents off to bed while he cleaned up the dinner dishes. It was the least he could do. His thoughts kept drifting back to Eve. He did miss her and really needed to hear her voice. After he finished cleaning up the kitchen he decided to give her a call and wish her a goodnight.

Eve missed Mike as well but didn't want to intrude on his time with his parents, so she decided to curl up with a book on the sofa. She was so engrossed in the book she damn near jumped out of her skin at the sound of her phone ringing. When she looked at the caller ID, a smile crept across her face.

"Hi sweetie," she answered, "Are you enjoying time with your parents?"

"Yes I am. I didn't realize how much I've missed them until I was here, so thanks for pushing me to visit."

"Anytime. Stick with me, kid, and I'll keep you on the right path."

"Oh, don't you worry. I plan on sticking *very* close."

"Down, boy, or you might need to take a cold shower tonight."

"That's already on the agenda, but I really needed to hear your voice and wish you a goodnight."

"Well, I'm glad you called. What do you have planned for the rest of the evening?"

"My parents have turned in for the night and I just finished cleaning up the dinner dishes. I think I might watch some news and then turn in myself. My parents are early risers, so we'll be up at the crack of dawn doing chores."

"You're such a good son."

"I try to be. What were you doing before I called?"

"I was doing some light reading. I'll probably go to bed after I finish this chapter."

"What are you wearing?" Mike asked.

"Wouldn't you like to know?" Eve teased.

"Yes I would. That's why I asked, smarty pants. So…"

Eve giggled. "I'm wearing a beige tank top and some shorts."

"Mmmm, I'm picturing you right now, sexy lady."

"Oh Lord, that cold shower is probably screaming for you."

"It most definitely is. Well, I'll let you get back to your book, and will call you tomorrow evening once I return, so goodnight, Miss Townsend, and have pleasant dreams of me."

"I will do just that."

Mike had a permanent grin on his face after speaking with Eve. He was glad to have this time to reflect about what their next step should be. After talking to his parents, he was now very anxious to tell Eve exactly how he felt about her and what he hoped they could become to each other. He could barely concentrate on the news because he couldn't stop thinking about Eve, so he decided to take that cold shower and just go to sleep.

* * *

The next morning, Mike helped his mother prepare Sunday breakfast. This was a ritual for them ever since he was old enough to know what a spatula was and actually learn how to use it. Afterwards he helped his father with the chores that needed to be completed. He wondered if maybe his father should consider hiring some help on a regular basis. Mike might not always be available to help out and he didn't want the work to pile up.

After a long morning, Mark decided to take a nap, while Mike and Carla relaxed on the porch enjoying the afternoon sun. Carla had wanted to get some time alone with Mike because she was interested in learning more about his feelings for Eve. "I can't believe my Mikey is finally in love."

Mike glanced at his mother. "I can't believe it myself sometimes. When Eve stepped off that elevator and our eyes met, it was like nothing I had ever felt before. I couldn't take my eyes off her and I just stood there like an idiot. It was so embarrassing. Thank God for Sam because he broke the ice by introducing us and getting the conversation going." Mike let out a heavy sigh. "I didn't know it was possible to care about someone else this much and so quickly. I honestly cannot picture my life without Eve in it, and that scares me sometimes. The shooting occurred not more than five to ten minutes tops after I met her, and I was scared out of my mind. I definitely would have felt the loss if she didn't survive. Isn't that weird?"

"No, Son. You just happened to fall in love with Eve at first sight. It happens to the best of us. Love isn't easy, you know. If it was, so many of us wouldn't constantly mess it up."

"*That,* I can agree with."

"I know it can be overwhelming to all of a sudden have such strong feelings for someone you didn't even know from one moment to the next. Just enjoy and cherish the experience, because not everyone is lucky enough to get the opportunity."

"You always know the perfect thing to say, Mom."

"What can I say, it's a gift, dear." Mike smiled.

"I can't wait for you and Dad to meet her. It would be nice for Eve to have the two of you to turn to for advice. She must have a huge hole in her heart after losing her parents."

"Well, it's not an easy thing, losing a parent, let alone both of them at the same time. I'm sure she needs her mother right now to help her through this new relationship that's developing between the two of you *and* especially when she was hurt during the shooting."

"I hadn't thought of that. She just moved here from San Francisco to start a new job at Colby Designs only weeks before the shooting. She doesn't have anyone out here, other than Sam and me."

"*What*? How is she handling everything?"

"Remarkably well, but I'm sure there are some residual effects from the trauma that will always be there. We weren't dating at the time because the case was still ongoing, but Sam and I tried to be there for her as much as we could without overstepping our bounds."

"Eve is very lucky to have you and Sam in her corner. It seems that you've shared quite a bit together in a short time span. I assume you saved her life as well, which probably helped the two of you bond that much more quickly."

"You're probably right about that. I'm just glad that Eve didn't allow herself to become paralyzed by the experience. She could have easily succumbed to that, given her circumstances. Underneath all of her strength she has a vulnerability about her that makes me feel protective of her. I just want to take all of her pain away."

"It must have been difficult, not being with her while the case was still ongoing."

"You have no idea. Every day I had to stop myself from calling her or dropping by her apartment unannounced. If she had called Sam or I on her own that would have been different, but she never asked for help."

"It was probably confusing for her, and she already had enough to deal with."

"I figured that. I'm just glad it worked out in the end. I'm anxious to see what the future holds for us."

"I'm happy that you're happy, Mikey... I guess you'll be heading back home in a couple of hours. Your father should be waking up from his nap soon, so you'll get to spend some time with him before you leave. Let's go inside. It's a little too chilly for me."

"I'm gonna stay outside for a few more minutes. I'm enjoying the crisp air." Mike reflected on his conversations with his parents over the past day and a half. Falling in love was a new experience for him, but things *were* moving fast. Most men wouldn't discuss their love life with their parents, but then again, most men didn't have the type of connection Mike had with his. He didn't want to mess this up. He would take his mother's advice and hope for the best.

Mike headed upstairs to see if his father was awake with the hopes of spending some time with him before he went back home. He was in luck and ran into Mark just as he was about to come downstairs. "Hey Dad, are you up for starting a game of chess?"

"Sure, I'll set up the chess board in the den and you can grab us a couple of beers." Mike just stared at his father. "What are you staring at? Just sneak them out of the kitchen. You're a detective. Don't you know how to be crafty?"

"I'll see what I can do, but if mom is in the kitchen you know you're out of luck."

Carla was reaching for something in the pantry when Mike entered the kitchen. "Let me get that for you, Mom."

"Thanks, Mikey. Did I hear your father come downstairs?"

"Yep, we're going to get a chess game going before I leave."

"Uh-huh. Well, don't think you're sneaking him a beer," chastised Carla without skipping a beat.

"What?"

"Don't what me, boy. Grab a couple of water bottles and go."

Mike took two water bottles and met up with his father in the den. Mark looked up when Mike entered the den carrying the water bottles and frowned. "Argh! That woman!"

Mike had to chuckle at his dad's annoyance. "Sorry, Dad, but she's just looking out for your health." Mark shot his son a look that told Mike to let it go.

They enjoyed their game of chess for about two hours. Then it was time for Mike to head out, so Mark secured the chess board in a safe place until Mike returned to continue the game.

Mike gave his parents a giant hug. "Mom, Dad, I *loved* hanging with you guys. I really missed you. Sorry again for being out of touch for so long."

"We understand, Son, just don't let it happen again," chided Carla, grinning from ear to ear. Her son was in love and she was thrilled. "We really are looking forward to meeting Eve, so you hurry up and bring her over here."

"I'm working on it. I'll call you tomorrow to check in, since it might be too late to call tonight by the time I get home."

"Okay, bye, Son. Drive safely," added Mark.

"I will, don't worry."

* * *

On the drive home Mike thought about Eve. He wondered if he would get back to town before she went to sleep. He wanted to see her, to hold her and so he decided to go for it. When Mike was about fifteen minutes away from Eve's apartment, he dialed her number.

"Hello?"

"Hey pretty lady, it's me."

"Mike, are you home already?"

"Actually, I'm about fifteen minutes away from you."

"What are doing all the way over here?"

"I wanted to see you. Is that okay? It's not too late, is it?"

"Of course not."

"Great, I'll be there in a few minutes."

Eve hung up the phone with a smile on her face. The thought of seeing Mike always had that effect on her. When Mike arrived, he gave her the biggest kiss imaginable.

"Wow, and hello to you too," she said, still trying to catch her breath.

"Hey beautiful," replied Mike. Then he pulled her into his arms and gave her the biggest hug ever. "Oh, that's just what the doctor ordered," murmured Mike. "You feel so good. I wish we could stay like this forever."

Eve looked up at Mike and smiled. "You seem to be in a good mood tonight. I take it you enjoyed your time with your parents."

"I most definitely did. It was a wonderful visit. I got to spend the weekend with my three most favorite people in the world."

"Ooh, I get to share top billing with your parents. I feel so special."

"You *are* special to me, Eve. I think you know that by now." Mike always made Eve feel special, and to hear him say it made her feel flushed and speechless. "I better get going," suggested Mike.

"Yeah, you still have a bit of a drive ahead of you."

"Goodnight, Ms. Townsend."

"Goodnight, Detective."

* * *

The time Mike spent with his parents helped to clear his head. Talking out loud about his feelings for Eve and the direction he wanted to take their relationship convinced him that he was ready to tell Eve that he was in love with her. Eve was the missing puzzle piece of his life, his soul mate. He finally felt whole and complete, and he believed she felt the same way. He planned to cook Eve a special dinner at his place at the end of the week. It didn't seem possible that they actually experienced what they had in such a short time, but he knew that what they shared with each other was real; they both did.

# Chapter 22

Lori knocked on Eve's office door then entered. "Hi Eve, you wanted to see me?"

"Yes, Lori. Please have a seat."

"Okay… This feels a little ominous."

"No, quite the opposite, and I think you will be pleased. It's regarding the hotel chain project. I want you to be in charge of procuring the artwork to be displayed throughout the hotels."

"Really, wow, thank you, Eve. This is certainly a surprise. I appreciate your confidence in me."

"Of course, I'm sure you'll be great. You'll need to put a team together and can choose whomever you feel would be an asset. You have plenty of time, of course, before the project reaches the design phase, but I wanted to give you the heads-up so you wouldn't feel rushed."

"Thanks again. I'll get started right away." Eve's phone rang. "Oh, let me go so you can take your call. We can continue this at another time," offered Lori.

"We'll talk later." Eve answered up her phone as Lori exited her office. "Eve Townsend speaking."

"Hey pretty lady."

"Hi there, handsome. To what do I owe the pleasure?"

"I hope you don't have plans this Friday evening because I'd like us to have dinner together."

"You're in luck, I happen to be free this Friday."

"Great, I'll pick you up at your place around five thirty."

"Where are we going?"

"My house, I'm cooking us dinner."

"Oooh, how exciting. I finally get to see where you live. I can't wait."

"Me neither."

* * *

Sam returned to his desk just as Mike finished his call with Eve. "The chief is not happy that we had to set aside that money-laundering case without linking it to the Gennaros."

"It couldn't be helped, Sam. He knows we tracked down every lead we could find."

"Yeah, and I'm sure he knows that it was also *the Gennaros* who got rid of every lead we found, which only fuels his anger."

"Tell me about it. You ready to get out of here?"

"Sure, I could use a drink right about now. Dan and Marty are still out in the field, but they will meet us at the bar later… Hey, are you seeing Eve this weekend *again*?"

"Yes, and I'm cooking dinner for her at my place on Friday."

"*Your* place? Eve hasn't been to your house yet?"

"Nope, this will be her first time. I'm a little anxious, as you know we've been spending our entire time together out in public to reduce the chances of us taking things too far before getting to know each other."

"And I tip my hat off to you for showing such restraint. It's not usually in your nature to hold back in the presence of a beautiful and sexy woman."

"It has *not* been easy. We've had a close call or two, so I'm a little nervous about being alone with her. But I do plan on telling Eve how I feel about her, so if she feels the same way and is ready to take it to the next step…"

"Say no more, my friend. I get the picture. I wish you luck, although, I don't think you're gonna need it."

"I pray you're right, my friend." Mike started to gather his belongings. "We should get going. The first round is on me."

* * *

Mike pulled into his driveway. "So here we are at last, pretty lady."

"It's lovely, Mike. I can't wait to see inside." Eve's eyes glinted with anticipation as they exited the car. Holding hands, they walked up the steps of a one-story brick house that led to the front porch, where Eve spotted the rocking bench and beautiful potted plants. She smiled at Mike. "This is looking less and less like a bachelor pad with each passing minute," she proclaimed.

"Then prepare to be stunned." Mike unlocked the front door and they entered. "Welcome to my home, Eve." He watched as Eve's eyes scanned the room. He could see that she was pleased with what she saw. "As you can probably guess, this is the living room, and over here to the left I have a minibar."

"Wow, I am stunned. I didn't know what to expect, but I certainly didn't expect this."

He pulled Eve close. "I'm glad you approve, as I hope you will be spending quite a bit of time here."

"I love it, and I'm sure I'll love the rest of the place too."

"Okay, so we'll complete the grand tour and then I'll get dinner started."

Eve turned to walk across the room and gasped when she spotted the drawing she made of Mike and Sam.

"It's a stunning piece of art, wouldn't you say? It was given to me by a beautiful and gifted artist."

Eve turned back to face Mike. She was touched that he had it framed and hung on his living room wall for all to see. "Mike, you didn't tell me you were going to do that." She was grinning from ear to ear.

"Sam and I wanted it to be a surprise for you to see your work displayed."

"It's a wonderful surprise. Thank you. I love it."

Mike pulled Eve back into his arms and they kissed. The smell of her perfume started to make Mike a little heady. He wanted to take her right then and there, and Eve was hardly putting up a fight. He pulled away, breathless.

"I think we had better quit while we're ahead."

"Do we have to?" Eve asked while delivering little kisses on Mike's cheeks, lips, and neck.

"Eve, please, you're killing me. And yes, we definitely have to stop."

"Okay, let's finish the tour then." She smiled, led Mike across room and stopped in front of a door. "What's behind this door, I wonder?"

Mike chuckled. "Cute. This is a bedroom, *my* bedroom. As I'm sure you've figured out."

"Well, let me see it."

Mike pushed open the door and reluctantly escorted Eve inside.

"Nice, sweetie, you have very good taste."

"Thanks. Through this door is the master bathroom."

"Ooooh, so clean. It looks like it's hardly been used."

"Now, truth be told, I'm not a slob by any means, and I don't always pick up my clothes, or do the dishes right away, but I did straighten the place up a little for you, of course. I couldn't have you walking into a pigsty on your first visit."

"Of course not, and I appreciate it. But I can still see that you have a beautiful home, even if things were strewn all over the place. Now show me the rest."

They exited the bedroom and Mike directed Eve down a hallway and entered another room. "This is the guest bedroom, and next to it we have the guest bathroom. Across from this bedroom is my study."

"Very nice, Detective. I love it here."

"Good, because I want you to feel at home."

"I already do. Now, let's get dinner started. I'm hungry."

Mike and Eve chatted away while Mike prepared dinner. She was impressed with how skilled he was in the kitchen. He didn't exaggerate when he told her that he learned how to cook from his mom. She liked watching him in action and thought to herself how natural this felt and how she couldn't imagine not having Mike in her life. She wanted to be around him all of the time and really missed him when she wasn't. Eve was struck by how quickly she'd fallen in love with this man and wondered if she should tell him so tonight. It was the first time that they were truly alone with complete privacy, and it was a great opportunity to have a serious discussion.

"This is really nice, Mike, just the two of us hanging out."

"It's a nice change of pace," Mike agreed. "We've been running all over town for weeks."

"Well, we had our reasons."

Mike glanced up at Eve. "And we should be proud at our restraint, but I figured we could use a quiet night in."

"Good call…Wow, the steaks smell wonderful. Are they almost ready?"

"Yep, any minute now. So you can get comfortable and I'll set up the table."

"Do you need any help?"

"Absolutely not. You are my guest, so just sit back and relax."

"Yes, sir! You can cater to my every whim all evening if you want. I won't put up a fight," Eve said with a slight grin on her face. Mike raised an eyebrow and was half-tempted to reply, but decided to let that one go, though not before giving Eve a sly glance that made her giggle.

Mike created a wonderful candlelit dinner consisting of two perfectly grilled steaks, roasted red potatoes, steamed vegetables, a tossed salad and red wine. Altogether, they created their own little piece of heaven.

After dinner they retreated into the living room to relax on the sofa. "Mike, dinner was incredible. Thank you. You really are a great cook. A girl can get spoiled if you keep this up." Eve noticed that Mike had a serious look on his face. "Hey you, why are you so pensive all of a sudden?" Mike hesitated. He was working out what he wanted to discuss in his head. "Mike, tell me," she coaxed gently.

He gathered his thoughts and decided it was now or never. "Eve, I had an ulterior motive for wanting some alone time with you tonight." Eve raised both eyebrows with curiosity. "I know that we've only been dating just over a month, but I honestly can't imagine my life without you in it. I don't know what I'd do if I ever lost you."

Eve was touched; she was just thinking the same thing about Mike earlier. "Well, I have no intention of going anywhere," she replied while caressing his face.

Mike quivered inside at her touch and reached out to hold her hands in his. "Eve, I knew something was missing in my life, but didn't know what it was until you stepped off the elevator that fateful morning. Then everything became crystal clear. I can't explain it, but I knew that you were the answer to *everything*." Mike paused briefly. "You might have already figured this out, but I've fallen in love with you, Eve Townsend."

Eve was overwhelmed by Mike's words. Tears threatened to form. "Mike, I… I love you too, so much. I've wanted to tell you so many times... but was afraid you would think it was too soon or would pull away from me, like most men do at the sound of those three little words."

"I'd never pull away from you. You're the love of my life, Eve," Mike whispered just before his mouth claimed hers. Their lips were not strangers to each other, but this kiss set off an electric jolt that rippled through their bodies. They looked into each other's eyes in silence, except for the sound of their ragged breathing. There was no need for any more words. They'd waited for what seemed like an eternity for this, and the wait was definitely over. Their mouths sought each other's with a need that had to be answered, and they urgently began undressing each other.

He picked Eve up off the sofa, carried her across the room with the intention of taking her into the bedroom, but they didn't make it that far. Mike pressed Eve back against the living room wall and her fingernails raked up and down his back. He moaned with pleasure as his kisses traveled from her lips and down her neckline until they landed on her breasts. Eve gasped as his lips brushed her nipples teasingly, hardening at his encouragement. Mike's mouth engulfed Eve's. One of his hands moved down her body and across her left hip and thigh. He lifted up her left leg and wrapped it around his waist and she held onto him for dear life. His searching fingers found their way to the brown curls between her thighs and he touched, flicked and stroked her until she cried out his name.

Oh, how she ached for him. He was driving her crazy. "Mike... please... I need you," Eve whispered, then cupped Mike's buttocks and pushed him closer as she arched her hips against him, causing him to groan. It was too much, and he had to have her.

"I need you too, Eve." Eve unbuckled his pants, and it was evident how much he needed her. Mike wrapped Eve's other leg around his waist and entered her. Delicious waves swept over them.

"Oh my God," Eve whimpered. She tightened her muscles around Mike, causing him to shudder.

He started to thrust inside of her slowly at first, and Eve's whole body quivered with delight. Their bodies were entwined and their lips were locked in a passionate, hungry kiss. She dug her fingers in his hair and clasped him closer. Mike plunged deeper inside of her and his thrusts became more rapid and urgent. Weeks of need and want overtook Mike and Eve, and ecstasy swept over them, carrying them to that ultimate release.

They clung to each other as Mike eventually carried Eve into the bedroom. His hunger for her hadn't abated. That was just the appetizer, and now he was ready for the main course. Mike gently lowered Eve onto the bed and just stared at her with loving eyes. Mike wanted to learn and memorize all of the curves of Eve's beautiful body.

*This is what heaven must feel like,* Eve thought to herself, smiling up at him. She was mesmerized by Mike's physique; he was handsome and strong, and she felt safe in his arms.

This time they would take their time with each other. He lowered himself across Eve's body and gently kissed her lips, savoring their sweet taste as if for the first time. He nibbled at her lips in a playful manner that made her giggle.

Eve gingerly ran her fingers through Mike's hair, her nails gently scratching his scalp, which sent shivers up and down his spine, making him groan with desire. Mike's soft, flirty kisses slowly traveled over her chin and down her throat, sending small electric pulses through her body, causing her to whimper his name. He could feel the rise and fall of her chest as her pulse began to quicken. Eve's hands ventured down from his hair, landing on his muscular shoulders, massaging and caressing him. Mike's kisses followed a course directly to her cleavage, and then he claimed one of her breasts.

"Mmmm." Eve sighed, and threw her head back.

*So sweet*, Mike thought. Her nipples responded to the familiar feel of his warm mouth and the teasing nature of his tongue. He made sure to pay equal time to her other breast, savoring her taste and causing a warm sensation to form deep down in the pit of her stomach.

His hands started to skillfully move downward in a sensuous motion over her abdomen, her waist and hips and then finally her thighs, until he reached his target, where she was warm and moist. Mike was making Eve crazy and she wanted him inside of her. Eve proceeded to massage his back then let her hands travel toward his lower spine and then to his buttocks. She moved her hands across his hips and inner thighs, lingering dangerously close to his manhood in a teasing manner, making his lower body jolt toward her. Mike's mouth left her breasts as he pulled her head upward to face his and kissed her with a need that couldn't be denied. Eve's teasing hand enclosed around him and she stroked him until he cried out her name.

Mike wanted to play with her a little more but he couldn't stand it any longer, and apparently neither could she. "I love you so much. Take me, Mike," Eve commanded in a soft, urgent voice, and Mike was willing to obey.

He placed himself between her thighs and entered her. "Oh God, Eve. I love you." The fullness and sensation alone made Eve weak. Mike's thrusts were gentle at first so as not to overexcite himself; he wanted it to last as long as possible. Eve arched her hips and began to move in motion with him. She threw her head back out of sheer pleasure as a delightfully sweet sensation overtook her. Mike threw her arms up over her head and clasped his hands in hers, continuing to thrust in a steady motion.

"Oh Mike, don't ever stop," she whispered, her head spinning.

Mike was trying to control himself, but she felt so incredible that he didn't know if he could hold on until she reached her climax. Eve instinctively tightened her muscles around him, making Mike take in a sharp breath and stutter in a raspy voice, "Oh God... Eve, don't... it's too much." Eve relaxed her muscles and slowed her movement until she heard him breathe out in relief. She would let him dictate the pace, for now anyway. "I love making love to you, my sweet Eve."

Eve wrapped her legs around Mike's back and drew him in deeper, causing Mike to release her hands and wrap his arms underneath and around her body, drawing her tightly against his. Eve then wrapped her arms around Mike's neck, drawing his face closer to hers. He kissed her like never before as his seeking tongue pried opened her lips in search of hers. Eve clung tightly to Mike as he angled his thrusts in search of her sweet spot. When he found it she gasped, which signaled him to forge ahead. Mike was insatiable as he urgently drilled inside of her. Eve felt as if she was soaring higher and higher. Mike quickened his pace until they both came apart together. Eve trembled against him in complete fulfillment.

Mike and Eve had never felt anything like this before in their lives. They were both too exhausted for words and lay entangled in bed and pleasantly numb as they drifted asleep. They became one that night.

# *Chapter 23*

Eve opened her eyes to find Mike staring at her. This made her smile. "Good morning, Detective."

"Good morning, beautiful. Waiting to make love to you was extremely difficult, but it was definitely worth the wait. I could *really* get used to waking up to your beautiful face."

"Me too, last night was *incredible*."

"So much so, a part of me wants to spend the whole day in bed making love to you," stated Mike.

"Sounds like a plan to me, but why do I get the feeling you have another idea in mind?" surmised Eve.

"There's an amusement park in Queens but it's the last day, so… if you want to go…"

"I love amusement parks. Yes, let's go," Eve replied in a kid-like manner.

Mike leaned into Eve and kissed her so deeply that they almost abandoned the amusement park idea altogether.

"We'd better get out of here before I change my mind." Mike groaned. "Let's take a quick shower, then we can swing by your place so you can change into something more comfortable. I'm sure you'd rather not run around the park in your work clothes and heels."

Mike watched Eve as she climbed out of bed and headed toward the bathroom. She turned back around. "You're not going to join me?" Eve yearned to feel Mike's body against hers.

"Hon, if I join you in the shower we will *definitely not* leave this house today."

She sauntered back to him and lay across his chest. "Point taken. I'll be quick," she added, and kissed him lightly on the lips.

"Babe, you're killing me." Mike groaned.

Eve smiled then pulled herself up and spirited off to the bathroom. Mike remained in bed, completely enthralled by Eve's beauty. That quick physical interaction elicited an immediate arousal, which made him half-tempted to join her anyway, but he didn't dare.

After Eve finished with her shower, she dressed while Mike took his turn.

"Okay, I think we're all set to go, so let's hit the road, pretty lady."

After a quick stop at Eve's apartment, they enjoyed a nice, leisurely morning drive. They were like giddy teenagers going out on their first date, casting flirtatious glances and sneaking kisses at red lights. After Mike parked the car and they entered the park, Eve stared in wonder, looking like a little girl who was going to the amusement park for the first time. Mike chuckled inside; he loved seeing her happy and was glad he came up with the idea.

"So what do you want to do first?" he asked.

"Hmm, how about a rollercoaster," she offered with a glint in her eye.

"The rollercoaster, are you sure you want to start with that?"

"Yep, it's almost time for lunch, so we might as well get it over with before we start filling our bellies with food."

"Ah, smart lady, I knew there was a reason I fell in love with you," Mike said with a wink.

They made their way through the crowds to get to the rollercoaster area. Once seated, Mike and Eve looked at each other with anticipation, and when the ride took off they held each other's hands. They started to go up, up, and up and Mike got his cell phone ready to capture the descent. This would be their first picture together, but only the first of many. The rollercoaster reached the peak and then down they went. Everyone's arms went up in the air and they all screamed their hearts out. Eve shouted, "Whoo Hooooooo," and Mike had to chuckle because the little girl had returned. He snapped the selfie that captured all of the happiness they were feeling inside for each other. They were in love and without a care in the world.

They left the ride, holding hands doubled over with laughter. Since they skipped breakfast, they were famished and woofed down hotdogs and French fries, while washing them down with ice-cold beer, which never tasted so good. "Now that our bellies are full, what does your heart desire?" Mike asked.

"Well, what's your favorite amusement park game?"

Mike got a glint in his eye as he grabbed Eve's hand. "Come with me."

"Where are you taking me?"

"You'll see when we get there." Mike stopped at a booth titled "Sharp Shooter" and Eve watched Mike get himself set up with his machine gun.

"This is your favorite game?" she asked, incredulous. "Sharp Shooter?"

"Yeah," he responded.

"Seriously, *this* is your favorite game?" she asked again, suspiciously and with more emphasis.

"Yes, why do you keep asking me that?"

"So you're not pulling my leg? A shooting game? Really?"

"Okay, wiseass… I know… what did you expect? I'm a detective. It's my thing."

"Well, Mr. Detective, I'd better get a damn good prize from you doing *'your thing.'*" Eve got her cell phone ready to take a picture of Mike in action. Mike got into position, took aim and let it rip until he had shot out every piece of that red star and with a couple of bullets to spare. He turned around to face Eve. "So how do you like that?" he asked proudly.

"Never doubted you for a second," Eve replied proudly, and planted him with a kiss. She showed him the picture she took. "How do you like that? You look pretty good from the rear, Detective." Mike blushed.

"Which prize to do you want?" asked the game attendant, interrupting their private moment.

Mike looked to Eve. "Pick whichever one you want, babe."

Eve scanned her choices until her eyes locked on a giant mocha brown and white stuffed kitten. "I want that one," she replied, and her eyes lit up as the game attendant handed it to her. "Thank you." Eve turned to Mike, "And thank *you,* sweetie."

"Let me get a picture of you with the kitten. Goodness, the thing is almost half your size."

"I know." Eve posed with her stuffed animal, and then they continued with their fun quest. Next stop was *Eve's* favorite game, Skee-ball.

"Skee-ball… so this is *your thing,* I presume," teased Mike.

"You presume right, so prepare to be whooped," challenged Eve.

"Oh really now, you think so?" goaded Mike.

"Oh, I know so, mister. So cut the yapping and get your tokens ready."

Surprised by her confidence, Mike shot Eve a look, wondering if he was being played. They inserted their tokens and the machines dispensed nine balls each. Eve took the first ball and landed it right in the fifty-point hole. "Yes," she exclaimed, pumping her fist and looking directly at Mike, who just stood there with his mouth gaping. "So what are you waiting for? Let's see what you've got," she challenged.

Mike took his first turn and only landed the ball in the twenty-point hole. He glanced at Eve and knew he was in trouble.

Eve smiled and patted him on the back. "That's okay, sweetie, you've got eight more chances." They continued with their games, and every time Mike looked over at Eve's progress her balls were landing in either the forty or fifty-point holes. He could only get his in the twenty and thirty-point holes, and when it was all over Eve had indeed whooped Mike's butt, as promised. She beat him four hundred and ten to his two hundred and thirty points. Eve did a little dance as the machine dispensed their tickets, and Mike got a video of it. Blackmail videos always came in handy.

"Let's go again," Mike insisted.

"Are you sure?"

"Yeah, I just needed to get warmed up, but I'm ready now."

Eve chuckled to herself as Mike inserted the tokens into the machines. Although Mike's score improved slightly, he still met the exact same fate as he did in the first game because Eve also improved her score.

Mike pulled Eve into his arms. "I have to say that I'm impressed."

"Thank you. You're not upset that I beat you... *twice*... are you?"

"Rub it in, why don't you? But no...Well... *maybe* a little embarrassed, but I'll survive. Hey why don't we combine our tickets and you can pick out something." Mike handed Eve his tickets and they went to the counter to choose a prize.

Eve handed the game attendant their tickets. "Hi, what can we get with these?"

The game attendant counted the number of tickets Eve gave him then pointed to a section of medium-sized stuffed animals and toy cars and trucks. "You can choose any one of those."

Eve glanced at Mike. "I'd like the red race car please." After the game attendant handed Eve the race car, she handed it to Mike.

"Babe, you didn't have to get me this."

"I wanted to." Eve could see the appreciation on Mike's face, and that made her happy.

"Thanks, I'll keep it on my dresser so I can see it first thing every morning and think of you."

They left the arcade and continued to wander around the park, taking turns carrying Eve's kitten, snacking on pretzels and cotton candy and stealing kisses every chance they got. They were having so much fun that they were like kids in a candy store. It was starting to get dark, so they decided to go on one last ride, the giant Ferris wheel. It seemed like the perfect way to end the day. The view of the park from the top was beautiful with all of the lights and scores of people milling about. It was very romantic, and Eve cuddled with Mike, feeling very happy in his embrace. Neither said a word as they each replayed the events of the past two days in their minds. Their relationship had taken a giant step forward.

They were almost to the top when the Ferris wheel started to slow down. The ride was coming to an end and they were letting everyone off. When they reached the top, they could hear fireworks going off and Eve noticed them behind Mike and off into the distance. They watched them in awe. It was quite beautiful seeing them from the sky that way without anything blocking their view. Before the firework display ended, Mike turned back to face Eve, reached out to caress her face and leaned in to kiss her, softly and slowly, tracing the shape of her lips with his. It was as if they were in their own private world. Mike made sure to capture this moment with his cell phone. They would have wonderful memories of this day to relive in the future.

When they left the amusement park, they went back to Eve's apartment. They couldn't keep their hands off each other and barely made it into Eve's bedroom. They made love all night and fell asleep, wrapped in each other's arms, and exhausted from all of their weekend activities.

*  *  *

When Mike awoke Sunday morning he just stared at Eve's beautiful face, looking so peaceful and content.

She opened her eyes to find him smiling at her and let out a small giggle. "Good morning, sweetie. Why do I feel a sense of déjà vu? Should I always expect to find you watching me sleep when I wake up?"

"Absolutely. Did you sleep okay?"

"Like a baby. So, what do you have planned today? Isn't it football with the guys?"

"Yeah, but it's still early, so I have plenty of time to head back to the house. Plus I'm not quite ready to leave you yet this morning. Are you hungry?"

"I'm starving, especially since we didn't have dinner last night."

"Well, let's take a shower and then I'll make us breakfast."

"Let me make breakfast, Mike. It's the least I can do after that wonderful meal you prepared Friday evening."

"No, no, no. I'm still catering to you this weekend. You can make me breakfast another time."

Eve relented as she followed Mike to the bathroom. They ran the water and as they stepped into the shower, Mike whispered in Eve's ear, "I hope you are fully rested, Ms. Townsend." Mike's tone made his intentions very clear, and her stomach clenched with desire. The warm water cascaded over their bodies and Eve's wet hair framed her face. Mike was also starving, but not for food. He towered over Eve, giving her a full frontal view of his masculinity as the water trickled down his tanned torso, which glistened in the bathroom light.

Eve's heart started to race and her eyes traveled from Mike's feet up to his head, and then her eyes met his. "Do you like what you see?" he asked in a hoarse voice.

"Very much so," Eve replied with a smile.

While Eve was giving Mike the once-over, he too was captivated by her physique. Watching the water stream down her full round breasts made him want to devour her. Pressing her against the shower tiles, Mike leaned in and kissed her deeply while navigating his hands down her body.

"Mmmm, your skin is so smooth."

Mike's lips followed the same path as his roaming hands and settled on her stomach. As his hands caressed her hips and thighs, his tongue played havoc with her navel, causing Eve to tremble. She was ready for him and he was definitely ready for her. He stood up, lifted both of her legs, wrapping them around his waist, and made his way inside of her. Eve wrapped her arms around Mike's neck and his mouth claimed hers. They created a synchronous rhythm together that no other could duplicate. Eve had never felt anything like this with anyone else before, and she completely surrendered herself to him. Mike never knew that making love could ever feel like this. For as many women as he'd dated, none had ever captured his heart and soul as Eve had. It was overpowering and intoxicating, and they both found themselves reaching that crescendo together in complete harmony. Mike didn't release himself right away. He wanted to stay connected to her, and they remained in each other's embrace for several minutes.

"I guess we should actually take that shower now, huh," Mike said reluctantly.

"I guess so," Eve replied, not wanting to let go either.

She unwrapped her legs from around his waist and Mike gently helped her land on her feet. They began to lather each other up, taking the opportunity to cop a feel every now and then in a playful manner.

Eve subtly positioned Mike against the tile wall in preparation for a treat. Mike paid so much attention to her needs that she decided to return the favor. She took her time lathering up his chest, lingering at his nipples and twirling the hairs on his chest. Mike, surprised by her initiative, was pleasantly aroused and let out a soft moan. Eve also saw the physical evidence of her maneuvers and let her soapy hands travel to his curly black mound. Mike gasped and his breathing started to quicken as Eve wrapped her hands around him. "Oh my God, Eve." Mike groaned with desire as she began to work in the rich lather. She continued to caress him in a purposeful and efficient manner, causing his heartbeat to quicken. Mike could feel every nerve ending tingle and his soul expanding. *What sweet ecstasy,* he thought as he felt the blood rushing to his head and his body started to shudder. Responding to Mike's reaction, Eve quickened her strokes until he cried out as the explosion erupted. Mike was weak in the knees with complete satisfaction and planted Eve with a kiss that denoted his appreciation.

"I love you, Eve."

"I love you, Mike."

After rinsing, they dried off and got dressed. Mike prepared a continental breakfast fit for royalty. They were damn near starving by that point, and since breakfast was Eve's favorite meal of the day she had everything you could possibly want or need in her refrigerator. They had, after all, worked up quite an appetite over the past couple of days. They gobbled their food like they hadn't eaten in months. Once they were finally sated, Mike gathered his things and Eve walked him to the door. They shared one long-lasting kiss before Mike left to go hang with the boys.

* * *

Mike finally arrived home around eleven thirty in the morning. He had just enough time to decompress from his whirlwind weekend-long date with Eve before the guys arrived and descended upon him. Sam was waiting for Mike, since he had promised to help him prepare for Sunday afternoon football with the guys. "Hey, look what the cat dragged in," announced Sam when Mike walked toward the porch.

"Ha, ha, very funny. I'm sorry I'm late, were you waiting long?"

"No, don't worry about it. I take it your date with Eve went well, given that it started Friday evening and you're just getting back home *now*."

"It did go well, *very* well," Mike responded as they entered the house. "It was... I... I can't even find the words to describe it."

"You don't have to, it's written all over your face. Plus, I already know how much you love her, Mike. I guess I have to find another wingman, huh?"

Mike didn't answer right away. He just paused and took a breath, and Sam wondered what was on his friend's mind. "I told her how I felt, Sam. I mean, I said *the* words... and Eve said them too."

"Well, it's about time..." Mike continued to stand there in silence, biting his lip. "Why do I get the feeling there's more?" asked Sam.

"Promise not to say anything to the guys when they arrive, okay?"

"Sure, of course I won't. What's up?"

"Eve and I finally made love... I've been with other women but I've never experienced anything like this, Sam. To be honest, I'm a little scared. I never cared about whether the girl would stick around or not, but I care if Eve does."

"Well, the experience is quite different when it's not just about having sex, isn't it? When genuine feelings are involved, there's risk and a fear of losing that love. That's why most people avoid it like the plague, the way *you* used to."

"You've got that right." Just then they heard car doors closing and loud talking. Mike glanced over his shoulder. "I guess the guys have arrived... and not a word, Sam."

"I promised, didn't I? Especially the part about you being *scared...*"

Mike shot Sam a look and opened the door just as the guys were coming up the porch steps. It appeared that they brought everything you could possibly need for a day of football: beer, nuts, chips and pizza.

"Yo, buddy, what's up? Haven't seen you outside of work in ages, man," proclaimed Dan. Dan Winters was a fellow detective with average height and dirty blond hair that he kept combed back and away from his face.

"I know, I know, I've been busy."

"That's what we hear. So when are we gonna meet this new woman that's been keeping you so *busy*?" asked Marty as they all gathered in the living room. Martin (Marty) Dent, the youngest of the group and Dan's partner, had shaggy brown hair that gave him the appearance of being unkempt. Although on the skinny side, Marty could hold his own in the field.

"Her name is Eve, and you'll meet her in due time, guys. Look, the Vikings and the Browns game is about to start, so let's give it a rest for now. Pass me a beer."

"Okay, we'll let it go, *for now.*" It was kickoff Sunday, so harassing Mike about Eve could wait until halftime.

Even though he was hanging with the guys watching football, Mike was still thinking about Eve and missing her. How was he supposed to get through the day without her? His preoccupation was causing him to miss the entire first half of the game.

"Did you see that?" exclaimed Dan. "Yo, Mike, what are you doing... are you on the phone?"

Mike looked up just in time to see the replay.

"Dude, you've been MIA for weeks spending all of your time with Eve and you can't even focus on *our* day without texting her?" complained Marty.

Not only was he texting her, but he had saved the picture he took of them on the rollercoaster as the background image on his phone. Marty grabbed his phone out of Mike's hand and found the pictures he took of them at the amusement park. They were impressed with how beautiful she was and understood why he was blowing them off for the past couple of weeks.

"Wow dude, she's gorgeous."

"Man, you ain't kidding. Look at her," added Dan.

"Hey guys, control yourselves," warned Sam as Mike snatched back his phone.

"Or I might have to have a talk with Kinsey and Grace," added Mike. "I don't think they'd appreciate you ogling my girl."

"Relax, man, we didn't mean anything by it," replied Marty.

"Yeah, sorry Mike," added Dan. Knowing Mike the way they did, they *had* to meet the woman who was having this profound effect on their friend. She was obviously not one of his fly-by-night chicks, and it actually seemed pretty serious. "Hey, all of those pictures are of you two at the amusement park, that's not the amusement park over in Queens, is it?"

"Yeah, it is, so what about it?"

"But yesterday was the last day... so those pictures are from yesterday, which means you spent *this* weekend with her as well. Man, this is the real deal, you and Eve?" Marty asked.

"It *is*, so cut the crap."

"We hear you, and I'm happy for you. It's about time you found someone special," Dan added. "Now we just need to find someone for Sam."

"Oh hells no, don't get any ideas about trying to fix *me* up," ordered Sam.

"Maybe Eve has a friend that she can introduce you to," Marty added, ignoring Sam's protest.

"What did I just say?" Sam warned.

"She's new in town. She just moved here a couple of months ago from San Francisco," Mike interjected.

"Then how in the hell did you meet her? I know you play the field, but damn you're quick. Are you scoping the airports as the honeys come off the plane or what?"

Mike shot Marty a look. "She works at Colby Designs and was one of the victims of the shooting. Sam and I met her when we went there looking for Lucas Coles."

"I knew she looked familiar," exclaimed Dan, "she came to the precinct the following week when you guys were re-interviewing the victims." Mike and Sam nodded in agreement. "You should definitely try to arrange something with all of us so we can meet her, maybe next weekend. If she's new in town and hasn't had the chance to make friends here yet, maybe she'll hit it off with Kinsey and Grace."

"That's true, I didn't think of that. I wasn't actually interested in sharing her just yet, if you know what I mean. But I'll talk with Eve and get back to you," offered Mike.

"Hey, halftime is over and the game is about to resume," announced Sam. "We can settle this later after the games are over." They finished watching the one o'clock game and at four o'clock the boys were glued to the TV watching their hometown team, the New York Giants play the Redskins, while Eve was glued to the TV watching her old hometown team, the San Francisco 49ers play the Cardinals.

* * *

After the guys left, Mike called Eve to say goodnight. He really just wanted to hear her voice because he missed her like crazy. He was half tempted to run back over to her apartment but didn't want to appear like some obsessive nut that couldn't go an entire day without his woman. *His woman*—they were actually a couple now. She made him happier than he ever thought possible. He placed the toy race car that Eve had won for him on top of his dresser and fell asleep looking at the pictures he took of them having the time of their lives this past weekend.

# Chapter 24

"I think the meeting went well, Eve," Nathan announced as the remaining team mates exited the conference room.

Eve glanced up while gathering her notes. "I agree. The whole department is buzzing about us landing this project, and they don't plan on letting anything fall through the cracks. Everyone had their game faces on today, that's for sure."

"We've come a long way. I think everyone has managed to bounce back and recover quite well, don't you agree?"

"Yes, I do."

"Including you, Eve. I… umm hear that you are involved with one of the detectives… McGarrett, I think."

Eve just looked at him. "Nathan! Is this your attempt at gossip?"

"Oh no, please forgive me if I'm prying. I was just curious. But I'm happy for you, if it's true, that is."

"Yes, it is. We have been dating, for a little over a month now."

"That's great. I wish you both well."

"Thanks, Nathan."

* * *

Eve had agreed to meet Mike's friends, and to his surprise, she didn't hesitate to accept the invitation but was honored to receive it.

She looked beautiful as always, but Mike felt that Eve managed to look beautiful in whatever she was wearing, even if it was nothing at all.

At a red light, Eve placed her hand over Mike's. "Sweetie, are you okay?"

"Yeah, of course," Mike lied.

Eve smiled. "Are you sure? You seem a little nervous to me."

Mike glanced at Eve. He couldn't fool her for one second. "Okay, I'll admit I'm a little nervous."

"It will be fine, sweetie, and we'll have a good time. So relax." Eve's touch definitely had a soothing effect on him. He was certain that everyone would love her, but your closest friends were generally a reflection of you, and he hoped that Eve liked them. He wanted to make a good impression on her. Eve wasn't just *some* woman—she was *the* woman.

They arrived at the ranch and it was a full house. Sam had arrived earlier to let the others in while Mike picked up Eve. Kinsey and Grace came right over and Mike introduced them.

"You don't mind if we steal her, do you, Mike?" asked Grace. Grace, Dan's wife of two years, had wavy brown shoulder-length hair and a slender physique due to many days of surfing on the Island of Hawaii. She had lived on the mainland for most of her adult life but always managed an occasional trip back home for family visits.

"You see her all the time," added Kinsey, also a brunette, whose locks cascaded past her shoulders. She was born and raised in New Jersey until her college years. She made New York her home after meeting her boyfriend, Marty Dent, at NYU and then they decided to move in together after graduation. They had been happily cohabitating for the last five years. Kinsey maintained her figure through weekly hours of self-defense and kickboxing classes.

Mike *did* mind, but it didn't matter because they were already escorting her across the room and *away* from him. He looked at Sam. "What just happened? Those two..."

"Relax, Mike. Let her hang with the girls. Look, she's having a good time… They're probably talking about you."

"God forbid. What do you think they're telling her?" Mike asked nervously, given his playboy ways before meeting Eve.

"They're probably warning her away from you." Mike shot Sam a look. "Relax dude, you know I'm just kidding. They're probably not even thinking about you."

Mike noticed Dan and Marty approaching them. "I see our girls have kidnapped yours already. They didn't waste any time, did they?"

"No they didn't. I barely got the introductions out before they were off. I need a drink. I'll be right back." Mike quickly walked to the minibar and poured himself a Scotch and water while eyeing the girls. He caught Eve's attention and she smiled. His heart melted. *Relax, Mike—she's okay and enjoying herself. You have nothing to worry about.* Mike took his drink and returned to the guys.

"So Mike, tell us a little bit about Eve. What does she do for a living?" asked Dan.

"Well, you already know that she works for the architect design firm, Colby Designs. She originally worked at the San Francisco branch but was just promoted and transferred here to manage the design department. She's also a very talented artist herself. She produced the drawing of Sam and I that's hanging on the wall over there." Mike pointed to the beautifully framed portrait of him and Sam and was proud to boast about Eve's credentials.

"I was wondering where that came from. It's really good. So… she's smart and talented as well as beautiful," added Marty. "That must be new for you, Mike. You don't normally go for the intelligent ones." Mike's eyes narrowed as Marty continued, "Are you sure you can handle her?" Marty had a smirk on his face that irked Mike, along with his snide remark.

"I don't need to handle Eve, Marty, so I'd advise you to tread lightly," warned Mike.

"I didn't mean anything by it, man."

"Of course you did, Marty," admonished Dan. Marty was his partner and he loved him like a younger brother, but he had always been a little jealous of Mike, which became apparent when he slipped these little insults into the conversation. "Let's cool it, guys, the girls are coming back."

Eve could see some tension in Mike's demeanor. She knew that he was a little nervous, but this was more than nerves; he seemed upset. So she wrapped her arms around his waist when she reached him and she immediately felt his body relax as he smiled at her. She had the feeling he was also a little annoyed with the girls for stealing her away from him and decided to stick close to him for a while.

"So what have you girls been talking about?" asked Sam.

"Oh, we were just filling Eve in about all of Mike's women," joked Kinsey, unaware of the altercation that had just occurred between Marty and Mike. Mike's eyes almost popped out of his head and Eve could feel him tense up again. Whatever happened before they arrived obviously got under his skin.

"She's just joking, sweetie. You know all of those other women don't matter as long as it's just you and me *now*."

Mike caressed her hair and looked into her brown eyes. "It's definitely just *you* and me, babe." He leaned in and gave her a soft and loving kiss. Everyone was caught off guard and shocked by Mike's open display of tenderness. They were not used to seeing him so enamored. He always had some chick on his arm, but those women never earned an introduction party with his friends.

"OMG, get a room," mocked Marty.

"Oh, be quiet," admonished Kinsey. "What's the matter with you?" she hissed in his ear. Marty just rolled his eyes.

"You guys don't mind if I steal Mike away for a bit?" Eve had a feeling Mike needed to talk.

"Oh no, you two lovebirds go and spend some time together, we'll catch up later," replied Grace.

*Thank goodness*, thought Mike. Mike and Eve found a spot on the sofa and immediately cuddled up to each other. They were automatically physically drawn to each other, and neither one of them could fight it even if they tried.

"So... do you want to tell me why you're upset?" Eve asked.

"Why would you think I'm upset?"

"So... you're *not* upset," she persisted while caressing Mike's hand. *God Almighty, if she only knew how good that felt.*

"Well, maybe I'm a little irritated," he admitted.

Eve still felt he was annoyed with the girls; he seemed to want to stick close to her.

"I know you were a little nervous about tonight. Does it have anything to do with that?"

"I just want you to feel comfortable with my friends and hopefully see them as your friends someday."

"That's very sweet of you. So far everyone has been very kind to me. I like them... but did something *specific* happen to irritate you?"

"That *fucking* Marty pissed me off," Mike hissed. "He has a tendency to make snide remarks usually directed at me for some reason, but I don't normally let him get to me."

"But this time you did. Maybe he said something that got under your skin and hit a little close to home?"

Mike sighed and closed his eyes before answering, "Yeah, he made a comment about how I don't normally go for beautiful women that are also smart and talented, and implied that I wouldn't be able to handle or keep up with you."

Eve shook her head in disbelief. "Why would he say something like that *tonight* of all nights? I thought he was a friend."

"Sometimes I wonder about that myself. Marty never thinks before he opens his mouth, at least *not* when it comes to me."

"Well, you don't actually believe what he said, do you?"

"I just know that I can't lose you, Eve."

"Mike, I'm not going anywhere."

He looked into Eve's eyes and held up his pinky. "Promise, with a pinky swear."

"I promise," Eve responded and she hooked her pinky with his. "We should probably go mingle; we don't want to appear antisocial."

Mike had other ideas on his mind, but he couldn't be selfish. The whole point of tonight was so that Eve could meet his friends and possibly become part of the group. So far, she was getting along with everyone nicely, and they all seemed to like her, especially the girls.

"Where's Sam? I haven't spoken with him since the memorial service." Eve glanced around and spotted him over by the bar, so they decided to go chat with him. She also wanted Sam's presence for Mike's sake to help keep him calm. Eve was catching up with Sam when Mike noticed Marty approaching them and groaned under his breath.

"Hey guys, sorry to interrupt... Mike, can we talk?"

Mike glanced at Eve and she squeezed his hand in encouragement. "Sure, Marty." He turned to Sam and Eve. "I'll be back in a few."

Sam and Eve watched them as they walked down the hallway and hoped that they would work it out. Sam turned back to Eve. "Did Mike tell you about what happened with Marty, before you and the girls returned?"

"Yeah, and it really pissed him off too. What's up with Marty, anyway? I really hit it off with Kinsey, and would hate to have our friendship hindered because of her boyfriend. Do I need to be concerned about him?"

"No, he's pretty harmless. He's a little younger than the rest of us and has a tendency to try to act tough but ends up sticking his foot in his mouth instead. Plus, Dan and I think he's a little jealous of Mike." Eve had a feeling there was more to be concerned about. Maybe it was female intuition, but she kept that opinion to herself as she watched Mike and Marty talk. Who was she to judge someone she had just met? But negative first impressions were generally hard to overcome.

"So, what's up, Marty?" Mike was not in the mood for anymore of his nonsense that evening.

"Look man, I wanted to apologize for what I said earlier. It was insensitive and uncalled for." Mike wasn't sure if Marty's apology was sincere or not. He didn't respond immediately, and Marty could sense Mike's skepticism. "Honestly, I'm sorry. I'm just not used to you having *actual* feelings for someone, and my attempt to be funny at your expense was inappropriate. I can see that you really love her, and it's obvious that she feels the same way. I'm happy for you both. So, are we good?" Marty reached out his hand to Mike. Mike shook his hand reluctantly.

"Sure, we're good." Marty's apology seemed genuine enough, so he decided to let it go, at least for the rest of the evening. He didn't want anything or anyone to make things uncomfortable for Eve, and he wanted this conversation over with.

"So Eve, how are you doing?" Sam asked. "We haven't seen much of each other since the memorial service except in passing, and I wanted to thank you personally for that beautiful drawing that you did of me and Mike."

"You're welcome, Sam. It was kind of you to frame and hang it on the wall. I was so touched. I feel like a real artist, having my work displayed for all to see."

"Well, both Mike and I believe that you are an artist. It's time you believe that too. You know, Ms. Townsend, you make my friend very happy. And he loves you very much, just in case you needed a second opinion."

"I love him very much too, Sam, more than I thought possible... To be honest, it's a little scary."

Sam chuckled inside at having the same conversation with Mike last weekend. "It's scary to open your heart to someone, but I think the rewards are worth the risk."

"I agree... Are you speaking from experience?"

"Well, that's a conversation for another time."

"Oh? Well I look forward to that conversation." Sam smiled mischievously. While Eve was chatting with Sam, she couldn't help but wonder if Mike was okay. She was about to get her answer when she noticed Mike and Marty approaching them.

"So, did you boys patch things up?" Sam asked.

"Yep, we're fine, and I apologized. I was being a complete ass," Marty answered, "and Mike was cool enough to accept my apology." Eve could tell that Mike was not completely over it and was putting up a brave front, probably for her sake.

As the evening progressed, everyone could sense that Mike was in better spirits. Eve had a definite calming effect on him that no woman had provided before. It was as if they were two halves of a whole and were a perfect match for each other.

The evening winded down and everyone started to trickle out. All of Mike's friends loved Eve, which wasn't a surprise to him—he expected as much. He was more concerned with his friends making a good impression on her because he wanted her to like *them*. It never mattered to Mike before whether the women he was dating liked his friends or not or vice versa. This revelation about himself and his past behavior concerning women made him stop to think about the kind of person he was, which made him see why Marty made that comment towards him earlier. Marty only said what everyone else was probably thinking, subconsciously anyway. It seemed he was emotionally disconnected in his previous relationships with women, and wondered if he was that way with his friends or even his parents. He didn't think his selfish behavior transcended to them, but if so, he would make sure to strive to become a better person, a better man, all because of his love for Eve. She was meant to come into his life, and he thanked God that she did.

Dan, Marty, Grace, and Kinsey were headed out and the girls were hugging Eve goodbye and making future lunch plans.

"Hey man, we're headed home. I'm glad we finally got to meet Eve. We had a good time," said Dan. "It's obvious how she's affected you, my friend. She's special, and a keeper. I'm happy for you both."

"Thanks Dan, that means more to me than you know."

Dan turned to Eve. "It was a pleasure to finally meet you."

"Likewise, Dan."

"Same here," added Marty. "I hope to make a better impression the next time, and I apologize again for my rude behavior earlier."

"It's water under the bridge, Marty. Don't give it another thought," said Eve.

"You might regret letting him off the hook so easily, my friend," joked Kinsey.

Marty whipped his head around to face her. "Hey, whose side are you on anyway?"

"Yours baby, always," replied Kinsey while throwing her arms around Marty's neck. Everyone laughed at poor Marty's expense.

"Okay everyone, laugh it up. Listen, let's get out of here before we overstay our welcome," suggested Marty, not happy about being the butt of the joke. But he brought it on himself, so he sucked it up. "Goodnight Eve, Mike. Catch you later, Sam."

"Goodnight guys, thanks for coming. We really appreciate it," added Mike.

Grace quickly approached Mike as the others were heading out to their cars. "Hey, I just wanted to tell you that Eve is wonderful. It's obvious that the two of you love each other very much. Guard what you have and don't let her get away, or I'll *never* forgive you," she whispered.

"Thanks Grace, and don't worry, I don't plan on letting her get away." Dan honked the car horn repeatedly, calling out for Grace to hurry up. She quickly hugged Mike and Eve then ran out the door. Mike and Eve waved as they drove off.

"Well you two, I'm wiped, so I'm going to leave you two love birds to yourselves," announced Sam, giving Eve a big hug. "It was great to see you again. Welcome to our dysfunctional family."

"Thanks, Sam."

"Goodnight, partner," added Mike.

As soon as Sam left, Mike pulled Eve into his arms. "Alone at last. Did you have a good time?"

"I most certainly did, but I'm just sorry that you were so stressed about it. I know that you were worried for me and you didn't enjoy yourself as much as you could have at the beginning of the evening. But at least you relaxed as the night progressed."

"Please forgive me. I shouldn't have allowed Marty to piss me off so easily. I hope that I didn't mar the evening for you."

"You didn't. Everyone was lovely, *even* Marty in the end, so it all worked out fine."

"I love you, Eve," Mike said softly while pulling her closer. "Is there any way I can convince you to stay with me tonight?"

"I'd *love* to stay with you, Detective."

A smile crossed Mike's face. "I was hoping you'd say that."

* * *

"Hey Mike, wait up," Dan called out as Mike was heading out of the station. Mike turned around at the sound of his voice.

"Hey Dan, what's up? I was just on my way to meet Eve for lunch."

"Well, speaking of Eve, I wanted to tell you again that it was great meeting her over the weekend. The girls loved her, and I think they're all going to become good friends."

"Thanks, I hope so for Eve's sake. It would be nice if she had some girlfriends to hang out with. Although I wouldn't mind her spending all of her time with just me, but I guess I can't be selfish that way, huh?"

"Nope, but to be honest, I don't really know what to expect from you. I'm still trying to get used to you even being in a committed relationship. But I think you picked the right woman for it. You might have hit the jackpot with this one, my friend. So *don't* screw it up."

"From your mouth to God's ears. I don't know what I'd do if I *did* mess things up. But I'll make it my mission not to." Mike glanced at his watch. "Listen, I really have to go, I'm already running late."

"Okay, tell Eve hi and that the girls will probably contact her soon for lunch or something."

"I will."

Dan turned around and flinched at finding Marty standing right in front of him. "Whoa man, how long have you been standing there? Why do you have to sneak up on people?"

"I just got here. Where's *he* running off to?" Marty asked, nodding in Mike's direction.

"Oh, he's meeting Eve for lunch."

"Humph, let's see how long that lasts," Marty mumbled under his breath.

"What was that?" asked Dan.

"Nothing, I hope he has a good time, that's all."

"I do too, let's get back to work." Dan heard exactly what Marty said. It seemed Marty's heartfelt apology had been short-lived, but he decided not to blast him about it *this time*. Dan was in a good mood and decided to keep it that way.

# *Chapter 25*

Mike planned on visiting with his parents this coming weekend and invited Eve to join him. "So you're okay with spending the weekend with my parents?"

"Yes, I'm fine with it."

"You don't think it's too soon? I don't want you to feel pressured in any way, especially since you literally just survived meeting all of my closest friends. You can meet my parents at any time, so I won't be offended if you're not ready," Mike babbled.

"I seem more ready than you are at this moment."

"Don't get me wrong, I'm good. I just want to make sure that you are that's all."

"Sweetie, it's *okay*. I *want* to meet your parents."

"That's good, because I really want you to, and they've been dying to meet you too. They will be thrilled that I've brought you along."

"Wait, they don't *know* that I'm coming with you?"

"Nope, I didn't want to get their hopes up just in case you weren't ready."

"So I'm a surprise?"

"Yes, but a good one, I assure you."

"Okay then, let's not keep them waiting."

During the drive, Mike filled Eve in on the discussion he had with his mother about her. "So I send you to visit with your parents and you spend the entire time talking about me?" Eve asked.

"Not the entire time, but the majority of the time, mostly with Mom. I mentioned you to the both of them at dinner, but Mom and I had a lengthy discussion the following morning. She wanted to know more about you because she could see how happy you've made me. Plus they had to know why I hadn't visited with them and wanted to make sure I had a worthy excuse."

"What in the world did you two talk about?"

"I told her how we met and that you had gotten hurt during the shooting." Mike noticed a slight cloud pass over Eve's eyes at the mention of the shooting and decided to move off the topic quickly. "She was concerned for your well-being, and I assured her that you had recovered and were in good health. But we mostly talked about the status of our relationship and how fast things were moving. That's when I decided that I was going to tell you how I felt about you, which is why I planned our special dinner." Eve smiled at the memory of that wonderful weekend, when their relationship went to another level.

"I'm glad that you're able to talk with your mom about such things. Most men wouldn't bother confiding in their *mommies*," she replied with a sly grin.

"My *mommy*, oh that's nice. Keep that up and I'll tell my *mommy* that you were teasing me. That wouldn't make a good impression on her, you know."

"You spoiled brat," responded Eve while punching Mike in the arm.

"*Ouch*! Now I can add abuse to the list of offenses," Mike teased and Eve giggled at his silliness.

They arrived at Mike's parents' home and decided that Mike would go in alone and then surprise them with Eve. "Hey Mom, Dad, I'm here. Where are you guys?" he called out, and several moments later he heard their footsteps approaching.

"Mikey, good, you're here before lunch. So we can all eat together." Mike couldn't conceal the mischievousness in his eyes, at least not from Carla. "What's that look about?"

"What look?"

"Boy, don't you play with me. I saw those eyes of yours glinting. What are you up to?"

"I was just hoping that you made enough food."

"I made a ton, like I always do."

"Well, that's good," Mike announced as he headed back toward the front door, "because, we have another mouth to feed." Mark and Carla looked at each other, puzzled. Then Mike opened the door and Eve walked inside.

Carla's hand flew to her face. "Oh my goodness, is this Eve?" Eve smiled at both Carla and Mark. She was touched by the happiness on Carla's face at her arrival, even though she was not expected.

"Yes, Mom and Dad, this is Eve." Before Eve could say a word she was enveloped in Carla's arms as she gave her a big hug. It made her think about her own mom, and she fought back tears.

"She's absolutely beautiful, Mikey." Eve blushed at Carla's effusiveness and Mike beamed from ear to ear.

"It's nice to meet you both," Eve finally responded, overwhelmed by the attention.

"It's lovely to finally meet you, dear," replied Carla.

"Yes, welcome to our home. I hope you don't mind hanging out with us old folks for the weekend?" added Mark.

"Old folks?" Carla asked, incredulous. "Speak for *yourself.*"

Eve had to giggle. They were too cute for words. Mike just stood back and watched everything unfold. Eve didn't realize it, but she had officially just become a part of his family without breaking a sweat.

"Come with me, Eve, darling." Carla picked up Eve's overnight bag and started to guide her towards the staircase. "We can talk more privately upstairs while we get you settled in your room."

"What, not you too?" protested Mike. "We just got here."

Eve knew exactly what Mike was referring to. "I met Mike's friends last weekend, and as soon as we arrived at the house the girls spirited me away."

Carla looked at Mike. "Well, this is different. I'm your mother, and you get to see Eve all the time." Carla proceeded to guide Eve upstairs.

"That's the same excuse the girls used. *Women!*" exclaimed Mike, which made Carla and Eve stop in their tracks and turn back to face him with stern looks on their faces.

Mike's mouth dropped open and his father snickered. "Uh, oh, you're in trouble now, Son." Mike shot his father a look of annoyance.

Carla pointed her finger at Mike, and then she and Eve proceeded upstairs.

Mark turned toward his son. "Look now, cool it with the nonsense. It was hard enough to win when it was only the two of us against her one, now Carla's got someone to double-team against us with."

"I heard that," Carla called out.

"See what I mean," Mark whispered.

Eve and Carla heard that too and just looked at each other. "They never learn, dear," Carla said while shaking her head. "Let's put your things in Mikey's room."

"Where is Mike going to sleep?"

"In the room with you, dear."

Eve looked at Carla in disbelief. "You don't mind us sharing a room together?"

"Of course not. We might be older, but we're not prudes."

Eve had to laugh. She had a feeling she would be doing a lot of that this weekend. "You are just too much Carla."

Carla helped Eve unpack while engaging in friendly chit-chat. She wanted Eve to feel comfortable with them. It could be daunting for a young woman to meet the parents of the man she's involved with, and she wanted Eve to know that she was not the typical "possessive mom" and wanted her to feel welcomed in their home.

Mike decided to wait a bit before taking his things upstairs. He knew that his mother was using this time to bond with Eve, and he didn't want to intrude.

Carla and Eve passed Mike as they were headed back down the stairs. "We'll get lunch ready, Mikey, and then we'll eat once you've finished unpacking," Carla announced.

"Thanks, Mom, I won't be long." Mike winked at Eve and grabbed her hand for a split second before heading upstairs. Mike noticed that his mother set Eve up in his room. *Thank heavens. Mom, you're the best*, he thought.

Everyone enjoyed lunch, and Mike and Eve were oblivious to Carla's watchful eye. She was curious to see how Mike and Eve interacted with each other and was thoroughly convinced of the love they shared. They made a beautiful couple, and Eve was a delightful young woman. Not at all like some of those airheads that Mike had briefly dated in the past. Carla could tell that Eve was special to Mike when he first mentioned her to them, and after seeing them together Carla knew their son was definitely in love for the first time.

After lunch, Eve helped Carla with the dishes while Mike helped his father with the chores. "Eve is lovely, Son," Mark told Mike as they prepared to mow the lawn.

"Thanks, Dad. She's everything to me, and it means a lot that you and mom approve."

"Carla loves this. No offense to you, but she always wanted a daughter too. Having Eve around can fill that void for her."

"I hope Mom can fill a void for Eve as well. A girl needs a mom on occasion."

"Oh, I think Carla has got that covered."

"I'm sure she does. I knew you two would love her. It's hard not to. There's something about Eve that makes you feel calm and stable."

"Coming from you, that says a lot. In regards to relationships, you are the *least* stable person I know, jumping from one girl to the next without forming any long-lasting connections. We were getting worried about you for a while there. We were beginning to think that you would become a permanent bachelor and we would never have any grandchildren to spoil."

"Well, maybe all of our lucks are changing thanks to Eve."

Mark did a double take at Mike. "Wow, is it that serious? Are you thinking about having children already?"

"Eve would make a great mom, and yes, it's too soon to be making plans, of course, but as far as I'm concerned I think that she could be the one."

"Have you discussed this with Eve?"

"Oh God no, I'm not crazy. She's been through a lot in the past couple of months, and her world has been pretty much turned upside down. I don't want to add any pressure."

Mark patted Mike on the back. "Well, I'm happy that you both found each other."

Carla and Eve had finished cleaning the dishes and were relaxing on the front porch while the boys were mowing the lawn out back. "Eve, dear, I'm glad that Mikey brought you along with him this weekend. It was a nice surprise."

"Thanks, Carla. It's nice to be included in your family time. You've both made me feel very welcomed."

"Mikey told us that you lost both of your parents in a car accident and that you've just moved out here only a couple of months ago. It couldn't have been easy going through everything without having moral support. I want you to know that if you ever need an ear, you have mine. And anything you confide in me will stay between us."

Eve was touched by Carla's offer. "Thanks, I just might take you up on that."

"It's too bad we hadn't met before the shooting. You probably could have used a shoulder to lean on, as well as a helping hand."

Eve glanced back up at Carla. "Mike told me that he mentioned the shooting to you."

"Is it still difficult for you to talk about? Mike said that you were handling things very well but was concerned that you might be experiencing residual emotional trauma from it all." She noticed that Eve was fidgeting with her fingers ever since she mentioned the shooting. It obviously still bothered her, which was to be expected.

"I try not to think about it too much except for the fact that it brought Mike into my life. I just focus on the positive outcome and thank God for those of us that were lucky enough to survive."

"Well, that is a very healthy attitude to have. I am very grateful because you've made my son very happy."

Eve smiled as tears threatened to form. "Thank you, Carla." They chatted for the rest of the afternoon while Mike and his father resumed the chess game they started during Mike's last visit.

Carla decided to start dinner preparations and had a thought. "Eve, Mike normally helps me with the meals."

"I know, and you've taught him well. He's a wonderful cook."

"If you don't mind hanging out with me a little longer, I'd love it if you helped me this time."

"I would be honored," Eve replied. They informed Mike that he was spared dinner duty this one time, and he and Mark decided to watch the news together instead.

Dinner was a delightful affair. They enjoyed wonderful conversation where Mike's parents regaled Eve with childhood stories, which thoroughly embarrassed him, but he took it in great stride. After dinner, Mike and Eve retreated to his room for some alone time.

As soon as they entered the bedroom Mike scooped her up, carried her to the bed and lay down beside her. "I finally have you all to myself. You're so popular with everyone that I can barely get any time alone with you. Should I start making appointments?"

"Michael McGarrett, don't tell me you're jealous?"

"Why would *I* be jealous?"

"Maybe it's because you're not the center of everyone's world."

"Well, you might be right on that account, but as long as I'm a part of your world I'll be just fine."

Eve reached up to caress Mike's face. "Always, my love." Mike smiled and gave Eve a gentle kiss, then started to run his fingers through her hair.

"So... did you enjoy the time you spent with my parents?" he asked.

"I most certainly did. They are just adorable. I hope we're as adorable at that age." Mike liked that Eve thought of them as being together for that long into the future.

"Mom and Dad *are* pretty cute, but I'd *never* tell them that. They would get swelled heads, especially Mom."

"Stop picking on them," she chastised. "They made me feel loved, as if I were their own child." Mike noticed the melancholic tone in Eve's voice.

"You're thinking about your parents, aren't you?" Eve shook her head yes, but didn't say anything. "I didn't want to suggest this to you before you actually met my parents, but maybe you could look at them as surrogate parents. I know that no one could ever replace your mother, but Dad told me that mom always wanted a daughter."

"Is it possible that Carla could look at *me* as her daughter?"

"Are you kidding? From the way she acted today, it's a sure bet."

"You think so?" she asked, like a little girl who needed her mommy. It almost broke Mike's heart.

"I know so," he assured her.

"We did have a nice talk, and she said that I could come to her if I ever needed someone to confide in."

"I told you, she's smitten already. I know how that feels; you're hard to resist, pretty lady." Mike kissed Eve long and sensuous this time. "Aarrgghh, I want to make love to you so much."

"Mike, we can't, they'll hear us."

"I know, especially Mom. She's got ears like a bat.

Eve slapped Mike in the arm. "Stop that! You're just terrible tonight."

"But it's *true*," he insisted.

"No comment," replied Eve. She wanted to make love too but didn't feel comfortable doing so with his parents within earshot, so they talked for the rest of the evening, stealing long, passionate kisses before turning in for the night.

* * *

Mark could tell Carla was still on a high from spending the day with Eve. She was quiet the entire time they were cleaning up the dinner dishes. He knew she was probably already planning Mike and Eve's entire future even though they had just met the young woman that morning. If Carla knew that Mike was already thinking about having children with Eve, there would be no stopping her. She has waited a long time for her baby boy to finally fall in love.

"Did you enjoy your time with Eve today, honey?" Mark asked, even though he already knew the answer.

"Yes I did. Isn't she perfect for Mikey? She seems to make him stop and take notice for a change. He was always on the go, never taking the time to appreciate life, just barreling through everything at full steam."

"She has grounded him a little..."

"Without stifling him," added Carla.

"Exactly," agreed Mark.

"Like I said, she's perfect for him, and makes him *very* happy."

* * *

The next morning, Mike awoke first. He looked over at Eve and she was still fast asleep. He carefully got out of the bed so as not to disturb her and went to check if his parents had gotten up and gone downstairs. They weren't in their bedroom, and then he heard his mom fiddling around downstairs in the kitchen. He didn't know where his father was, but he wasn't upstairs, and that was all that mattered.

Mike wanted to make love to Eve without them hearing, but he had to wake her up first. He tickled her nose, and Eve's hand went up and lightly brushed her face. Mike tickled it again, snickering to himself as she wiggled her nose and started to stir. She turned toward him and he leaned in and kissed her delicately. Eve sighed and Mike kissed her again with a little more intensity. Eve blinked and opened her eyes to find Mike staring right at her, smiling mischievously. "Hi, what are you up to?" she asked.

"I was trying to wake you up. *I want you.*" Eve quickly glanced toward the door.

"Don't worry, they're both downstairs. I checked already."

Eve shook her head. "You're like a kid trying to make out with his girlfriend after sneaking her into his bedroom."

"You make me *feel* like a kid again." He had ached for Eve all night, so much so that he dreamt about her. Eve melted. She had been too embarrassed to give herself to him last night in his parent's home, but she was definitely over that now.

He kissed her with such passion that Eve felt as if Mike was going to devour her. They made love as if they were being deprived, and the intensity of Mike's thrusts showed how ravenous he was. Eve was overwhelmed by the wealth of emotion and feeling that swept over her.

"Wow, what in the world got into us?" Eve asked breathlessly. "I really hope your parents didn't hear us. How embarrassing..."

"I know, we were a bit out of control, even for us. Maybe it's because we're sneaking behind my parents' back. But I don't think we were *that* loud."

"I certainly hope not," replied Eve, blushing at the thought.

Mike wanted to remain in bed with his arms wrapped around Eve. But if they didn't make an appearance soon, it would be like advertising to his parents what they were doing.

"Are you hungry?" he asked.

"Not so much. I'm still stuffed from the meal your mom prepared last night."

"Well, breakfast is less formal, so we can eat at our leisure or skip it altogether, but we should at least get downstairs to avoid unnecessary questions."

"I'll race you to the shower," Eve announced as she jumped out of the bed and ran into the bathroom before Mike could catch her.

Mike and Eve weren't fooling anyone once they finally joined Mark and Carla downstairs. They were still giddy from their bedroom *and* shower activities and could barely make it through breakfast without casting furtive smiles and glances and touching each other's hands. Mark and Carla just looked and smiled at the two lovebirds. Mike decided to help his mom clear the table and wash the dishes while Mark took the opportunity to spend some alone time with Eve.

"So, Mom... I take it that all of the time you've been spending with Eve means that you like and approve of her," Mike stated.

"Yes, Mikey, I like her a lot. She's absolutely wonderful."

"I knew you would... I still can't believe I found her, Mom. Sometimes I think I must be dreaming. My life is completely different now."

"Love can do that to you, especially when it's with the right person."

"Eve is the *perfect* person."

"I couldn't agree more, and that's exactly what I told your father last night." Carla gave Mike a wink, and he just smiled at his mother's approval.

Mark and Eve got comfortable in the living room. "So we finally have some time to spend together, Eve. Between Mike and Carla, I thought I'd never get the chance."

"You sound like Mike did yesterday evening."

"Well, it appears you are a very popular person. You've made both my son and wife very happy." Mark paused for a second and leaned forward. "I hope I'm not misspeaking when I say this, but... I think Carla is looking at you as a daughter." Slightly taken aback by Mark's directness, Eve didn't respond right away and just looked at him. "Oh, I haven't scared you, have I? You're not going to run for the hills now, are you? The both of them would *kill* me."

Eve laughed. "Oh no, I'm honored that Carla would think of me as a daughter. I don't doubt what Mike and I have, but isn't it a little too early for..." Eve struggled to find the right words. She, herself, had thought of having a future with Mike, but didn't think they were at that stage in their relationship yet. She didn't want to jinx what they had by forcing things. If they were meant to be, they *would* be.

"You don't have to explain, I understand." Mark patted Eve's hand for added reassurance. "On a slightly different note, Carla told me that you lost your parents a couple of years ago."

"Yes, in a car accident."

"I'm sorry about that, and I don't mean to bring up bad memories. I only want to mention that if you ever need us for parental guidance, we are here for you, Eve. You are part of our family now." Mark reached out and embraced Eve, and she thought that she would break down and cry right then and there. Mike and Carla entered the living room just in time to witness the tender moment.

"Hey Dad, what's going on in here?" asked Mike, approaching Eve.

"What did you do to this poor girl, Mark?" demanded Carla jokingly. "Why is she crying?"

"Oh stop it you two, I haven't done anything to her," defended Mark.

"It's okay, they're happy tears," Eve added while giving Mark a wink.

"I'm glad to hear that," Mike added while wiping away a small tear from Eve's cheek. "Hey babe, I was thinking that we would head home soon. You don't mind if we leave before having lunch, do you? We're all having such a good time, so I hate to break up the party."

"There will be plenty of other parties, so don't you worry about it. But why the rush to leave early?" asked Carla. Eve was wondering the same thing.

"I want to show Eve a little bit of where I grew up, and we could stop for lunch in town along the way." Mike looked down at Eve. "That's if you *want* to go on the tour, of course."

"I'd love to see where you grew up," Eve agreed, smiling up at him, "but I do hate to leave your parents so soon."

"Mike will just have to bring you along on his next visit," Carla suggested. "Come, dear, I'll help you pack so the two of you can get going, because the day will slip away faster than you realize."

After Mike and Eve packed their bags, everyone hugged each other goodbye while Mark and Carla told Eve how much they enjoyed their time with her.

The tour consisted of where Mike attended high school and college, and he showed Eve several tourist highlights. They took pictures at each location to build upon the photo album that Mike was putting together. They ate a late lunch at a local diner and took a short walk before heading home.

*  *  *

Over the next month, Mike and Eve's relationship blossomed while they shared their favorite activities with each other. Mike took Eve to the racetrack and on small hiking trips. Mike joined Eve on some of her morning runs and she taught him the basics of how to play tennis. Everything seemed to be working out for them and they were practically joined at the hip.

# Chapter 26

There was a knock at Eve's office door. "Come in," announced Eve.

Anna, one of Eve's team members, opened the door and peeked inside the office. "I'm not disturbing you, am I?"

"No, don't be silly, come in. What do you need?"

"You're still dating Detective McGarrett, right?"

"Yes."

"Well, I don't want to scare you, but I was in the cafeteria and saw him on the news talking about some hostage situation." Eve's eyes widened. "Don't be alarmed, Ms. Townsend, he's okay."

"Oh, thank goodness." Eve exhaled a sigh of relief.

"He's a hero yet again, it seems," continued Anna.

"Really? What did he do now?" Eve felt a mixture of pride and fear all at the same time.

"He aided in the rescue of hostages; a couple of thugs tried to hold up a convenience store. No one got hurt. Everyone is safe and sound, including Detective McGarrett. I just figured you'd want to know about it."

"Yes, thank you, Anna."

"No problem. You're a lucky woman, Eve. Good looks and bravery all rolled into one."

"I *am* lucky." A smile spread across Eve's face.

"Well, *he's* damned lucky too, I might add. You're beautiful, smart and strong. The two of you make a great couple."

Eve was touched by the sentiments. "That's very kind, thank you."

"You're welcome, but I just call it like I see them. I'll get out of your hair now."

After Anna left, Eve started to think about the hostage situation. Sure, Mike was okay, *this time*, but the events could have easily turned out very differently. A sliver of fear coursed through her body. It had only been a couple of months since she and Mike started dating, but they were a part of each other's lives now. He *is* a detective, which is how they met in the first place, but she didn't know what she would do if something ever happened to him. Did he always have to be the hero? Would she be able to deal with him being in constant danger? *Stop it! You're overreacting.* Eve decided to call Mike, just to hear his voice and confirm for herself that he was okay.

Mike felt his phone buzzing in his pocket. Eve's name and beautiful face displayed across the screen. He smiled as he answered. "Hey pretty lady, what can I do for you?"

"Hey handsome, I just needed to hear your voice."

Mike sensed an uneasiness as Eve spoke. "Is everything okay, Eve? What's wrong...? Oh, you saw the news, didn't you?"

"Well, one of my coworkers did and filled me in about the hostage situation. I just needed to make sure you were okay."

"I'm fine, babe." Mike tried to assuage Eve's fear but he could sense it wasn't working. "Hey, I'm on my way back to the station and I have to write up my report. How about I stop by your apartment this evening and we can talk about this. I can tell you're still worried."

"I'm not hiding it very well, am I?"

"No, I can hear it in your voice. But we'll talk tonight, okay? Please don't stress about this."

"I'll try not to. I'm proud of you. I'll see you later. Bye, sweetie."

"Thanks. Bye, pretty lady."

After Mike hung up, Eve tried to focus on her projects. No need to work herself up when Mike and all of the hostages were okay.

* * *

Mike arrived at Eve's just after five thirty in the evening and she was in a much better place emotionally after they last spoke. He greeted her with a passionate kiss. "Wow, what was that for?" she asked, still enveloped in his arms.

"It felt like you needed that, and so did I, to be honest." He leaned in to rub her nose with his.

"You're right, but I'll always need that, regardless of the situation."

"You seem better, more relaxed. Are you sure you're okay? Because, as you can see, I am safe and sound, and in one piece. Come, let's sit down." Mike led Eve over to the sofa and sat her on his lap. She wrapped her arms around him and looked down at him adoringly. Her favorite place to be was in Mike's arms. He stroked the side of her face with the back of his hands. "So, that hostage situation really scared you, didn't it?" he asked.

She nodded her head yes. "Of course it did. It must have been scary for you too."

"A little, but I'm trained to deal with those types of situations, Eve. I *am* a detective, babe. It's my job to protect the innocent."

"I know, and you're very good at it, having been rescued by you myself."

"But it must have brought up some bad memories for you though, and made you think about the shooting?"

"Yeah, it mostly reminded me just how dangerous your job is, but I also had to remind myself that it's how we met and I might not be alive today if you weren't so good at what you do."

"But that doesn't exactly make it any easier for you to deal with, does it?"

"No, and I'm sure it will get easier... but… must you *always* be the hero? Couldn't someone else have gone inside to take down the bad guys?"

"In this case, I guess so. Sam, for instance, could have taken point, but it's not in my nature to take a backseat, Eve. I hope you can understand that and trust that I will make the correct decisions for the situation I'm dealt with at the time."

She let out a long sigh. "I can and I will, as long as you promise me that you won't take any *unnecessary* risks."

"I can do that. I'm lucky; I have a damn good partner to rely on, so no unnecessary risks are needed."

"And I need you to trust me too."

"In what way?" Mike asked, perplexed.

"To let me know if a case gets too hairy. I don't want you to keep things from me or lie to me under the guise of 'protecting' me, as men *love* to do. It always causes more harm than good."

"Eve, you know that I can't always discuss the details of a case with you."

"I don't want details of cases, Mike. I want to know how the cases are *affecting* you or if they might impact *our* lives in some way. I'm a big girl and I can handle anything, no matter how bad it might seem, as long as *we* are okay."

"I know that you're strong, Eve. So yes, I promise to trust and be honest with you."

"Thank you. Okay, enough talk." Eve leaned in, twisted her fingers into Mike's hair and kissed him passionately. He easily returned the favor. All of the raw emotions from the day came to the forefront, and they lost themselves in each other.

Eve decided to put her fears aside and focus on her and Mike's future together instead. She had no choice; she had fallen in love with him.

* * *

Kinsey and Grace waited anxiously for Eve to arrive for their lunch date. The girls were also excited to spend more time with Eve, *away* from the guys. They immediately bonded with her at the party and were eager to jumpstart their newfound friendship. Eve arrived at the restaurant, scanned the room and spotted Grace waving her over.

"Hey girls, sorry I'm a little late. I'm still getting used to commuting in this city." They hugged and kissed.

"Don't worry about it, we weren't waiting long," Kinsey replied.

"I have to say I was really looking forward to this," Eve said.

"So were we," Grace added, "It's nice to just have girl time."

The waiter appeared and was more than happy to take their orders. It wasn't luck that he got their table. He had to bargain away one of his kidneys to one of the waitresses for the chance to wait on these three beauties. He was hoping to be lucky enough to get a number. He had his favorite but will be disappointed to discover that none of the ladies are available. He openly flirted with them before heading off to place their orders with the chef.

"Ooooh, I think you have an admirer, Eve," Kinsey teased.

"Oh stop, he was flirting with all three of us."

"But with *you* the most," Kinsey insisted, "I think he likes you."

"Unfortunately for him, my heart belongs to Mike."

"Speaking of Mike," Grace chimed in, "we're both so happy he found you. We've never seen that man happier."

"He makes me very happy, too. It's nice to be able to talk about it with people who know him, other than his parents. You can give me a different perspective and can relate to dating detectives." Eve needed some guidance dealing with the hazards of Mike's job. Kinsey and Grace could provide her with that.

"Eve, are you okay with Mike's profession?" Kinsey asked, sensing a bit of concern in Eve's voice.

"Yes, actually, I am, but it scares me sometimes. Doesn't it scare the two of you?"

"Of course, but not as much now as before," answered Grace.

"How do you handle it?"

Kinsey and Grace looked at each other. They sympathized with Eve's plight. She's afraid of losing her man. "We just do, sweetie, with a lot of patience and understanding. We don't have a choice if want to be with Dan and Marty," Grace replied.

"And we can see why you're extra concerned, given Mike's propensity for heroics," stated Kinsey.

"Tell me about it," said Eve, "I guess it's hypocritical of me to wish Mike did something else. If he wasn't such a great detective, we never would have met. I love him and I don't want anything to happen to him."

Grace reached across the table to hold Eve's hand. "That's understandable and a reasonable reaction. Listen—don't beat yourself up about this. You are entitled to your feelings. It will just take some time for you to work through them. Just don't bottle it up inside. We're here for you if you need us, and Mike is, too."

"Oh, I wasn't planning on discussing this with Mike—well, not *again*, anyway."

"Why not? Are you afraid of how he'll react?" Kinsey asked.

"No, I don't want to worry him and make him self-conscious while he's out in the field. It can become more of a distraction, which would really put him in danger."

"Okay, but you can still talk to us if you need to."

"Thanks—"

"Ahem." The waiter cleared his throat upon arriving with their drinks. Eve didn't mind that their conversation was interrupted. The girls had helped her work through some issues and they were starving. The waiter took their orders while continuing to flirt with them.

After the waiter left, Eve glanced at Kinsey. "What did I tell you?" Kinsey quickly announced. "He likes you, Eve." Eve and Grace just shook their heads in defeat. There was no convincing Kinsey otherwise.

"Now, back to what we were discussing before he interrupted us," Grace interjected. "I hope we were able to help you, Eve?"

"Oh, yes. It helps just knowing there's someone who can relate to what I'm struggling with. I appreciate it more than you know. But enough about me, what do you girls do?"

"Well, I have a Bachelor's in computer science," offered Kinsey, "I work in the Cybercrime division of my company."

"Ooh, how exciting. Do you get to catch bad guys on a regular basis?" Eve asked.

"Well, I focus more on making sure I keep the bad guys out of our systems so I don't have to deal with them personally, thank goodness."

"You must be pretty busy given the increase in corporate hacking these days," Eve added.

"Tell me about it, it seems to get worse and worse each day."

"So what about you Grace?"

"I'm a Kindergarten school teacher."

"Aw, it must be nice working with little ones."

"It is, and very rewarding. To get to mold them at the early stages of their learning development, there are just no words to describe it. I love it."

Eve smiled. "I can see it written all over your face as you spoke about them. It's obvious how much you love your students. I'm so glad we got to do this, girls."

"We are too, Eve," stated Grace, and Kinsey nodded in agreement.

# Chapter 27

Mike and Eve were relaxing at the ranch and Mike decided to ask Eve a very special question. "Eve, you know that I love you very much, right?"

"Of course I do. I feel it every time we're together and you make sure to tell me, *frequently*, I might add. So, why would you need to ask me that?"

"I need something from you and I want to get you in the right frame of mind, so bear with me please, because I have a couple of questions that I'd like you to answer."

"A *couple* of questions? Intriguing..."

Mike smiled. "Question number one, when we're not together, do you wish that we were?"

"Always. I miss you when you're not with me."

"Good answer."

"I thought so, it was an easy one."

Mike smiled again. "Here's question number two: When you go to sleep at night and awake in the morning, do you wish that I was with you holding you in my arms?"

"Most definitely."

"That's two for two, you're on a roll babe... and I feel the same, by the way."

"Of course you do," she quipped, and threw Mike a wink.

"Question number three, will you marry me?" Mike reached into his pocket and produced a little black box. He opened it to reveal a beautiful fourteen-karat white gold diamond ring.

Eve gasped and her mouth dropped open. Caught up in Mike's playful banter, she was shocked by his sudden and serious proposal. "Mike, what is this? I didn't expect... I don't know what to say."

"You should say yes, of course," Mike offered, dangling the diamond ring in front of her teasingly.

"But I... I don't think—" She stopped abruptly.

Mike put the ring down, moved closer to Eve, and placed her hands in his while trying to ignore the knot that was forming in his stomach. "Hey babe, talk to me. Why are you hesitating? You *do* love me, right?"

"Of course, you *know* I do, but don't you think it's too soon for us to be talking about marriage? We've only known each other for three months. Most people barely get engaged after a year of dating, and we're *still* getting to know each other."

"I don't agree, Eve. There's no set timetable when it comes to love. We're perfect for each other. It's as if we've known each other forever, and I firmly believe that we are destined to be together."

His heartfelt plea almost changed her mind especially since she wanted to marry Mike, more than anything, but Eve had to follow her instincts. "I agree, but that doesn't mean we should make hasty decisions that could ruin what we have, and what we could possibly have in the future. Yes, we're in love, but we should also take the time to really get to know each other, just as we did before making love for the first time. Our whirlwind romance is scary enough as it is, so why put the added pressure of marriage on our plates so soon into the relationship? We have plenty of time, our entire lives."

"So you're not saying that you *don't* want to marry me, just that we should wait a while?"

"That's exactly what I'm saying, sweetie. I would love to become Mrs. Michael McGarrett. I just don't want us to do something that we're not ready for and that we might regret."

Relief washed over Mike. He understood Eve's point, thought about it for a moment and came up with a compromise. "Well... then would you consider moving in with me?"

"What?"

"Hear me out. Living together would allow us the additional time to get to know each other and really learn how to live with each other under the same roof."

Eve had to admit that Mike was not one to give up easily. Being with Mike on a daily basis did sound appealing. "Okay... I'll think about it."

"Thanks, babe." Mike kissed Eve, grateful that she didn't immediately shoot down his second proposal.

* * *

Eve thought it over for a couple of days and decided to accept Mike's proposal to move in with him. She would keep her apartment just in case the new arrangement didn't work out and she needed someplace to retreat to, plus they could also use it as a getaway to have some time for themselves in the city.

* * *

Mike crept up behind Eve as she was packing her clothes and slipped his arms around her waist. "Are you almost done yet?" he asked while nuzzling her neck.

"Mike, I thought you were going to *help* me pack."

"I am helping," he responded as he continued to deliver kisses up and down her neck.

Eve groaned with pleasure from his touch. "How is this helping?"

"Well, moving can be stressful, so I'm providing you stress relief."

Eve had to chuckle at his feeble excuse to slack off and fool around. His hands started to roam and Eve quickly grabbed them. If she didn't stop him they'd never finish. "Michael McGarrett, behave yourself!" she admonished.

"I don't want to behave." Eve turned to face him. "I want to kiss you," Mike continued.

"If I give you one kiss, will you be satisfied enough to get to work?"

"I'll *never* be satisfied with just *one* kiss from you, Eve."

"You're so spoiled."

"Well, whose fault is that?"

"Oh my goodness, *fine*, you can have one kiss. But don't get carried away."

A big smile spread across Mike's face. He'd won this round and didn't waste any time collecting his prize, and, of course, had every intention of getting *very* carried away. He pulled Eve closer and kissed her deeply. His hands resumed roaming up and down her back in a caressing motion that made Eve weak in the knees. Eve pulled away and held herself at arm's length.

"Whoa there, cowboy, we have a lot more work to do. Do you want me to move in with you or not?"

"More than anything, babe."

"Really, even more than stealing kisses? Because I can stop packing and just remain here and kiss you all afternoon, then send you back home *alone*." Eve eyed him with a wry smile.

Mike squinted at her. "I see where you're going with this."

"I thought you might. So are you going to help me or not? The quicker we get this done, the more time we'll have together at home in *our* bed."

Mike's eyes gleamed. "Where do you want me to start?" he quickly acquiesced.

"Why not start with those two top drawers?"

Eve watched as Mike opened the first drawer. The smile returned as his eyes roamed over Eve's intimate apparel. "Anything for you, babe," he replied.

"That's what I thought," Eve answered.

Mike thoroughly enjoyed his newfound duties, but didn't linger as he would have done originally. Visions of Eve wearing one of those nighties, but more importantly, visions of him ripping them off her that evening spurred him into action. They finished packing and headed out.

Eve had to admit that she was excited as they pulled up to the ranch house. It was her home now, with Mike. They grabbed some boxes from Mike's truck and carried them to the porch. Mike put the key in the door, instructed Eve to wait on the porch and then placed the boxes inside. Then he turned around and swept Eve up in his arms.

"Mike, what are you doing?"

"I'm going to carry you over the threshold."

"That's for your bride, after you've gotten married."

"Well then, practice makes perfect." He carried her inside and spun her around in a circle while Eve squealed with delight with a firm grip around Mike's neck. "Welcome home, pretty lady," he announced. Finally, Eve was here, and Mike was overjoyed that he'd get to fall asleep and wake up with this beautiful woman every day.

Eve leaned in and kissed him. "Thank you, babe."

"Before we get you all settled and moved in, I'm going to make you a promise. If after three months of living together we're still madly in love, I will propose to you again, and hope that I get the answer I long for." Eve just smiled, slightly overwhelmed by how her life had changed in just three months. Mike carried Eve directly into the bedroom. Unpacking would have to take a backseat for now.

* * *

Mike and Eve had survived their first week under the same roof, and pretty much spent every spare moment alone in bed. They felt like newlyweds and couldn't get enough of each other.

"Eve, hurry up, the kids will start arriving soon." Eve was dressing in the bedroom while Mike prepared for the arrival of the trick-or-treaters.

"I'm almost done." Eve grabbed her hat and emerged from their bedroom. Eve was breathtaking in her Halloween costume. "So… what do you think?" she asked after putting on her hat.

"Are you kidding me? You're gorgeous, my little cowgirl. You're lucky children are on the way, or we wouldn't even be talking right now. These kids are going to get more of a treat than they bargained for, especially with that mini jean skirt."

"I'm glad you like it. You don't look so bad yourself, cowboy." The doorbell rang, and they could hear the clatter of kids' voices. "The first arrivals are here; I'll grab the bucket of candy."

Mike was right on target—the kids were very appreciative of their costumes and house decorations. Some of the parents also showed signs of appreciation, which Eve took in stride. Mike, on the other hand, was not happy with the attention thrown in Eve's direction, and his displeasure was written all over his face.

"You can stop scowling now," Eve said, after they handed out the last of the candy.

"You're gonna tell me it wasn't obvious that some of those fathers were ogling you?"

"Of course I noticed. Some of the mothers were ogling you too, but *they're* not important, *we* are. Besides, I was probably a surprise for them. They're not exactly used to you having a partner in crime, in residence, Mr. Bachelor, you probably never even handed out candy before, have you?"

"You're right... as usual." Mike flashed a big smile. "See, the scowl is gone."

"That's much better. Now let's go. We don't want to be late for Dan and Grace's party. Kinsey and I want to get there a little early to see if Grace needs some help with any last-minute preparations."

When Mike and Eve arrived at the party, Dan greeted them at the door. "You two look great."

"Thanks man, nice Batman costume," Mike replied.

"Where is Grace?" Eve asked, while hugging Dan hello.

"She's upstairs, waiting for you. I'll send Kinsey up too, once she and Marty arrive."

"Okay, see you later, babe." Eve gave Mike a quick peck before heading upstairs. She knocked on Grace's bedroom door. "Hey Grace, it's Eve. Can I come in?"

"Yes, yes, come." Eve entered and they both eyed each other.

"Sexy Robin, I should have guessed!" exclaimed Eve. "You and Dan are perfect as Batman and Robin."

"Thanks sweetie." Grace beamed as she hugged Eve. "But check *you* out. Sexy cowgirl... Mike must be beside himself."

"Oh, he is, believe me." They chuckled amongst themselves just as Kinsey knocked on the door.

"What's all the laughing about in there?" she called out.

"Get in here, Kinsey," responded Grace.

Kinsey entered and both Grace and Eve let out a whistle in unison. "Look out, sexy nurse in the house," exclaimed Eve.

"*Me*, look at the two of you," she responded. "The guys are in trouble for sure."

"That's exactly what we were laughing about. So how do I look? Am I a presentable hostess?" Grace asked, striking a pose.

"Just gorgeous," Kinsey replied.

"Great, I'll grab my purse and we can head downstairs."

The men were deep in conversation when they noticed the girls descending the stairs. Mike, Dan and Marty all stared at their beautiful women. Marty was also transfixed at the sight of Eve in her cowgirl costume. She was absolutely beautiful. He had an unexpected but instant physical reaction to her, and desire coursed through his veins. He quickly diverted his gaze to Kinsey as the girls reached them. He pulled Kinsey into his arms and planted a big kiss on her.

"Whoa Doc, you missed me already? I only left you about five minutes ago."

"How could I resist my sexy nurse?" he replied nervously, trying to push Eve's image out of his mind.

The girls glanced at each other, smiling at their private joke.

"What's with the looks?" Dan asked, not wanting to be kept out of the loop.

"Don't you worry about it, sweetie," Grace answered deftly and turned her attention to Mike and Marty. "The two of you look very handsome." Dan just shook his head in defeat.

"Thanks, Grace, you look beautiful," Mike replied.

"Yeah Grace, Dan had better stick close tonight," stated Marty, "and…you look lovely too, Eve," he added.

Both Eve and Grace thanked Marty. "Now you all go mingle and enjoy yourselves," added Grace. "Dan and I have to make the rounds, so we'll catch up to you later." As Dan and Grace walked away to greet other guests, Marty took the opportunity to extricate himself and Kinsey from Mike and Eve. He needed to put some distance between them.

"Looks like it's just you and me, cowboy," announced Eve.

"That's just fine with me. I've wanted to get you alone ever since we arrived." Mike pulled Eve close and they kissed little flirty kisses and giggled like kids.

Marty and Kinsey watched them from across the room, but the distance did nothing to abate his attraction for Eve. "Don't they look adorable?" Kinsey asked. "I'm so happy Mike found her."

"Yeah, adorable... cowboy and cowgirl, *how original.* He lives in a ranch house for goodness' sake. He couldn't come up with something else?"

"What is your problem, Marty?"

He turned to face Kinsey. "Listen, I wouldn't get too happy with your newfound friendship with Eve just yet if I were you. That relationship probably won't last long anyway. She'll probably be out of the ranch and back in her own apartment in no time."

Kinsey gave Marty a sharp look. "What would make you say such a thing?"

His unexpected desire for Eve unnerved him, and Marty was not too keen on Eve and Kinsey getting so close, which might bring him into constant proximity with her as well. "When was the last time Mike had a *real* relationship, if *ever*? Why should Eve be any different from the other gorgeous women he's had on his arm?" he answered. These were his actual true feelings, which he had no intention of sharing again after the last time he stuck his foot in his mouth when first meeting Eve, but he needed to say something to cover his ass.

"*Martin Dent*, that's a terrible thing to say. Eve *is* different because Mike actually *loves* her. She's here to stay, so get used to it," admonished Kinsey.

"I need a drink, do you want one?" he snapped, done with the conversation.

"Sure..." Kinsey responded as Marty stalked off. She was left wondering what the hell that was all about.

Mike and Eve watched Marty stomp off toward the bar. "What's up with him?" Eve asked.

Mike shook his head. "Who the hell knows with Marty sometimes?"

"I'm going to go see if Kinsey is okay."

"I knew that was coming. Oh, go ahead, and I'll go see what's up with Marty."

Eve made her way over to Kinsey, who was sulking at Marty's unkind words and his abrupt departure. It was clear he didn't want to hear anything she had to say on the matter, and he pretty much dismissed her by walking off.

"Kinsey, is everything okay? We saw Marty stomp off. Mike went to check on him."

"I don't know what's eating him *this time*. He made some offhand remark about you and Mike again, but *please* don't say anything to Mike. I don't want them getting into it at Grace and Dan's party."

"Don't worry, I won't. Should I even ask what Marty said?"

"Please don't, I don't want to upset you."

"It's *that* bad?"

"Well, it's *that* petty and doesn't warrant repeating. What he said wasn't against you personally, rather more against Mike, but what's new? I just don't understand what it is about Mike that sets Marty off, but I set him straight, which is why he stalked off, supposedly getting us drinks. He hasn't returned, so maybe Mike is talking some sense to him. I just hope he checks himself and doesn't say anything stupid like he did when we all first met you."

Grace appeared at the tail end of the conversation. "Hey, what's up? Where are the boys?"

"We thought Dan was with you," replied Eve.

"He went to get something to drink."

"Then he's probably with the other two," answered Kinsey. "That's where Marty was supposedly headed, and Mike followed suit."

"Well, maybe it's a good thing Dan is with them," said Eve.

"Why is that?" asked Grace.

Kinsey sighed. "Marty is being *Marty*, let's just leave it at that, please," she replied, shaking her head. Grace flashed Eve a concerned look but decided to let it go for now.

Dan found Mike and Marty at the bar, discussing work. Marty had deftly maneuvered the conversation with Mike to the Gennaro case as a distraction. The last thing he needed was for Mike to know what he said to Kinsey and that he had the hots for Eve.

Mike was complaining about how every lead he and Sam found turned up as dead ends. "It was as if the Gennaros were one step ahead of us," he continued, "removing all possible witnesses that could testify against them. As far as Sam and I are concerned, these actions only reinforced our suspicions. If we weren't on the right track, Lucas Coles wouldn't be dead and the bank managers wouldn't have disappeared. Unfortunately, this also fueled the chief's desire to lock the Gennaro family away and—" Mike stopped abruptly and turned around at the sound of Eve's voice, so he ended the conversation. "Look, the girls are coming this way, so we need to the change the topic. I don't want Eve to hear us talking about the Gennaros, and most definitely not about Lucas Coles. I don't want to bring up memories of the shooting for her when she's worked so hard to move past it."

"Sure, man, we understand," Dan replied.

"Hey guys, we thought you were bringing us drinks," announced Grace, "but you just left us hanging instead. What's up with that?"

Dan said, "Sorry, we got to talking shop, you know how it goes."

Eve approached Mike from behind and wrapped her arms around his waist. He turned his face to meet hers and she kissed his cheek. Mike seemed tense, and she searched his face. "Is everything okay?" she whispered. Eve was concerned with Marty's tantrum and wondered if he repeated the inappropriate comments he made to Kinsey about them to Mike. She didn't realize Mike had another reason to be tense.

"Everything is cool, babe."

"Are you sure?"

"Yeah..."

Eve glanced at Marty, then back at Mike but decided to let it go. Marty seemed to have calmed down and Kinsey was at his side, so there was no need to press the issue. She decided not to mention the comments to Mike because she didn't want to upset him. She recalled the hurt and worried look on his face when she rejected his marriage proposal, and it tugged at her heart. Eve didn't want Marty's unkind words to cause Mike to doubt her feelings for him. She agreed to move in with him and they were very happy with this next phase of their relationship. She loved Mike and she wasn't going anywhere. Eve and Mike rejoined the others in conversation and the remainder of the evening proceeded as if nothing ever happened.

* * *

"I guess I can finally get out of this costume," said Eve once they returned home.

"Hold on there," Mike responded, grabbing Eve by the waist and turning her around to face him, "I thought I could help you with that."

"Oh really," she responded while wrapping her arms around Mike's neck as they stared lovingly into each other's eyes.

Mike responded by kissing Eve. They had talked enough all day *and* evening. All he wanted to do was rip that costume off and make love to her. Eve received his message loud and clear when she found herself being lifted off the ground and carried into the bedroom.

# *Chapter 28*

Eve felt particularly thankful on this Thanksgiving Day. She got to watch the Macy's Thanksgiving Day Parade with Mike in person, for the first time. It would be the first of many new holiday experiences that Mike planned on introducing her to. Afterward, they drove up to Mike's parents' home, where Eve helped Carla to prepare a Thanksgiving feast to remember. While the ladies cooked, Mike and his father continued with one of their chess games. Mike was again exempt from helping Carla prepare the meal, but he figured this gave Eve more quality time with his mom, something he knew they both needed.

"Eve dear, I see that you and my Mikey are doing okay."

Eve stopped peeling the sweet potatoes and looked up at Carla. The wide grin on her face was enough of an answer, but she provided Carla with a response nonetheless. "Yes, we are. Better than okay, in fact."

"I'm pleased, but not surprised. Mikey has never been happier, and I know that's all because of you."

"I've never been happier either." Eve glanced around and lowered her voice. "Can I tell you something in confidence, Mama Carla?"

"Of course, dear."

"Mike asked me to marry him."

"What? Wait, the two of you are engaged? Why didn't you say anything? Where's the ring?"

"Oh no, no, we're not engaged yet."

"Well, I don't understand..."

"Don't be upset, but I turned him down. I thought it was too soon. That's why we decided to move in together instead to give us the time to really get to know each other."

"I see... I'm surprised Mikey didn't mention this to me, and he seems okay, but… I'm sure he was not happy that you turned down his proposal."

"No, he wasn't, but he understood. It was his idea that we move in together. He's hoping to convince me at a later date that we should get married."

"Do you *need* convincing? Don't you want to marry my son?"

"Of course I do. I want to marry him more than anything. It's the timing I have an issue with. I just don't want us to do something we're not equipped to handle. I don't want anything to ruin what we have now."

"So you don't want to rush things."

"Exactly. My life has been turned upside down for the last couple of months. I just want to catch my breath and enjoy my new life with Mike."

"I understand, sweetie. Like you said, so many things have changed for you simultaneously. If you didn't have to deal with your move, the new job, and that *God-awful shooting*, then maybe the whirlwind romance wouldn't freak you out so much."

"Isn't it crazy that Mike and I are already discussing marriage after dating for only three months?"

"Listen, I'm going to give you the same advice I gave my son when you first started dating. There is no timetable on love. Each couple and their relationship is different, so you have to make decisions that are best for the two of you... You and Mikey will be okay."

Eve put down the peeler and potatoes, walked over to Carla and hugged her. "Thanks, Mama Carla. I needed someone to talk to about this. I'm glad it was you."

"I'm glad too, dear."


"So Dad, when do I get to win one of these chess games?"

"When you learn to play better."

"Thanks a lot."

"I just call it like I see it."

Mike smirked, while making his next move. "You know, I asked Eve to marry me."

Mark's head snapped up. "Say what?"

"You heard me," replied Mike, grinning.

"Okay, so what's the verdict?"

"She said no, for *now* anyway."

"Did you propose before or after you moved in together?"

"Before; she moved in as a compromise. So we could get to know each other better."

"So that's what she was concerned about when turning you down?"

"Yeah... and that we could be rushing things. I think she's overwhelmed by everything she's experienced since moving to New York six months ago. So I'll wait and make another attempt on New Year's Eve."

"You're going to propose at the New Year's Eve party in front of *everyone*?" Mark asked, incredulous. "You know she's a little shy. Why would you put her on the spot like that?"

"Well, I didn't look at it that way. But I warned her that I was going to propose again in three months. So she knows it's happening."

"But she doesn't know it's happening at the party in front of *everyone*. You might want to rethink that plan of yours, Son."

"Okay, okay, I'll play it by ear. I mean we do live together now, so I should have a better sense of how she's feeling by then."

"If you say so. It's your move," replied Mark.

"What? When did you make yours?"

"I *can* do two things at the same time, you know."

Mike perused the chessboard. "Oh, I guess I won't be winning this game either, huh?"

"Nope, it doesn't look like it, but there's always the next time."

"That's what you always say." Mike sulked while his father chuckled at his expense.


"So, who is going to say grace before we eat this wonderful meal?" Carla asked.

"I will," volunteered Mike. Everyone joined hands. Mike glanced over at Eve, squeezed her hand and then gave her a quick wink. They closed their eyes and lowered their heads. "Blessed Father," Mike began, "we are thankful for this opportunity to share this special day with each other as a family. I am always thankful for my wonderful parents and the three of us are especially thankful for Eve, the newest addition to our quirky crew." Everyone chuckled and Mike squeezed Eve's hand again. "This is Eve's first Thanksgiving away from her own family and we are honored to fold her into ours. Lord, also, please look after those who aren't as blessed and lucky as we are, which should remind us to never take what we have for granted. Amen."

"Amen," responded Carla, Mark, and Eve in unison.

"That was beautiful, Mike," Eve whispered. "Thank you."

Mike smiled.

* * *

Black Friday, the day after Thanksgiving, was the official countdown to Christmas, and Eve was nervous about what to get Mike as a gift. She wanted it to be special, since it was their first Christmas together.

"Eve, honey, are you okay? You seem lost in thought. Christmas shopping is supposed to be fun," stated Kinsey.

Grace said, "Actually, any kind of shopping is supposed to be fun."

"I know, ladies, but I want to find the perfect gift for Mike. It is our first Christmas together."

"Well, don't put pressure on yourself. I'm sure Mike will love anything you give him because it's coming from you, plus you still have a month to decide," reminded Grace.

"You're absolutely right… and just think, six months ago we didn't even know each other and here we are picking out Christmas gifts together. I can't imagine not having any of you in my life."

"We feel the same way, sweetie," replied Kinsey. Both Grace and Kinsey embraced Eve in a hug, and then proceeded to attempt to find the best gifts for their loved ones.

After shopping the entire day, Eve still hadn't found the right gift for Mike, but was able to check a couple of people off her list, so all was not lost. By the end of it all, Eve knew exactly what she wanted to give Mike, and it was not something she could find in any store.

* * *

While Eve was out shopping with the girls Mike decided to take advantage of this time to shop for her present, but he was experiencing the same angst as Eve, trying to determine the perfect gift for her. He didn't bother discussing it with the guys, as he knew they would be no help, except for maybe Sam, who knew Eve more personally than Dan and Marty. If Mike hit a roadblock, he would solicit Sam's opinion.

He was perusing through a jewelry store on the East Side and stopped in his tracks. He was completed captivated, much like when he saw Eve for the first time. He knew it was perfect.

The salesperson approached Mike. "Can I help you, sir? Would you like to see take a closer look at that one?" she asked, anticipating an easy sale.

Mike glanced up at her nametag. "Yes, thank you, Elena," he replied.

Elena unlocked the glass case and removed a beautiful gold chain necklace with an infinity symbol attached. It sparkled like Eve's eyes, Mike thought. "Is this for someone special?" Elena asked.

"Yes, for someone *very* special, and it's perfect for her. I'll take it."

"I'm sure she'll love it. Follow me to the register and I'll ring this up for you." As Mike followed suit, Elena thought, *I wish all of my sales were this easy. Then this would be a great holiday season.* She placed the necklace inside of a small jewelry box. "Would you like me to gift wrap it for you?" she asked as Mike handed her his credit card.

"No, thank you, I want to personally gift wrap this gift."

Elena rang up the charge and Mike signed the receipt. "Well, she is a lucky lady to have someone love her so much." Elena handed Mike his credit card, placed the jewelry box inside a shopping bag and handed it to him.

"Believe me, I'm the lucky one," Mike replied just before leaving the store.

* * *

Stephanie Gennaro burst into the house like a tornado in search of her father. "DAD," she yelled at the top of her lungs.

Nicholas winced at the sound of his sister's voice, indicating her return home from school for the Christmas break. He would have to contend with her insufferable need to have anything she wanted for damn near an entire month. But maybe her arrival was fortuitous, as it would give their father someone else to focus on instead of his own recent failures. Stephanie was always the favorite anyway, made obvious by the fact that Angelo never denied her whatever she asked for. The youngest and only daughter was spoiled rotten. Talk about a cliché. Then Nicholas heard Angelo greet Stephanie with love and affection, behavior that was never bestowed upon him.

"Hi Daddy, did you miss me?"

"Of course I did, my little sweet pea. I'm just glad I get to have you back home for an entire month." Stephanie looked just like her mother, his dear Lily, and Stephanie's presence always took him back to a time when he and Lily were young and happy. "I take it the chauffer is still gathering your belongings from the car?"

"Yes, and he knows to take them up to my room. I hope I didn't over pack. Where are my brothers? Why aren't they here to welcome me home?" Stephanie asked, always needing to be the center of everyone's attention.

"Anthony is taking care of business at the office, and Nicholas, well, he's upstairs somewhere, sulking as usual, and so I get to have you all to myself."

Stephanie cooed at her father's devotion. "I see nothing has changed. So what did Nick do now?"

"Nothing you need to worry your pretty little head about. Come. Join me in the dining room for lunch. I had the cook prepare all of your favorites."

"You're too good to me, Daddy!"

Nicholas heard this entire exchange while listening at the top of the stairwell. His *little sweet pea.* He wanted to barf. He was also *so* hungry he could gnaw his fingers off, but didn't dare join those two for lunch and be succumbed to their dribble. He'd wait for Tony to return from the office before acknowledging his sister's arrival.

* * *

"That freakin' Sam gets to be on vacation in hot Atlanta while we're here in cold ass New York inundated with drunken assholes and depressed, suicidal victims," complained Marty.

Dan said, "He is allowed to visit with his family, you know. He's only been gone a week, for Christ's sake."

"Yeah man, don't be a hater," added Mike.

Marty just shot them dirty looks while the boys laughed at his expense, *once again.* He was so tired of them.

"Are you fools always like this?" asked Greg.

"Yep, so get used to it. You're stuck with us while we're partnered up until Sam returns," answered Mike.

"Well, Marty is right about one thing. People lose their minds around the holidays, and Christmas Eve is no joke," Greg replied. "Today was especially off the charts."

"Tell me about it. But it's almost over, and after I finish up this paperwork I'm headed home to my girl." Mike was all smiles at the mere thought of Eve.

"This is unchartered territory for you, isn't it, Mike, spending the holidays with just *one* woman?" Marty meant this as a dig, of course, but even *he* couldn't get under Mike's skin today.

"Correction, one *special* woman, and don't you forget it," Mike answered.

310

* * *

Mike and Eve were relaxing on their sofa admiring their tree on Christmas Eve. The blinking lights were almost hypnotic as they reveled in their solitude and peaceful quiet. It had been a busy couple of days, delivering gifts to friends and family, and they had racked up a multitude of gifts themselves that they proudly displayed under their beautifully decorated Christmas tree. They felt very blessed as they turned in for the night.

Eve opened her eyes to find Mike staring right at her. "Good morning, sweetie. Merry Christmas," she said.

"Merry Christmas *indeed*," Mike replied, then leaned in and gave Eve a kiss. "I've been waiting for you to wake up," he continued, grinning from ear to ear. "I almost took measures into my own hands."

"I can see that. You want to go and open up the gifts, don't you?"

"Yes," he replied instantly.

Eve laughed. "What are you, *four*?"

"Yep, on Christmas morning I am, so come on, woman." Mike leapt out of bed, threw the covers off Eve, grabbed her hands and pulled her out of the bed.

"Okay, okay, I'm coming," Eve protested as Mike continued to guide her into the living room until they were in front of the tree.

Mike immediately knelt down on his knees. "I'll start separating the gifts. I'll put yours over there, mine over here, and the ones for the both of us in the middle."

Eve knelt down next to Mike as he worked on the gifts. Mike glanced up to find Eve smiling at him. "What's so funny?" he asked.

"You're just so damn cute. Who would have thought that underneath this strong detective was a little kid at heart?"

"Well, let's just keep that between you and me, alright? I have a reputation to uphold."

"My lips are sealed."

They started on their piles, displaying their gifts to each other and taking pictures. Mike's enthusiasm was infectious, and Eve started to prance around and model some of the lovely pieces of clothing she received. Then they opened the gifts they received as a couple. Mike normally spent Christmas morning alone, so sharing this experience with Eve was a special treat for him, which accounted for his more-than-usual childlike behavior that morning.

They were down to the last two unopened gifts, which Mike had carefully saved for the end, the presents they had bought for each other. Mike looked at Eve adoringly, and all childlike qualities were gone for this special moment as he handed her his gift.

"I hope you like it, Eve. The moment I saw it, I thought of you. It represents what you and our relationship mean to me."

Eve could see the love in Mike's eyes as he spoke. She carefully ripped off the wrapping paper to display a beautiful jewelry box. Her eyes danced as she glanced up at Mike while he watched with anticipation. She opened the box and found herself staring at a lovely gold necklace with an infinity symbol. Eve knew the meaning of the symbol and was touched beyond words. Her eyes glistened with tears.

"It's beautiful, Mike. I love it, and I love you." She leaned forward and gave Mike a thank you kiss he wouldn't soon forget.

"I love you too, Eve, until infinity." They stared into each other's eyes lovingly, and Eve knew at that moment that she wanted to spend the rest of her life with this man.

"Now, you open my gift," Eve demanded as she reached over to retrieve it from under the tree and then handed it to him. "I really hope you like it."

Mike shook the present, as if trying to figure out what it was. "I wonder what's inside," he cooed, the little kid resurfacing.

Eve had to laugh. "Stop shaking it and open it already, silly."

Mike ripped off the wrapping paper and opened up the flat, rectangular box. When he looked inside, he saw the edges of a frame. He smiled and pulled out a beautifully framed drawn portrait of him and Eve. They were embraced in a playful and loving manner while staring into each other's eyes as they were just doing moments earlier. He couldn't stop staring at it. He was enthralled.

"Wow, babe, I *love* it. When did you draw this? How did you do it without me noticing? And where were you hiding it all of this time? This is incredible, thank you, sweetie."

"You're welcome." Eve was grinning from ear to ear. Mike's reaction and appreciation was more than she could hope for. The drawing was a labor of love that represented how Eve felt about Mike and their relationship.

"I love you so much, Eve Townsend." Mike put the portrait safely aside and crawled over to Eve. He embraced her in his arms and kissed her passionately. They spent the remainder of the morning making love on the living room floor, right in front of the Christmas tree.

This was the best Christmas *ever*.

## *Chapter 29*

Mike and Eve's New Year's Eve party was in full swing. Mike approached Eve while she was standing by the bar conversing with Grace.

"Hey babe," he announced, and nuzzled her on the neck. "I have a surprise for you, so don't go anywhere, okay?"

"A surprise? How exciting. Can you give me a hint?"

"Nope, just wait here. You'll know soon enough."

Eve glanced nervously at Grace as Mike walked over to the DJ. He asked him to lower the music and called for everyone's attention because he wanted to say a few words.

"First of all, Eve and I would like to thank everyone for joining us tonight to celebrate the end of a year and ring in the new one. Personally, this was a *great* year for me because I was lucky to have met the lovely Miss Eve Townsend." Mike glanced in Eve's direction and winked at her. Eve was slightly unnerved by the attention as all eyes pinned on her, but she winked back at Mike and just focused on him. "Eve means the world to me," Mike continued, "and has brought so much to my life in the short time that I've known her. Even though we haven't been dating that long, it seems that we were fated to be together, and because of that, I asked Eve to marry me *three months ago*. Being a smart and cautious woman, she turned me down, *but* did agree to move in with me." Mike started to walk toward her. "I also made a promise to Eve that if after three months of living together we were *still* madly in love with each other, I would ask for her hand in marriage again." Eve let out a short gasp as she knew instantly what Mike's surprise was. Once he reached her, Mike got down on one knee and presented her with the ring. "Eve, you are the missing puzzle piece in my life, and my soul mate. I love you, and there is no one else I want to spend my life with. Will you give me the honor of becoming my wife?"

Eve knelt down along with Mike with tears in her eyes. "Yes, it would be my honor to become your wife, Detective." Mike pulled Eve into his arms and they kissed. Everyone started clapping and whistling and they all continued celebrating the coming New Year.

Eve unexpectedly caught Marty staring at her from across the room. She was taken aback not only by the way he was looking at her, but also by the slightly startled look in his eyes when he realized she had busted him. Eve wondered what that was all about. She loved Kinsey, but her boyfriend's treatment toward Mike did not make Eve a fan of his. Now he was watching her and giving her the creeps, so Eve decided to keep her distance from him as much as possible.

"Hey babe, where did you go?"

Eve refocused on Mike at the sound of his voice and smiled. "Oh, I was just thinking about the last six months of my life." This wasn't a lie. It was exactly what she'd been thinking about before she caught Marty eyeing her from across the room. "Just think, six months ago we didn't even know each other existed, and now we're engaged," she added.

"We were meant to be together, Eve. I firmly believe that."

Marty now watched *both* Mike and Eve from across the room. "And you said they wouldn't last," stated Kinsey, breaking Marty's train of thought.

"Say what?" Marty snapped.

"You heard me."

"Please don't start, Kinsey."

"Fine, let's just go and congratulate them."

Marty shot Kinsey a look and decided to keep his mouth shut and to not respond. He did not want to approach Eve after having been caught staring at her. He was afraid of what she was thinking of him and if she would mention the instance to Mike. He reluctantly grabbed Kinsey's hand and made his way across the room with trepidation.

Eve spotted them approaching and a low groan escaped her throat. Mike heard this and glanced in the direction she was looking and spotted Marty and Kinsey. He knew that groan wasn't meant for Kinsey, so Mike wondered what Marty might have done to upset her. It was bad enough that Marty took potshots at him personally, but Mike was not going to allow him to harass Eve.

"Congratulations," announced Kinsey while embracing Eve in a giant bear hug. "I have to say I'm not surprised by the engagement," she continued.

"Thanks, sweetie," replied Eve. "I've never been happier."

"Yeah, congrats," added Marty, appearing and sounding less enthused. He did *not* need this right now. Eve was looking exceptionally hot, and he was still feeling things for her that he shouldn't.

Eve hooked her arms with Mike's and pulled herself closer to him. Mike could feel the tension in Eve's body and noticed that Marty also looked uncomfortable while Kinsey seemed completely unaware. Something was definitely amiss, and he would have to get to the bottom of it, but not tonight. Tonight was about ringing in the New Year with his fiancée. "Thanks, man," Mike replied. "I'm the luckiest man in the world. Now if the two of you will excuse us,

I'd like to dance with my fiancée." Mike sensed he should get some distance between Marty and Eve.

"No problem, you love birds go party," answered Kinsey.

Eve winked at Kinsey as Mike led her to the dance floor. Mike could feel Eve's body relax, and his suspicions were confirmed. Eve was definitely uneasy around Marty, and he'd find out why.

"See, that wasn't so bad now, was it?" Kinsey asked Marty.

"Let's just dance," replied Marty, anxious to distract himself from sexual thoughts of Eve. He took Kinsey's hand and led her to the opposite side of the room from where Mike and Eve were located. *What in the hell is wrong with me?* Marty thought. Kinsey is beautiful and the best girlfriend, better than he deserved. He had better get over his attraction for Eve before Kinsey actually realized that she could do better than *him*.

"Do you mind if I cut in?"

Mike and Eve looked up to Sam's smiling face. "Sam!" exclaimed Eve as she threw herself into his arms.

"Now that's what I call a warm welcome," Sam responded.

"We missed you these past couple of weeks. I hope you had a nice vacation with your family," replied Eve.

"Yeah, man, welcome home," added Mike. "I'm glad you got back in time for the party."

"I hear congratulations are in order. Sorry I missed the proposal. I'm so happy for the two of you."

"Thanks, Sam. I'm glad you're back too," added Eve. "I get worried about this one running off half-cocked on cases without you here to back him up and keep him in check."

"*Please*, he runs off half-cocked even when I'm here," answered Sam.

"Hey!" interjected Mike. "I just convinced this pretty lady into spending the rest of her life with me. Don't you go scaring her into changing her mind," warned Mike.

Eve turned to Mike. "You couldn't scare me away if you tried," she assured him.

"That's good to know," Mike responded, pulling Eve close.

"Alright, that's my cue to leave. You two lovebirds carry on with whatever you were doing before I arrived. I see some honeys I'd like to connect with, myself."

"Okay, Sam, we'll catch up later," said Mike before turning his attention back to Eve. Sam could tell by the look Mike gave him that he had something specific to catch him up on.

"It's almost countdown time, so you might want to remind your guests to get ready," announced Dan.

"Thanks for the heads-up." Mike signaled for the DJ to lower the music. "Everyone, I'd like to inform you that the New Year is fast approaching. So refill your glasses, find that special person and get ready to ring in the New Year." Mike made his way back to Eve just in time for the countdown.

"Ten, nine, eight, seven, six, five, four, three, two, one... HAPPY NEW YEAR!" everyone resounded in unison. Horns blew and streamers flew across the room while "Auld Lang Syne" blared at high volume.

"Happy New Year, Eve."

"Happy New Year, Mike."

Mike pulled Eve into his arms and they kissed passionately. "This will be the best year ever because this is the year you will become my wife, Eve. I love you so much."

"I love you too, sweetie."

* * *

New Year's Eve was a blast, and Mike and Eve spent the following morning lazily in bed, recovering from a very late night as a newly engaged couple. Later that afternoon, Eve decided to call her friends in San Francisco and apprise them of her engagement while Mike called his parents to inform them that Eve had accepted his proposal.

Just as Eve reached for her phone, it started to buzz, then Bonnie's face appeared on the screen. Eve smiled as she answered the call. "You must be a mind reader. Happy New Year, my friend."

"Happy New Year, Eve," Bonnie replied. "How am I a mind reader?"

"I was just about to call you and *voila*, you rang. I have some news to share."

"Oh, good news, I hope."

"Definitely good. I hope you're sitting down."

"Girl, stop teasing me and spill it."

"Okay, Mike and I are getting married," Eve blurted while grinning from ear to ear.

"*What*? Oh my God! Congratulations! When did this happen?"

"Last night, at the New Year's Eve party. I wish you were here to celebrate with us."

"He proposed in front of everyone?"

"Yep."

"That detective of yours has got balls, I'll give him that," stated Bonnie.

"Yes, that does seem to be his MO, being bold and taking chances."

"You sound a little bothered by that."

"Well yeah, given his profession, he tends to boldly throw himself into dangerous situations. It's a bit scary sometimes."

"Can you live with that, Eve?"

"Yes."

"Wow, you didn't even hesitate, but good answer."

"Are you testing me, Bonnie?"

"Damn straight. When you marry someone you need to be able to accept *all* that comes along with them."

"Well, if it came down to not having Mike in my life, there is no contest. I love him."

"Good. You know, I always thought you'd make your way back to San Francisco, back to us, but now that you're marrying Mike your future will be in New York."

"When I accepted this job, I viewed it as a stepping stone, but I figured I'd end up back home in California at some point too, but ever since the first day I met Mike those thoughts started to dissipate over time."

"As it should... You're getting married and your life is in New York now, but I'll still miss not having my best friend around."

"I miss you too, Bonnie, more than you know. I really hope you, Charles, and Caroline can make it to the wedding, but I'll understand if you can't."

"Are you kidding? I wouldn't miss it for the world. You just provide the date and I'm there. I'm sure Caroline and Charles will make sure they can attend as well. Wait until I tell them, they're gonna flip."

"Thank God, I couldn't imagine getting married without you guys. Once Mike and I set the date, I'll call you to make arrangements."

"Okay, my friend, we'll talk later."

"Bye, Bonnie." Mike walked in the bedroom just as Eve was ending her call with Bonnie.

"So you gave Bonnie the good news, huh?"

Eve stood up. "Yes, and she's ecstatic for us."

"I presume you'll ask her to be your maid of honor?"

"Yes, and I'd like Caroline and Charles to be in the wedding party, if that works out with who you have in mind."

"I think we can make room for everyone. Sam will be my best man, of course. Dan, Grace, Kinsey, and... even *Marty* can be in the wedding party, if he can behave himself."

Eve wasn't too keen on Marty being involved in anything in her life, but how could she suggest excluding him without raising questions and hurting Kinsey's feelings? "That's perfect," she replied, "everyone is paired up. All we need is to set the date, and then we can start making some real plans."

"We're on the same page. I don't want to wait too long to make you my wife, Eve. I've already waited three months, too long as it is."

"Oh, you big baby... crying over three months of waiting."

"That's right, I'm crying. You didn't have to torture me like that."

"Well, you got what you wanted in the end, didn't you?"

Mike gathered Eve into his arms. "I wouldn't have settled for anything less," Mike replied. He suddenly took on a serious tone. "Eve, I want to ask you about something and I don't want you to be afraid to be completely honest with me."

This sudden change in Mike's tone concerned Eve. She leaned back and searched his face for some clue as to what he was feeling, but wasn't able to discern anything. "Of course, Mike. Why would I be afraid to be honest with you about anything?"

"Well, it's the topic that might make you hesitant. Not to deceive me, for any reason, but maybe to protect someone dear to you."

Eve didn't have a clue what Mike was talking about. "Just ask me," she implored.

"Umm, is there a problem between you and Marty? I picked up on some tension from you last night at the party."

Eve was taken aback; she hadn't realized that her uneasiness around Marty was that evident, and hoped that Kinsey hadn't picked up on it too. Her delay in answering Mike's question only confirmed his suspicions.

"Eve, please answer me. If Marty is causing you any problems, I want to know. He can be a real bastard sometimes, and it's one thing for me to deal with it, but I won't have him treating you as such."

"It's nothing like that, *really!*"

"Then what is it like?" urged Mike.

Eve sighed heavily. Marty was the last person she wanted to be talking about. Mike felt her body tense. "He just gives me the creeps. Plus, I don't like the way he treats you. He doesn't seem much like a real friend to you. But you tolerate him and Kinsey loves him, so who am I to pass judgment? I don't know him as well as the rest of you do."

"Are you sure that's all there is? He hasn't *done* anything to you, has he?"

"No. Absolutely not! I wouldn't keep something like that from you *or* Kinsey. He hasn't said or done anything improper to me; we barely speak aside from pleasantries."

Mike searched Eve's face and could clearly see that the mere mention of Marty distressed her. "So why does he give you the creeps, Eve?"

Eve had to admit that she couldn't pinpoint a specific reason aside from the way she caught him staring at her at the New Year's party. She struggled to mention it, not wanting Mike to jump to any conclusions causing him to confront Marty, which would ultimately hurt Kinsey.

Mike could see Eve battling with something, so he pressed her firmly. "Eve, answer me. I can see it in your eyes, there's something, so *tell me.*"

Eve released a breath in frustration. "Okay. Last night, right before Marty and Kinsey came over to congratulate us, I caught him staring at me from across the room. But it wasn't like catching a friend's eye across the room where they wave or acknowledge you. He looked startled that I had caught him staring, and that felt weird." Eve shivered at the memory. "I could easily be making more out of this than necessary, Mike. So please, let's just drop this."

Mike saw Eve shiver while she recalled the incident, much like she did when she described Lucas Coles to him and Sam when they first met her. Lucas also gave her the creeps, and with good reason. Look what he turned out to be, a murdering son of a bitch, but Mike kept these thoughts to himself. The last thing Eve needed was a reminder of Lucas Coles. Her instincts were spot on about Lucas, and he wondered if they were just as accurate about Marty, only she was dismissing them because of their friendship and his relationship with Kinsey.

"Sure, honey, we can drop it. I don't want you to be upset about my questions, okay? I just wanted to make sure my future bride was not being harmed." Eve smiled tentatively and Mike pulled her into his arms for reassurance. He would definitely take this up with Sam, who would help him get to the bottom of it.

* * *

Eve perused the examples of artwork laid before her. "Lori, do you have a preference for which pieces we should use for the hotel?"

"Well, I'm kind of partial to these two, as they fit the color scheme and decor the best, but I love all of them, to be honest."

"I agree. There's something about these two that make them stand out from the rest. We should use them as focal points and place them strategically in the hotel. You did good work putting this together, Lori. Money was definitely not wasted on purchasing these pieces. They will do the hotel justice, and hopefully help promote the artist as well."

"Thank you, Eve. That really means a lot to me."

"You don't have to thank me. You have an exceptional eye, which is why you were chosen for this task, and you did not disappoint." Eve closed the folder containing the photos of the artwork and the light caught her ring, which made it sparkle.

"Hey, is this an engagement ring you're wearing?" Lori asked while taking Eve's left hand in hers.

"Yes, Mike proposed on New Year's Eve."

"Congratulations! I'm so happy for you, but why haven't you announced it to everyone?"

"I don't want a big fuss… plus… my relationship with Mike reminds people of the shooting, and I don't want to rub my happiness is everyone's noses."

"I'm glad something good came out of that horrific day, *everyone* is. Lucas turned out to be a crazed nut, but he brought you and the detective together, and no one is upset with that."

"Yeah, it's funny how things work sometimes. If Lucas wasn't a person of interest for the NYPD, Mike never would have shown up here at Colby and we wouldn't be planning our lives together now."

"Have you set a date?"

"No, not yet, but I get the feeling Mike wants it to happen sooner rather than later."

"Well, by that big grin on your face, I'd say you don't have a problem with that plan."

"Am I that obvious? I'm really trying to keep my cool at work."

"Don't worry. You're good, except when you're talking about it. Then it shows all over your face and your eyes get all sparkly. It's cute, *and* you deserve it."

"Thanks, Lori. Again, good work on this project. It's a big one, so your diligence is much appreciated."

"Thank you, Eve." As Lori exited Eve's office, she turned back to see Eve admiring the engagement ring with the biggest smile across her face.

* * *

Sam joined Mike in one of the conference rooms. "Hey, Sam, close the door behind you. I need your advice, and maybe your help with something."

"Sure, anything, tell me what's up."

"I think there's something up between Marty and Eve."

Sam shook his head in disbelief. "Say what? You're not saying they're—"

"Oh no," Mike interrupted, "it's nothing like that."

"Then you'd better start over."

"I sensed some tension between Marty and Eve, more so from Eve, during the New Year's Eve party. Right before you arrived that evening, I noticed that she seemed uncomfortable around him and that she physically tensed in his presence."

"Well, who wouldn't," Sam joked.

"Sam, I'm being serious."

"Sorry, man, but you know I'm right, that dude is a freakin' pain in the ass sometimes. Look, I sensed you needed to talk to me about something at the party that night, is this it?"

"Yes, but I wanted to speak with Eve first to make sure that I wasn't imagining things."

"So, I guess you weren't imagining things?"

"No, she admitted, with a little coaxing on my part, that he gave her the creeps and that she didn't like the way he treated me and that he didn't act like that great of a friend. She tried to downplay the situation."

"Well, she *is* right about Marty *not* being that great of a friend, but do you think she's lying about the severity of it all?"

"To herself, yes, but maybe subconsciously. I think she's trying to protect Kinsey's relationship with Marty. If Eve acknowledges that Marty has done something to her or just that he's made her uncomfortable, well, that could cause problems in Kinsey's relationship as well as between her and Kinsey."

"Kinsey will go on the defensive and defend her man, yada, yada, yada..."

"Now you see the dilemma. I told Eve not to worry about it, that I wasn't upset with her for not confiding in me and that I just wanted to make sure she was okay. We're about to start our lives together, we have a wedding to plan and I don't want anything to interfere with her happiness."

"Understandable, but if there really is an issue, Mike, we can't just sweep it under the rug. It has to be dealt with. Eve isn't the type of person to judge someone's character unfairly. It's one thing to not like the way Marty treats you, and it's quite another to be creeped out by him."

"Yes, so this tells me that there is some merit to her feelings."

"I say we keep a close eye on him when Eve's around or if the subject of her comes up in conversation to see if he does or says anything we should be concerned about, and then deal with the situation accordingly."

"I agree." Mike let out a breath. "Thanks for the extra pair of eyes on the situation. I don't trust myself to be objective where Marty is concerned."

"No problem, partner."

* * *

"So, have you asked Bonnie to be your maid of honor yet?" Mike asked.

"Yep, and she was ecstatic. Kinsey, Grace, and Caroline agreed to be bridesmaids, so I'm all set." Eve beamed at the prospect of having all of her closest friends celebrate one of the most important days of her life.

"Good, I am too. Sam will be my best man, and Dan, Marty, and your friend Charles are the groomsmen. We got lucky; it looks like everyone is all paired up."

"It's not luck, Mike; it's fate. Everything is supposed to work out for us."

# *Chapter 30*

Mike had heard Eve's cab pull up while he was putting the finishing touches on his surprise. He'd raced to the bedroom to await Eve's entrance. She entered to find the living room dimly lit and to the sounds of soft music. "Oh my..." she gasped. There were lovely bouquets of flowers strategically placed throughout the room with rose petals leading a trail to the bedroom. She smiled to herself. It was her birthday after all, and Mike, of course, wouldn't let an opportunity for romance slip past him. Eve made a beeline for the bedroom in search of her wonderful fiancé. He heard her footsteps approach the bedroom door as she undoubtedly followed the trail he left for her. When the door opened, the look on Eve's face was worth all of his efforts.

"Mike," she exclaimed while running into his arms, "everything looks wonderful."

"Happy birthday, my love."

"Thank you, sweetie, you're too good to me."

"It's easy, you're my angel," he replied, gazing into her eyes.

Eve's lips found Mike's, and they were locked for several minutes while savoring each other. Mike was the first to pull away.

"Whoa, if we keep this up we won't make it to dinner."

"Dinner? You cooked too?"

"Hell yeah, and I've made all of your favorites. I tried to plan everything to be ready by the time you arrived home from work, so let's get a move on while it's still hot." Mike turned Eve around and marched her out of the bedroom and into the kitchen. Once there, Eve was in awe.

"You've definitely missed your calling, my love. You must have been a chef and event planner in your other life. This is absolutely breathtaking."

"I'm glad you approve," Mike replied as he pulled out a chair for Eve to sit in at the kitchen table, although it no longer looked like their kitchen, but instead a four-star restaurant. Mike grabbed the bottle of Dom Pérignon he had chilling in the refrigerator. After opening it, he poured two glasses and prepared to make a toast. "Here's to you, my beautiful fiancée, on your twenty-seventh birthday. I hope to make it the most memorable one for you yet."

"I believe you have surpassed all previous memories already, Mike."

Their glasses clinked, and both took a sip of the champagne. "Enjoy your drink and I'll prepare our plates," added Mike as he sauntered over to the stove to retrieve the delicious meal he'd prepared in Eve's honor.

As Eve watched Mike, it reminded her of the first meal he'd cooked for her, the night they professed their love for each other for the first time and then proceeded to display that love to each other all night long. Eve was getting hot and bothered just thinking about it, and used her free hand to fan herself.

"Hey, what are you thinking about, pretty lady?"

"Huh? Oh, just thinking about you, sweetie," she said, smiling.

"Dare I even ask?" Mike started to fill their plates with cedar plank salmon, yellow rice, grilled vegetables and a lovely garden salad.

"Well, I was just remembering the first time you cooked for me and *all* of the activities that followed."

"Ah, I see that I *do* have a lot to live up to tonight, don't I?" Mike asked with one eyebrow raised.

"Oh, I'm not worried at all." Eve eyed the wonderful meal before her and then glanced up at Mike's expectant gaze. "This looks and smells divine. I can't wait to dig in."

After dinner, they retreated into the living room, listening to the music Mike had carefully arranged as they continued to sip their champagne.

"Thank you, Mike, for this birthday surprise. Everything was incredible, and that dessert, chocolate molten lava cake. Oh my God! That was to die for." Eve's head was resting comfortably on Mike's shoulder, with her legs curled up on the sofa.

"You're welcome, babe. You know I aim to please... Eve, I'd like us to finally set the date for our wedding tonight."

Eve sat upright to face Mike. "Eager beaver, aren't we?"

"You know that I am. So, how about it? How does six months from now sound? I don't think I could wait much longer than that, but wanted to at least provide us enough time to plan properly."

"You want to get married in July or August?"

"Yes, August sounds good. My birthday is in July, and I'd rather not have our wedding in the same month, so early August would be great, *unless* you have any objections or other preferences."

"No, the date doesn't matter to me; I just want to be your wife. So early August it is. What about the first Saturday of the month?"

"Okay, let's see what that date is." Mike whipped out his cell phone and opened the calendar. "It's the sixth. I think we have our wedding date. Now we can start making the arrangements." Mike was like a kid in a candy store, much like he was on Christmas morning.

It was very endearing to Eve to see him so excited to marry her. She felt very much loved at that moment.

"So, Detective, on Saturday, August sixth, I will become Mrs. Michael McGarrett."

"I can't wait."

* * *

"Are you ready to go see my parents, Eve?"

"I'm more than ready. This is important to me."

"And it will be important to them too. They will be honored to walk you down the aisle. They love you like their own daughter."

"I know, and I love them too, so much—" Eve's voice broke as she struggled not to cry. "I just wish my parents could be here to see us get married too. I really miss them at times like this."

"I know, babe, but they are with you, right here." Mike tapped Eve's heart with his finger.

"You're right." Mike embraced Eve in a hug for added support.

"Okay, so let's get going."

Mike and Eve arrive at his parents' home and they were immediately embraced by Mark and Carla and were showered with congratulations.

"We're so happy," cooed Carla.

"Yeah, Son, your gamble paid off, you lucky dog."

"Thanks Dad, Eve is worth any gamble." Eve blushed several shades of red.

"Stop embarrassing the girl, Mikey," admonished Carla.

"Hey, I only speak the truth."

They gathered in the living room while Carla headed out to the kitchen to retrieve the coffee she had prepared. Once she returned, they each poured a cup for themselves.

Eve gathered her thoughts while they all took sips of their coffee. Carla eyed Eve, and then put her cup down on the table.

"Is there something on your mind, dear?" she asked.

Eve smiled as she placed her cup down. Carla didn't miss much, that's for certain. "Yes, actually, and it's *very* important... I would be honored if you and Daddy Mark would both walk me down the aisle."

Mark and Carla looked at each other, slightly shocked. They looked at Mike and then back at Eve. "Oh dear, we are the ones who are honored. Are you sure you want both of us and not just Mark?"

"I'm very sure. The both of you have welcomed me into your family and have treated me like your very own daughter. Walking me down the aisle would symbolize the both of you giving me to your son."

"That sounds lovely," replied Carla.

"Your wish is our command, darling girl," added Mark, sounding very much like his son in that moment.

Eve jumped up and ran into Mark and Carla's arms. "Thank you. This means a lot to me. I love you both so much."

"We love you too, sweetheart."

"Hey! What about me? I am the groom-to-be, after all. I want some hugs too," Mike jokingly complained.

"Then get over here," chided Carla.

Mike didn't miss a beat and was immediately scooped up in the embrace. "Well Eve, you are officially on your way to becoming part of this kooky family," said Mike.

"I wouldn't have it any other way, sweetie."

# *Chapter 31*

"So, how was your first Valentine's Day like with Mike?" asked Kinsey, once they arrived at the bridal boutique.

"It was wonderful, and more meaningful given we're planning our lives together. We discussed having a family."

"Already?" Grace replied.

"Well, it wasn't the first time. We talked about kids on one of our early dates. It was more general then, but we went into more detail this time."

"Mike actually wants to be a father. Who would have thought? I'm still getting used to him being in love, and now picturing him as a dad, wow. Times have surely changed," stated Kinsey.

"Don't I know it? Hey, Bonnie should be calling me on Skype in a few minutes," Eve informed the girls, "then we can choose the perfect bridesmaid dress."

Grace said, "This is so exciting. I still can't believe you and Mike are getting married in just a little over five months."

"Mike sure doesn't play around, does he?" added Kinsey.

Eve casually started to look through the dress racks. "Oh no, he pinned me down on my birthday to set a date, so August sixth it is. He doesn't even want me to plan anything for his birthday in July and says the wedding is more than enough of a birthday present for him. He'd rather us to just spend a nice quiet evening while we're in the midst of all of this wedding hoopla." Eve turned to face Kinsey and Grace. "Thanks for helping me with sending out the invitations."

"No problem, you know we've got your back. Your maid of honor is in San Francisco and can't help with the day-to-day stuff and assist you with the local arrangements, so we are here to pick up the slack. I *have* been through this before, you know?" replied Grace. "Just to make sure, you and Mike *have* gotten your marriage license, right?"

"Yes, it was one of the first things we accomplished, and we also secured the minister. We've also chosen the flavor of our wedding cake and placed the order with a bakery, which wasn't easy given the time frame, and we'll work on the dinner menu tomorrow." Eve's phone chimed. "Oh, here's Bonnie now." The girls huddled around Eve. "Hey Bonnie and Caroline, we're all here at the bridal shop. Meet Grace and Kinsey." Everyone waved and said their hellos. "So we all know what to do, right?"

"Definitely, we'll each pick out the dress we like, find out if it's available in purple, then share it with everyone for a group consensus," stated Bonnie.

The girls found two dresses that appealed to everyone's liking and ultimately chose the perfect bridesmaids' dress.

# Chapter 32

Anthony hugged his baby sister while her luggage was being brought into the house and taken upstairs to her room. "I can't believe you've already graduated college, Stef."

"Sorry to disappoint you, big brother. I know you didn't think I could do it," Stephanie quipped.

"That's not true. Why would you say something like that?"

"Oh please, we both know that you and Nicholas think I'm a flake. That I'm Daddy's little girl who gets anything and everything she wants by batting her eyelashes."

Anthony was hurt by her accusations. He had to admit that Nicholas did have those opinions, but he never imagined that Stephanie thought he felt the same way. "Sorry to disappoint *you*, sis, and I'd appreciate you not judging me unfairly when you are clearly sensitive to being judged yourself. I have only ever wanted the best for you and have done anything I could to facilitate that, and you know it."

Thoroughly chagrined, Stephanie realized she owed her brother an apology. "I'm sorry, Tony. *You* might not feel that way, but I *know* that Nicholas does. He barely spoke to me during my visit over Christmas break. It was as if he was deliberately avoiding me. I know that you were busy with work, but what was his excuse? He doesn't even work in the business with you and Daddy. I can tell from Dad's behavior that he and Nick were on the outs again, but how is that *my* fault?"

"Don't take it personally Stef, he's been steering clear of me as well. He obviously needs some time on his own to deal with things, so try not to be so hard on him. You don't understand what it's like to feel Pop's wrath, and I unfortunately got a little taste of it myself. Believe me, it doesn't feel good, and that is all Nick has ever felt from him, so let's cut him some slack, Okay?"

"Okay." Stephanie wrapped her arms around her big brother. "You always look out for us, what would we ever do without you, Tony?"

"You'll never have to find that out, sis." Anthony protectively cradled his sister in his arms wishing he could find a way to protect Nicholas better, but Nicholas didn't always make that easy to accomplish.

At the top of the stairwell, Nicholas watched Anthony and Stephanie engaged in conversation. He heard his name several times and wondered what the hell they were talking about and why they were talking about him in the first place. He'd been pretty successful limiting his exposure to Stephanie over the holiday break, but she was home for good now, and he was going to have to find a way to deal with her permanent presence.

* * *

Nicholas entered the library and stopped in his tracks at the sight of Anthony. Anthony glanced up just as Nicholas turned away in retreat. "Nick, wait a second." Nicholas sighed and turned back around.

"What do you want, Tony?"

"Why are you being so hostile? I know you were upset and hurt by Pop's treatment toward you regarding Lucas's melt down and possibly implicating us in the money-laundering scheme, but that was *months* ago. Why do you remain so angry with *me*? I supported your idea and Pop was upset with me too when it all fell apart, and it took a while for us to get back to some semblance of normalcy."

"Well, goodie for you, *big brother*. Pop still treats *me* like shit. I don't know why I'm surprised, since it's his normal treatment of me, only now it feels worse. You got his trust back and get to continue working with him while I get the seething death stare every time he catches sight of me. To top it all off, Stef is back and he's all lovey dovey and smiles with *her*, and I'm sick of it."

"Look, I'm sorry, Nick, but we're not responsible for how Pop treats you. We're your brother and sister, and we love you. Why push us away and isolate yourself? It's not very mature, and that's one of Pop's biggest complaints. Why not prove him wrong instead of fostering his bad opinion of you?"

"So that's your sound advice, be more mature? Pop isn't perfect, you know. Everyone has an Achilles' heel, and Stef is *his*. Mark my words, Tony. His blind devotion to her whims and needs will be his and *all* of our downfalls one day. So, you know what you can do with your *unsolicited* advice, Tony." Nicholas turned and stalked off.

# Chapter 33

Mike and Eve eagerly awaited her friends' arrival at JFK Airport. Eve was like a little girl waiting for her friends to come outside to play after finishing their homework.

"Look at you. Your eyes are practically popping out of your head, Eve."

"Well, what do you expect? They're my best friends since high school and college, and I haven't seen them in over a year."

"I know. It's just adorable seeing you like this."

Eve spotted them as they entered the gate area. "There they are," she exclaimed as she raised her hands and waved to catch their attention. Bonnie noticed her immediately and she, Caroline and Charles made their way over to them. They were all hugs and kisses, and then Eve made the introductions. "Mike, meet Charles, Caroline, and Bonnie, my very best friends in the whole world."

Mike hugged the women and shook Charles's hand. "It's nice to finally meet all of you. Your arrival has put a smile on this beautiful woman's face, so you must try to visit more often."

"Well, Mike, I've never seen Eve so happy, which I presume is *your* doing," added Bonnie.

"I certainly hope so, I try my best." Mike gave Eve a tender kiss.

"Okay now, you guys have plenty of time for that," Charles chimed in.

Caroline kindly swatted Charles on the arm as a reprimand.

Eve giggled. "The two of you never change, do you?"

"Nope, and you love it," answered Charles.

"Yes I do, now let's get you guys to the house. You must be tired from the trip, and probably hungry."

"Now you're speaking my language sista, let's get moving," Charles added.

Mike had to chuckle to himself. Eve's friends were a trip, and he had the feeling they were going to have a great time together this weekend.


You have a lovely home," said Caroline, looking around.

"Thanks. We brought you here first so we could give you a quick tour and have lunch before taking you to the hotel," stated Mike. "After we get you unpacked and settled you'll meet the rest of the gang at the hotel before the dinner rehearsal."

"That sounds great," added Bonnie. "I can't wait to meet everyone."

"Um, Eve, I'm not sure if I should mention this... but... um... Jackson said to give you his congratulations," stated Caroline.

Eve whirled around. "Jackson, Jackson Harper? How does he know about the wedding?"

"God only knows. He approached Charles and me saying that he was offended that he didn't get an invite and how we always go to great lengths not to include him in our activities, not to mention he was not pleased that you were dating someone other than *him*, and so quickly." Caroline rolled her eyes. "Can you believe him? Who would want his creepy ass around?"

"Who's Jackson Harper?" Mike asked, concerned with Eve's reaction.

"He's a *stalker* if you ask me," answered Caroline. "He's always had the hots for Eve but can't take *no* for an answer. That man had the nerve to show up at her going-away party, *without* an invitation I might add, and proceeded to harass Eve. Charles had to intervene just to get him to back off. I guess Jackson was feeling desperate since Eve was leaving San Francisco indefinitely and didn't know if he would ever see her again."

"Caroline, please, you're upsetting Eve," admonished Bonnie.

"You don't think that he'll show up here this weekend, do you?" Eve asked, clearly shaken.

"Would he do that?" Mike asked. "Showing up uninvited to a party is a far cry from crashing a wedding."

"I don't think he'd go that far," replied Charles.

"Charles, don't be so naïve, *of course* he would. He's relentless, *and* don't forget, a stalker," Caroline snapped.

"He did joke about the fact that my moving across the country wouldn't do much good and he had half a mind to chase me all the way here to New York," added Eve.

"What did I tell you, *stalker*," Caroline insisted.

"You've never mentioned him before, Eve," said Mike.

"Quite frankly, I haven't thought about him since the going-away party. At the time, I figured out of sight out of mind and he would finally move on to someone else, but apparently not. That was just wishful thinking on my part, I guess." Eve looked completely dejected at the prospect of Jackson still pursuing her.

"You don't think he was actually serious about following you out here, do you?" asked Bonnie.

"Maybe I did for a fleeting second, but overall I thought he was joking, but now, given what I've experienced with the shooting, I've learned to not dismiss any type of creepy behavior from *anyone*. You never know when someone might flip out."

Mike put his arms around Eve for comfort. "If it'll make you feel better, I can put a trace on Jackson to monitor any sudden travel arrangements."

Eve glanced at Charles. "I know you grew up with him and you think he's harmless, but I'd feel better if Mike put a trace on his movements, at least until after the wedding. Would you be okay with that?"

"Of course, sweetie, this is *your* weekend and you should be happy, not worried about being stalked. Do whatever you need to do."

"Okay, I'll make the call now. You guys continue with the tour and I'll join you when I'm done. I'll protect you, sweetie, please don't worry." Mike kissed Eve on the forehead and retreated into the study.

"Oh, Eve, I hope I didn't ruin your weekend by opening up my big mouth about Jackson," Caroline said. "You're not upset with me, are you?"

"No, don't worry about it. We should know what we're dealing with. I feel better already knowing that Mike is handling it."

"I'm glad," Caroline responded. "Mike is quite the looker, and very protective of you. I can see why you fell so hard and so quickly," she added.

"I guess he's *alright*, if you like that type," Charles offered grudgingly.

"What type would that be, drop-dead gorgeous with a body to match?" quipped Caroline. Charles shot her a look. "What, you sound jealous to me, Charles."

"I am *not* jealous of Mike. I just met the man, for Christ's sake. As long as he makes Eve happy, that is all I care about," he responded, glaring at Caroline.

Bonnie and Eve watched intently at this exchange, finally witnessing some real action between these two.

"Is there something the two of you would like to share with us?" asked Bonnie.

Caroline and Charles both glanced at each other.

"No, what are you talking about?" asked Caroline.

"There's nothing to share," stammered Charles.

"If the two of you say so," replied Eve.

"Well, back to Mike," Bonnie said, "the photos you showed us don't do him justice at all. He *is* very handsome indeed."

Eve was all smiles. "I know."

Mike decided to run a background check on this Jackson Harper in addition to putting a trace on his movements. Eve's experience with Lucas gave her a unique perspective. Most people just ignored odd behavior because they're too close to the person to be objective until it's too late. How was Jackson finding out their activities if they weren't providing it to him personally? He was obviously going to enough trouble to obtain it, so Mike was glad that Caroline had mentioned it. After he finished his phone call, Mike rejoined Eve and her friends and kept their focus on the tour and their upcoming plans for the day.

* * *

Mike and Eve helped Charles, Caroline, and Bonnie get settled at the hotel and then introduced them to Sam, Dan, Marty, Kinsey and Grace at the church for the wedding rehearsal.

"Look at those two, aren't they disgusting?" Sam joked with Bonnie. Eve and Mike were cuddling and kissing.

"I think they are cute. I love seeing her so happy," replied Bonnie.

"Yep, not gonna lie, Mike has never been happier himself. Eve is perfect for him."

"Hey everyone," Grace called out, "let's head over to the restaurant. I don't want us to be late for our reservation."


Everyone was famished and thoroughly enjoyed their meal, plus everyone was on their best behavior, even Marty, to Mike's relief, but he wondered how long that would last.

"Hey, where did you drift off to?" Eve asked, interrupting his reverie.

"Just thinking how lucky we are, having all of our friends here to celebrate our marriage."

"Well, let's thank them." Mike and Eve stood up and tapped their glasses to get everyone's attention.

"We wanted to thank all of you for being here with us," Mike began. "I know my lovely bride-to-be is overjoyed that you, Charles, Bonnie, and Caroline, were able to join us this weekend." Mike wrapped his arm around Eve's waist and pulled her close. "I am so in love with this woman…"

Marty squirmed in his seat at the sight of Mike and Eve so lovey-dovey. This weekend was making him crazy, but he had to keep his cool so he wouldn't become unhinged. The touch of Kinsey's hand on his brought him back to the present, and he noticed that Eve was speaking now.

"I am over the moon for this man and I am grateful for my childhood friends, my new friends, and my soon-to-be in-laws. My family has grown, and I feel blessed. Thank you everyone." Everyone clapped and cheered as Mike pulled Eve in for a kiss. Marty just closed his eyes and exhaled.

* * *

Bonnie and Kinsey planned a girl's day for Eve. They completed their dress fitting and then enjoyed a spa treatment, which included massages, mani-pedis and facials at Eve's apartment.

The guys were at their tuxedo fittings. Charles was getting some last-minute adjustments to his tuxedo while Mike, Dan, Sam and Marty were eyeing themselves in the mirror, testing out their neckties. Marty was having trouble with his and the guys were busting his chops. If he had it his way, he wouldn't have been a part of the wedding party at all, but couldn't find a good enough excuse to decline without arousing suspicions. Marty didn't like being the butt of the jokes, and since he was not comfortable with this wedding and being so up close and personal to Mike and Eve's love, he decided to take it out on Mike in his usual fashion.

"Look, why don't you guys just focus your attention on Mike? He needs all the help he can get. I mean getting married after dating *so* many women must be daunting to him." He knew that saying this in front of Charles, one of Eve's best friends, would embarrass Mike.

Charles was completed dumbfounded at Marty's behavior. Wasn't he supposed to be a friend of Mike's? He was part of the wedding party, after all.

Mike had enough of Marty's bullshit and whirled around to confront him. "Are you seriously starting this shit up again? What is your problem?" He didn't have to tolerate Marty's nonsense, especially when he knew that Eve was not comfortable around him. Mike had half a mind to blindside him with that piece of information but decided to let it slide, for Kinsey's sake, as well as for Eve.

Seeing the potential danger in allowing this to escalate, Sam interceded, "Marty, why don't you rein in it before I come over there to help adjust that tie around your neck. It looks like it may need some tightening." He pinned Marty with a cold stare to let him know he meant it. He then steered Mike away from Marty and whispered, "Don't let that fool get to you. He's just jealous that you're getting married before he even had the nerve to pop the question to Kinsey himself."

"You're probably right, Sam. I just can't believe he had the gall to pull this crap the day before my wedding. Maybe Eve's being uncomfortable around him is justified."

Dan made his way over to Charles. "Please don't let Marty's childish behavior give you the wrong impression of Mike. Marty tends to be spiteful and vindictive towards him. We all think he's a bit envious and I'm sure this was just an attempt to embarrass Mike in front of you."

"The only person who should be embarrassed is Marty," stated Charles. "I've seen Mike with Eve, and it's obvious how much he loves her. I'm not concerned."

Dan patted Charles on the shoulder. "I knew I liked you. Anyone who can see through Marty's bullshit is alright in my book."

Marty walked away with a slight grin on his face, pleased with himself for getting under Mike's skin *again*.

*　*　*

Sam and Dan wanted to give Mike a bachelor party at the ranch house but Mike wasn't into it, so they opted to go out for drinks instead, at a local tavern. Meanwhile, the girls' spa day continued into the evening accompanied by music. "I wonder if the guys are having as much fun as we are," Caroline pondered.

"I certainly hope so, and I pray that Marty isn't causing any problems. He's been acting weird all weekend," answered Kinsey.

"When is he *not* acting weird?" stated Grace. Eve was thinking the same thing.

"Hey, stop picking on my man." Kinsey grabbed a nearby rag and threw it at Grace.

Grace ducked. "Then he shouldn't make it so easy. Honestly, Kinsey, he can really act immature sometimes. You can do a lot better, sweetie."

"What! Now I need to get rid of my boyfriend. How did this get turned around on me?"

Despite her feelings regarding Marty, Eve felt bad for Kinsey, but more importantly did not want to spend her bachelorette party focused on that asshole. "Kinsey is right. This is not the time or place for this."

"You're right, and I'm sorry… to both of you," stated Grace. "I shouldn't have said that to you, Kinsey, and this is *your* night, Eve. We should be focused on you."

"I second that," added Caroline. She would have to get the scoop on this Marty guy from Eve and Charles at another point and time. She had the feeling there was *more* to the story.

Sam made sure that Charles got back to the hotel and got Mike home in one piece. He took his best man duties seriously. Once Sam was back on the road, Mike called Eve. Eve would be spending the night at her apartment, so Mike wouldn't see her until the next morning during the wedding ceremony. It would be their first night apart since Eve moved in with him and he missed her. Eve picked up the phone on the second ring. She thought it was one of girls but was pleasantly surprised at the sound of Mike's voice.

"Well, hello there, Detective. You had better not be drunk-dialing me right now," she teased.

Mike smiled. "I wouldn't dream of it. I have had a few, but I'm by no means wasted. Sam made sure of that for fear you would kill him if I showed up at our wedding tomorrow morning hung over."

"I will thank him personally. So, to what do I owe the pleasure?"

"I just wanted to hear your voice. I miss you. I'm used to you being here with me, but I'm all alone."

"I'm all alone here too, so I'm glad you called, sweetie. I miss you too. Did you have a nice time with the boys? Did everyone *behave*?"

Mike knew that Eve was referring to Marty, but he didn't want to upset her by informing her of Marty's latest antics and have her worrying all night. "Yes, the guys took really good care of me. I take it you had a fun time, especially spending it with Bonnie and Caroline."

"Definitely. I've missed them so much. It was a *fantastic* day."

"You sound really happy, babe."

"I am, because I'm going to become your wife tomorrow morning."

"And nothing will make my happier. I can't wait, pretty lady. Good night, my love."

"Good night, my love."

# *Chapter 34*

It was a beautiful day for a wedding, and the reception hall was decorated to perfection. It was a scene straight out of a fairy tale. Eve awoke happier than she ever thought was possible because it was her wedding day. She had plenty of time before the wedding, so she lay in bed for a little while, letting her mind wander to thoughts of Mike and the life they were about to embark on together as husband and wife.

The girls picked Eve up and escorted her to the church. They were getting ready in the changing area when there was a knock at the door. "If that's Mike..." complained Bonnie as she headed toward the door.

"I have a package for Eve," a voice from the other side of the door announced. All of the girls exchanged looks of curiosity.

"Well, it's not Mike *this time*, but mark my words: That man will be paying you a visit before the ceremony," stated Bonnie just before opening the door. She took the box and thanked the delivery man. "Hold on for minute," Bonnie stated. She grabbed her purse and tipped the gentleman before sending him on his way. "It looks like flowers," she handed the box to Eve.

Eve opened it and her eyes lit up. "They're beautiful, lilies, and in my favorite color."

"I wonder who they're from," mused Grace, "do you think they're from Mike?"

"I don't think so," surmised Bonnie, "I think Mike would bring them to you personally. Although, these would have to be from someone close enough to you to know to send you purple lilies. I think they're from Malcolm, who's probably feeling guilty for not making it here in person."

"There has to be a card somewhere... ah, here it is." Eve opened up the envelope and pulled out the card. She glanced up at Bonnie. "When you're right, you're right. It *is* from Malcolm."

"Well, read it," urged Kinsey.

"Okay, it says, 'To my beautiful Eve, congratulations on your special day. I'm sorry I couldn't be there with you to share in your joy. Love, Malcolm.' Huh, short but sweet. Are any of us really surprised by this? I mean really... I haven't heard one word from Malcolm since before my parents died and all I get is this short note. This is just par for the course with him." Eve put the box of flowers down on the dresser. "I have a wedding to get ready for, ladies, and the only man on my mind this morning is my future husband."

"But it must hurt, Eve. Malcolm was like a brother to you," replied Caroline.

"But he's not *here*, is he?"

"No, you're right, we have more important things to take care of," answered Caroline apologetically just as there was another knock at the door.

"Any guesses as to who that might be?" asked Bonnie as she sauntered over to the door. "Who is it?" she sang.

"It's Mike, open up. I want to see my fiancée."

Bonnie turned to face the rest of the girls and they all burst out laughing.

"When you're right, you're right," replied Eve.

"Men are too predictable for their own good," Bonnie answered.

"Hey, what's going on in there? Are you going to open up the door or not?" Mike insisted.

Bonnie turned back toward the door. "Absolutely not, Michael McGarrett—you know it's bad luck to see the bride before the wedding."

"Is Eve in her wedding dress yet?"

"No."

"Then it's not bad luck, is it?"

Bonnie turned to face the ladies again. "Men are also too *smart* for their own good too sometimes." They all burst out laughing again.

"Ladies *please*, take pity. I just need to see Eve's beautiful face."

"Oh, Bonnie, stop torturing my man," said Eve.

Even Bonnie couldn't deny Mike's heartfelt plea. She opened the door and let him in, and his eyes caught Eve's immediately. "We'll give the two of you some privacy, but keep it brief. You have a wedding to attend."

"Thank you, Bonnie," replied Mike as he walked across the room, never taking his eyes off Eve's. Once the ladies left, Mike pulled Eve into his arms. "I thought they'd never leave."

"You are too much, Michael McGarrett... Are you okay, sweetie?"

"Yes, I just missed you. I haven't seen you since yesterday, after the girls kidnapped you, and it's the first night we've spent apart after moving in together. I needed to see you and couldn't wait any longer."

"I missed you too. I'm glad you dropped by, but don't tell Bonnie that." Eve giggled. She was on cloud nine gazing into the eyes of her soon-to-be husband.

"It's our little secret." Mike caressed Eve's face while staring into her eyes adoringly. They shared a tender, passionate kiss that left them both breathless with anticipation. Mike couldn't believe Eve would soon become his wife. This was the happiest day of his life, and he couldn't wait to show her just how happy he was later that evening.

*  *  *

Sam straightened Mike's tie while trying to keep him calm before the ceremony. "Wasn't this tie straight earlier? What the hell have you been up to?"

"I was just with Eve."

"Dude, you're about to get married. You'll have her for the rest of your life. Can't you go without her for two minutes?"

"No, I can't, and not to change the subject, but I take it there's no news on Jackson Harper?" Mike asked.

"You *are* changing the subject, but it's all good. Our Mr. Harper is still in San Francisco and nowhere near your beautiful bride-to-be. Some interesting things came up in his background check, but we can discuss that *after* you return from your honeymoon."

Mike's eyes squinted. "Okay, but nothing I should be concerned about, I hope?"

"Not immediately, no, but things you might want to be aware of for future use, if needed, but *after* you return from your honeymoon. And I'll continue to monitor his movements while you're away."

"Thanks Sam, you're the best."

"Damn straight, that's why *I'm* the best man."

Mark entered the room. "You two lovebirds don't mind if I cut in, do you?"

"Very funny, Dad."

"Only *you* could get away with that, Mr. McGarrett," Sam chuckled as he headed for the door.

Mark patted Sam on the back on his way out. "You know I couldn't resist."

Sam chuckled. "I'll give the two of you some father-and-son time."

Mark turned to Mike. "So, my boy is about to become a husband. I couldn't be more proud."

"Thanks, Dad. I couldn't be happier."

"Your mother and I know that we raised a good man, so I'm only going to remind you to make sure that you treat Eve right."

"Dad, come on, you know I will. Eve is the love of my life. She's very precious to me."

"You'd better, because she is precious to us too. We already consider her our daughter, and soon that will become official... Carla and I never thought this day would come, with you gallivanting around with all of those different women, never holding down a relationship for more than a couple of months."

"That was before Eve, Dad. It's not like I was using those women, I was just dating like any man my age. There was no need for me to be in a relationship that wasn't real, so I didn't bother until I met the right woman, someone that meant something to me."

"I'm not criticizing you, Mikey, just saying we were worried, because it took you long enough. We'd like some grandchildren to spoil before we're too old to do so."

"You and mom will never be too old… You've been a great role model for me. I only hope that I can be half the husband and father that you are."

"Come here, my boy." Mark pulled Mike into his arms.

"Dad, are you crying?"

Mark released Mike. "Yeah, so what of it? Don't ever be afraid to cry in front of Eve. It's not a sign of weakness, as most men believe. It just shows that you can be vulnerable and sensitive. Women like it, so remember that."

"I will. Thanks, Dad."

* * *

Carla joined the ladies in the dressing room. "Wow, you are all visions of loveliness, especially you, my beautiful Eve."

"Thanks, Momma Carla. I'm almost ready. I just have to put on the dress."

"Well, we have something for you before you do that, my dear."

"Oh really?" Eve shrieked in delight.

"Of course, girl, you didn't think we'd forget the traditional gifts of something old, something new, something borrowed, and something blue, did you?"

Caroline approached Eve. "I guess I'll start. This is from all of us. It's something new, and we hope you like it sweetie."

Eve unwrapped the present, which contained a charm bracelet. "It's lovely. I can't wait to add charms to it from the honeymoon."

"That's what we figured," added Caroline. "It could be a reminder of how you spend your time in Hawaii. Every time you glance at it you will be flooded with fond memories of your honeymoon."

"It's perfect. Thanks, ladies."

"Okay, here is the something borrowed," Bonnie announced. "It's something of mine you've always admired, Eve, so I thought you could wear them on your special day." Bonnie then handed Eve a pair of earrings.

Eve pulled Bonnie into her arms. "Oh, Bonnie, this is so thoughtful. I can't believe you remembered I liked them."

"Of course I remembered, and I thought to myself that if the perfect occasion arises I would lend them to you. What better occasion could there be than your wedding day? I'm so happy for you, my friend and soul-sista for life."

"Thank you so much, I'm putting them on right now. How do they look?"

"Perfect, of course."

"Now for something blue," announced Kinsey, "which can also be considered new if you like." She handed Eve a tiny box.

Eve looked between all of the women. "I can't even imagine what this could be." She opened the box and grinned. "A toe ring, it's adorable, look at the tiny blue rhinestones. Now whose idea was this?" Eve asked while slipping it onto one of the toes on her left foot.

"Kinsey's, of course," stated Grace. "Who else would come up with a toe ring for goodness' sake?"

"Hey, what's that supposed to mean?" asked Kinsey.

"It means that only you could come up something so unorthodox and whimsical at the same time," answered Eve. Kinsey was all smiles at the compliment. Leave it to Eve to make Kinsey's kooky ways sound appealing, Grace thought.

"It's my turn. I have the something old, of course," Carla said as she sat next to Eve. "Eve, sweetie, Mark and I knew you were the one for our son as soon as your name came out of his mouth. His eyes sparkled with joy and happiness, and I loved you for that, even before I met you." Carla pulled out a small box from her purse. "My mother gave this to me on my wedding day, which is passed down from mother to daughter. I've looked at you as my own daughter from the very first time we met, and I'd like you to have this precious heirloom, so that you can pass it down to your daughter on her wedding day."

Carla handed Eve the box. Eve opened it to view a lovely locket embroidered with beads and filled with two pictures, one of Carla and the other of Eve. "Oh, Momma Carla, it's beautiful. I'm so honored to carry on your family tradition. I'll cherish it forever. Thank you, I love you so much." Eve hugged Carla, and the embrace lasted several seconds.

"I know you're missing your mom and dad right now, but they are here with you, watching over you on this blessed day." Tears of happiness streamed down Eve and Carla's faces.

"Okay, okay, you two, enough crying, you're going to mess up your makeup," admonished Bonnie. "Now let's get you in that beautiful wedding gown."

They all cooed as Eve stood before them in her wedding dress. She looked like a princess and she felt like one.

"Mike is just going to die when he sees you, Eve," stated Caroline.

"My son is a very lucky man," agreed Carla.

* * *

The bridal party prepared to start the wedding procession while Mike and Sam waited for their arrival at the altar. The music started and the butterflies in Eve's stomach performed their familiar dance, a performance she expected would never end. Mike was so nervous with anticipation and couldn't wait to see Eve, but he had to endure the arrival of the bridesmaids, the groomsmen, the flower girl and ring bearer before he got his wish.

Then the moment he was waiting for arrived as Eve appeared with his mom and dad. She was so beautiful. He couldn't believe this woman was about to become his wife. Eve was a vision as Mark and Carla walked her down the aisle. Mike's heart swelled. He struggled to hold back tears, despite his father's words earlier, but he didn't hold back the biggest smile ever seen when his and Eve's eyes locked onto each other. All of his nerves dissipated because his dream was about to come true.

Eve was so happy, surrounded by so many people that loved her, but the greatest love of all was waiting for her at the altar. She didn't think she could ever love someone so much, and she prayed that this wasn't all a dream, because it certainly felt like one.

Once they arrived at the altar, Mark and Carla kissed Eve and handed her to Mike. Mike and Eve took each other's hands, and then Mike mouthed, "I love you." Eve did the same. They couldn't take their eyes off each other.

Everyone took their seats, and Father Thompson began, "A wedding is a sacred event, but above all else it is a promise of what is to be, and a marriage is a clasping of hands and a blending of hearts and family. Dearly beloved, we are gathered here today to join this man and this woman in holy matrimony, which is a holy estate and not to be entered into lightly. Michael and Eve will proclaim their love with their own vows."

Mike and Eve faced each other. "Eve, I never realized how empty my life really was until you were standing right in front of me. From that moment on, I was complete. You've changed me, Eve, and you've changed my life forever. You're a part of me now, one half of a whole. So I promise to make sure that every day of your life is better than the day before. I love you wholeheartedly, and with every breath I take. These are the vows I pledge to you."

Eve looked at Mike adoringly and then stated her vows. "Mike, people might say that this is happening too fast and that we couldn't possibly have fallen in love this quickly. But we both know deep in our hearts that time has very little to do with it, and *you* told me in no uncertain terms that there was no set timetable for love. I never knew that it was possible to love another human being as much as I love you, Mike. There are no words that could ever describe what you mean to me and how you make me feel. You are the love of my life and I can't imagine my world without you in it. These are the vows I pledge to you."

Father Thompson continued, "Michael, do you take Eve to be your wife, to live together in God's ordinance in the holiest state of matrimony? Will you love her, comfort her, honor and keep her in sickness and in health, for richer or poorer, for better or worse, in sadness and in joy. To cherish and bestow upon her your heart's greatest devotion, and forsaking all others keep yourself only onto her as long as you both shall live?"

"I most certainly do."

"Eve, do you take Michael to be your husband, to live together in God's ordinance in the holiest state of matrimony? Will you love him, comfort him, honor and keep him in sickness and in health, for richer or poorer, for better or worse, in sadness and in joy. To cherish and bestow upon him your heart's greatest devotion, and forsaking all others keep yourself only onto him as long as you both shall live?"

"Without question, I do."

"We will now exchange the rings." Sam handed the rings to Father Thompson. "May these rings be blessed as a symbol of this union. These two lives will now be joined in one unbroken circle, and may these rings on their fingers symbolize the spirit of love in their hearts." Father Thompson handed Mike his ring.

"Eve, with this ring I thee wed," said Mike as he placed the ring on her finger.

Father Thompson handed Eve the other ring.

"Mike, with this ring I thee wed," said Eve as she placed the ring on his finger.

"By the power vested in me by the state of New York and almighty God, I now pronounce you husband and wife. What God has brought together let no man tear asunder. Michael, you might kiss your bride."

Mike pulled Eve into his arms and they shared a long and passionate kiss that brought forth applause and whistles.

Once the lovebirds came up for air, Father Thompson said, "In the joyful spirit of this wedding, I now present to you Mr. and Mrs. Michael McGarrett." Mike and Eve walked down the aisle hand in hand with the biggest smiles any two people could possibly have, followed by the wedding party. Mike and Eve's happiness was infectious, and everyone gathered around them lavishing them with hugs and kisses and tears of joy. The guests proceeded to the reception while the photographer took pictures of the wedding party and Mike's parents. Afterwards, Mike and Eve joined their guests in the reception hall.

The newly Mr. and Mrs. Michael McGarrett danced their first dance to "Always and Forever." Mike and Eve looked into each other's eyes, each seeing the hope and promise of a wonderful life and future together. Mike wanted to remember Eve like this forever.

"Well, Mrs. McGarrett, how does it feel to be a married woman?"

"Absolutely wonderful," Eve answered.

"I'm the happiest man on earth, and I can't wait to show you just how happy I am."

"Neither can I."

After a couple of minutes the wedding party joined them on the dance floor.

Marty found himself glancing at Eve while he was dancing with Kinsey. Eve was a beautiful bride, but she belonged to Mike, and he had to somehow deal with his attraction for her or he could lose Kinsey and ruin his friendships with the guys.

"Hey, where are you right now?"

Marty blinked at the sound of Kinsey's voice. "Huh? What did you say, hon?"

"I asked where you were. You're like a thousand miles away."

"Oh, I was just noticing how happy the newlyweds look."

"They are very happy, that's for sure." Kinsey wondered how long she had to wait for her own marriage proposal from Marty. They had definitely been together for much longer than Mike and Eve, and Mike, the perpetual bachelor, had no problems marrying the woman he loved. Suddenly, Kinsey was the one a thousand miles away.

After the song finished, Mark and Mike swapped dance partners. Mark used this time alone with Eve to tell her how much he loved her as a daughter. He was grateful to her for making his son so happy, and officially welcomed her into their family.

Carla was so happy for her only son. She told him how proud she was of him for recognizing real love and grabbing onto it with both hands. She warned him to never let Eve get away and to always treat her right, or he would have to answer to *her*. After the song finished, everyone returned to their seats in order to enjoy the deliciously catered meal.

Sam stood up. "Alright everyone, if I could have your attention, it's time for me, the best man, to say a few words. Mike and I have been partners at the NYPD and best friends for the last three years, and I know from experience that there is nothing he wouldn't do for the people he loves. So you, my dear Eve, are in good hands, because Mike will protect you with his life. I have never seen my friend as happy as he is now, and that is because of you. I was blessed to have witnessed the two of you fall in love, right before my eyes since the day we met you, Eve, and I am honored to be your friend. May the two of you be happy and in love for the rest of your lives." Everyone held up their glasses... Sam turned to Bonnie, "Maid of honor, it's your turn to toast the happy couple."

Bonnie stood up and looked lovingly at the bride and groom. "I have known Eve since we were in high school, and she has always had this light that emanated from her soul and shone brightly on the rest of us. But she has never shone as brightly as she does today, and that's because she found Mike, her soul mate. Mike and Eve's love makes me feel safe and it gives me hope that everything is going to be okay. Here's to hope and love." Everyone held up their glasses...

After the toasts, some of the guests headed to the dance floor to get their groove on while Mike and Eve made their rounds, going from table to table greeting their guests.

They wheeled out the most beautiful wedding cake you could ever imagine. It was a four-tiered chocolate fudge cake with creamy chocolate frosting that was donned with pearl-like decorations that surrounded the base of each layer and red roses that cascaded from top to bottom. Mike and Eve cradled the knife in both of their hands and cut the first slice. They each took a piece of the slice and fed it to each other simultaneously, followed by a kiss. It was the most delicious piece of cake the two of them had ever eaten.

All of the single ladies lined up for the bouquet toss. Eve tossed the bouquet over her shoulders and Caroline caught it. She proceeded to jump up and down, waving the bouquet around in triumph. Charles had an immediate look of panic on his face and Eve struggled not to burst out in laughter.

Then the men lined up to catch the garter. Mike removed it from Eve's leg and tossed it over his shoulder, and of course, it landed right at Charles. Caroline sat in the chair and enjoyed every minute of Charles having to put the garter on her. Charles enjoyed it too, although he tried to feign indifference and act cool in front of everyone.

"Bonnie and I believe that Charles and Caroline are together, like a couple," Eve whispered to Mike.

"No kidding? They haven't confirmed one way or the other?"

"Nope, for some reason they're choosing to keep their relationship or whatever is happening between them under wraps."

"Or so they think," quipped Mike.

Eve laughed. "I know. The poor things don't realize how obvious they are." Eve turned to Mike. "I'm ready to go, sweetie, aren't you?"

"You don't have to ask me twice," Mike said. "You know I want you all to myself."

"Okay, give me a couple of minutes to say goodbye to Bonnie, Caroline and Charles. They're flying back home tomorrow, and I don't know when I'll see them again."

"Of course, go do your thing. I'll say goodbye to the guys."

Eve tracked down Charles and the girls and gave them big hugs and kisses. She was so blessed to have such great friends. Afterward she hugged her new in-laws, who also showered her with kisses.

Everyone lined up in front of the church, and when Mike and Eve exited, everyone tossed rose petals at them as the newlyweds ran hand in hand to the car.

# *Chapter 35*

Mike and Eve arrived at the ranch. He unlocked the door, picked her up and carried her over the threshold. Once inside, he spun her around in a circle just as he did when she first moved in. "Welcome home, Mrs. McGarrett," he announced. Eve leaned in and kissed Mike deeply. Mike continued to hold Eve in his arms. "Eve, I want last night to be the first and only night we spend apart. I missed you so much. It was unbearable. It just wasn't the same without you here with me."

"You won't get any arguments from me, my love."

Mike carried Eve into their bedroom, where he finally set her down on her own two feet. He wasted no time and teasingly planted a sweet kiss on Eve's lips. His hunger for her was evident by the smoldering look in eyes. Mike unzipped her dress and slowly pushed the straps off her shoulders and down her arms while letting his hands graze across her skin until the dress fell to the floor. His touch sent a shiver through her entire body. He removed Eve's hair clamp and she shook her head, which allowed her hair to fall to her shoulders.

"You are so beautiful. I love you, Mrs. McGarrett."

"I love you, Mr. McGarrett."

Instantly, Mike's hands were in Eve's hair grasping her head, and his mouth covered hers. The speed of his movements took Eve by surprise, but his seductiveness caused an immediate response. Eve moaned at Mike's probing tongue. She began to undo his shirt buttons and Mike withdrew his hands from her hair in order to remove his blazer and shirt. Their need for each other intensified, and Eve went to work on Mike's pants while he deftly undid her bra snaps. Both pant and bra dropped to the floor.

Mike wrapped his arms around Eve's waist and pulled her against him, and the feel of their naked bodies against each other was almost too much to bear. Their mouths quickly found each other again, and their deep longing for each other was evident by the voraciousness of their kiss. Eve's fingers gripped Mike's hair as he pushed his erection against her. He moaned at the physical connection, he needed her. He guided Eve toward the bed and gently pressed her back against the mattress. Mike pulled off his boxers and stood over her. Eve raised her arms, framing her head while admiring his physique.

Mike couldn't tear his eyes off her as they raked over her body hungrily. Eve was truly the sexiest woman alive. He removed her panties and crawled onto the bed. He trailed kisses up her inner thighs until he reached her special place. Eve arched her back as electric currents spread through her veins. Mike briefly teased her clitoris and she began to moisten. His kisses proceeded to travel up her torso and settled on her breasts. He was completely on top of her now and Eve instinctively raised her knees. Their bodies melded into each other. His lips closed around her nipple and it hardened under his command. Her physical response to his sensual assault increased his arousal. Mike started to grind on top of Eve and she moved with him. He began to caress the other breast while sucking on the first. The sensations were overwhelming and Eve ached for him. As if reading her mind he entered her.

"Mike!" Eve gasped.

"Oh, Eve," Mike murmured, and he began to thrust in and out of her with a commanding grind. Eve's legs automatically tightened around Mike's lower back, and she pulled him in deeper with each thrust. They found a natural but frenzied rhythm while kissing each other hard. Mike's hands were in Eve's hair and Eve was scratching her nails along Mike's back, which she knew made him crazy. It was impossible for them to last much longer. They were in complete ecstasy. Their moans of pleasure grew louder. Eve's body started to quiver, which sent Mike over the edge as he sensed her approaching orgasm.

"Don't stop, don't stop," she pleaded.

Mike pounded faster while they devoured each other.

"Oh God!" Eve cried out as she threw her head back and stiffened. "I love you," she said breathlessly as she climaxed.

"Eve! My love!" Mike called out as his orgasm violently ripped through him, and then collapsed on top of her.

Still clinging to each other, both were breathing heavily while their hearts continued to thump hard at a rapid pace. After a minute, Mike slowly pulled out of Eve but continued to lie on top of her, still wanting the feel of her body against his. Mike stared down at Eve and said, "I love you, wife." Eve caressed his face and he gently kissed her lips. If only they could stay like this forever. The gentle kiss became more fervent, and soon they were devouring each other once again. They continued to make love all night long, as newlyweds should.

* * *

Mike and Eve awoke entwined with each other and thoroughly exhausted. Mike stared at Eve while she slept. Her hair was wildly displayed across her pillow and she looked sexy as hell. He couldn't believe that she was his wife now. Before Eve, no one would have thought that Michael McGarrett would have ever gotten married, and here he was, the happiest married man alive.

Eve's eyes finally opened, and she smiled at the sight of Mike's handsome face. *What could be better than this?* she thought to herself.

"So, what can I do for you this morning, Mrs. McGarrett?"

"You will never tire of calling me that, will you?"

"Absolutely not, it's music to my ears. So, what can I get you?" Eve snuggled closer to Mike and kissed him deeply. "Mmmm, coming right up, pretty lady."

"It was a good idea to have a later flight," Mike murmured.

"I know. Lord knows we never would have made a morning one, especially since we can't seem to make it out of bed. We would have missed our entire honeymoon," answered Eve.

"Well, we don't have a choice now. We have to get up if we expect to make our flight, and we have just enough time to eat something, shower and dress. You shower first while I fix us something to eat and throw our luggage in the trunk."

Both clamored out of bed and Mike couldn't resist slapping Eve on her bottom.

"Hey!" Eve yelped in surprise, then teasingly stuck her tongue out at him and scurried into the bathroom.

Mike laughed to himself. *Eve is lucky we're pressed for time, or I would have helped myself to that tongue of hers*, he thought. As Mike headed out of the bedroom, his cell phone rang. Sam's face appeared on the screen. He shook his head while answering. "Dude, you know I'm on my honeymoon, right?"

"Of course, and I'm calling to make sure the two of you get out of bed and actually make it to Hawaii."

"Thanks for the assist, but we're on track. Although we *are* cutting it close. We'll have to do some multitasking, but we should make it to the airport on time. Eve is in the shower now, and I'm entering the kitchen as we speak."

"Good, then my job is done. You won't hear from me unless the world is coming to an end. So enjoy your new wife, my friend, and I'll see you when you return."

"Oh, I'm enjoying my new wife all right."

"TMI... TMI..." replied Sam then he hung up.

Mike laughed. *Sam walked right into that one*, he thought as he proceeded into the kitchen to whip up a couple of sandwiches. By the time he finished, Eve had arrived dressed in a pale blue sundress and ready to eat. "Well, aren't you adorable. Ready for Hawaii?"

"Yes, I am *so* ready," Eve replied, twirling in a circle for Mike's benefit.

After they finished eating, Mike showered and dressed. They both completed their checklist and headed off to the airport.

# Chapter 36

"I hope you and your lovely wife enjoy the island of Kauai, Mr. McGarrett," the bellboy gushed.

Mike tipped him. "Oh, we intend to."

Eve, a little tired from the long flight and the lack of sleep during their wedding night, flopped herself onto the bed. It felt heavenly.

"Hey, babe," Mike called out. "Are you hungry?"

Eve leaned up and braced herself on her elbows as Mike approached her. "I'm starved. The flight meal just didn't cut it for me."

"I agree... I was thinking that we could have dinner downstairs at the restaurant. We need sustenance to give us strength for when we return to our room and *continue* our honeymoon." Eve just shook her head and smiled. Her new husband had a one-track mind. "We can unpack tomorrow," Mike continued, "and explore the island *if* we're in the mood to venture out of this villa."

"That sounds fine to me. Just give me a minute to freshen up, and then we can head down."

They were very happy and impressed with their accommodations. The villa was magnificent, and dinner was superb. They discussed what activities they were interested in, that took place *outside* of their bedroom, of course, while exploring the island of

Kauai. After dinner, Mike and Eve showered together and made love all night.

Of course, it was no surprise that they never made it out of their bedroom the following day. Mike made sure to put the "Do Not Disturb" sign on the door, and they spent the entire time in bed, with some light conversation, and ordered room service to get them through the day.

On the third day of their honeymoon they finally emerged out into the world, spending a leisurely morning on the beach.

Mike and Eve were lip-locked while stretched out on their sun lounges. "Although we've ventured out of our bedroom, it seems as though our activities have remained the same," whispered Eve on one of the rare occasions they came up for air.

"Well, we *are* on our honeymoon after all." Mike's hands slowly traveled down Eve's body and settled on her belly.

"I'm not complaining, just stating a fact. At least we're getting some fresh air and enjoying the outdoors. The beach is absolutely beautiful."

"Is it? I haven't noticed," Mike murmured, planting little kisses on Eve's face. "Do you have enough sunscreen on? I won't be able to touch you if you let this beautiful body get sunburned."

"Oh and we can't have that, can we?"

"Absolutely not!" Mike stated emphatically as he grabbed the sunscreen from their bag. "Turn over onto your stomach and I'll start with your backside." Eve complied and then Mike undid her bikini straps and began to sensually apply the sunscreen to her back and arms.

"That feels wonderful," Eve murmured, and her subtle moans of pleasure caused a wry smile to cross Mike's face. His hands moved down to her buttocks, and Eve suspected he was enjoying himself immensely as he lingered there a little longer than necessary. He finally finished with the back of her legs and then requested she turn over onto her back.

Eve carefully held her bikini top in place and turned over. "I just can't get enough of you Mrs. McGarrett," said Mike, and his mouth immediately claimed hers. While kissing her, he moved her bikini top down.

After coming up for air, Mike squeezed some sunscreen into his hand and began to apply it to Eve's breasts. Eve gasped and quickly looked around. "No one is looking, sweetie, relax," assured Mike, and then leaned in for another kiss. His fingers played with Eve's nipples and she relinquished her will to him. Her fingers gripped his hair and she returned his kiss with intensity, ignited by the glorious sensations that rippled through her body at his touch.

Mike lifted his head. "You're evil," Eve murmured.

"And you love it. Lean up and I'll tie the straps on your bikini." Eve sat up, bracing herself with her elbows. Mike watched her breasts heave up and down from her heavy breathing and smiled. After he finished tying her straps, he gently pushed her back against the lounge, leaned over her and whispered in her ear, "I'm not done with you yet, Mrs. McGarrett."

The electric connection between them was palpable. This man was seducing her, on the beach in broad daylight for the entire world to see. *Truly evil*, Eve thought.

Mike applied additional sunscreen to his hands and massaged it onto her stomach in gentle, caressing circular moves. Their eyes were locked onto each other as if no one else existed and the rest of the world had faded away. Mike began to massage her feet and Eve knew she was in trouble for sure. She moaned and her eyes closed involuntarily as her body melted into the lounge chair. She was completely at Mike's mercy and didn't care. His hands skillfully traveled up her calves, past her knees and landed on her thighs. He applied additional sunscreen and went to work, massaging deeply and methodically. His thumbs seemed to have a mind of their own as his hands reached the top of her thighs. Eve gasped and her eyes flew open as his thumbs lingered very near her private area. Just close enough to send shivers of delight throughout her body. Mike could feel the tension build in her legs.

"Oh my God!" she exclaimed, "Mike. You're. Wicked," she announced breathlessly, tightly gripping the arms of the lounge chair.

"You have no idea," he responded. Mike positioned himself over Eve so as to obscure her from view from the other beachgoers. He cradled her head with one hand while the other continued to make its way to his final destination. His thumb reached underneath Eve's bikini bottom and made contact. He debated whether to ease his fingers inside of her, but decided to save that pleasure for himself.

"Mike," she moaned, and started to breathe heavily.

Her hands slid into his hair and she pulled his face toward hers. His mouth started to devour hers. Eve's entire body tingled from Mike's continuous touch, and she struggled not to move against him, slightly aware that they were still in public. God, he was driving her crazy, and it was pure, sweet torture. It was clear that he intended to make her have an orgasm, but she wanted him inside of her. His thumb and his mouth were relentless, and her head started to swirl. Eve could feel his hardness against her thigh and knew Mike resisted the urge to enter her only because they were exposed. She felt like she was falling and rising simultaneously, and she wanted to scream out, but she couldn't. They were restricted, which only added to the intensity of the experience. She didn't know how much more she could take.

"Mike, I want you," Eve pleaded, and she felt herself building and lifting up for takeoff.

"You will have me soon enough, my sweet," he answered hoarsely just before reclaiming her mouth. He could feel that her body was on the verge of exploding, and his fingers and mouth picked up the pace.

Eve started to whimper, which turned into groans, the sounds lost in their kisses. Her fingers gripped his hair more tightly as she started to erupt. Her body jerked as her orgasm ripped through her, leaving her breathless, her body still yearning the feel of her husband inside of her.

They gazed into each other's eyes for several seconds.

"I love you, Mrs. McGarrett."

"I love you, Mr. McGarrett."

Mike pushed himself off Eve and stretched out his hand. "Let's go out into the water, my love."

"You're in the mood to swim?" Eve asked incredulously after what they just experienced.

"Swimming is not what I have in mind."

Eve stared at him. She should have known better; the look in his eyes explained it all. She took his hand and followed him into the ocean. She was about to get what she wanted and needed. Looking like children about to get themselves in trouble, they waded out just far enough for a little privacy, even though they weren't fooling anyone on the beach who happened to glance in their direction.

"I *have* to have you *now*. It was all I could do to control myself on the beach, Eve."

"Please take me," she replied, wrapping herself around her husband.

Her body hadn't recovered from his last assault, and she ached for him badly. She grasped his neck and flung her head backwards from pure pleasure as he entered her. Both moaned in unison. When she leaned back upward, his lips found hers and they continued their rhythmic dance in the water together.

After their morning activities at the beach, they spent the afternoon visiting art galleries and buying souvenirs for their friends.

They spent the remaining days of their honeymoon exploring the island. They enjoyed the wonderful and spectacular views of Kauai via a helicopter tour and the vast scenery under water while snorkeling as well as hiking and relaxing in the salon and spa.

* * *

Sam felt his phone buzz. He pulled it out of his pants pocket and saw Mike's name. "Hey man, shouldn't you two be on your way to the airport?"

"Yeah, listen; I only have a few minutes to talk while Eve is in the bathroom."

"Okay, what's up?"

"I'm just checking for an update on Jackson Harper."

"There's nothing new to report. He remained in San Francisco, and as I told you before you left, we'll discuss what I uncovered in the background report when you return. I hope you haven't been thinking about this guy during your honeymoon."

"No! Of course not! Eve has been the *only* thing on my mind, believe me. It's just that now we're coming back home and I want to make sure we're not coming back to any problems with this guy. It's bad enough I have to worry about Marty's behavior."

"Hey, Marty behaved during the wedding, so maybe that situation has resolved itself. But other than that, it's all good here, so have a safe trip home. Look, I hate to cut you off, but I have somewhere to be, my friend."

Mike snickered. "Okay Sam, I won't hold you up."

"Much appreciated. I'll see ya when I see ya."

* * *

*So, you're on your way back home from your honeymoon. It's just as well. I should have paid you a visit much, much sooner, before you met him. I thought I made it clear that I planned to follow you to New York, and that farewell kiss, mmm, that kiss. I know you enjoyed it as much as I did, even though you tried to feign indifference, but you're taking this game of playing hard to get a little too far, my sweet Eve. Married or not, you will always be mine, not his. This marriage won't last long, one way or the other. Not if I have anything to say about it.*

* * *

Mike and Eve returned home after having the best time of their lives.